THE WALLS OF THE UNIVERSE

Tor Books by Paul Melko

Singularity's Ring
The Walls of the Universe

Paul Melko

The WALLS of the UNIVERSE

A Tom Doherty Associates Book
New York

THE WALLS OF THE UNIVERSE

Part 1 of this novel appeared in somewhat different form as "The Walls of the Universe" in *Asimov's Science Fiction*.

A Tor Book
Published by Tom Doherty Associates, LLC
175 Fifth Avenue
New York, NY 10010

Tor® is a registered trademark of Tom Doherty Associates, LLC.

ISBN-13: 978-0-7653-1997-5

Printed in the United States of America

For Stacey,
of course

ACKNOWLEDGMENTS

Many thanks go to the readers of *Asimov's Science Fiction,* who voted "The Walls of the Universe" the best novella of 2006.

Part One

CHAPTER 1

The screen door slammed behind John Rayburn, rattling in its frame. He and his dad had been meaning to fix the hinges and paint it before winter, but just then John wanted to rip it off and fling it into the fields.

"Johnny?" his mother called after him, but by then he was in the dark shadow of the barn. He slipped around the far end and any more of his mother's calls were lost among the sliding of cricket legs. His breath blew from his mouth in clouds.

John came to the edge of the pumpkin patch, stood for a moment, then plunged into it. Through the pumpkin patch was east, toward Case Institute of Technology, where he hoped to start as a freshman the next year. Not that it was likely. There was always the University of Toledo, his father had said. One or two years of work could pay for a year of tuition there.

John kicked a half-rotten pumpkin. Seeds and wispy strings of pumpkin guts spiraled through the air. The smell of dark earth and rotten pumpkin reminded him it was a week before Halloween and they hadn't had time to harvest the pumpkins: a waste and a thousand dollars lost to earthworms. He ignored how many credits that money would have bought.

The pumpkin field ended at the tree line, the eastern

edge of the farm. The trees—old maples and elms—abutted Gurney Road, beyond which was the abandoned quarry. He stood in the trees, just breathing, letting the anger seep away.

It wasn't his parents' fault. If anyone was to blame, it was he. He hadn't had to beat the crap out of Ted Carson. He hadn't had to tell Ted Carson's mom off. That had entirely been him. Though the look on Mrs. Carson's face had almost been worth it when he told her her son was an asshole. What a mess.

He spun at the sound of a stick cracking.

For a moment he thought that Ted Carson had chased him out of the farmhouse, that he and his mother were there in the woods. But the figure who stood there was just a boy, holding a broken branch in his hand.

"Johnny?" the boy said. The branch flagged in his grip, touching the ground.

John peered into the dark. He wasn't a boy; he was a teenager. John stepped closer. The teen was dressed in jeans and a plaid shirt. Over the shirt he wore a sleeveless red coat that looked oddly out-of-date. He had sandy blond hair and brownish eyes.

John's eyes lingered on the stranger's face. No, not a stranger. The teen had *his* face.

"Hey, Johnny. It's me, Johnny."

The figure in the woods was him.

"Who . . . who are you?" John asked. How could this be?

The stranger smiled. His smile. "I'm you, John."

"What?"

"Who do I look like?" the stranger said. He opened his arms, palms up, as if to share an intimate comment.

John's head spun for a moment. "You look like . . ." Me, he almost said. A brother. A cousin. A hallucination. A trick.

"I look just like you, John. Because I am you." John took a step back. The stranger continued, "I know what you're thinking. Some trick. Someone is playing a trick on the farm boy. No. Let's get past that. Next you're going to think that we're twins, and that one of us was put up for adoption. Nope. It's much more interesting than that."

The thought of twins *had* crossed his mind, but he didn't like the stranger's manner, his presumption. "Explain it, then."

"Listen, I'm really hungry. I could use some food and a place to sit down. I saw Dad go into the house. Maybe we can sit in the barn and I can explain everything."

There was something desperate in his words. He must want something from John. There had to be some twist, some gimmick. John just couldn't see it yet. And that bothered him.

"I don't think so," he said.

"Fine. I'll turn around and walk away," the stranger said. "Then you'll never get to hear the story."

John almost let him go. He glanced left and right. No one was in the woods, lurking and laughing. If this were a joke, he couldn't see the punch line. If this were a scam, he couldn't see why he was the mark. He couldn't see the logic, and that ate at him. What harm was there in hearing the story?

"Let's go to the barn," he said finally.

The stranger's smile was genuine. "Great!"

John headed back toward the barn, the stranger at his side. John eased away from him. As they walked through the pumpkin patch, John noted that their strides matched, that they were the same height. He pulled open the back door of the barn, and the young man entered ahead of him, tapping the light switch by the door.

"A little warmer," he said. He rubbed his hands together and turned to John.

The light hit his face squarely, and John was startled to see the uncanny match between them. In the dark, it had been easy to think their looks were close but not *exact*. The sandy hair was styled differently and was longer. The clothes were odd; John had never worn a coat like that. The young man was just a bit thinner as well. He wore a blue backpack, so fully stuffed that the zipper wouldn't close all the way. There was a cut above his eye. A bit of brown blood was crusted over his left brow, clotted but recent.

He could have passed as John's twin.

"So, who are you?"

"What about a bite of something to eat?"

John went to the horse stall and pulled an apple from a bag. He tossed it to the young man. He caught it and smiled at John.

"Tell the story and I might get some dinner from the house."

"Did Dad teach you to be so mean to strangers? I bet if he found me in the woods, he'd invite me in to dinner."

"Tell," John said.

"Fine." The young man flung himself on a hay bale and munched the apple. "It's simple, really. I'm you. Or rather I'm you genetically, but I grew up on this same farm in another universe. And now I've come to visit myself."

"Bullshit. Who put you up to this?"

"Okay, okay. I didn't believe me either." A frown passed over his face. "But I can prove it. Hold on a second." He wiped his mouth with the back of his hand. "Here we go: That horse is named Stan or Dan. You bought him from the McGregors on Butte Road when you were ten. He's stubborn and willful and he hates being saddled. But he'll canter like a show horse if he knows you have an apple in your pocket." The young man turned to the stalls on his left. "That pig is called Rosey. That cow is Wilma. The chickens are called Ladies A through F. How am I doing so far?" He smiled an arrogant smile.

"You stole some of your uncle's cigarettes when you were twelve and smoked them all. You killed a big bullfrog with your BB gun when you were eight. You were so sickened by it you threw up and haven't used a gun since. Your first kiss was with Amy Walder when you were fourteen. She wanted to show you her underwear too, but you ran home to Mommy. I don't blame you. She's got cooties every-where I go.

"Everyone calls you Johnny, but you prefer John. You have a stash of *Playboys* in the barn loft. And you burned a hole in the rug in your room once. No one knows because you rearranged your room so that the nightstand is on top of it." He spread his arms like a gymnast who'd just stuck a landing.

"Well? How close did I come?" He smiled and tossed the apple core into Stan's stall.

"I never kissed Amy Walder." Amy had gotten pregnant when she was fifteen by Tyrone Biggens. She'd moved to Montana with her aunt and hadn't come back. John didn't mention that everything else he'd said was true.

"Well, was I right?"

John shrugged. "Mostly."

"Mostly? I nailed it on the head with a hammer, because it all happened to me. Only it happened in another universe."

How did this guy know so much about him? Who had he talked to? His parents? "Okay. Answer this. What was my first cat's name?"

"Snowball."

"What is my favorite class?"

"Physics."

"What schools did I apply to?"

The man paused, frowned. "I don't know."

"Why not? You know everything else."

"I've been traveling, you know, for a while. I haven't applied to college yet, so I don't know. As soon as I used the device, I became someone different. Up till then, we were the same." He looked tired. "Listen. I'm you, but if I can't convince you, that's fine. Let me sleep in the loft tonight and then I'll leave."

John watched him grab the ladder, and he felt a twinge of guilt at treating him so shabbily. "Yeah, you can sleep in the loft. Let me get you some dinner. Stay here. Don't leave the barn, and hide if someone comes. You'd give my parents a heart attack."

"Thanks, John."

He left him there and sprinted across the yard to the house. His mother and father stopped talking when the door slammed, so he knew they'd been talking about him.

"I'm gonna eat in the barn," he said. "I'm working on an electronics experiment."

He took a plate from the cabinet and began to dish out the lasagna. He filled the plate with enough to feed two of him.

His father caught his eye, then said, "Son, this business with the Carson boy . . ."

John slipped a second fork into his pocket. "Yeah?"

"I'm sure you did the right thing and all."

John nodded at his father, saw his mother look away. "He hates us because we're farmers and we dig in the dirt," John said. His mother lifted her apron strap over her neck, hung the apron on a chair, and slipped out of the kitchen.

"I know that, Johnny . . . John. But sometimes you gotta keep the peace."

John nodded. "Sometimes I have to throw a punch, Dad." He turned to go.

"John, you can eat in here with us."

"Not tonight, Dad."

Grabbing a quart of milk, he walked through the laundry room and left out the back door.

He stopped short as he pulled open the barn door. The stranger was rubbing Stan's ears, and the horse was leaning into him, loving it.

"Stan never lets anyone do that but me."

The stranger—this other John—turned with a half smile on his lips. "Just so," he said. He took the proffered paper towel full of lasagna, dug into it with the extra fork John had fetched.

"I always loved this lasagna. Thanks."

The tone, the arrogance, of the stranger annoyed him. His smile . . . Did John look like that? He expected the stranger to keep talking, to keep goading him, but instead he remained silent, chewing on his dinner.

Finally John said, "Let's assume for a moment that you are me from another universe. How can you do it? And why you?"

Through a mouth of pasta, the stranger said, "With my device, and I don't know."

"Elaborate," John said, angry.

"I was given a device that lets me pass from one universe to the next. It's right here under my shirt. I don't know why it was me. Or rather, I don't know why it was us."

"Stop prancing around my questions!" John shouted. He was impossible! He wouldn't give a straight answer. "Who gave you the device?"

"I did!" The stranger grinned.

John shook his head, trying to understand. "You're saying that one of us—yet another John—from another universe gave you the device."

"Yeah. Another John. Nice-looking fellow."

Again that smile. John was silent for a while, just watching the stranger wolf down his food. Finally John said, "I need to feed the sheep." He poured a bag of corn into the trough. The stranger lifted the end of it with him. "Thanks." They fed the cows and the horse afterwards, then finished their own dinners.

John said, "So if you are me, what do I call you? If we were twins we'd have different names. But really, we're the same person exactly. Closer than twins." Twins had identical genetic material but from the moment of conception had slightly differing environments that might turn on and off different genes. Presumably John and this other John had identical genetic material and indentical environments, up to a point.

"My name is John, just like yours. I am you, but you may not like to think of me as John Rayburn. I think of you as John Farm Boy. But you gotta remember there's an infinite number of us. It's going to be hard to keep track of all us John Rayburns if we ever get together." The stranger laughed. "How about you think of me as John Prime for now? We'll keep track of ourselves relative to our downstream and upstream universes."

"Who gave you the device?"

"John Superprime," Prime said with a smile. "So do you believe me yet?"

John was still dubious. It made a bizarre sense, but then so did any of those made-up science fiction stories he'd read at the drug-store. Anything could be believed and made to sound coherent. "Maybe."

"All right. Here's the last piece of evidence. No use denying this." He pulled up his pant leg to reveal a long white scar, devoid of hair. "Let's see yours," John said.

John looked at the scar, and then pulled his jeans up to the knee. The cold air of the barn drew goose bumps on his calf everywhere except the puckered flesh of his own identical scar.

When John had been twelve, he and Bobby Walder had climbed the barbed-wire fence of Old Mrs. Jones to swim in her pond. Mrs. Jones had set the dogs on them, and they'd had to run naked across the field, diving over the barbed-wire fence. John hadn't quite cleared it.

Bobby had run off, and John had limped home. The cut on his leg had required three dozen stitches and a tetanus shot.

"Now do you believe?" Prime asked.

John stared at the scar on his leg. "I believe. Hurt like hell, didn't it?"

"Yes," Prime said with a grin. "Yes, it did, brother."

CHAPTER 2

John sat in the fishbowl—the glass-enclosed room outside the principal's office—ignoring the eyes of his classmates and wondering what the hell John Prime was up to. He'd left his twin in the barn loft with half his lunch and an admonishment to stay out of sight.

"Don't worry," he'd said with a smirk. "Meet me at the library after school."

"Don't let anyone see you, all right?"

Prime had smiled again.

"John?" Principal Gushman stuck his head out of his office. John's stomach dropped; he was never in trouble.

Mr. Gushman had a barrel chest, balding head, and perpetual frown. He motioned John to a chair and sat behind the desk, letting out his breath heavily as he sat. He'd been a major in the army, people said. He was strict. John had never talked with him in the year he'd been principal.

"John, we have a policy regarding violence and bullying."

John opened his mouth to speak.

"Hold on. Let me finish. The facts of the matter are these. You hit a classmate—a younger classmate—several times in the locker room. He required a trip to the emergency room and stitches." Gushman opened a file on his desk.

"The rules are there for the protection of all students. There can be no violence in the school. There can be no exceptions. Do you understand?"

John stared, then said, "I understand the rule. But—"

"You're a straight-A student, varsity basketball and track. You're well liked. Destined for a good college. This could be a blemish on your record."

John knew what the word "could" meant. Gushman was about to offer him a way out.

"A citation for violence, as stated in the student handbook, means a three-day suspension and the dropping of any sports activities. You'd be off the basketball and track teams."

John's throat tightened.

"Do you see the gravity of the situation?"

"Yes," John managed to say.

Gushman opened another folder on his desk. "But I recognize this as a special case. So if you write a letter of apology to Mrs. Carson, we'll drop the whole matter." Gushman looked at him, expecting an answer.

John felt cornered. Yes, he had hit Ted, because he was a prick. Ted needed hitting, if anyone did; he had dropped John's clothes in the urinal. He said, "Why does Mrs. Carson want the letter? I didn't hit her. I hit Ted."

"She feels that you showed her disrespect. She wants the letter to address that as well as the violence."

If he just wrote the letter, it would all go away. But he'd always know that his mother and Mrs. Carson had squashed him. He hated that. He hated any form of defeat. He wanted to tell Gushman he'd take the suspension. He wanted to throw it all in the man's face.

Instead, John said, "I'd like to think about it over the weekend if that's okay."

Mr. Gushman's smile told John that he was sure he'd bent John to his will. John went along with it, smiling back. "Yes. You may. But I need a decision on Monday."

John left for his next class.

The city library was just a couple of blocks from the school. John wandered through the stacks until he found Prime at the center study desk in a row of three on the third floor. He had a dozen *Findlay Heralds* spread out, as well as a couple books. His backpack was open, and John saw that it was jammed with paper and folders.

To hide his features, Prime wore a Toledo Meerkats baseball hat and sunglasses. He pulled off his glasses when he saw John, and said, "You look like crap. What happened to you?"

"Nothing. Now what are you doing? I have to get back to the school by five. There's a game tonight."

"Yeah, yeah, yeah." Prime picked up the history book. "In every universe I've been in, it's always something simple. Here George Bush raised taxes and he never got elected to a second term. Clinton beat him in '91." He opened the history book and pointed to the color panel of American presidents. "In my world, Bush never backed down on the taxes thing and the economy took off and he got elected to his second term. He was riding even higher when Hussein was assassinated in the middle of his second term. His son was elected in 1996."

John laughed. "That joker?"

Prime scowled. "Dubya worked the national debt down to nothing. Unemployment was below three percent."

"It's low here too. Clinton did a good job."

Prime pointed to a newspaper article he had copied. "Whitewater? Drug use? Vince Foster?" He handed the articles to John, then shook his head. "Never mind. It's all pretty much irrelevant anyway. At least we didn't grow up in a world where Nixon was never caught."

"What happened there?"

"The Second Depression usually. Russia and the U.S. never coming to an arms agreement. Those are some totalitarian places." He took the articles back from John. "Are there Post-it notes in this world?"

"Yes. Of course."

Prime shrugged. "Sometimes there aren't. It's worth a fortune. And so simple." He pulled out his notebook. "I have a hundred of them." He opened his notebook to a picture of the MTV astronaut. "MTV?"

"Yep."

"The World Wide Web?"

"I think so."

"Rubik's Cube?"

"Never heard of it."

Prime checked the top of the figure with a multicolored cube. "Ah ha. That's a big moneymaker."

"It is?"

He turned the page. "Dungeons and Dragons?"

"You mean that game where you pretend to be a wizard?"

"That's the one. How about Lozenos? You got that here?"

"Never heard of it. What is it?"

"Candy. South African diamond mines?"

They worked through a long list of things, about three-quarters of which John had heard of, fads, toys, or inventions.

"This is a good list to work from. Some good moneymakers on this."

"What are you going to do?" John asked. This was his world, and he didn't like what he suspected Prime had in mind.

Prime smiled. "There's money to be made in interdimensional trade."

"Interdimensional trade?"

"Not in actual goods. There's no way I can transport enough stuff to make a profit. Too complicated. But ideas are easy to transport, and what's in the public domain in the last universe is unheard of in the next. Rubik sold one hundred million Cubes. At ten dollars a cube, that's a billion dollars." He lifted up the notebook. "There are two dozen ideas in here that made hundreds of millions of dollars in other worlds."

"So what are you going to do?"

Prime smiled his arrogant smile. "Not me. We. I need an agent in this world to work the deals. Who better than myself? The saying goes that you can't be in more than one place at a time. But I can."

"Uh-huh."

"And we split it fifty-fifty."

"Uh-huh."

"Listen. It's not stealing. These ideas have never been thought of here. The people who invented these things might not even be alive here."

"I never said it was stealing," John said. "I'm just not so sure I believe you still."

Prime sighed. "So what's got you so down today?"

John said, "I may get suspended from school and kicked off the basketball and track teams."

"What? Why?" Prime looked genuinely concerned.

"I beat up a kid, Ted Carson. His mother told my mother and the principal. They want me to apologize."

Prime was angry. "You're not gonna, are you? I know Ted Carson. He's a little shit. In every universe."

"I don't have a choice."

"There's always a choice." Prime pulled a notebook out of his bag. "Ted Carson, huh? I have something on him."

John looked over Prime's shoulder at the notebook. Each page had a newspaper clipping, words highlighted and notes at the bottom referencing other pages. One title read: "Mayor and Council Members Indicted." The picture showed Mayor Thiessen yelling. Another article was a list of divorces granted. Prime turned the page and pointed. "Here it is. 'Ted Carson Picked Up for Torturing a Neighbor's Cat.' Apparently the boy killed a dozen neighborhood animals before getting caught." He glanced at John.

"I've never heard anything about that."

"Then maybe he never got caught here."

"What are we going to do with that?" John asked. He read the article, shaking his head.

"Grease the gears, my brother." Prime handed John the newspaper listing of recent divorces. "Photocopy this."

"Why?"

"It's the best place to figure out who's sleeping with who. That usually doesn't change from one universe to the next. Speaking of which, how does Casey Nicholson look in this universe?"

"What?"

"Yeah. Is she a dog or a hottie? Half the time she's pregnant in her junior year and living in a trailer park."

"She's a cheerleader," John said.

Prime glanced at him and smiled. "You like her, don't you? Are we dating her?"

"No!"

"Does she like us?"

"Me! Not us," John said. "And I think so. She smiles at me in class."

"What's not to love about us?" Prime glanced at his watch. "Time for you to head over to the school, isn't it?"

"Yeah."

"I'll meet you at home tonight. See ya."

"Don't talk to anyone," John said. "They'll think it was me. Don't get me in trouble."

"Don't worry. The last thing I want to do is screw up your life here."

After the game John left a copy of the stats with Coach Jessick and then met his father in the parking lot.

"Not a good game for the home team," his father said. He wore his overalls and a John Deere hat. John realized he'd sat in the stands like that, with manure on his shoes. Soft country and western whispered tinnily from the speakers. For a moment John was embarrassed; then he remembered why he'd had to fight Ted Carson.

"Thanks for picking me up, Dad."

"No problem." He dropped the truck into gear and pulled it out of the lot. "Odd thing. I thought I saw you in the stands."

John glanced at his father, forced himself to be calm. "I was down keeping stats."

"I know; I saw. Must be my old eyes, playing tricks."

Had Prime not gone back to the barn? What was that bastard doing to him?

"Gushman called."

John nodded in the dark of the cab. "I figured."

"Said you were gonna write an apology."

"I don't want to," John said. "But . . ."

"I know. A stain on your permanent record and all." His father turned the radio off. "I was at the U in Toledo for a semester or two. Me and college didn't get along much. But you, Son. You can learn and do something interesting with it. Which is really what me and your mother want."

"Dad—"

"Hold on a second. I'm not saying what you did to the Carson boy was wrong, but you did get caught at it. And if you get caught at something, you usually have to pay for it. Writing a letter saying something isn't the same as believing it."

John nodded. "I think I'm gonna write the letter, Dad."

His father grunted, satisfied. "You helping with the apples tomorrow? We wait any longer and we won't get any good ones."

"Yeah, I'll help until lunch. Then I have basketball practice."

"Okay."

They sat in silence for the remainder of the trip. John was glad his father was so pragmatic.

As they drove up to the farmhouse, John considered what he was going to do about Prime. He'd gone out in public; John was sure of it. That was too far.

His dad pulled the truck into its spot next to the house, and John slid out of the front seat.

"Where you going?" his dad called.

"Check on stuff in the barn," John replied over his shoulder. He slammed open the door. The barn was dark, except for a bulb above the center post. Prime was nowhere to be seen.

"Where are you?" John called.

"Up here," he heard. There was a faint glow from the loft.

"You went to the football game," John said as he climbed the ladder. He expected Prime to deny it.

"Just for a bit," he said. "It was no big deal."

"My dad saw you."

"But he didn't realize it was me, did he?"

John's anger faded just a notch. "No, no. He thought he was seeing things."

"See? No one will believe it even if they see us together."

"But . . ."

"Nothing was harmed, John. Nothing," Prime said. "And I have something else. This Ted Carson thing is about to go away."

"What do you mean?"

"A bunch of cats have gone missing over there."

"You went out in public and talked to people?" It was worse than John thought. "Who saw—"

"Just kids. And it was dark. No one even saw my face. Three cats this month, by the way. Ted is an animal serial killer. We can pin this on him and his mom will have to back off."

"I'm writing the letter of apology," John said.

"What? No!"

"It's better this way. I don't want to screw up my future."

"Listen. It'll never get any better than this. The kid is a psychopath and we can shove it in his parents' faces!"

"No. And listen. You have got to lay low. I don't want you wandering around town messing up things," John said. "Going to the library today was too much."

Prime smiled. "Don't want me hitting on Casey Nicholson, huh?"

"Stop it!" John raised his hand. "That's it. Why don't you just move on? Hit the next town or the next universe or whatever. Just get out of my life!"

Prime frowned. He paused for a moment, as if considering something important. Finally, he lifted up his shirt. Under his gray sweatshirt was a shoulder harness with a thin disk the diameter of a softball attached at the center. It had a digital readout that said "7533," three blue buttons on the front, and dials and levers on the sides.

Prime began unstrapping the harness and said, "John, maybe it's time you saw for yourself."

CHAPTER 3

John looked at the device. It was tiny for what it was supposed to do.

"How does it work?" he asked. John envisioned golden wires entwining black vortices of primal energy, X-ray claws tearing at the walls of the universe as if they were tissue.

"I don't know how it works," John Prime said, irritated. "I just know how to work it." He pointed to the digital readout. "This is your universe number."

"Seven-five-three-three?"

"My universe is 7433." He pointed to the first blue button. "This increments the universe counter. See?" He pressed the button once and the number changed to 7534. "This one decrements the counter." He pressed the second blue button and the counter flipped back to 7533. He pointed to a metal lever on the side of the disk. "Once you've dialed in your universe, you pull the lever and—pow!—you're in the next universe."

"It looks like a slot machine," John said.

Prime pursed his lips. "It's the product of a powerful civilization."

"Does it hurt?" John asked.

"I don't feel a thing. Sometimes my ears pop because

the weather's a little different. Sometimes I drop a few centimeters or my feet are stuck in the dirt."

"What's this other button for?"

Prime shook his head. "I don't know. I've pressed it, but it doesn't seem to do anything. There's no owner's manual, you know?" He grinned. "Wanna try it out?"

More than anything, John wanted to try it. Not only would he know for sure if Prime was full of crap, but he would get to see another universe. The idea was astounding. To travel, to be free of all this . . . detritus in his life. Ten more months in Findlay was a lifetime. Here in front of him was adventure.

"Show me."

Prime frowned. "I can't. It takes twelve hours to recharge the device after it's used. If I left now, I'd be in some other universe for a day before I could come back."

"I don't want to be gone a day! I have chores. I have to write a letter."

"It's okay. I'll cover for you here."

"No way!"

"I can do it. No one would know. I've been you for as long as you have."

"No. There's no way I'm leaving for twelve hours with you in control of my life."

Prime shook his head. "How about a test run? Tomorrow you're doing what?"

"Picking apples with my dad."

"I'll do it instead. If your dad doesn't notice a thing, then you take the trip and I'll cover for you. If you leave tomorrow afternoon, you can be back on Sunday and not miss a day of school." Prime opened his backpack wider. "And to make the whole trip a lot more fun, here's some spending money." He pulled out a stack of twenty-dollar bills.

"Where did you get that?" John had never seen so much money. His bank account had no more than three hundred dollars in it.

Prime handed him the stack of cash. The twenties were crisp, the paper smooth-sticky. "There's got to be two thousand dollars here."

"Yep."

"It's from another universe, isn't it? This is counterfeit."

"It's real money. And no one in this podunk town will be able to tell me that it's not." Prime pulled a twenty out of his own pocket. "This is from your universe. See any differences?"

John took the first twenty off the stack and compared it to the crumpled bill. They looked identical to him.

"How'd you get it?"

"Investments." Prime's smile was ambiguous.

"Did you steal it?"

Prime shook his head. "Even if I did steal it, the police looking for it are in another universe."

John forced aside a wave of panic. Prime had his fingerprints, his looks, his voice. He knew everything there was to know about John. Prime could rob a bank or kill someone and then escape to another universe, leaving John holding the bag. All the evidence of such a crime would point to him, and there was no way he could prove that he was innocent.

Would Prime do such a thing? He had called John his brother. In a sense they were identical brothers. And Prime was letting John use his device, in effect stranding him in this universe. That took trust.

"Twenty-four hours," Prime said. "Think of it as a vacation. A break from all this shit with Ted Carson."

The lure of seeing another universe was too strong. "You pick apples with my father tomorrow. If he doesn't suspect anything, then maybe I'll take the trip."

"You won't regret it, John."

"But you have got to promise not to mess anything up!"

Prime nodded. "That's the last thing I'd want to do, John."

Prime was sprawled in the loft. A hay straw clung to the side of his face.

John nudged him in the thigh.

He jerked awake clutching at his chest as if he were having a heart attack. No, John realized, Prime was reaching for the device, still strapped to his chest under his clothes.

"Damn, it's early," Prime said, brushing at his hair.

"Don't let my dad hear you cursing," John said.

"Right, no cursing." Prime stood, stretching. "Apple picking? I haven't done that . . . in a while."

"It couldn't have been that long ago," John said. "A year? You'll remember soon enough."

"Yeah."

Prime peered out a small window. John could hear his father puttering out to the orchard on the tractor.

"What's up between you and your dad? Anything heavy?" Prime asked.

John took off his coat and handed it to Prime, taking his in return. John shook his head. "We talked last night about the Carson thing. He wanted me to write the letter."

"So that's it. What about your mother?"

"She was pissed with me before. She still may be. We haven't talked since Thursday."

"Anything happening this afternoon?" Prime took a pencil out and started jotting things down.

"Nothing until tomorrow. Church, then chores. Muck the stalls. Homework. But I'll do that."

"What's due for Monday?"

"Reading for physics. Essay for English on Gerard Manley Hopkins. Problem set in calculus. That's it."

"What's your class schedule like?"

John began to tell him, then shook his head. "Why do you need to know that? I'll be back."

"In case someone asks."

"No one's gonna ask." John pulled Prime's jacket on after struggling to get his arms through the right holes. Why were there no sleeves? he wondered. He used his binoculars to gaze out at the sun-filled orchard. "I'll watch from here. If anything goes wrong, you pretend to be sick and come back to the barn. You'll brief me and then we switch back."

Prime smiled. "Nothing's gonna happen. Relax." He pulled on gloves and climbed down the ladder. "See ya at lunch."

John's hands shook as he watched Prime walk across the barnyard toward the orchard. What had he gotten himself into? And yet the mystery of it was a magnet and he was the iron filings. He had to understand what this John was about. It was a conundrum.

Prime cast a glance over his shoulder and smiled, while John watched with his binoculars. He raised his hand and waved at John's father.

John's father barely glanced at Prime, and said something.

Prime nodded, then gripped a branch and pulled himself into the tree. His foot missed a hold, and he slipped.

"Careful there," John heard himself say.

Prime made it into the tree and began pulling apples. He said something and John's father laughed in reply. John felt a twinge of jealousy as he watched his father laugh. He wondered what Prime had said. Then John realized that if his father was laughing at Prime's jokes, there was no danger of being found out.

The precarious nature of John's situation bothered him. Effectively, Prime was him. And he was . . . nobody. Would it be that hard for someone to slip into his life? He realized that it wouldn't. He had a few immediate relationships, interactions that had happened within the last few weeks that were unique to him, but in a month those would all be absorbed into the past. He had no girlfriend. No real friends, except for Erik, and that stopped at the edge of the court. The hardest part would be for someone to pick up John's studies, but even that wouldn't be too hard. All his classes were a breeze, except for Advanced Physics, and they were starting a new module on Monday. It was a clear breaking point.

John wondered what he would find in another universe. Would

there be different advances in science? Could he photocopy a scientific journal and bring it back? Maybe someone had discovered a unified theory in the other universe. Or a simple solution to Fermat's last theorem. Or . . . But what could he really do with someone else's ideas? Publish them under his own name? Was that any different from Prime's scheme to get rich with Rubik's Square, whatever that was? He laughed and picked up his physics book. He needed to stay caught up in this universe. They were starting quantum mechanics on Monday after all.

"Here's lunch."

John looked up from the physics book, startled.

Prime handed John a sandwich.

"You went inside?" John asked, alarmed. "You weren't supposed to go inside."

Prime shrugged. "Your mom didn't notice either."

John took the sandwich. Prime looked different. He was covered in sap, there was a scratch on his cheek, and his clothes were grimy. "You look happy," John said.

Prime started. He looked down at himself, then smiled. "It felt good. I haven't done that in a while."

Around a bite of sandwich, John said, "You've been gone a long time."

"Yeah," Prime said. "You don't know what you have here. Why do you even want to go to college?"

John laughed. "It's great here for the first fifteen years; then it really begins to drag."

"I hear you."

John handed Prime his jacket. "What will I see in the next universe?"

Prime caught his eye. "So you're gonna take me up on the offer?" he asked.

John thought about it for a moment longer. He had to know whether Prime was a crackpot or the giver of a fabulous gift. If

Prime was nuts, John had lost nothing and could go about getting rid of him. If Prime's device worked, the whole universe was open to him.

"Yeah, I think so. Tell me what I'll see."

"It's pretty much like this one, you know. I don't know the exact differences."

"So we're—one of us, I mean—in the next universe?"

"Yeah. I wouldn't try to meet him or anything. He doesn't know about us."

"Why'd you pick me to talk to? Why not some other me? Or why not all of us?"

"This is the most like home," Prime said. "This feels like I remember."

"In one hundred universes this is the one that is most like yours? How different are we from one to the next? It can't be too different."

"Do you really want to hear this?"

John nodded.

"Well, there are a couple types of us. There's the farm boy us, like you and me. Then there's the dirtbag us."

"Dirtbag?"

"Yeah. We smoke and hang out under the bleachers."

"What the hell happened there?"

"And sometimes we've knocked up Casey Nicholson and we live in the low-income houses on Stuart. Then there's the places where we've died."

"Died?"

"Yeah. Car accidents. Tractor accidents. Gun accidents. We're pretty lucky to be here, really."

John looked away, remembering something. It was the time he and his father had been tossing hay bales and the pitchfork had fallen. Then John recalled the time he had walked out on Old Mrs. Jones' frozen pond and the ice had cracked and he'd kept going. And the time the quarry truck had run him off the road. It was a fluke really that he was alive.

"I think I'm ready. What's the plan?"

Prime lifted up his shirt and began unbuckling the harness. "You leave from the pumpkin field. Select the universe one forward. Press the toggle. Spend the day exploring. Go to the library. Figure out what's different. If you want, write down any money-making ideas you come across."

"I don't think so," John said. It seemed too much like cheating.

"Fine. Then don't. Tomorrow, flip the counter back to this universe and pull the lever. You'll be back for school on Monday."

"Sounds easy enough."

"Don't lose the device! Don't get busted by the police! Don't do anything to draw attention to yourself."

"Right."

"Don't flash your money either. If anyone recognizes you, go with it and then duck out. You don't want to make it hot for our guy over there."

"Right." John swallowed. What if it did work? What if . . . ?

"Johnny, you look a little nervous. Calm down. I'll keep you covered on this end." Prime slapped him on the back, then handed him the harness.

John pulled off his shirt and shivered. He passed the two bands of the harness over his shoulders, then connected the center belt behind his back. The disk was cold against his belly. The straps looked like a synthetic material.

"It fits."

"It should," Prime said. "I copied some of my materials for you in case you need them." He pulled a binder from his own bag, opened it to show John pages of clippings and notes. "You never know. You might need something. And here's a backpack to hold it all in."

Prime paused as he handed it over.

"What's wrong?" John asked.

"I haven't been away from the device in a long time. It's my talisman, my escape. I feel naked without it. You gotta be careful with it."

John realized how much trust Prime was placing in him. "Hey," he said. "I'm leaving my life in your hands. How about a little two-way trust?"

Prime smiled grimly. "Okay. Are you ready? I've got twelve thirty on my watch. Which means you can return half an hour past midnight. Okay?"

John checked his watch. "Okay."

"Toggle the universe."

John lifted the shirt and switched the number forward to 7534. "Check."

"Okay. I'll watch from the loft." Prime climbed the ladder, then turned. "Make sure no one sees you."

"Right," John said. What would someone think if he or she saw John disappear into thin air? He stopped himself; he was acting like the device would actually work. He'd find out soon enough.

John's foot landed awkwardly on a clump of dirt. The backpack shifted on his shoulders. He felt silly, suddenly. He'd look the putz when the device failed to send him across universes. Prime would laugh at him. Still he had to know.

He found his spot. His heart raced. This was it. He looked up at the barn window. Prime was there, watching. He waved.

John waved back; then he lifted up his shirt. Sunlight caught the brushed metal of the device.

John hesitated. Soon enough.

He pulled the switch and the world lurched.

John's ears popped and his feet caught in the dirt. He stumbled and fell forward, catching himself on his gloved hands. He wasn't in a pumpkin patch anymore. Noting the smell of manure, he realized he was in a cow pasture.

He worked his feet free. His shoes were embedded in the earth. He wondered if there was dirt lodged in his feet now. It looked like the dirt in the current universe was a couple centimeters higher here than in the old one. Where did that extra dirt go? He shook his feet and the dirt fell free.

It worked! He felt a thrill. He'd doubted to the last second. He'd expected the other John to suddenly yell, Tricked ya! but here he was, in a new universe.

He paused. Prime had said there was a John in this universe. He spun around. Cows grazed contentedly a few hundred yards away, but otherwise the fields were empty, the trees gone. There was no farmhouse.

McMaster Road was there and so was Gurney Road. John walked from the field, hopped the fence, and stood at the corner of the roads. Looking to the north toward town, he saw nothing but a farmhouse maybe a mile up the road. To the east, where the stacks of the GE plant should have been, he saw nothing but forest. To the south, more fields.

Prime had said there was a John Rayburn in this universe. He'd said that the farm was here. He'd told John he'd been to this universe.

John pawed up his jacket and shirt and tried to read the number on the device. He cupped his hand to shield the sun and read 7534. He was where he expected to be, according to the device. There was nothing here.

The panic settled into his gut. Something was wrong. Something had gone wrong. He wasn't where he was supposed to be. But that's okay, he thought, calming himself. It's okay. He walked to the edge of road and sat on the small berm there.

Maybe Prime had it wrong; there were a lot of universes and if all of them were different that was a lot of facts to keep straight.

John stood, determined to assume the best. He'd spend the next twelve hours working according to the plan. Then he'd go back home. He set off for town, a black mood nipping at his heels.

CHAPTER 4

John Prime watched his other self disappear from the pumpkin field and felt his body relax. Now he wouldn't have to kill him. This way was so much better. A body could always be found, unless it was in some other universe. He didn't have the device, of course, but then he'd never need it again. In fact, he was glad to be rid of it. John had something more important than the device; he had his life back.

It had taken him three days of arguing and cajoling, but finally Johnny Farm Boy had taken the bait. Good riddance and good-bye. John had been that naive once. He'd once had that wide-eyed gullibility, ready to explore new worlds. There was nothing out there but pain. He was alive again. He had parents again. He had money— $125,000. And he had his notebook. That was the most important part. The notebook was worth a billion dollars right there.

John looked around the loft. This would be a good place for some of his money. If he remembered right, there was a small cubbyhole in the rafters on the south side of the loft. He found it and pulled out the bubble gum cards and slingshot that were hidden there.

"Damn farm boy."

John placed about a third of his money in the hiding

place. Another third he'd hide in his room. The last third he'd
bury. He wouldn't deposit it like he'd done in 7489. Or had that been
7490? The cops had been on his ass so fast. So Franklin had been
looking the wrong way on all those bills. John had lost eighty thousand dollars.

No, he'd be careful this time. He'd show legitimate sources for
all his cash. He'd be the talk of Findlay, Ohio, as his inventions
started panning out. No one would suspect the young physics ge-
nius. They'd be jealous, sure, but everybody knew Johnny Rayburn
was a brain. The Rubik's Cube—no, the Rayburn's Cube—would
be John's road to fame and riches.

He climbed down from the loft. Stan whinnied at him, tossing
his head to get his attention and maybe an apple.

"Of course you can have one, Stan," John said.

John took an apple from the basket and reached out to the
horse. Suddenly John's eyes were filled with tears.

"Hold yourself together, man," he whispered as he let Stan gingerly chomp the apple from his hand. His own horse was dead, at
his own hand.

He'd taken Dan riding and had tried the fence beyond the back
field. They'd galloped through the grass, throwing mud behind them.
John had felt Dan leap, felt the muscles twist and clench. They
had flown. But Dan's hind left hadn't cleared it. The bone had broken, and John ran sobbing to his farm.

His father met him halfway, a rifle in his hand, his face grim.
He'd seen the whole thing.

"Dan's down!" John cried.

His father nodded and handed the rifle to him.

John took it blankly, then tried to hand it back to his father.

"No!"

"If the leg's broken, you must."

"Maybe . . ." But he stopped. Dan was whinnying shrilly; John
could hear it from where they stood. The leg had been horribly
twisted. There was no doubt.

"Couldn't Dr. Kimble look at him?"

"How will you pay for that?"

"Will you?"

His father snorted and walked away.

John watched him tread back to the house until Dan's cries became too much for him. He turned then, tears raining down his cheeks.

Dan's eyes were wide. He shook his head heavily at John; then he settled when John placed the barrel against his skull. Perhaps he knew. John fished an apple from his pocket and slipped it between Dan's teeth.

The horse held it there, not biting, waiting. He seemed to nod at John. Then John had pulled the trigger.

The horse had shuddered and fallen still. John sank to the ground and cried for Dan for an hour.

But here he was. Alive. John rubbed Dan's muzzle.

"Hello, Dan. Back from the dead," John said. "Just like me."

His mother called him to dinner, and for a moment he froze with fear. They'll know, he thought. They'll know I'm not their son.

Breathing slowly, he hid the money back under his comic book collection in the closet.

"Coming!" he called.

During dinner he kept quiet, focusing on what his parents mentioned, filing key facts away for later use. There was too much he didn't know. He couldn't volunteer anything until he had all his facts right.

Cousin Paul was still in jail. They were staying after church tomorrow for a spaghetti lunch. John's mother would be canning and making vinegar that week. His father was buying a turkey from Sam Riley, who had a flock of twenty or so. The dinner finished with homemade apple pie that made the cuts on John's hands and the soreness in his back worth it.

After dinner he excused himself. In his room he rooted through

Johnny Farm Boy's book bag. John had missed a year of school; he had a lot of makeup to do. And, crap, an essay on Gerard Manley Hopkins, whoever the heck that was.

John managed to get through church without falling asleep. Luckily the communion ritual was the same. If there was one thing that didn't change from one universe to the next, it was church.

He expected the spaghetti lunch afterwards to be just as boring, but across the gymnasium John saw Casey Nicholson sitting with her family. That was one person he knew where Johnny Farm Boy stood with. She liked him, it was clear, but Johnny Farm Boy had been too clean-cut to make a move. Not so for John. He excused himself and walked over to her.

"Hi, Casey," he said.

She blushed at him, perhaps because her parents were there.

Her father said, "Oh, hello, John. How's the basketball team going to do this year?"

John wanted to yell at him that he didn't give a rat's ass. But instead he smiled and said, "We'll go all the way if Casey is there to cheer for us."

Casey looked away, her face flush again. She was dressed in a white Sunday dress that covered her breasts, waist, and hips with enough material to hide the fact that she had any of those features. But he knew what was there. He'd seduced Casey Nicholson in a dozen universes at least.

"I'm only cheering fall sports, John," she said softly. "I play field hockey in the spring."

John looked at her mother and asked, "Can I walk with Casey around the church grounds, Mrs. Nicholson?"

She smiled at him, glanced at her husband, and said, "I don't see why not."

"That's a great idea," Mr. Nicholson said.

John had to race after Casey. She stopped after she had gotten out of sight of the gymnasium, hidden in the alcove where the restrooms were. When John caught up to her, she said, "My parents are so embarrassing."

"No shit," John said.

Her eyes went wide at his cursing; then she smiled.

"I'm glad you're finally talking to me," she said.

John smiled and said, "Let's walk." He slipped his arm around her waist, and she didn't protest.

CHAPTER 5

John reached the outskirts of town in an hour, passing a green sign that said: "Findlay, Ohio. Population 6232." His Findlay had a population in the twenty thousand range. As he stood there, he heard a high-pitched whine grow behind him. He stepped off the berm as a truck flew by him, at about forty-five miles per hour. It was in fact two trucks in tandem pulling a large trailer filled with gravel. The fronts of the trucks were flat, probably to aid in stacking several together for larger loads, like a train with more than one locomotive. The trailer was smaller than a typical dump truck in his universe. A driver sat in each truck. Expecting to be enveloped in a cloud of exhaust, John found nothing fouler than moist air.

Flywheel? he wondered. Steam?

Despite his predicament, John was intrigued by the engineering of the trucks. After ten more minutes of walking, past two motels and a diner, he came to the city square, the Civil War monument displayed as proudly as ever, cannon pointed toward the South. A few people were strolling the square, but no one noticed him.

Across the square was the courthouse. Beside it stood the library, identical to what he remembered, a three-story building, its entrance framed by granite lions reclining on brick pedestals. There was the place to start figuring this universe out.

The library was identical in layout to the one he knew. John walked to the card catalog—there were no computer terminals— and looked up the numbers for American history. On the shelf he found a volume by Albert Trey called U.S. *History and Heritage: Major Events That Shaped a Nation.* He sat in a low chair and paged through it. He found the divergence in moments.

The American Revolution, War of 1812, and Civil War all had the expected results. The presidents were the same through Woodrow Wilson. World War I was a minor war, listed as the Greco-Turkish War. World War II was listed as the Great War and was England and the United States against Germany, Russia, and Japan. A truce was called in 1956 after years of no resolution to the fighting. Hostilities had flared for years until the eighties, when peace was declared and disarmament accomplished in France, which was split up and given to Germany and Spain.

But all of those things happened after Alexander Graham Bell developed an effective battery for the automobile. Instead of internal combustion engines, cars and trucks in this universe used electric engines. That explained the trucks: electric engines.

But even as John read about the use of zeppelins for transport, the relatively peaceful twentieth century, his anger began to grow. This universe was nothing like his own. John Prime had lied. Finally, he stood and found the local telephone book. He paged through it, looking for Rayburns. As he expected, there were none.

He checked his watch; in eight hours he was going back home and kicking the crap out of John Prime.

By the time the library closed, John's head was full of facts and details about the new universe. There were a thousand things he'd like to research, but there was no time. He stopped at a newspaper shop and picked an almanac off the shelf. After a moment's hesitation, he offered to buy the three-dollar book with one of the twenties

Prime had given him. The counterman barely glanced at the bill and handed John sixteen dollars and change. The bills were identical to those in his own world. The coins bore other faces.

He ate a late dinner at Eckart's Cafe, listening to rockabilly music. None of it was familiar music, but it was music that would be playable on the country stations at home. Even at ten in the evening, there was a sizeable crowd, drinking coffee and hard liquor. There was no beer to be had.

It was a tame crowd for a Saturday night. He read the almanac and listened in to the conversations around him. Most of it was about cars, girls, and guys, just like in his universe.

By midnight, the crowd had thinned. At half past midnight, John walked into the square and stood behind the Civil War statue. He lifted his shirt and toggled the number back to 7533.

He paused, checked his watch, and saw it was a quarter till one. Close enough, he figured.

He pressed the button.

Nothing happened.

There was no sensation of shifting, no pressure change. The electric car in the parking lot was still there. The device hadn't worked.

He checked the number: 7533. His finger was on the right switch. He tried it again. Nothing.

It had been twelve hours. Twelve hours and forty-five minutes. But maybe Prime had been estimating. Maybe it took thirteen hours to recharge. John leaned against the base of the statue and slid to the ground.

He couldn't shake the feeling that something was wrong. Prime had lied to him about what was in Universe 7534. Maybe he had lied about the recharge time. Maybe it took days or months to recharge the device. And when he got back, he'd find that Prime was entrenched in his life.

He sat there, trying the switch every fifteen minutes until three in the morning. He was cold, but finally he fell asleep on the grass, leaning against the Civil War Memorial.

He awoke at dawn, the sun in his eyes as it streamed down Washington Avenue. He stood and jumped up and down to revive his body. His back ached, but the kinks receded after he did some stretches.

At a donut shop off the square, he bought a glazed and an orange juice with the change he had left over from the almanac. A dozen people filed in over the course of an hour to buy donuts and coffee before church or work. On the surface, this world was a lot like his.

John couldn't stand the waiting. He walked across the square and climbed the library steps and yanked at the door. It was locked, and he saw the sign showing the library's hours. It was closed until noon.

John looked around. There was an alcove behind the lions with a bench. No one would easily see him from the street. He sat there and tried the device. Nothing.

He continued to try the lever every ten or fifteen minutes. As he sat on the steps of the library, his apprehension grew. He was going to miss school. He was going to miss more than twenty-four hours. He was going to miss the rest of his life. Why wouldn't the device work like it was supposed to?

He realized then that everything Prime had told him was probably a lie. He had to assume that he was the victim of Prime's scheming, trapped in another universe. The question was how he would return to his life.

He had the device. It had worked once, to bring him from Universe 7533 to Universe 7534. It would not allow him to return because it wasn't recharged yet. It took longer than—he checked his watch—twenty hours to recharge the device apparently.

He stopped. He was basing that logic on information he got from Prime. Nothing that Prime had said could be used as valid information. Only things that John had seen or gotten from a valid source were true. And Prime was not a valid source.

The twelve-hour recharge time was false. John had assumed

that it meant the length of time was what was false in Prime's statement. What if there was no recharge time at all?

There were two possibilities that John could see. First, there was no recharge time and he was being prevented from returning to his universe for some other reason. Second, the device no longer worked. Perhaps he had used the last of its energy source.

For some reason he still wanted to believe Prime. If it was simply a mechanical issue, then he could use intelligence to solve the problem. Maybe Prime was truthful and something happened to the device that he didn't know about. Maybe Prime would be surprised when John never returned with the device, effectively trapping Prime in John's life. Prime might even think that John had stolen his device.

But mechanical failure seemed unlikely. Prime said he had used the device one hundred times. His home universe was around 7433. If he'd used it exactly one hundred times, that was the distance in universes between John's and Prime's. Did that mean he only used the device to move forward one universe at a time? Or did he hop around? No, the numbers were too similar. Prime probably moved from one universe to the next systematically.

John decided that he was just too ignorant to ignore all of Prime's information. Some of it had to be taken at face value.

The 100 number indicated that Prime only incremented the universe counter upward. Why? Did the device only allow travel in one direction?

John played with the theory, fitting the pieces together. The device was defective or designed in such a way that only travel upward was allowed. Prime mentioned the recharge time to eliminate any possibility of a demonstration. There was perhaps no recharge time. The device was of no value to Prime, since he planned to stay. That explained the personal questions Prime had asked; he wanted to ease into John's life. Some things Prime knew, but other things he had to learn from John.

The fury built in John.

"Bastard!" he said softly. Prime had screwed him. He'd tempted John with universes, and he had fallen for it. And now he was in another universe, where he didn't exist. He had to get back.

There was nothing to do, he realized, but test the theory.

He pulled his backpack onto his shoulders and checked around the bench for his things. Then, with a quick check to see if anyone was looking, he toggled the device to 7535 and pulled the lever.

He fell.

CHAPTER 6

Monday morning at school went no worse than expected. John Prime barely made it to homeroom and ended up sitting with the stoners by accident. He had no idea what the word "Buckle" meant in the Hopkins poem. And Mr. Wallace had to flag him down for physics class.

"Forget which room it is?" Mr. Wallace asked.

"Er."

There was no Mr. Wallace in Prime's home universe, and he had to dodge in-jokes and history between him and Johnny Farm Boy; the class was independent study! Prime realized he'd have to drop it. He was grateful when a kid knocked on the door.

"Mr. Gushman needs to see John Rayburn."

Mr. Wallace took the slip of paper from the acne-ridden freshman. "Again? Read the assignment for tomorrow, John. We have a lot to cover." The man was disappointed in him, but Prime couldn't find the emotion to care. He hardly knew him.

Prime nodded, then grabbed his stuff. He nudged the freshman hall monitor as they walked down the hall. "Where's Mr. Gushman at?"

The freshman's eyes widened like marbles. "He's in the front office. He's the principal."

"No shit, douche bag," Prime said.

Prime entered the fishbowl and gave his name to the reception-ist. After just a few minutes, Mr. Gushman called him in.

Prime didn't have anything on Gushman. He'd come to Findlay High School in the time Prime had been away. The old principal had fucked a student at his old school and that had come out in one of the universes that Prime had visited. That bit of dirt would be no good in this universe.

"Have you got the letter of apology for Mrs. Carson?" Mr. Gush-man asked.

Prime suddenly realized what the meeting was about. He'd not written the letter.

"No, sir. I've decided not to write the letter."

Mr. Gushman raised his eyebrows, then frowned. "You realize that this will have grave consequences for your future."

"No, I don't think so. In fact, I've contacted a lawyer. I'll be su-ing Ted Carson." Prime hadn't thought of doing that until that mo-ment, but now that he'd said it, he decided it was a good idea. "I'm an honor student, Gushman. I'm a varsity player in two sports. There will be fallout because of this. Big fallout."

"It's 'Mr. Gushman,' please. I'll have your respect." His knuckles were white, and Prime realized that Gushman had expected him to cave. Well, maybe Johnny Farm Boy would have caved, but not him. He had dirt on the education board members. He had dirt on the mayor. This would be a slam dunk for him.

"Respect is earned," Prime said.

"I see. Shall I have your mother called or do you have trans-portation home?"

"Home? Why?" Prime said.

"Your three-day suspension starts right now." Prime had forgot-ten about that. He shrugged. Johnny Farm Boy would have shit a brick at being expelled. To Prime, it didn't really matter.

"I can take care of myself."

"You are not allowed on school property until Thursday at noon.

I'll be sending a letter home to your parents. I'll also inform Coach Jessick that you are off the roster for basketball and track."

"Whatever."

Mr. Gushman stood, leaning heavily on the desk. His voice was strained as he said, "I expected better of you, John. Everything I know about you says that you're a good boy. Everything I've seen since you walked in this door has made me reevaluate my opinions."

Prime shrugged again. "Whatever." He stood, ignoring Gushman's anger. "We done here?"

"Yes. You are dismissed."

At least he didn't have to worry about learning basketball. And three days was enough time to get started on his plans. He smiled as he passed the receptionist, smiled at the dirtbags waiting in the office. This was actually working out better than he expected.

Prime took the two o'clock Silver Mongoose to Toledo, right after he stood in line at the Department of Motor Vehicles trying to convince the clerk to file the paperwork for his lost license.

"I am positive that it won't turn up," Prime said.

"So many people say that and then there it is in the last place you look."

"Really. It won't," he said slowly.

The clerk blinked at him, then said, "All righty, then. I'll take that form from you."

He was tempted to rent a car, but that would have raised as many eyebrows as hiring a patent lawyer in Findlay. Prime had to go to Toledo to get his business done. Three days off school was just about perfect.

As the northern Ohio farmland rolled by, he wondered how hurt he'd be if he had to transfer out right now. He was always considering his escape routes, always sleeping on the ground floor, always in structures that were as old as he could find. His chest itched where the device should have been. It was Johnny Farm Boy's problem now. Prime was free of it. No one would come looking for him here. He blended right in. No police would come barging in at 3:00 A.M. No FBI agents wanting his device.

What an innocent he'd been. What a piece of work. How many times had he almost died? How many times had he screwed up within centimeters of the end?

For a moment, he had a twinge of guilt for the displaced John. Prime hoped that John figured out a few things quickly, before things went to hell. Maybe he could find a place to settle down just like Prime had. Maybe I should have written him a note, he thought.

Then he laughed to himself. Too late for that. Johnny Farm Boy was on his own. Just like he had been.

The first lawyer Prime visited listened to him for fifteen minutes until she said she wasn't taking any new clients. Prime almost screamed at her, "Then why did you let me blather on for so long?"

The second took thirty seconds to say no. But the third listened dubiously to Prime's idea for the Rayburn's Cube. He didn't even blink at the cash retainer Prime handed over for the three patents he wanted him to research and acquire.

Prime called Casey from his cheap hotel.

"Hey, Casey. It's John!"

"John! I heard you were expelled for a month."

"News of my expulsion has been greatly exaggerated."

"What happened?"

"Just more of the Ted Carson saga. I told Gushman I wasn't going to apologize, so he kicked me out of school. You should have seen the colors on his face."

"You told Gushman no?" she asked. "Wow. He used to be a colonel in the army."

"He used to molest small children too," Prime said.

"Don't say that."

"Why? He sucks."

"But it's not true."

"It could be true, probably is in some other universe."

"But we don't know for sure."

Prime switched subjects. "Listen, I called to see if you wanted to go out on Saturday."

"Yeah, sure," she said quickly. "Yeah."

"Movie?"

"Sounds good. What's playing?"

"Does it matter?"

She giggled. "No." After a moment, she added, "Didn't your parents ground you?"

"Oh, shit!"

"What?"

"They don't know yet," Prime said. He looked at the cheap clock radio next to the bed: eight thirty. "Shit."

"Do you think we can still go out?"

"One way or another, Casey, I'll see you on Saturday."

"I'm looking forward to it."

He hung up.

His parents. He'd forgotten to call his parents. They were going to be pissed. Damn. He'd been without them for so long, he'd forgotten how they worked.

He dialed his home number.

"Mom?"

"Oh, my God!" she yelled. Then to his father she said, "Bill, it's John. It's John."

"Where is he? Is he all right?"

"Mom, I'm okay." Prime waited. He knew how Johnny Farm Boy would play this. Sure, he'd never have gone to Toledo, but Prime could play the suspension for all it was worth. "Did you hear from Gushman?"

"John, yes, and it's okay. We understand. You can come home. We aren't angry with you."

"Then, Mom, you know how I feel. I did the right thing, Mom, and they took everything away from me." It was what Farm Boy would have said.

"I know, dear. I know."

"It's not fair."

"I know, Johnny. Now where are you? You've got to come home." His mother sounded pitiful.

"I won't be home tonight, Mom. I've got things to do."

"He's not coming home, Bill!"

"Give me the phone, Janet." Into the phone his father said, "John, I want you home tonight. We understand that you're upset, but you need to be home, and we'll handle this here, under our roof."

"Dad, I'll be home tomorrow."

"John—"

"Dad, I'll be home tomorrow." He hung up the phone and almost chortled.

Then he turned on Home Theatre Office and watched bad movies until midnight.

"It turns *this* way, *this* way, and *this* way!" Prime made the motions with his hands for the fourth time, wishing again that he'd bought the key-chain Cube when he'd had the chance.

"Why?" Joe Patadorn was the foreman for an industrial design shop. He scratched his bald head with the nub of his pencil. He was dressed in blue coveralls with "Joe" stitched on the breast. The office and shop near the river smelled of machine oil. A pad of paper on his drafting board was covered in pencil sketches of cubes. "Rotate against what? It's a cube."

"Against itself! Against itself! Each column and each row rotates."

"Seems like it could get caught up with itself."

"Yes! If it's not a cube when you try to turn it, it'll not turn."

"And this is a toy people will want to play with?"

"I'll handle that part."

Joe shrugged. "Fine. It's your money."

"Yes, it is."

"We'll have a prototype in two weeks."

They shook on it.

His errands were finally done in Toledo. His lawyer was doing the patent searches and Patadorn was building the prototype. If Prime was lucky, he could have the first batch of Cubes ready to ship in a month. Too late for Christmas, but he didn't need a holiday for the fad to catch on.

From the bus stop he hiked the three miles to the farm, and stashed his contracts in the loft with the money there. When he was climbing down, he saw his dad standing next to the stalls.

"Hey. Am I in time for dinner?" Prime asked.

His father didn't reply, and then Prime realized that he was in trouble.

His father's face was red, his cheeks puffed out. He stood in overalls, his fists at his hips.

"In the house." The words were soft, punctuated.

"Dad—"

"In the house, now." His father lifted an arm, pointing.

Prime went, and as he entered the house, he was angry too. How dare Bill order him around?

His mother was waiting at the kitchen table, her fingers folded in a clenched, white mound.

"Where were you?" his father demanded.

"None of your business," Prime said.

"While you're in my house, you'll answer my questions!" his father roared.

"I'll get my things and go," Prime said.

"Bill . . . ," his mother said. "We've discussed this."

His father looked away, then said, "He pranced into the barn like he'd done nothing wrong."

His mother turned to him. "Where were you, John?"

He opened his mouth to rail, but instead he said, "Toledo. I had to . . . cool off."

His mother nodded. "That's important."

"Yeah."

"Are you feeling better now?"

"Yes . . . no." Suddenly he was sick to his stomach. Suddenly he was more angry with himself than with his father.

"It's okay," she said. "It's okay what you did, and we're glad you're back. Bill?"

His father grunted, then said, "Son, we're glad you're back." And then he took Prime in his big farmer arms and squeezed him.

Prime sobbed before he could fight it down, and then he was bawling like he hadn't since he was ten.

"I'm sorry, Dad." The words were muffled in his shoulder. Prime's throat was tight.

"It's okay. It's okay."

His mother joined them and they held on to him for a long time. Prime found he didn't want to let go. He hadn't hugged his parents in a long time.

CHAPTER 7

John's arms flailed and his left foot hit the ground, catching his weight. He groaned as his leg collapsed under him. He rolled across the grass.

Grass? he thought as the pain erupted in his knee. He sat up, rocking as he held his knee to his chest. He'd been on the steps of the library and now he was on a plain. The wind blew the smell of outside: dirt, pollen, clover.

He tried to stretch his leg, but the pain was too much. He leaned back, pulling off his backpack with one hand, and looked up at the sky, breathing deeply. It hurt like hell.

The device had worked. He had changed universes again. Only this universe had no library, no Findlay, Ohio. This universe didn't seem to have anything but grass. He fell because the steps he'd been standing on weren't in the universe he was in now.

He checked the readout on the device. He was in 7535. He'd gone forward one universe.

John looked around him but didn't see anything through the green-yellow grass. It rustled in the wind, making sounds like sandpaper rubbing on wood.

John stood gingerly on his other leg. He was on a broad plain, stretching for a good distance in every direction. There were small groves of trees to the north and east. To the west and south, the grass stretched as far as he could see.

There was no library to use to figure out what was different in this universe. No humans at all, maybe. A Mayan empire? If he wanted to find the differences, he'd have to do some field research.

He sat back down. No, he thought. He had to get back to his life. John Prime had some answers to give and a price to pay. It was Sunday afternoon. He still had half a day to figure out how to get back to his universe.

His knee was swelling, so he took off his coat and shirt. He ripped his T-shirt into long strips and used that to wrap his knee as tightly as possible. It wasn't broken, but he may have sprained it.

He took the sandwich that he had packed on Saturday from his backpack and unwrapped it. He finished it in several bites and rinsed it down with some of the water in his water bottle. The taste of the sandwich made him angry. Prime was eating his food and sleeping in his bed.

John spent the afternoon nursing his knee and considering what he knew, what he thought he knew, and what Prime had told him. The latter category he considered biased or false. What he knew, however, was growing.

Universe 7535 was the second one he'd visited. The device clearly still worked. His going from 7534 to 7535 proved that.

It was also support for his theory that the device only allowed travel to universes higher in number than the one a traveler currently resided in. But not proof. Hypotheses required repeatable experimental proof. He'd used the device to move forward through two universes. He'd have to do it a couple more times before he was certain that was the way the device worked.

He took a blade of grass and chewed on it. This was an unspoiled universe, he thought. Which gave him another piece of data. Universes sequentially next to each other could have little in common. John couldn't even begin to guess what had happened for a universe to not have North America settled by the Europeans.

There'd been no library steps here, so he had fallen three meters to the ground. More data: There was no guarantee that a man-made object in one universe would exist in the next. Nor even natural objects. Hills were removed or added by machines. Rivers were dammed and moved. Lakes were created. What would happen if he jumped to the next universe and the steps were there? Would he be trapped in the cement that formed the steps? Would he die of asphyxiation, unable to press the lever because he was encased in the library steps?

The thought of being entombed, blind and without air, horrified him. It was no way to die.

He would have to be careful when he changed universes. He'd have to be as certain as possible that there was nothing solid where he was going. But how?

Movement caught his eye and he looked up to see a large beast walking in the distance. It was so tall he saw it from his seat in the grass. A cross between a rhinoceros and a giraffe, it munched at the leaves of a tree. It was gray, with legs like tree limbs, a face like a horse. Leaves and branches gave way quickly to its gobbling teeth.

No animal like that existed in his universe.

John watched, amazed. He wished he had a camera. A picture of this beast would be a nice addition to his scrapbook. Would it be worth cash? he wondered.

Ponderously the beast moved to the next tree in the grove.

John looked around him with more interest. This was no longer a desolate North America. There were animals here that no longer existed in his time line. This universe was more radically different than he could have imagined.

The wave of the grass to the west caught his attention. The grass bobbed against the wind, and he was suddenly alert. Something was in the grass not twenty meters from him. He realized that large herbivores meant large carnivores. Bears, mountain lions, and wolves could be roaming these plains. And he had no weapons. Worse still, he had a bum knee.

He looked around for a stick or a rock, but there was nothing. Quickly he gathered the notebook into the backpack. He pulled his coat on.

Was the thing closer? he wondered. He glanced at the grass around him. Why hadn't he thought of that earlier?

John felt beneath his shirt for the device. He glanced down and toggled the universe counter up one to 7536. But he dared not pull the lever. He could be under the library right now.

He looked around him, tried to orient himself. The library entrance faced east, toward the Civil War Memorial. If he traveled east sixty meters, he'd be in the middle of the park and it was unlikely that anything would be in his way. It was the safest place he could think of to do the transfer.

Suppressing a groan, he moved off in an easterly direction, counting his steps.

At fifty-two steps he heard a sound behind him. A doglike creature stood five meters away from him in his wake in the grass. It had a dog's snout and ears, but its eyes were slits and its back was arched more like a cat's. It had no tail. Its fur was tan with black spots the size of quarters along its flank.

John froze, considering. It was small, the size of a border collie. He was big prey, and it may just have been curious about him.

"Boo-yah!" he cried, waved his arms. It didn't move, just stared at him with its slit eyes. Then two more appeared behind it.

It was a pack animal. Pack animals could easily bring down an animal larger than a pack member. John saw three of them, but there could be a dozen hidden in the grass. He turned and ran.

The things took him from behind, nipping his legs, flinging themselves onto his back. He fell, his leg screaming. He felt weight on his back, so he let the straps of his backpack slide off. He crawled forward another meter. Hoping he'd come far enough, he pulled the lever on the device.

A car horn screeched and a massive shape bore down on him.

John tried to scramble away, but his hand was stuck. As his wrist flexed the wrong way, pain shot up his arm.

He looked up, over his shoulder, into the grille of a car. John hadn't made it into the park. He was still in the street, the sidewalk a meter in front of him.

John got to his knees. His hand was embedded in the asphalt. He planted his feet and pulled. Nothing happened except pain.

"Buddy, you okay?" The driver was standing with his door open. John's eyes were just over the hood of the man's car.

John didn't reply. Instead he pulled again and his hand tore loose with a spray of tar and stones. The impression of his palm was cast in the asphalt.

The man came around his car and took John's arm. "You better sit down. I'm really sorry about this. You came outta nowhere." The man led him to the curb, then looked back and said, "Jesus. Is that your dog?"

John saw the head and shoulders of one of the cat-dogs. The transfer had caught only half the beast. Its jaws were open, revealing yellowed teeth. Its milky eyes were glazed over. Blood from its severed torso flowed across the street. A strand of intestine had unraveled onto the pavement.

"Oh, man. I killed your dog," the motorist cried.

John said between breaths, "Not . . . my . . . dog. . . . Chasing me."

The man looked around. "There's Harvey," he said, pointing to a police officer sitting in the donut shop that John had eaten in that morning. Well, not the same one, John thought. This wasn't the same universe, since this car was gas powered.

"Hey, Harvey," the man yelled, waving his arms. Someone nudged the police officer and he turned, looking at the blood spreading across the street.

Harvey was a big man, but he moved quickly. He dropped his donut and coffee in a trash can at the door of the shop. As he approached he brushed his hands on his pants.

"What happened, Roger?" he said. He glanced at John, who was too winded and too sore to move. He looked at the cat-dog on the street. "What the hell is that?"

He kicked it with his boot.

"This young man was being chased, I think. I nearly clipped him and I definitely got that thing. What is it? A badger?"

"Whatever it is, you knocked the crap out of it." Harvey turned to John. "Son, you okay?"

"No," John said. "I twisted my knee and my wrist. I think that thing was rabid. It chased me from around the library."

"Well, I'll be," said the officer. He squatted next to John. "Looks like it got a piece of your leg." He lifted up John's pant leg, pointed to the line of bite marks. "Son, you bought yourself some rabies shots."

The officer called Animal Control for the carcass and an ambulance for John. The white-uniformed Animal Control man spent some time looking for the other half of the cat-dog. To Harvey's questions about what it was he shrugged. "Never seen nothing like it." When he lifted up the torso, John saw the severed arm straps of his backpack on the ground. He groaned. His backpack, with seventeen hundred dollars in cash, was in the last universe under the other half of the cat-dog.

A paramedic cleaned John's calf, looked at his wrist and his knee. She touched his forehead gingerly. "What's this?"

"Ow," he said, wincing.

"You may have a concussion. Chased by a rabid dog into a moving car. Quite a day you've had."

"It's been a less than banner day," John said.

"'Banner day,'" she repeated. "I haven't heard that term in a long time. I think my grandmother said that."

"Mine too."

They loaded him into the ambulance on a stretcher. By the time the door had shut on the ambulance, quite a few people had gathered. John kept expecting someone to shout his name in recognition, but no one did. Maybe he didn't exist in this universe.

They took him to Roth Hospital, and it looked just like it did in his universe, an institutional building from the fifties. He sat for fifteen minutes on an examining table off of the emergency room. Finally, an older doctor came in and checked him thoroughly.

"Lacerations on the palm. The wrist has a slight sprain. Minor. The hand is fine." Looking at John's knee, he added, "Sprain of the right knee. We'll wrap that. You'll probably need crutches for a couple days."

A few minutes later, a woman showed up with a clipboard. "You'll need to fill these forms out," she said. "Are you over eighteen?"

John shook his head, thinking fast. "My parents are on the way."

"Did you call them?"

"Yes."

"We'll need their insurance information."

John stood wincing and peered out the door until she disappeared. Then he limped the other way until he found an emergency exit door. He pushed it open and hobbled off into the parking lot, the bleating of the siren behind him.

John shivered in the morning cold. His knee was the size of a melon, throbbing from the night spent on the library steps. The bell tower struck eight; Prime would be on his way to school right now. He'd be heading for English class. John hoped the bastard had done the essay on Gerard Manley Hopkins.

John had slept little, his knee throbbing, his heart aching. He'd lost the seventeen hundred dollars Prime had given him, save eighty dollars in his wallet. He'd lost his backpack. His clothes were ripped and tattered. He'd skipped out on his doctor's bill. He was as far from home as he'd ever been.

He needed help.

He couldn't stay here; the hospital probably called the police on his unpaid bill. He needed a fresh universe to work in.

Limping, he walked across to the Ben Franklin, buying new dungarees and a backpack.

Then he stood in the center of the town square and waited for a moment when no one was around. He toggled the universe counter upward and pressed the lever.

John climbed the steps to the library. This universe looked just like his own. He didn't really care how it was different. All he wanted was to figure out how to get home. He'd tried the device a dozen times in the square, but the device would not allow him to go backward, not even to universes before his own.

He needed help; he needed professional help. He needed to understand about parallel universes.

As he browsed the card catalog, it soon became apparent the Findlay library was not the place to do a scientific search on hypothetical physics. All he could find were a dozen science fiction novels that were no help at all.

He was going to have to go to Toledo. U of T was his second choice after Case. It was a state school and close. Half his friends would be going there. It had a decent, if not stellar, physics department.

He took the Silver Mongoose to Toledo, dozing along the way. A local brought him to the campus.

The Physics Library was a single room with three tables. Stacks lined all the walls and extended into the middle of the room, making it seem cramped and tiny. It smelled of dust, just like the Findlay Public Library.

"Student ID?"

John turned to the bespectacled student sitting at the front desk. For a moment, he froze, then patted his front pockets. "I left it at the dorm."

The student looked peeved, then said, "Well, bring it next time, frosh." He waved John in.

"I will."

John brought the catalog up on a terminal and searched for "Parallel Universe." There wasn't much. In fact, there was nothing at all in the Physics Library. He was searching for the wrong subject. Physicists didn't call them parallel universes of course. TV and movies called them parallel universes.

He couldn't think what else to search for. Perhaps there was a more formal term for what he was looking for, but he had no idea what it was. He'd have to ask his dumb questions directly of a professor.

John left the library and walked down the second-floor hall, looking at nameplates above doors. Billboards lined the walls, stapled and tacked with colloquia notices, assistantship postings, apartments to share. A lot of the offices were empty. At the end of the hall was the small office of Dr. Frank Wilson, Associate Professor of Physics, lit and occupied.

John knew associate professors were low on the totem pole, which was probably why Wilson was the only one in his office. And maybe a younger professor would be more willing to listen to what John had to say.

He knocked on the door.

"Come on in."

He entered the office, found it cluttered on all sides with bookshelves stacked to bursting with papers and tomes but neat at the center, where a man sat at an empty desk reading a journal.

"You're the first person to show for office hours today," he said. Professor Wilson was in his late twenties, with black glasses, a sandy beard, and hair that seemed in need of a cut. He wore a gray jacket over a blue oxford.

"Yeah," John said. "I have some questions, and I don't know how to ask them."

"On the homework set?"

"No. On another topic." John was suddenly uncertain. "Parallel universes."

Professor Wilson nodded. "Hmmm." He took a drink of his

coffee, then said, "Are you one of my students? Freshman physics?"

"No," John said.

"Then what's your interest in this? Are you from the creative writing department?"

"No, I . . ."

"Your question, while it seems simple to you, is extremely complex. Have you taken calculus?"

"Just half a semester. . . ."

"Then you'll never understand the math behind it. The authorities here are Hawking, Wheeler, Everett." He ticked them off on his fingers. "You're talking about quantum cosmology. Graduate-level stuff."

John said quickly before Wilson could cut him off again, "But my question is more practical. Not theoretical."

"Practical parallel worlds? Nonsense. Quantum cosmology states that there may be multiple universes out there, but the most likely one is ours, via the weak anthropic principle. Which means since we're here, we can take it as a given that we exist. Well, it's more complex than that."

"But what about other universes, other people just like us?"

The man laughed. "Highly unlikely. Occam's razor divests us of that idea."

"How would I travel between universes?" John said, grasping at straws against the man's brisk manner.

"You can't; you won't, not even remotely possible."

"But what if I said it was? What if I knew for sure it was possible?"

"I'd say your observations were manipulated or you saw something that you interpreted incorrectly."

John touched the wound in his calf where the cat-dog had bitten him. No, he'd seen what he'd seen. He'd felt what he'd felt. There was no doubt about that.

"I know what I saw."

Wilson waved his hands. "I won't debate your observations. It's a waste of my time. Tell me what you think you saw."

John paused, not sure where to start and what to tell, and Professor Wilson jumped in. "See? You aren't sure what you saw, are you?" He leaned forward. "A physicist must have a discerning eye. It must be nurtured, tested, used to separate the chaff from the wheat." He leaned back again, glanced out his window onto the quad below. "My guess is that you've seen too many Schwarzenegger movies or read too many books. You may have seen something peculiar, but before you start applying complex physical theories to explain it, you should eliminate the obvious. Now, I have another student of mine waiting, one I know is in my class, so I think you should run along and think about what you really saw."

John turned and saw a female student standing behind him, waiting. His rage surged inside him. The man was patronizing him, making assumptions based on his questions and demeanor. Wilson was dismissing him.

"I can prove it," he said, his jaw clenched.

The professor just looked at him, then beckoned the student into his office.

John turned and stalked down the hall. He was asking for help, and he'd been laughed at.

"I'll show him," John said. He took the steps two at a time and flung open the door to the quadrangle that McCormick Hall faced.

"Watch it, dude," a student said, almost hit by the swinging door. John brushed past him.

John grabbed a handful of stones and, standing at the edge of the quadrangle, began flinging them at the window that he thought was Wilson's. He threw a dozen and started to draw a crowd of students, until Wilson looked out the window, opened it, and shouted, "Campus security will be along in a moment."

John yelled back, "Watch this, you stupid bastard!" He toggled the device forward one universe and pulled the lever.

CHAPTER 8

John Prime awoke in the night, gripped by the same nightmare, trapped in darkness, no air, his body held rigid. He sat up and flung the covers away from him, unable to have anything touching him. He ripped off his pajamas as well and stood naked in the bedroom, just breathing. It was too hot; he opened the window and stood before it.

His breathing slowed as the heavy air of the October night brought the smells of the farm to him: manure and dirt. He leaned against the edge of the window, and his flesh rose in goose pimples.

It was a dream he'd had before, and he knew where it came from. He'd transferred near Lake Erie, on a small, deserted beach not far from Port Clinton, and ended up buried in a sand dune. He'd choked on the sand and would have died there if a fisherman hadn't seen his arm flailing. He could have died. It was pure luck that the guy had been there to dig his head out. He'd never transferred near a body of water or a river again.

That hadn't been the only time either. In Columbus, Ohio, he'd transferred into a concrete step, his chest and lower body stuck. He'd been unable to reach the toggle button on the device and had to wait until someone wandered by and called the fire department. They'd used a jackhammer to free him. When they'd turned to him, demanding how he'd been trapped, he'd feigned unconsciousness and transferred out from the ambulance.

After that, each time he touched the trigger he did so with the fear that he'd end up in something solid, unable to transfer out again, unable to breathe, unable to move. He was nauseated, his stomach kicking, his armpits soaked, before the jumps.

It was the cruelest of jokes. He had the most powerful device in the multiverse, and it was broken.

"No more," he said to himself. "No more of that." He had a family now, in ways he hadn't expected.

The confrontation with his parents had been angry, then sad, and ended with all of them crying and hugging. He'd meant to be tough; he'd meant to tell his parents that he was an adult now and could take care of himself, but his resolve had melted in the face of their genuine care for him. He'd cried, goddamn it all.

He'd promised to reconsider the letter. He'd promised to talk with Gushman again. He'd promised to be more considerate to his parents. Was he turning into Johnny Farm Boy?

Prime had gone to bed empty, spent, his mind placid. But his subconscious had pulled the dream out. Smothering, suffocating, his body held inflexible as his lungs screamed. He shivered, then shut the window. His body had expelled all its heat.

He slipped back into bed and closed his eyes.

"I'm becoming Johnny Farm Boy," he whispered. "Screw it all."

Prime helped his father around the farm the next day. He took it as penance for upsetting his parents. They still thought he was Johnny, and so Prime had to act the part, at least until his projects started churning.

As they replaced some of the older wood in the fence, Prime said, "Dad, I'm going to need to borrow the truck on Saturday night."

His father paused, a big smile on his face. "Got a big date, do you?" He said it in such a way that Prime realized he didn't think his son really had a date.

"Yes. I'm taking Casey Nicholson out."

"Casey?" His father held the plank as Prime hammered a nail into it. "Nice girl."

"Yeah, I'm taking her to a movie at the Bijou."

"The Bijou?"

"I mean the Strand," Prime said, silently yelling at himself for sharing details that could catch him up. The movie theater was always called the Palace, Bijou, or Strand.

"Uh-huh."

Prime took the shovel and began shoring up the next post.

"What movie you gonna see?"

Before he could stop himself, he answered, "Does it matter?"

His father paused, then laughed heartily. "Not if you're in the balcony, it doesn't." Prime was surprised; then he laughed too.

"Don't tell your mother I told you, but we used to go to the Strand all the time. I don't think we watched a single movie."

"Dad!" Prime said. "You guys were . . . make-out artists?"

"Only place we could go to do it," he said with a grin. "Couldn't use this place; your grandpa would have beat the tar out of me. Couldn't use her place; your other grandpa would have shot me." He eyed Prime and nodded. "You're lucky we live in more liberal times."

Prime laughed, recalling the universe where the free-love culture of the sixties hadn't ended until AIDS had killed a quarter of the population and syphilis and gonorrhea had been contracted by 90 percent of the population by 1980. There dating involved elaborate chaperone systems and blood tests.

"I know I'm lucky."

CHAPTER 9

The wind shoved at him, and, unprepared for it, John staggered into a snowdrift. He hurried to zip up his coat, then stuffed his hands into his pockets. Snow? It was only October.

He pulled himself up, leaning against the wind, and turned quickly to survey his locale. He was still on campus, but the place was desolate; the trees that had been holding leaves in the last universe were empty and black here. Dark clouds roiled above the roof of the physics building. The windows were broken out or boarded up, the doors chained shut. He smelled something burning, acrid. It was still the University of Toledo, but something was wrong here.

The snow was powdery and fine, and he guessed that it was near freezing and much colder with the windchill. John had no hat, and the wind pulled the heat from his forehead, giving him an instant headache. He turned away from the wind, but it still ripped through his coat. It was his fall coat, not his winter one. He walked with the wind, toward the center of campus.

He passed between two buildings. Ahead of him was a large open area, empty. Again the trees were black and dead, not like hibernating trees but like dead and rotten ones, as if they had not been alive for years.

He walked across the open space, staring up at the gnarled limbs. Ahead of him was a large building, the Student Union, he saw by the carved words above the door. Next to the door was a large sign, painted in red.

"The University of Toledo is closed during the current crisis until further notice." It was dated three years prior. The sign was weathered and beaten.

What crisis would close the school? John wondered. He walked around the Student Union and found himself looking down onto a river that ran toward the northeast. He knew this was the Ottawa River and that it would ultimately dump into Lake Erie on the north side of the city. The river was frozen over.

John was cold, but he was growing accustomed to the wind. He followed the river to the southwest. There were no other footprints in the snow. No one had passed here since the snow had last fallen. He had no idea when that might have been. There was a bridge behind him, and it had not been plowed. But then university facilities would not bother plowing if the campus was closed.

Ahead of him he heard an engine running, evidence of someone alive in this universe. John ran through the snow, feeling it collect in his shoes at his ankles. He rounded a building and saw an army truck, surrounded by soldiers parked on one of the campus roads. They held weapons and watched a line of civilians standing at the back of the truck.

A sign was posted near the truck: "UT Food Drop-Off, Tuesday, Thursday, Saturday."

As each person shambled forward, a soldier dropped two cans into their hands or their bag if they'd brought one. It was a food line.

John stood near the back of the line and watched.

Someone nudged him and said, "Line starts back there." John turned on the man, dressed in a bulky red coat and toboggan hat. Even under the coat, John could tell the man was thin.

"I'm not here for food," John said.

"No other reason to be out," the man replied. "Line's in back."

"What's happening here?" he asked.

"Food, maybe enough to last until I get up there. Probably not."

"Why won't you get any food?"

"'Cause I didn't get up at four A.M. like the rest of these yahoos. I slept in and so I'm late. Which ain't so bad. The wife has a card for the Ottawa Hills High School drop. We're right by there, so we're always first in line."

John couldn't guess how this universe came to be. Food lines and ration cards were not something that happened in the United States.

"Don't you think it's early for winter?" John asked.

"Early?" The man laughed. "It ain't early for winter. It's late for summer. Three years late." He nudged the guy in front of him. "You hear that, Rudy? Boy thinks winter is here early."

Rudy turned and cast an eye on John, then grunted. "Boy looks well fed, Stan."

Stan looked at John then, his eyes suddenly appraising him. "You a hoarder, son? That why you don't need food?"

John didn't like the way things were going, so he walked forward, knowing the two couldn't follow him or else they'd lose their places in line.

He stood away from the line and watched as person after person took their two cans of food. John saw that the cans were soup. The truck held dozens of boxes of Campbell's Chicken Noodle Soup.

A soldier saw him, noticed that he was watching, and stepped up to him.

"Why you loitering?" he said, his weapon held against his chest.

"I'm waiting, sir. Not making any trouble," John said.

The soldier nodded, relaxing. "Don't wait too long, okay?"

John nodded. The soldier stood there watching the line, not moving back to where he'd been standing. John ventured a question. "Do you think you'll have enough food?"

The soldier glanced at the truck, then at the length of the line. "I hope so. It's no fun when there isn't. Last week we had oranges—I have no idea where they came from—and we ran out. We had to push the crowd back and run before they tipped over the truck."

"Don't oranges come from Florida?" John asked.

"Not anymore. They plowed the last of the fields under last year. Planting wheat and soybeans. Farms in Kansas didn't get one crop in this year."

"It's nuclear winter, isn't it?" John said, half to himself.

The soldier looked at him. "Course it is. What do you think?"

John shrugged, then said, "What do you think caused it, in your opinion? What did you hear through the army?"

John and the soldier watched as a young woman and her daughter, maybe three or four years old, took their two cans. John could have eaten two cans of soup in a single sitting. How could the two of them and whoever else was at home survive on that?

"Same as was in the papers. Fucking Pakistanis. I can't blame the Indians, though their bombs did all the damage. If someone nuked Washington, I'd say nuke them right back. But the last count I heard was one hundred and seventeen bombs. Not a centimeter of Pakistan worth living on and the rest of the world cold."

John nodded. A nuclear winter was the result of the debris kicked up by nuclear explosions into the atmosphere. The dirt particles, so small by themselves, in bulk curtained the world from sunlight, causing a long winter. In this case, it had lasted three years already. A similar thing had wiped out the dinosaurs. A meteor had struck the Earth, cooling it enough that most of the dinosaurs died out.

"Any idea when it'll be over?" John asked. A nuclear winter would end slowly as the debris washed out of the sky.

"They're still saying a decade before it warms up again. I heard the scientists have some ideas on how to clean up the sky. Maybe it'll be less than that, but I ain't counting on it. We'll be driving through Texas into Mexico soon; I just know it."

"War?"

"Hell, yes. Mexico's gonna be a paradise. I have a cousin in Dallas who says the temperature never got above sixty this summer. Who'd have thought it? I spent a summer there when I was a kid. Hottest place I've ever been, just gullies and cactuses. Everything melting in the sun. If Texas is getting cold, then the only place to go is south, just like the Canadians did to us."

An officer waved at the soldier, told him to come back to the truck. They'd stopped handing soup out for the moment, and John saw why. The truck had been only half as full as he thought. The boxes filled only the back of the truck. The front was empty.

The soldier saw what was up as well. He motioned to John. "Step on back, friend. You might want to move along."

John backpedaled away as he felt the sound travel up the line like a force. "No food," he heard. "That's the last of it." And the line of waiting people transformed into a throng of voices. They surged at the truck, a hundred angry men and women.

"On the truck," the officer said. The soldiers stopped the advance with their weapons, lowering their rifles and aiming at the group. John didn't want to be in the mob, nor between them and the soldiers.

"Stop right there, people! More food is on the way," the officer said.

"Liar!"

"We've been waiting for hours."

The officer motioned all the soldiers into the truck, and the truck jumped away from the crowd. "More food will be here soon!" he shouted.

The crowd milled for a moment. John saw Rudy and Stan, their voices raised, shaking fists at the departing truck. Then Stan caught sight of the woman and the little girl, who had gotten the last of the soup. He jumped forward, running after the two who were walking slowly through the snow toward a bridge that crossed the Ottawa River.

John ran after Stan, knowing he meant to take their food.

There was a shot and the woman collapsed against the little girl, who slid over the side of the embankment toward the river. Stan shoved his gun back into his coat and grabbed the woman's bag. The army officer, hanging on to the tail of the truck, watched dispassionately. The truck didn't stop.

John slid in the snow next to the woman. Red welled from her wool coat, blackening the fabric, running onto the snow in bright rivulets.

"You shot her!" John cried.

Stan looked at him, shrugged, and walked away.

A small crowd of people gathered around them, peering down at the bleeding woman.

"Someone call an ambulance," John said. "She's been shot."

An old woman laughed. "No ambulances, don't you know?" She turned and walked off.

"Momma!"

John looked over the edge of the embankment. The little girl lay on the ice. He pointed at a young man standing in the circle and said, "You! Apply pressure here." He reluctantly complied, pushing on the woman's abdomen, trying to staunch the blood.

John slipped and slid down the embankment to the girl. He placed his foot on the ice slowly, then all his weight. It held, and he carefully stepped to the girl. Her leg was twisted oddly, and he knew she had broken it.

He lifted her carefully, then looked for a way up. Next to the bridge was a rocky trail, not too snowy, that led up the slope. He fell once, hearing the child cry out as he did, then managed to get to the top of the riverbank. The crowd was gone.

Even the man who'd been holding back the blood was gone, bloody footprints marking his retreat.

John laid the girl down next to her mother's face.

"Momma?" she said pitifully.

The woman's breathing was shallow, but she was alive. No ambulances, the old woman had said. Authorities looked the other way over killings for food. John was sure he could get no help in this universe for the woman.

And if she died, so would the child.

"Do you have a family, child?" John asked softly. She stared at him blankly. "Do you have a father or brothers or sisters?"

The girl shook her head. "No, just Momma."

"What's your name?"

"Kylie. Kylie Saraft."

John tried to think back to the severed cat-dog carcass. The thing had dove at him and been clinging to his back as he fell. The slice had looked perpendicular to the beast's torso, perhaps a meter behind John. That meant the device had a field of radius of one meter, at least.

"Hug your mother," John said. Kylie looked at him for a moment, her eyes hard. John wondered what atrocities she had seen in her short life. Then she took John's hand and slid against her mother's body, groaning when her leg flexed suddenly.

John toggled the universe counter forward to 7539, slipped in beside the two on the ground. He pulled them as tight as he could. They felt like skeletons. He could easily feel the ribs of both of them, the bones in their arms.

There was no one in this universe for them. They'd been left for dead. No family, no medical help. If he didn't help them, they would die. He had to do this.

Grasping them both, he pulled the lever.

"Jesus," someone said.

John stood. The snow was gone, except for the bits that clung to his legs and the woman's back. The daughter and the woman had come through with him. All of them, no bloody stumps. The field of the device seemed to have covered him, the woman and the girl, and a pile of snow.

"What happened to you, man?"

John turned to the students looking on. The woman was lying on a footpath that followed the Ottawa River; a half-dozen students stood around them.

"This woman's been shot. We need an ambulance."

"No way, man," the student said. He wore black denim pants, a black jeans jacket. An earring dangled from his left ear, and a stocking cap, also black, covered his head. He looked around, as if he could find an ambulance that way.

"Does anyone have a phone?" John said. "This woman is bleeding to death."

A female student, holding her books in front of her like a shield, pointed to a lamppost ten meters away. "Security phone's over there."

John ran over and picked the phone up. It began to ring immediately. "Campus security."

"Yes. There's a woman shot at this location. And a little girl with a broken leg. Send an ambulance."

"Please state your name."

"Is the ambulance coming?"

"Yes."

John hung up the phone. The chill of the other universe had left him. It was a warm October day here. No food riots, no shootings over two cans of Campbell Chicken Noodle. He watched the crowd of well-fed students gather around the woman and her child.

The girl had sat up and was looking at all the strange faces, perhaps wondering where all the snow had gone. Within a minute, John heard the wail of sirens. He looked down at his blood-soaked jacket and realized he'd have to answer a lot of questions.

He pulled his jacket off, turned it inside out, and walked away. What more could he do?

He'd brought them to a universe where food was plentiful. Sure, he'd ripped them out of their home universe. But there was no one there for them. It was better for them in this next universe, John was certain, though he had no idea what this universe was like. It seemed close enough to his own. There would be Welfare and services for the two. They would survive. He'd helped them.

John Prime had done the same thing to him, he realized. Guilt and anger knotted his stomach. He'd saved their lives, damn it! He hadn't kidnapped them. He'd saved them. It was nothing like what Prime had done to him.

The ambulance pulled up and two EMTs began working on the woman. Moments later a university police car arrived.

John continued walking. He needed someplace to clean up. Ahead of him was the field house. He assumed it would have a locker room. Maybe he could fake his way in as he had at the Physics Library in the earlier universe. His shirt and jacket were soaked in blood. His shoes were soaked with melted snow and squeaked as he walked.

The field house was an old building adjacent to the quad he had walked through to get to the Student Union. McCormick Hall was there; he saw the telescope observatory rising above the other buildings.

There was no one barring his way into the locker room, so he slipped in and found the showers. There were a couple guys changing clothes, but no one noticed him.

John stripped down and hung the device on a hook in the shower alcove. Then he wrung out his shirt and coat. Red swirls circled the drain and disappeared. He used his hands to wash the streaks of blood off the shower curtain.

Afterwards, he dried his clothes as best he could on the hand drier. He would have preferred a washing machine, but at least the blood was gone. As he leaned against the hand drier, he wondered what would happen with the woman and her daughter. He hoped that they would, if not understand, at least cope with being in another universe. Just like he was doing.

As he walked across the quad from the field house to McCormick Hall, John was taken aback by the juxtaposition of this same grass field with the one in the other universe. The trees weren't gnarled and hideous here; they still held a bouquet of colorful leaves, as students flung Frisbees or lounged around, on one of the last warm days of the year. Some of the students were even wearing shorts, and John compared these well-fed, fleshy children to the boney, malnourished people of the last universe. There the clouds roiled; here the sun shined.

He decided not to feel guilty about bringing the woman and her daughter here. If he could, he thought, he'd bring everyone from that universe here. The inhabitants of that universe thought they had to live with the world as it was, but they didn't. Here was a universe with food to spare. Did they realize that salvation and plenty was in the universe next door? If he had a device that was large enough, one that worked right, he could transfer thousands of people through.

A large enough device, he thought. If he had a device that worked, he'd get himself home. He looked for the physics building. He had what he needed to confront Wilson now.

CHAPTER 10

McCormick Hall looked identical. In fact, the same student guarded the door of the Physics Library, asked John the same question.

"Student ID?"

"I left it in my dorm room," John replied without hesitation.

"Well, bring it next time, frosh."

John smiled at him. "Don't call me frosh again, geek."

The student blinked at him, dismayed.

His visit with Professor Wilson had not been a total loss. Wilson had mentioned the subject that he should have searched for instead of parallel universe. He had said that the field of study was called quantum cosmology.

Cosmology, John knew, was the study of the origin of the universe. Quantum theory, however, was applied to individual particles, such as atoms and electrons. It was a statistical way to model those particles. Quantum cosmology, John figured, was a statistical way to model the universe. Not just one universe either, John hoped, but all universes.

He sat down at a terminal. This time there were thirty hits. He printed the list and began combing the stacks.

Half of the books were summaries of colloquia or workshops. The papers were riddled with equations, and all of them assumed an advanced understanding of the subject matter. John had no basis to understand any of the math.

In the front matter of one of the books was a quote from a physicist regarding a theory called the Many-Worlds Theory: "When a quantum transition occurs, an irreversible one, which is happening in our universe at nearly an infinite rate, a new universe branches off from that transition in which the transition did not occur. Our universe is just a single one of a myriad copies, each slightly different than the others."

John felt an affinity for the quote immediately. He had seen other universes in which small changes had resulted in totally different futures, such as Alexander Graham Bell's invention of the electric motor. It almost made sense then that every universe John visited was one of billions in which some quantum event or decision occurred differently.

He shut the book. He thought he had enough to ask his questions of Wilson now.

The second-floor hallway seemed identical, right down to the empty offices and cluttered billboards. Professor Wilson's office was again at the end of the hall, and he was there, reading a journal. John wondered if it was the same one.

"Come on in," Wilson said at John's knock.

"I have a couple questions."

"About the homework set?"

"No, this is unrelated. It's about quantum cosmology."

Wilson put his journal down and nodded. "A complex subject. What's your question?"

"Do you agree with the Many-Worlds Theory?" John asked.

"No."

John waited, unsure what to make of the single-syllable answer. Then he said, "Uh, no?"

"No. It's hogwash in my opinion. What's your interest in it? Are you one of my students?" Wilson sported the same gray jacket over the same blue oxford.

"You don't believe in multiple universes as an explanation . . . for . . ." John was at a loss again. He didn't know as much as he thought he knew. He still couldn't ask the right questions.

"For quantum theory?" asked Wilson. "No. It's not necessary. Do you know Occam's Theory?"

John nodded.

"Which is simpler? One universe that moves under statistical laws at the quantum level or an infinite number of universes, each stemming from every random event? How many universes have you seen?"

John began to answer the rhetorical question.

"One," said Wilson before John could open his mouth. Wilson looked John up and down. "Are you a student here?"

"Uh, no. I'm in high school," John admitted.

"I see. This is really pretty advanced stuff, young man. Graduate-level stuff. Have you had calculus?"

"Just half a semester."

"Let me try to explain it another way." He picked up a paper-weight off his desk, a rock with eyes and mouth painted on it. "I am going to make a decision to drop this rock between now and ten seconds from now." He paused, then dropped the rock after perhaps seven seconds. "A random process. In ten other universes, assuming for simplicity that I could only drop the rock at integer seconds and not fractional seconds, I dropped the rock at each of the seconds from one to ten. I made ten universes by generating a random event. By the Many-Worlds Theory, they all exist. The question is, where did all the matter and energy come from to build ten new universes just like that?" He snapped his fingers. "Now extrapolate to the nearly infinite number of quantum transitions happening on the Earth this second. How much energy is required to build all those universes? Where does it come from? Clearly the Many-Worlds Theory is absurd."

John shook his head, trying to understand the idea. He couldn't refute Wilson's argument. He realized how little he really knew.

He said, "But what if multiple worlds did exist? Could you travel between the worlds?"

"You can't; you won't, not even remotely possible."

"But—"

"It can't happen, even if the theory were true."

"Then the theory is wrong," John said to himself.

"I told you it was wrong. There are no parallel universes."

John felt the frustration growing in him. "But I know there are. I've seen them."

"I'd say your observations were manipulated or you saw something that you interpreted incorrectly."

"Don't condescend to me again!" John shouted.

Wilson looked at him calmly, then stood.

"Get out of this office, and I suggest you get off this campus right now. I recommend that you seek medical attention immediately," Wilson said coldly.

John's frustration turned to rage. Wilson was no different here than in the last universe. He assumed John was wrong because he acted like a hick, a farm boy. He was certain John knew nothing that he didn't already know.

John flung himself at the man. Wilson's papers scattered across his chest and onto the floor. John grabbed at Wilson's jacket from across the desk and yelled into his face, "I'll prove it to you, goddamn it! I'll prove it."

"Get off me!" Wilson yelled, and pushed John away. Wilson lost his balance when John's grip on his jacket slipped and he fell on the floor against his chair. "You maniac!"

His breathing coming hard, John stood across from the desk from him. John needed proof. His eyes saw the diploma on the wall of Wilson's office. He grabbed it and ran out of the office. If he couldn't convince this Wilson, he'd convince the next. He found an alcove beside the building and transferred out.

John stood clutching Wilson's diploma to his chest, his heart still thumping from the confrontation. Suddenly he felt silly. He'd attacked the man and stolen his diploma to prove to another version of him that John wasn't a wacko.

He looked across the quad. He watched a boy catch a Frisbee, and then saw juxtaposed the images of him tripping and not catching it, just missing it to the left, to the right, a million permutations. Everything in the quad was suddenly a blur.

He shook his head, then lifted the diploma so that he could read it. He'd try again, and this time he'd try the direct approach.

John climbed the steps to Wilson's office and knocked.

"Come on in."

"I have a problem."

Wilson nodded and asked, "How can I help?"

"I've visited you three times. Twice before you wouldn't believe me," John said.

"I don't think I've ever seen you before," he said. "You're not one of my students, are you?"

"No, I'm not. We've never met, but I've met versions of you."

"Really."

"Don't patronize me! You do that every f—" John stopped himself, then continued slowly. "You do that every time, and I've had enough." His arms were shaking. "I don't belong in this universe. I belong in another. Do you understand?"

Wilson's face was emotionless, still. "No, please explain."

"I was tricked into using a device. I was tricked by another version of myself because he wanted my life. He told me I could get back, but the device either doesn't work right or only goes in one direction. I want to get back to my universe, and I need help."

Wilson nodded. "Why don't you sit down?"

John nodded, tears welling in his eyes. He'd finally gotten through to Wilson.

"So you've tried talking with me—other versions of me—in other universes and I won't help. Why not?"

"We start by discussing parallel universes or quantum cosmology or Multi-Worlds Theory, and you end up shooting it all down with Occam's razor."

"Sounds like something I'd say," Wilson said, nodding. "So you have a device."

"Yeah. It's here." John pointed to his chest, then unbuttoned his shirt.

Wilson looked at the device gravely. "What's that in your hand?"

John glanced down at the diploma. "It's . . . your diploma from the last universe. I sorta took it for proof."

Wilson held out his hand, and John handed the diploma over. There was an identical one on the wall. The professor glanced from one to the other. "Uh-huh," he said, then after a moment, "I see."

He put the diploma down and said, "My middle name is Lawrence."

John saw that the script of the diploma he'd stolen said "Frank B. Wilson" while the one on the wall said "Frank L. Wilson."

"I guess it's just a difference—"

"Who put you up to this? Was it Greene? This is just the sort of thing he'd put together."

Anguish washed over John. "No! This is all real."

"That device strapped to your chest. Now that's classic. And the diploma. Nice touch."

"Really. This is no hoax."

"Enough already. I'm on to you. Is Greene in the hall?" Wilson called through the door, "You can come out now, Charles. I'm on to you."

"There is no Charles. There is no Greene," John said quietly.

"And you must be from the drama department, because you are good. Two more copies of me! As if the universe can handle one."

John stood up and walked out of the office, his body suddenly too heavy.

"Don't forget the shingle," Wilson called, holding up the diploma. John shrugged and continued walking down the hall.

He sat on a bench next to the quad for a long time. The sun set and the warm summer day vanished along with the kids playing Frisbee with their shirts tied around their waists.

Finally he stood and walked toward the Student Union. He needed food. He'd skipped lunch at some point; his stomach was growling at him. He didn't feel hungry, but his body was demanding food. He just felt tired.

There was a pizza franchise in the Student Union called Papa Bob's. He ordered a small pizza and a Coke, ate it mechanically. It tasted like cardboard, chewy cardboard.

The Union was desolate as well, all the students driving home or heading to the dorms for studying and TV. John spotted a pay phone as he sat pondering what he would do next, whether he should confront Wilson again. John realized that he should have taken a picture of the man or demanded he write himself a note. But he would have told John that it was computer generated or forged.

John walked over to the phone and dialed his number. The phone demanded seventy-five cents. He inserted the coins and the phone began to ring.

"Hello?" his mother answered.

"Hello," he replied.

"Johnny?" she asked, surprised.

"No. Could I talk to John please?"

She laughed. "You sound just like him. Gave me a fright, hearing that, but he's standing right here. Here he is."

"Hello?" It was his voice.

"Hi, this is Karl Smith from your English class," John said, making up a name and a class.

"Yeah?"

"I missed class today, and I was wondering if we had an assignment."

"Yeah, we did. We had an essay on the poem we read, Tennyson's 'Maud.' Identify the poetic components, like the last one."

"Oh, yeah," John said. The poem was in the same unit as the

Hopkins one. He remembered seeing it. "Thanks." He hung up the phone.

This universe seemed just like his own. He could fit right in here. The thought startled him, and then he asked himself what was stopping him.

He walked to the bus station and bought a ticket back to Findlay.

CHAPTER 11

In the early hours of the morning, John slipped across Gurney, through the Walders' field, and found a place to watch the farm from the copse of maple trees. He knelt on the soft ground, wondering if this was where John Prime had waited for him.

John's arms tingled as he anticipated his course of action. He was owed a life, he figured. His had been stolen and he was owed another. He'd wanted his own back, and he'd tried to get it. He'd researched and questioned and figured, but he couldn't see any way back.

So he was ready to settle for second best.

He'd trick the John Rayburn here, just like he'd been tricked. Tease him with the possibilities. Tickle his curiosity. And if he wasn't interested, John would force him. Knock him out and strap the device on his chest and send him on.

Let him figure it out like John had. Let him find another universe to be a part of. John deserved his life back. He'd played by the rules all his life. He'd been a good kid; he'd loved his parents. He'd gone to church every Sunday.

Prime had pushed him around, Professor Wilson, the cat-dogs. John had been running and running and with no purpose. And enough of that. It was time to take back what had been stolen from him.

Dawn cast a slow red upon the woods. His mother opened the back door and stepped out into the yard with a basket. He watched her open the henhouse and collect eggs. She was far away, but he recognized her as his mother instantly. Logically he knew she wasn't his mother, but to his eyes she was. That was all that mattered.

His father pecked her lightly on the cheek as he headed for the barn. He wore heavy boots, thick ones, coveralls, and a John Deere cap. He entered the barn, started the tractor, and drove toward the fields. He'd be back for breakfast in an hour, bacon, eggs, toast, and, of course, coffee.

They were John's parents. It was his farm. Everything was as he remembered it. It was what he wanted.

The light in John's room turned on. John Rayburn was awake. He'd be coming out soon to do his chores. John waited until this John went into the barn; then he dashed across the empty pumpkin field for the barn's rear door. The rear door was locked, but if you jiggled it, John knew, it came loose.

John grabbed the handle, listening for sounds from within the barn, then shook it once for a few seconds. The door held. He paused, then shook it again, and it came open suddenly, loudly. He slipped into the barn and hid between two rows of stacked bales.

"Hey, Stan-Man. How are you this morning?"

The voice came from near the stalls. This John—he started thinking of him as John Subprime—was feeding his horse.

"Here's an apple. How about some oats?"

John crept along the row of bales, then stopped when he could see the side of John Subprime's face from across the barn. John was safe in the shadows, but he needed to get closer to him.

Stan nickered and nuzzled John Subprime's head, drawing his tongue across his forehead.

"Stop that," he said, with a smile.

John Subprime turned his attention to the sheep, and when he did so John slipped around the bales and behind the corn picker.

How could he trick himself? John wondered. He couldn't. He

couldn't do to another John what Prime had done to him. There was no duplicity in him. John wasn't a liar. He wasn't a smooth talker. He couldn't do what Prime had done to him, that is, talk him into using the device. John would have to do it some other way. And the only way he could think to do it was the hard way.

John lifted a shovel off a pole next to the corn picker. It was a short shovel with a flat blade. He figured one blow to the head and John Subprime would be out cold. Then John would strap the device to his chest, toggle the universe counter up one, and hit the lever with the end of the shovel. It'd take half the shovel with him, but that was okay. Then John would finish feeding the animals and go in for breakfast. No one would ever know.

John ignored the queasy feeling in his stomach. Gripping the shovel in two hands, he advanced on John Subprime.

John's faint shadow must have alerted him.

"Dad?" John Subprime said, then turned. "My God!" He shrank away from the raised shovel, his eyes passing from it to John's face. His expression changed from shock to fear.

John's body strained, the shovel raised above his head.

John Subprime leaned against the sheep pen, one arm raised.

He had only one arm.

Nausea washed through John's body, and he dropped the shovel. It clattered on the wood floor of the barn, settled at John Subprime's feet.

"What am I doing?" John cried. His stomach heaved, but nothing came up but a yellow bile that he spat on the floor. He heaved again at the smell of it.

He was no better than Prime. He didn't deserve a life.

John staggered to the back door of the barn.

"Wait!"

He ran across the field. Something tangled his feet and he fell. He pulled his foot free and ran into the woods.

"Wait! Don't run!"

John turned to see John Subprime running after him, just one arm, the right, pumping. He slowed five meters in front of John, then stopped, his hand extended.

"You're me," he said. "Only you have both arms."

John nodded, his breath too ragged, his stomach too tense, to speak. Tears were welling in his eyes as he looked at the young man he had contemplated clubbing.

"How can that be?"

John found his voice. "I'm a version of you."

John Subprime nodded vigorously. "Only you never lost your arm!"

"No, I never lost it." John nodded his head. "How did it happen?"

John Subprime grimaced. "Pitchfork. I was helping Dad in the barn loft. I lost my balance, fell. The pitchfork caught my biceps, sliced it. . . ."

"I remember." In John's universe, he'd been twelve and he had fallen from the loft while he and his father loaded it with hay. He had thought he could carry the bale, but he hadn't been strong enough and he'd fallen to the farmyard, knocking the wind out of himself, bumping the pitchfork over as he fell. The pitchfork had landed next to him, nicking his shoulder. His father had looked on in horror and then anger. The scolding from John's mother had been worse than the nick. "I just got a cut on my shoulder. In my world."

John Subprime looked confused. Then he laughed. "In one world I lose my arm, and in another I get a scratch. Don't that beat all." Why was he laughing?

"Yeah."

"Why don't you come inside and have some breakfast?"

John looked at him, unsure of how he could ask that. He yelled, "I was going to steal your life!"

John Subprime nodded. "Is that why you had the shovel? Then you saw my arm. No way you could steal my life. You've got two arms." He laughed.

"It wasn't just that," John said. "I couldn't bring myself to hurt . . ."

"Yeah, I know."

"No, you don't" John yelled. "I've lost everything!" He reached into his shirt and toggled the universe counter. "I have to leave."

"No. Wait!" John Subprime yelled.

John backed away and pulled the lever.

The world blurred and John Subprime blinked away.

There was the barn and the farmhouse, and off in the distance John's father on the tractor. Another universe where he didn't belong. He toggled the device and pulled the lever. Again the farmhouse. He didn't belong here either. Again he moved forward through the universes. The farmhouse was gone. And again. Then it was there, but green instead of red. He toggled the counter again and again, wanting to get as far away from his contemplated crime as possible.

The clouds flew around in chaotic fast motion. The trees he stood in were sometimes there, sometimes not. The farmhouse bounced left and right a foot, a half foot. The barn more, sometimes behind the house, sometimes to the east of it. The land was the one constant, a gently sloping field. Once he found himself facing the aluminum siding of a house. And then it was gone as he transferred out.

A hundred times he must have transferred through universe after universe where he didn't belong until finally he stopped and collapsed to the ground, sobbing.

He'd lost his life. He'd lost it all, and he'd never get it back.

He rested his head against the trunk of a maple and closed his eyes. After the tears were gone, after his breathing had slowed, he slept, exhausted.

CHAPTER 12

"Hey there, fella. Time to get up."

Someone poked him. John looked up into his father's face.

"Dad?"

"Not unless my wife's been hiding something from me." He offered a hand, and John pulled himself up. John was in the copse of maples, his father from this universe standing beside him, holding a walking stick. He didn't recognize John.

"Sorry for sleeping here in your woods. Got tired."

"Yeah. It'll happen." He pointed toward Gurney with his stick. "Better be heading along. The town's that way." He pointed north. "About two miles."

"Yes, sir." John began walking. Then he stopped. His father hadn't recognized him. Which meant what? John wasn't sure. He turned back to him. "Sir, I could use some lunch. If you have extra. I could work it off."

Bill Rayburn—John forced himself to use the name in his head; this man was not his father—checked his watch, then nodded. "Lunch in a few minutes, my watch and my stomach tell me. Cold cuts. As to working it off, no need."

"That's fine."

"What's your name?"

"John . . . John Wilson." He took Professor Wilson's last name spontaneously.

John turned and followed Bill across the pumpkin field toward the house. The pumpkins were still on the vine, unpicked and just a week until Halloween. Some of them were already going bad. John passed a large one with its top caved in, a swarm of gnats boiling out of it.

He remembered the joke his father had told him a week ago.

"How do you fix a broken jack-o'-lantern?" he asked.

Bill turned and glanced at him as if he were a darn fool.

"I don't know."

"With a pumpkin patch," John replied, his face straight.

Bill stopped, looked at him for a moment; then a small smile crept across his lips. "I'll have to remember that one."

The barn was behind the house, smaller than John remembered and in need of paint. There was a hole in the roof that should have been patched. In fact, the farm seemed just a bit more decrepit than he remembered. Had hard times fallen on his parents here?

"Janet, another one for lunch," Bill called as he opened the back door. "Leave your shoes."

John took his shoes off, left them where he always did. He hung his bag on a hook. It was a different hook, brass and molded, where he remembered a row of dowels that he and his father had glued into the sideboard.

John could tell Janet wasn't keen on a stranger for lunch, but she didn't say anything, and she wouldn't until she and Bill were alone. John smiled at her, thanked her for letting him have lunch.

She wore the same apron he remembered. No, he realized. She'd worn this one, with a red check pattern and deep pockets in front, when he was younger.

She served John a turkey sandwich, with a slice of cheese on it. He thanked her again as she did, and ate the sandwich slowly. Janet had not recognized him either.

Bill said to Janet, "Got some good apples for cider, I think, a few bushels."

John raised his eyebrows at that. He and his father could get a couple bushels per tree. Maybe the orchard was smaller here. Or maybe it had been hit with blight. John glanced at Bill and saw the shake in his hand. He'd never realized how old his father was, or maybe he had aged more quickly in this universe for reasons unknown. Maybe a few bushels was all he could gather.

"I should work on the drainage in the far field tomorrow. I've got a lake there now and it's going to rot my seed next season." The far field had always been a problem, the middle lower than the edges, a pond in the making.

"You need to pick those pumpkins too, before they go bad," John said suddenly.

Bill looked at him.

"What do you know of farming?"

John swallowed his bite of sandwich, angry at himself for drawing the man's resentment. John knew better than to pretend farm another farmer's fields.

"Uh, I grew up on a farm like this. We grew pumpkins, sold them before Halloween, and got a good price for them. You'll have to throw half your crop away if you wait until Sunday, and then who'll buy that late?"

Janet said to Bill, "You've been meaning to pick those pumpkins."

"Practically too late now," Bill said. "The young man's right. Half the crop's bad."

"I could help you pick them this afternoon." John said it because he wanted to spend more time there. It was the first chance he'd had in a long time to relax. They weren't his parents; he knew that. But they were good people.

Bill eyed him again appraisingly.

"You worked a farm like this, you say. What else you know how to do?"

"I can pick apples. I can lay wood shingles for that hole in your barn."

"You been meaning to do that too, Bill," Janet said. She was warming to John.

"It's hard getting that high up, and I have a few other priorities," Bill said. He looked back at John. "We'll try you out for the day, for lunch and dinner and three dollars an hour. If it isn't working out, you hit the road at sundown, no complaining."

John said, "Deal."

"Janet, call McHenry and ask him if he needs another load of pumpkins and if he wants me to drop 'em off tonight."

CHAPTER 13

John waited outside the county clerk's window, his rage mounting. How damn long did it take to hand over a marriage certificate? Casey was waiting for him outside the judge's chamber, nine months pregnant. If the man behind the glass wall took any longer, the kid was going to be born a bastard. And Casey's and John's parents had been adamant about that. No bastard. He'd said he'd take care of the kid and he meant it, but they wanted it official.

Finally the clerk handed over the license and the two notarized blood tests and John snatched them from his hand.

"Thanks," John said, turning and heading for the court building.

After the wedding he and Casey were driving up to Toledo to honeymoon on the last of his cash. In a week he was scheduled to start his GE job. He was going to work one of the assembly lines, but that was just until the book he was writing—*The Shining*—took off.

The trip to Toledo served the purpose of the honeymoon, as well as the fact that he had meetings regarding the screwed-up Rubik's Cube. It still irked him. The patent search had turned up nothing and they had built a design, one that finally worked, and they'd sunk ninety-five thousand dollars into a production run. Then they'd gotten a call from the lawyer in Belgium. Apparently there was a patent filed in Hungary by that bastard Rubik. The company Rubik had hired in New York to market the things had gone under and he'd never bothered to try again. Someone had gotten wind of John's product, and now they wanted a piece of the deal.

The lawyer had wanted to drop John like a hot potato, but he'd convinced him that there was still cash to be made from it. Some cash at least. He'd have to pay a licensing fee probably. Kiss some ass. But there was money to be made. The lawyer would stick it out with John, though the retainer was just about gone.

Casey waved as he rounded the corner on the third floor in front of the judge's office. Casey sat on a bench, her belly seeming to rest on her knees. Her face was puffy and pink, as if someone had pumped her with saline.

"Hi, Johnny," she said. "Did you get the paper?"

He hated being called Johnny and he'd told her that, but she still did it. Everybody used to call Johnny Farm Boy Johnny, so John was stuck with it. Some things just couldn't be changed.

He put on a smile and waved the certificate. "Yeah," he said. "Everything's ready." He kissed Casey on the cheek. "Darling, you look radiant." He'd be glad once the baby was out of her body; then she could start dressing the way he liked again. He hoped her cheerleading uniform still fit.

The ceremony was quick, though Casey had to dab her eyes. John wasn't surprised that none of Casey's friends were there. Getting pregnant had put a lot of stress on her relationships. Field hockey had been right out.

The judge signed the certificate and it was done. John was glad Casey's and his parents hadn't come. They'd wanted to, but John had axed that request. They had settled for a reception after the baby was born.

John knew his parents were disappointed in what had happened, and he hadn't wanted to face them during the ceremony.

They'd wanted him to go to college, to better himself. But those were the dreams they had for Johnny Farm Boy. John was a completely different thing.

They'd understand once the money started rolling in. They'd not be disappointed in their son anymore.

John slowly lowered Casey into the bucket seat of the Trans Am, a splurge with the last of his cash. He had to have decent wheels. The Trans Am pulled away and he headed for Route 16. "Glad that's over with," he said.

"Really?" Casey asked.

"Well, I'm glad it's over with and we're married now," he said quickly.

"Yeah, I know what you mean."

John nodded. He had to be careful what he said with Casey, what he shared. About the time she'd started showing and they'd had to tell their parents, John had wished he had the device, wished he could jump to the next universe and start over. John felt then he should have killed Johnny Farm Boy, hidden the body, and kept the device. Now the Cube had to work right. With John's money almost gone, he might not have another chance, no matter how good an idea the AbCruncher was. He'd wanted to come clean and tell Casey all about his past, but how could he? How could she believe him?

He was stuck here and he had to make it work. There were no other choices now. This was the life he'd chosen. He patted Casey's leg and smiled at her. He'd make some money, enough to set her and the kid up, and then he'd have his freedom to do what he wanted with his money. It would take a little longer now; there were some bumps in the road, but he'd succeed. He was Johnny Prime.

CHAPTER 14

Spring had arrived, but without the sun on his shoulders, John was chilly. He'd started working on the car in the morning and the sun had been on him, and now, after lunch, it was downright cold. He considered getting the tractor out and hauling the beat-up Trans Am into the sun. He finally decided it was too much trouble. It was late and there was no way he'd get the carburetor back together before dinner.

He'd bought the car for fifty dollars, but the car had yet to start. He'd need it soon. He started a second-shift job at the GE plant in May. And then in the fall he was taking classes at the University of Toledo.

He'd applied to the University of Toledo's continuing-education program. He couldn't enroll as a traditional freshman, which was all right with him, because of the fact that he'd taken the GED instead of graduating from high school. He wouldn't get into the stuff he wanted to learn until his senior year: quantum field theory, cosmology, general relativity. That was all right. He was okay where he was for the time being. If he didn't think about home, he could keep going.

With the plant job, washing-machine assembly line work from four until midnight, he'd have enough for tuition for the year. Plus Bill and Janet were still paying him three an hour for chores he was helping out with. He noted ironically to himself that in his own universe he wouldn't have been paid a dime. In September he'd get another job for pocket money and rent near the university.

He set the carburetor on the front seat and rolled the car back into the barn. This was a good universe, John had decided, but he wasn't staying. No, he was happy with Bill and Janet taking him in. They were kind and generous, just like his own parents in nearly every respect, but he couldn't stay here. Not for the long term.

The universe was a mansion with a million rooms. People didn't know they were in just one room. They didn't know there was a way through the walls to other rooms.

But John did. He knew there were walls. And he knew something else too. He knew walls came down. There were holes between worlds.

John had listed his major as physics, and he'd laughed when the manila envelope from the department had arrived, welcoming him and listing his faculty advisor as Dr. Frank Wilson. Professor Wilson's world was going to shatter one day, and John was going to do it for him.

John knew something that no other physicist in this world knew. A human could pass through the walls of the universe. Just knowing that it was possible, just knowing, without a bit of doubt—he needed only to pull up his pant leg and look at the scars from the cat-dog bite—that there were a million universes out there, was all it would take for John to figure the science of it out.

That was his goal. He had the device and he had his knowledge. He'd reverse engineer it, take it apart, ask the questions of the masters in the field, he would himself become one of those masters, to find out how it was done.

And then, once the secrets of the universe lay open to him, he would go back; he would kick the shit out of John Prime and take his own life back.

He smiled as he shut the barn door.

Part Two

Part Two

John Prime awoke from a nightmare of suffocation. Casey's elbow nudged him in the ribs.

"Your turn," she muttered.

At first Prime thought she was talking in her sleep, and he rolled over, pulling the covers with him. The second-hand bed squeaked as he moved. Then he heard Abby scream.

"Fuck," he said.

The alarm clock blazed 2:17. He had to get up in three hours for work at the plant. Why couldn't Casey feed the baby? He was the one bringing in the money. All she had to do was stay home with Abby all day.

Abby's screams turned to tiny shrieks. The Williamses upstairs would be complaining to the landlord if Prime didn't do something.

He sat on the edge of the bed, rubbed his eyes, then stood. He pulled on some shorts. He should have just started wearing pajamas; it wasn't like Casey and he had done it anytime recently.

He stumbled into the kitchenette and opened the refrigerator, glaring at the light. He found the fullest bottle of formula and nuked it for thirty seconds. By the time he made it to Abby's room, she was bright red and so angry her shrieks were nearly silent.

Prime lifted her to his shoulder, his own anger gone, his own resignation lifted away. She struggled against his neck for a moment and then went still, sobbing silently. The maternity nurses had been shocked when he'd asked to be present for the birth. That was a small difference between his universe and this one. But he had insisted, and Casey had been glad for him next to her. He had viewed the blotchy purple Abby with a mixture of feelings. Pride, yet fear. Joy, yet frustration. She was another millstone, just like his marriage, just like his job.

He sat in the wooden rocking chair his mother had given them. It squeaked reassuringly. Abby rooted for the plastic nipple, and fell silent save the slurping.

Would he have used the device if he still had it? Always it had been a getaway, a fail-safe. He had tried to stay before, vowing never to use the device again. He'd tried to make a life for himself. Every time he transferred out, he was terrified, guilty, depressed.

Now there was no choice. But would he have, if he could?

He pulled the nipple out of Abby's mouth, and the bottle sucked in air.

It was safe here. He had made it safe, for once. How many times had he almost died because of that damn device? It had even made him a murderer. His mind returned to Thomas and Oscar. It had been around 7450 or so, early on in Prime's flight. He had switched out after the police had busted in his door, having time only to grab his emergency bag.

In the dawn light, he had been surprised to see a well-worn path and in the distance a palisade. It looked like a Pleistocene universe, one of the unpopulated ones, where all of North America was mastodons and saber-toothed tigers. But there was a human-made structure.

He checked the sky: no contrails. He checked the horizon for power lines and cell towers. Nothing. The little transistor radio he had in the emergency pack emitted nothing but static.

"Weird," he muttered.

He started down the path.

As the palisade came into view, Prime caught the smell of burning wood and roasting meat. A guard, dressed in cured skins and armed with a twelve-foot-long pike, leaned against the gate. He didn't show surprise at Prime's arrival down the well-worn path, nor at Prime's clothes.

"Another one? And young," the guard said, shaking his head. "Welcome to Fort America, home of the truly free. Got anything on you?"

The man reached into Prime's jacket, and Prime jumped back.

The guard seemed about to press the point, then shrugged.

"Why would you, then? They never leave us with anything useful." He pulled out a clipboard and said, "Thomas has a spot in his crew for a tenderfoot. See that bunkhouse? Ask for him there."

Prime wondered at the way the guard had expected people to show up at the gate. Was that common? He spoke unaccented English, which seemed anachronistic in this wilderness world.

The gate was open, and inside were two longhouses and several smaller huts, built of logs and skins. A battlement ran around the inside of the outer wall. At the parapet at two-meter intervals leaned pikes with stone heads. What were these people fortified against?

The courtyard was empty except for a couple of women tending a cooking fire, slowly turning a spit. The quartered beast was nothing Prime recognized, too large for the hindquarters of a cow. The women eyed him dully.

Prime knocked on the rough wooden door of the first longhouse.

"Come in!" someone yelled.

Prime entered and found himself in a long room of bunk beds, rough-hewn from logs. The room smelled of sap and fresh wood. Two young men leaned against one bunk, talking.

"Who are you?"

"John. The guard at the gate sent me here."

"Jesus! Another one, and a kid," the first said. "You don't know metallurgy, do you, kid?"

"Uh, no."

"Oh, well. I'm Thomas; this is Oscar. I'm captain and he's lieutenant of this bunk." Thomas was tall and blond, like the quarterback of a football team. Oscar was shorter, with a shaved head.

Oscar said, "What have you got on you? Hand it over."

Prime backed away.

"Leave him alone," Thomas said. "They never drop anybody off with anything of value." To Prime he said, "Come on. We were just about ready to walk out to the mine. My crew is working a coal seam today, and they're probably loafing."

Thomas led him out the back of the bunkhouse and then through a smaller gate in the fort wall. This one was there for convenience, it seemed, as there was no guard. It was wide open, though it could have been closed with a wooden latch. They grabbed pikes as they passed through the gate. Prime grabbed one too.

"What universe are you from?" Thomas asked.

"Seven-four-three-three," Prime said.

"Yeah? I don't think we've got anyone from there. What did they nab you for? Hacking? Propagandizing?"

"I don't know."

Oscar looked at him sharply. "A dark grab. What makes you so special?"

"Nothing," Prime said.

"Yeah," said Oscar. "Nothing special."

They walked over a small hill and came to a river that cut through a shallow valley. Workers, standing knee-deep, were panning the water. Others were hacking at a seam of coal they had opened on the hillside, already half-exposed by the river. There were a dozen guards watching up- and downstream. A couple were positioned on the hills.

Thomas went to speak with a few of the workers, leaving Oscar with Prime.

"Gold for conductors. Coal for our steam engine," Oscar said. "We're thinking about a trip to the old Fort Pitt area to mine some iron."

Thomas came back to them holding a small nugget of gold. "A few meters of wire, at least," he said.

He led them up the far hill of the valley. Prime struggled to understand what they were doing: reconstructing a technological world in a primitive earth. Were they colonists? Were they running from something? Hiding here? They must have their own devices, maybe ones that worked right.

Oscar said, "We think we can build a transporter in about a hundred years. You'll still be a young man, and if you have any children after the sterilization wears off, your children might get back home."

Prime stopped. These people were from high-tech worlds. The primitive living wasn't a choice. These people were stranded, just like him.

"You people don't have a device? A transporter of your own?" he asked.

Thomas barked a laugh. "Of course they wouldn't let us have a device."

"But I have one," Prime said, then cut himself off. It was too late. Thomas and Oscar turned on him.

"You fucking liar," Oscar said.

"Yeah," Prime said. "Yeah. I was just kidding." His hand went inside his shirt, toggling the button for the next universe. He was on natural land, no man-made depressions. Prime would be all right if he transferred out here.

"What you got there?" Thomas said. Oscar grabbed him by the arm.

"Nothing!" Prime cried. He couldn't reach the lever, his arm caught in Thomas' viselike grip. Prime tried with his other hand, but Oscar batted it away.

Thomas nodded at Oscar, who pulled up Prime's coat and shirt.

They stared at the device strapped to Prime's chest, their faces stunned.

Oscar said, "Jesus, he has a portable."

"Where did you get that?"

"You stupid kid! What the fuck are you doing with a portable?" Oscar yelled, reaching under Prime's shirt for the device.

Prime kicked, connected with something, and rolled away.

Thomas' grip found Prime's shoulder and pulled him back like he was a sock puppet.

He pressed a knee against Prime's throat. He pulled a knife.

"Do you believe this?" he asked Oscar.

"Fuck it, no."

The knife cut at the straps holding the device. Prime flinched. He figured the next slice would open his belly.

Thomas stood with the device, leaving Prime to gasp and hold his throat.

Thomas and Oscar held the device between them, marveling, ignoring Prime as they had before.

"Frigate is going to shit when he sees this."

"We're going back home."

"Home? We're going anywhere we damn well please."

Prime pushed himself off the ground.

They stood holding the device as if it were a baby. Didn't they know how much trouble it had caused him? Didn't they know it was *broken*?

But Prime had earned that broken device; he had traded his own life for it, and damn it, these assholes weren't going to take it away.

Prime lunged at the device, snagging it from Thomas' grip. In a moment he was past them.

"Hey!"

A hand caught his leg, and he went down, Oscar and Thomas atop him.

"You're dead now," Oscar said. Thomas' knife loomed above him.

Prime's finger found the lever. He pressed it.

The world shifted in an explosion of blood. He squeezed his eyes shut. Hot liquid covered his chest and legs. Something hard—the broken knifepoint—scratched his cheek.

Prime stood, scrambling away, his gorge rising.

He wiped his eyes clear, and looked at what had come through with him. Thomas' hand, the front of Oscar's chest, and a foot littered the ground, bits of the men who had been in the radius of the field when Prime had pulled the button. Looking at the flesh, he realized that Oscar was dead and Thomas was maimed. On that primitive world, with a severed hand, he would probably die.

Prime spewed his lunch onto the ground.

After his stomach was empty, he stood and cleaned himself as well as possible. He'd found others who knew of travel between worlds, and they'd tried to kill him. Fuck them, he thought.

He had thought at first to bury the pieces of body but decided to leave them for the animals. What sympathy did the men deserve from him? Prime'd picked the next universe and left them there to rot.

He looked down, realizing Abby was asleep. He lifted her gently into her crib, where she rustled for a moment, then lay still. Sometimes it was best just to keep still, to stop running, and take the best bolt-hole you could find. The universes were too dangerous.

Prime could barely keep his eyes open the next morning. He flubbed his assembly twice, dropping bolts into the washer tub and having to stop the line to fetch them. He ignored the glares of his co-workers. Fuck 'em, he thought. Fuck 'em all. He'd be out of there as soon as things started shaping up.

Lunch didn't come soon enough, and when it did, his mind wouldn't focus on the words. Stephen King made it seem so easy. Prime had seen the movie twice, and he'd even skimmed the book. Writing *The Shining* should have been simple. He was taking every lunch hour to write, or rather remember. And there was no King in this universe. Prime had been sure to check. No way was the guy going to show up and accuse Prime of plagiarism. He should have brought a paperback edition with him.

"Hey."

What had happened in Room 237?

"Hey! Rayburn!"

Prime looked up. A teenager he vaguely recognized was addressing him from the next table where he sat with a few friends, all his age.

"You knocked up Casey Nicholson, didn't you?"

Prime ran cold. His hands twisted into fists.

Carson. Ted Carson. Prime remembered him now. The asshole who had gotten him expelled from school, or rather Johnny Farm Boy expelled.

Prime forced his anger down. He exhaled, then smiled. "Aren't you Ted Carson? The famous Ted Carson?"

Carson looked at him with confusion. "You know who I am, Rayburn!"

"You're famous!"

"What are you talking about?" His bluster was fading away.

"A lot of animals go missing in your neighborhood, I hear," Prime said.

Ted's face paled.

"You know anything about that? Seen any evidence, maybe?"

Prime smiled as Carson's neck tendons stood out. His jaw was so tightly clenched he couldn't speak. His friends cast glances at him; what had started as some gentle bullying had taken a turn they couldn't understand.

Prime could.

"What are you practicing for, killer?" Prime asked softly.

Carson broke the stare and glanced left and right at his friends. He stood and stormed off.

"Screw you, Rayburn," he shouted.

Prime shrugged and laughed. He glared at the remaining pack of summer interns.

"Well?" he said. "What do you want?"

They turned away, and Prime turned back toward his novel.

At quitting time, he felt his neck bristle and turned to see Ted Carson and a man with the same jowly face staring at him. Wouldn't you know it? Prime thought. Ted Carson's dad works at the plant too. Now he had two Carsons to deal with.

CHAPTER 16

His lab class was in the old physics building—Hermangild Hall—a stone edifice with wooden-floored hallways that echoed with voices and footsteps. John had traveled universes, but he still wasn't too sure of himself in crowds. He was still a small-town kid at heart. He turned and counted room numbers, realizing his lab was in the basement. He found a stairwell, and as he descended, the smell of mold and dust tickled his nose. Naked bulbs were strung along the ceiling, and he was certain he was lost.

"You look lost," someone said.

John turned to find a frizzy-haired woman standing in a doorway.

"Looking for physics lab? You're in the right place," she said.

"Uh, thanks," John said.

The room behind was fifteen meters long and five wide. Six black-lacquered tables were arranged in two rows, and a dozen students sat around them waiting for class. John found a seat at an empty table.

He felt someone at his elbow and turned to find the frizzy-haired woman had followed him.

"Can I sit here too?"

"I guess."

She dumped her bursting backpack on the floor next to John, then sat. She held out her hand.

"I'm Grace. Grace Shisler."

"John," he replied, shaking. "Ray—John Wilson."

"Is your middle name Ray?" Grace asked.

John blushed, embarrassed to have made a mistake with his alias. "No. It's just . . . It's irrelevant."

"Okay, John Ray, whatever you say."

John looked around for another table to sit at, but they were all full.

"Hey! Henry! Over here!" Grace shouted. Half the class craned their necks around, and John blushed again. He hated standing out.

Henry was a tall, gangly fellow, with dark hair and a slouch. He sat next to Grace and gave John a grunt in greeting.

"Henry's in Alcott," Grace said. "I'm in Benchley. We met at one of those mixer things they give for freshmen. Imagine that, both of us engineering majors. What dorm you in, John Ray?"

"It's just John. Um, I'm off campus," he said.

"How'd you swing that?" Grace asked. "All freshmen have to stay in the dorm. You're a freshman, aren't you? This is freshman physics lab."

"I'm a freshman, but nontraditional," John said. Without a high school diploma, without any sort of documentation at all, he'd been forced to take the GED and apply to the UT continuing-education program. If this universe had required any ID beyond his faked birth certificate, he would have been in big trouble.

"Cool, nontraditional," Grace said. Henry grunted. "What do you think of Higgins' class? I did everything he's covered so far in high school."

John nodded. The freshman physics class had been utterly useless to him, but there was no way he'd be able to understand the advanced physics he needed to master the device without starting with the basics. It was why he'd decided to attend the university, to understand enough to understand the device. But everything was so maddeningly irrelevant: engineering drafting, Electronics 101, freshman physics, European history, English! Of course, what school would offer a class on cross-dimensional travel? Maybe MIT.

"I wonder what's going to be on the quiz," Grace said. "I hope it's hard."

John glanced at her. She was smiling at him.

"You want us to sit somewhere else?" she asked.

John blushed for a third time. "No. I'm just—"

"—a little introverted?"

"A little. Not used to all this."

"Well, just sit back and relax," Grace said. "Leave the driving to me. I'm helping Henry acclimate to college too."

John glanced at Henry, who shrugged silently.

Grace was forced to, if not be silent, then at least keep her volume low as the teaching assistant explained the lab for the day. It was all about velocity, acceleration, and momentum. They dropped wooden disks down a ramp and measured the time it took for the disks to travel the length of the board at various angles. Henry worked the stopwatch, Grace recorded the times, and John dropped the disks. John was surprised to look up at the end of the class and find they were the last ones there, having worked through the ancillary material on friction.

"That was pretty cool," Henry said, the only opinion he had uttered all day.

"Yeah!" Grace said.

"It's like a pinball machine," John said.

"A what?" Grace asked.

"Pinball," he said. "The ramp is like the play field. The disk could be the ball. If we added bumpers and paddles . . ." He trailed off. "What?"

"What are you talking about? Pinball?" Grace asked.

"Oh," John said. "Never mind, something I saw as a kid . . . in Las Vegas. Hard to explain." He realized he'd found one of the anomalies that he had been tripping on now and again since he'd arrived in Universe 7650. Like the weird soda names: Pepsi and Dutch's. He was used to Zotz and Coke. And saying, "Good health!" when someone sneezed instead of, "God bless you." There was no pinball in this world.

"Oh, Vegas," Grace said. "Hey, you want to eat with us at the dining hall?"

John checked his watch. It was past five.

"Thanks, no," he said. "I have dinner at my apartment."

"Sure. Apartment food," Grace said. "I understand."

"See you next week," he said.

"Yeah, see you," Grace said.

Henry grunted.

John pried up the boards in the closet while the water for his ramen noodles boiled. He withdrew the lockbox, dialed the combination quickly, and opened it. The device was wrapped in a lambskin cloth.

It had taken him a while to stop wearing it, to put it aside. The day he had, he'd realized he was going to be staying in this universe for a long time. He took out the rest of the items in the box: a jeweler's tool set, a magnifying glass.

He realized that he needed one more thing now: a notebook. He and Henry had copied the numbers that Grace had written down during their experiment into their own notebooks. John Prime had had his own notebooks, but John hadn't bothered. He realized now that he needed to document everything.

He brought the magnifying glass close to the edge of the device, looking for some detail, some hint. He ran his finger across the edge. The metal was smooth and cold. There were no warm spots anywhere on the device.

John wished he had been nicer to Henry and Grace, but it scared him to befriend anyone in this universe. These people were all shades and shadows, copies of themselves, one of a billion identical people. What good was it befriending them? He was leaving one day.

The kettle whistled. He carefully packed the device and his tools away. There was a comfort in deciding to follow a meticulous scientific method in his analysis of the device. Sooner or later it would yield its secrets.

CHAPTER 17

"So explain this pinball thing you saw in Las Vegas."

"Why?" John said. He glanced at Grace from across the air table. They were doing a linear momentum problem in two dimensions: floating disks on an air table and bouncing them together.

"Henry wants to know," Grace said.

"Is that so?" John asked Henry.

Henry shrugged.

"He says he did a literature search on 'pinball' and couldn't find anything," Grace said.

John shook his head. "Would you launch the slug?"

Henry let the slug—the moving disk—fly. It zipped across the table toward the target disk. The camera overhead flashed four times. It whirred and dispensed a flimsy paper photograph of the disks twice before and twice after the collision. From that they would be able to calculate the linear momentum transfer between the two disks. John retrieved the target disk and replaced it with a disk twice the mass.

"Why are you checking up on me?"

Grace actually looked confused, and John realized he was being paranoid.

"We're not checking up on you! We're just—you know—interested," she said.

John sighed again. He should have changed lab partners after the first lab, but instead he'd stuck with Henry and Grace. He also should have kept his big mouth shut about things that were common in his universe and not here. Of course it was hard to know what those were until he got a blank stare in return, which meant it was better to not talk with anyone at all. But he was stuck with these two.

"It was just a game, not for betting, and there probably was only one of them ever made," John said. "And it was a long time ago, which is why you didn't find any reference."

"Explain," Henry said.

The slug hit the heavier disk and the camera flashed.

"Inclined plane, ball bearing, flippers," John said. "You bounced the ball off the scoring things until the ball slipped past you."

"I don't get it," Grace said.

"Yeah," Henry added.

John found himself explaining pinball while they bounced more disks together. They worked through six weights of disk, as well as three mystery weights, which they had to calculate via the equations of momentum.

"I'm gonna have to see it," Henry finally said, which was the most John had ever heard him say in one conversation.

"Well, we can't go to Las Vegas!" John cried, frustrated.

"We can build one," Grace said. "Henry and I are on Lab Squad."

"Lab Squad?"

"All the freshmen got a letter last year about Lab Squad," Grace said. "You must have thrown yours out. Lab Squad is the coolest student group in the engineering school. We help the senior and grad students in the lab with their work, and we get to do our own experiments during off-hours. We have keys."

"I didn't get that letter," John said.

"Oh, right, you're a nontraditional student," Grace said. "Good thing you know us. We can create a pinball project, and you can help us build a pinball . . . device."

"Pinball machine," John said automatically.

"I like 'pinball device' better," she said.

"It doesn't matter," John said. "We're not doing it." Anything like that, any exploitation of technology from across universes, felt too much like John Prime and his schemes for John to stomach.

"It's just a—," Grace began.

"No." John slammed the disks into their slot in the box. He shoved his notebook into his backpack and left the lab.

He wasn't going to become like Prime. There was no way John was doing something like that. Cross-dimensional trade. No way. Prime was an exploiter. He was a user, and John wasn't anything like that. And why were Henry and Grace pushing him? It was better if he just switched sessions and did lab on Mondays. He couldn't get too close to anyone in this universe. He was leaving, as soon as he figured out the device.

He found himself in the Student Union, cutting through to get to the far side of campus where his apartment was. A word on a bulletin board caught his eye: "Findlay". It was a ride share board. Someone needed a ride to Findlay, for gas. John had planned to go see Bill and Janet the next weekend anyway. He read the name on the board: "Casey Nicholson."

His hand hovered over the tab with her phone number on it. Oh, no, he thought. Not her.

He reached out and tore her phone number away.

CHAPTER 18

That Friday, John drove his car over to Benchley Hall, one of the undergrad women's dorms, but the U in front of it was jammed with cars. He parked at a student lot about a kilometer away, then walked back.

He was nervous, and he chided himself for it. She didn't know him; he didn't know her. The Casey he knew was far away. She was John Prime's now for all he knew. Prime certainly had shown interest in her.

But this Casey was an unknown factor. She might be completely different from the one John remembered. She might have the same name but a totally different genetic makeup. She might be dark haired and short, not the tall blonde he knew. She might be mean-spirited. She might be a lesbian. She might have a boyfriend.

She probably did have a boyfriend, a pretty girl like her.

John brooded as he walked the last hundred meters.

This was all a mistake, he was sure. He should be minimizing his problems, not adding to them. What would he say to her? We shared a class, but you don't remember me. I had a crush on another version of you. He'd sound like a total wacko.

The front atrium of the dorm was a madhouse of people: It seemed like everyone was going home for the weekend. Laundry and luggage were piled everywhere. John found the house phone and dialed Casey's extension.

"Hello?" someone said, definitely not Casey. Benchley Hall was all quads, so Casey shared the room with three other women.

"Is Casey there?"

"Is this Jack?"

"Uh . . . no. I'm her ride to Findlay."

"Oh, right. She'll be right down."

He hung up wondering if Jack was her boyfriend. Jack was probably on the football team. Or he was a medical student. Or he was a professor in the music college. Not any of whom John could compete with. Not that he would. She wasn't his Casey.

He stood by the elevators waiting. She got off, carrying a green duffel bag. Her hair was blond and bobbed, one of the current styles in this universe; he was glad she wasn't wearing a beehive. She wore baggy dungarees and cowboy boots. Her coat was a lettered jacket from Findlay High School. Casey looked just like he remembered.

"Casey?"

"John?"

"Yeah. I'm your ride. Can I carry your bag?"

She hitched it up her shoulder and said, "No. I got it. Let's go." They fought their way through the throng at the door. "This is worse than move-in day," she called over her shoulder.

"Johnny! Johnny!"

John turned at the shrill voice.

"Hey, Johnny," Grace said. She wore a shirt that said: "I'm Not Dead Yet." She had hold of the inside door behind him.

John looked back at Casey, holding the outside door, looking back at him, and then over his shoulder at Grace.

"Hey, Grace," he said, trying to not match her shrill, piercing tone.

"Did you hand in your lab notebook?"

"Yeah, I did," he said, turning again to look at Casey. She looked back at him with a smile. "I'll see you later," John said to Grace.

"Okay. Happy Freya Day! Bye, Casey!"

"Right."

Casey nodded and turned away. Then they were through and into the crisp evening air.

"How'd you know it was me coming off the elevator?" she asked.

"Your jacket."

"Oh, yeah," she said, looking down at the jacket. "As close as Findlay is, you'd think more people would be from there here at the university."

"Yeah."

"But not many people in my class went on to college." She looked at him. "You go to Findlay High?"

"Uh, no," he said. "But I know people who did."

"Where'd you go then?"

"School in Columbus. I know people in Findlay, though. That's where I'm heading for the weekend."

"Yeah? Who?"

"Bill and Janet Rayburn. They're my aunt and uncle."

"Yeah?"

"On McMaster."

"Yeah, I know them. They go to my church. They're over by the abandoned rock quarry. I've been there. The quarry, I mean." She looked around the U outside the dorm. "Where'd you park?"

"Not too close. Sorry. You sure I can't take your bag?"

"Yeah. Lead on."

After a moment, Casey said, "So you're Grace's Johnny?"

"What? I'm not her . . . I mean we're not . . ."

"She's got a thing for you, Johnny."

"She does not! It's professional between us."

"Uh-huh. You should hear her talk, and can she talk. You'd think you were Jesus Johnny Christ, but not a celibate one." She smiled at him.

"She's just my lab partner," John said, exasperated. "Besides, I thought she and Henry were a thing."

"You mean that guy who never talks?"

"That's the one."

Casey shrugged.

They reached John's car. "Over here," he said. He unlocked the trunk and took Casey's bag.

"A Trans Am?" she said.

"Yeah."

"I didn't picture you in a muscle car for some reason."

"It was cheap. I rebuilt it this summer," he said, suddenly defensive. "You don't like my car?"

"It's better than my car," she said with a smile. "You gonna let me drive?"

John shut the trunk and looked at her. Then he tossed her his keys. "Sure."

She smiled and ran around the car to the driver's side.

"You're a brave man."

For a smile like that, he would have let her do anything.

"So you're in physics? You must be smart," she said as she accelerated onto I-75.

He shrugged, though she probably couldn't see it from the driver's seat. The engine growled as she edged the car in front of a semi. The truck had a flat front, like all the trucks in this universe, and reminded him yet again of the 1950s of his universe. Everything had a retro feel to it here.

"I'm in psychology, but it sucks. Boring. It sounded a lot better in the guidance counselor's office," she said, and he laughed.

She'd taken the car through a series of back roads, not going straight for the interstate. At one point she had the car up to 115 kilometers per hour on a small road in the middle of nowhere.

"Psychology could be fun," John ventured, knowing he sounded like a fool as he said it.

"Yeah, whatever," she said, sliding the car around a slower Olds. "I'm thinking of switching to premed. My biology class rocks.

Speaking of which . . ." She turned on the radio and zipped through his presets. "Country, country, country, blues." She glanced over at him. "Don't you listen to rock and roll?"

John shrugged again. The truth was that the rock and roll of this world sounded like the golden oldies of his own. And the new hard reverb was impossible to appreciate. The only music that sounded decent to him was country. There was none of the heavy metal rock that he listened to when he was back home.

She rotated the dial to find the Toledo rock station.

"Bill and Janet seem like nice folks," she said. "I've met them at church stuff."

"Yeah, they're real nice," John said quickly, glad the conversation had turned away from his lack of taste in music. "I spent the last twelve months working the farm with them." He'd gone to church with them too but had never seen Casey there. He hadn't thought to look, maybe because he could never shake the feeling that this universe wasn't real.

"Farm boy, huh. You got that look to you."

"Do I? Don't I look like a physicist?"

"No. Not at all. You look like you should be driving a tractor or a pickup truck."

"Huh."

"Don't take it the wrong way," she said with a laugh. "I knew lots of farm boys in high school."

"Where you were a cheerleader and a flirt?" John asked, wanting to defend himself.

"Well, yeah. A girl's gotta do what a girl's gotta do. You know, I barely remember high school, and it's been like six months. All my friends were saying, 'Stay in touch,' 'Write every day.' Bullshit like that. None of them write. None of them call."

"They're busy."

"Having kids, getting married, working minimum-wage jobs. At least they can afford to buy cars. I have to bum a ride off a farm boy." She looked at him slyly, and John realized she was making fun of him.

"And I have to give rides to flirty cheerleaders for gas money."

"Touché." She paused, then said, "So what's this pinball device Grace keeps talking about? You guys are building it? I can't understand what she's talking about half the time."

"We're not—," John started; then he shrugged. "It's just a game I saw once. Played on a ramp with a metal ball. It's a game of skill and luck."

"Yeah?"

John spent fifteen minutes trying to explain how pinball worked. When he was done, Casey nodded and said, "Sounds cool. When you guys get it done, show it to me."

"We're not—," he said. "Okay, I will."

She fell silent after that, and John spent the next half hour super-aware of how close he was to her. Casey smelled good. She looked good. His body wanted to test all his other senses on her as well.

Three times he almost spoke up, wanting to ask her out, start the conversation again. The trip to Findlay was too damn short to waste it in silence.

Finally, forcing himself to say anything, he said, "Your roommate thought I was Jack." He instantly regretted saying it because he sounded too damn needy.

She laughed, though. "Jack? That is funny. He's some slobbery frat boy I gave the time of day to at a party. He's from Findlay too."

"Oh, then he's not a boyfriend."

She looked at John with her pale blue eyes, and he knew what she was thinking. He knew she dealt with such puppy dog affection like his on a regular basis.

"No, not a boyfriend. I'm unattached at the moment. I had a boyfriend back in Findlay, but he was a junior and long-distance relationships don't work."

"Findlay and Toledo aren't that far apart."

"It wasn't the *physical* distance, John."

She took the Findlay exit, taking Bigelow into the north side of town. Her family lived in an older house, built in the 1800s. It had three stories and a widow's watch. Two huge oak trees towered over the lawn.

She pulled up in front of the house and hopped out. John grabbed her bag and handed it to her.

"What time should I pick you up?"

"Tomorrow?" she asked with a smile.

"I thought we're heading back on Sunday."

"We are. But I thought you could come by on Saturday. Around eight?" She smiled and put the bag over her shoulder. On the porch, her mother had opened the door and was waving. Casey's dog, a golden retriever, raced at her.

"Okay," he said to her back.

He got back into his car, his heart pounding as fast as the engine. Saturday night. He had a date with Casey Nicholson Saturday night.

CHAPTER 19

"Here," Casey said, handing the baby to him. John Prime dropped his pencil to grab Abby.

"What?" he said. He realized Casey was dressed in slacks and was carrying a purse.

"I have lunch with Mom, remember?"

"I'm in the middle of something," Prime said. "I have to talk with the lawyers tomorrow." All his capital was still locked up in the Cube. If he could just work out a licensing arrangement with Rubik's people . . . Prime had rolled over on the name, but now the sticking point was the license fees. They were staggering, and Prime doubted he'd make a cent at what the heirs wanted from the deal. He had taken the day off to run the numbers.

"I told you last week about this," Casey said.

"I can't work and watch Abby at the same time!"

"Working?" Casey said. "That implies you get paid for this." She pointed at the thick binder of papers that represented the months-long arbitration.

A spike of anger surged through Prime. If he hadn't been trying to hold on to the squirming baby, he would have stood up and shouted at Casey. Instead, he hissed, "Screw that! I expect you to support me. This represents our fortune!"

Casey laughed shortly. "Define 'fortune.'"

"Millions!" Prime said. "You know what this could mean to us."

"John, you stole the idea, got caught, and now you're fighting for a scrap," she said. "It's not even worth your time."

"This is my deal! This is my fortune!" Prime shouted. The baby's lip jutted out and she let out a wail in unison with Prime.

Casey shook her head. "There's bottles in the fridge and diapers under the bassinet." She turned and headed for the door.

"How long are you going to be gone?"

Casey shrugged. "I dunno."

"I need to know."

"Lunch, then shopping," she said. "I could be a couple hours. Before dinner."

"You better be," Prime said.

"And if not?" Casey let the door slam behind her.

Prime fumbled with the knob, trying to keep Abby on his shoulder at the same time. By the time he had the door open again, she was down the stairs and out the apartment building door.

From the front window, he watched her get into the Trans Am and back out of the driveway they shared with the other three tenants. His anger grew as he tried to shush the screaming baby. Why didn't Casey understand? Why didn't she help him? This was important. This was what made all the suffering worth it.

If he had the device . . .

The Trans Am sped down their street. Prime turned away, then turned back. He had caught an outline in a parked car on the street. The sole occupant looked at him, caught his eye, then pulled out of his spot and sped away in the same direction Casey had gone.

For a moment, Prime could have sworn it was Ted Carson in that car. He shook his head. His subconscious was playing tricks.

At six, Abby resting on his chest, he dialed his mother-in-law.

"Oh, Casey left two hours ago," her mother said.

"Do you know where she went?" Prime asked. "I was expecting her."

"Oh, I don't know. Is that Abby I hear?"

"She's asleep."

"I was so sorry she didn't bring her to lunch. A girls' day out!"

Prime found himself gritting his teeth. "Yeah, too bad."

"I'll be over tomorrow. I bought a new outfit for Abby, and I want to see how it looks on her. She looks good in purple, doesn't she?"

"Yeah," Prime said. "If you see Casey, have her call me, please."

"I will. Bye-bye!"

Prime cradled the phone and craned his neck to look out the front window. The street was long in shadow, but there was no sign of Casey.

She had promised she would be back after lunch, and now it was dinnertime and he had gotten *nothing* done. It had been a mistake to settle with this Casey. There were better ones out there. Better universes. He should have taken his time and picked a better one. But the chance of finding a fucked-up universe or another one with castaways in it was too much. This universe had seemed close enough. And now he was shackled down with a baby and a dead-end job and lawsuits, while Johnny Farm Boy had the multiverse to explore. It wasn't fair.

Prime thought he heard something at the door and jumped. Abby squeaked, then rooted around, mewing. He patted her back, not wanting her to wake back up, because he knew it would be a twenty-minute ordeal to get her asleep again.

He listened for the scratch of a key in the door. Nothing. Perhaps it was just the neighbors walking down the hallway.

The floorboards outside creaked. Probably just Mr. Williams walking past. Not Casey.

Damn it! Where was she?

Prime craned his neck around again, slowly so that Abby

wouldn't stir, and scanned the street. He heard an engine rev, but it was two streets over.

Something rattled outside the window. He jumped. Abby snorted, then sobbed, in her sleep.

Prime's heart raced, and he could do nothing. He was helpless with the baby in his arms.

He rose, and gently lowered her onto the couch, wedging her into the corner of the ratty pillows. She could almost roll, but the couch was the best place for her; the crib was in their room. She stirred but didn't wake.

He slipped into the open kitchenette area and pulled a knife from the drawer. Then he edged next to the window, peering out at the twilight.

He exhaled. There on the fire escape was a tabby cat, licking its crotch. He banged the window with his palm.

"Scat!"

It jumped, and ran.

Abby yowled, and Prime cursed himself.

He raced to the couch and lifted her into his arms. She squalled into his ear. Prime caught the heavy smell of feces. She'd pooped her drawers in her sleep. He turned around and inspected her butt. Brown stains around the edges of the diapers meant the poop had leaked out.

"Shit," he muttered, looking around for the wipes. Diapers, wipes, and formula took the largest chunk of his paycheck right now. He hated using them.

Abby shrieked the entire time, from the moment he unsnapped her outfit to the moment he snapped it back on. Then she let out a huge sigh, as if being clean were all that mattered, and her cries disappeared.

"Great," Prime muttered.

Keys rattled in the door. Casey, carrying bags in each hand, kicked it open. Most were from the food store, but one was from the bookstore: more mysteries. They didn't have money for that!

"I'm back!" she called.

"Back late!" Prime shot back, before he could cut himself off. He didn't want to sound so angry.

"So? I said I was going shopping." Casey frowned a moment, then pushed the smile back on her face. "She was good for you, wasn't she?"

Prime looked down at the baby who had been shrieking for ten minutes straight. Abby was batting at the string of his hooded sweatshirt.

"No, she wasn't."

Casey took Abby from him, cooing at her. "Daddy's little girl was mean to Daddy? Was she? Was she?"

Prime groaned, looking through the bags for the receipt. He found it under a slab of pork. "We can't afford this!" He held up a book. "How many more books did you buy?"

"They're essentials," Casey said, using the same voice she was using with Abby. "Meat and mysteries are essential."

"Don't talk to me that way!"

"You'll startle the baby, John."

Prime glared, then began pulling food from the bags, slamming items into the shelves.

"Jesus, John! Why are you so angry?"

"Because— Because you left me here with a screaming child all day!"

"She's your daughter, John."

"Sometimes, I just—"

"Want to leave? Chuck it all and run? Yeah, I know what you want to do. I know you think I tricked you or something. Well, it wasn't my plan to be a pregnant teenager. I wanted to go to college. Well, we can't just run from her. We're here, and this is what we're stuck with."

"I know it! I know it! I chose this."

"There was another option, besides marrying me and having this kid?" Now Casey was screaming too, and Abby was angrier than ever.

"No! That's not what I meant!"

"What did you mean?"

"I—"

There was a thump, and Prime spun to look out onto the fire escape again.

"Someone's at the door," Casey said.

"Right," Prime said. He peered out the window, but the escape was empty.

Casey flipped the lock with her one free hand.

The door squeaked open, and she stood there staring into the hall.

"What is—"

Then she looked down and shrieked.

Prime leaped across the chair between him and the door. He pushed her aside, ready to take on whatever was there.

There was no one.

But a wet-furred animal lay on the doorstep: the tabby cat.

Its fur was matted with blood, and its neck was twisted the wrong way. It was dead.

Prime nudged the cat with his foot. It flopped over. A piece of wire had been wrapped around its throat.

"John, John, John," Casey was saying.

He turned and looked her straight in the eye.

"It's a prank, a filthy prank," he said. "Meant to scare us. It's all right. Take the baby to the bedroom. Lock the windows. Lock the door."

She nodded and ran to the back room.

Prime peered out the hallway, up and down the stairs. No one.

His heart was pounding. Casey had walked in five minutes prior and the cat hadn't been there. Now it was. Whoever had done this was nearby, waiting for a reaction. Waiting for him to show himself, to go running into the night in anger or fear.

Whoever.

Prime knew who was out there. Ted Carson, the only animal torturer he knew.

"Damn it," he whispered.

He glanced down the stairs. Had the door slammed shut between when they had heard the noise and Casey had opened the door? He couldn't remember. Had Carson stayed in the building? Perhaps he was lurking in the dead-end stairwell that led to the attic. Or had he run out the front?

Prime wedged the door open with the coat tree. Then keeping his face toward the door, he backed into the kitchen and reached blindly for the knife block. His fingers closed on the largest blade. The block had been a gift from his parents, good sturdy steel.

Prime pushed the coat tree out of the way, and exited the apartment. He stood in the hall, over the corpse of the cat, listening. He let the door shut and used his keys to lock the door. If Carson had gone down and out, Prime didn't care. If Carson had gone up, if he was lurking above, then Prime would finish this all now.

He took the steps two at a time in his stocking feet. He flattened himself against the wall, then inched forward until he could see just up the stairs.

Nothing.

Carson had gone the other way.

In the distance he heard the wail of a siren.

Then the padding of feet running away from the front door.

"Bye-bye, Carson," Prime whispered. He unlocked the apartment door, entered, and locked it again behind him.

"I called the police," Casey said. She'd not stayed in the bedroom like he'd said but stood in the kitchen with a second knife from the block.

Prime smiled at her, and she smiled back.

"Good thinking," he said.

John sunk his knife into the block with a thunk and pulled Casey into a tight hug.

CHAPTER 20

John Prime sat in his car outside his lawyer's office, shivering. The rain had soaked Prime as he ran out, leaving his suit shirt clinging to his body. It was over, and he didn't care.

What was he going to do about Carson?

The Rubik people had been so smug about it. They'd waited until halfway through the meeting to spring it.

"We've decided to license the Cube directly through our agents in New York," Lorraine Creifty had said. "We appreciate the . . . enthusiasm in your marketing plan, but we think a specialist, not a teenager with a high school diploma, can do a better job marketing it."

Prime's rebuttal had been halfhearted. He had yelled, he had screamed, and he had thrown the prototype against the wall, splintering it into twenty-six smaller cubes.

Not that it mattered. It had been spiraling down the toilet for three months.

Just like Carson.

Prime's mind wouldn't stop coming back to it. The fucker had been just outside their door. He had killed an animal. He was a psychopath.

Not that Prime was any different. He'd killed before too. In self-defense. That was different.

Creifty and her team pushed through the door of the law office. Through his fogged and streaked window, he watched them climb into a limousine. What had he been thinking? He was a kid, who's been whisked away from his life. He'd tried to make something of it, but he was nothing, just some farm boy, who'd tried to get rich quick.

What had he been thinking?

He put his car into gear and began the long drive back to Findlay. He didn't have the whole day off; he still had to work second shift at three in the afternoon.

He cast Creifty one last glance. They thought they knew how big it was going to be, but they didn't. He'd seen it. Nothing was going to prepare them for it. He shrugged. Let them have it. He didn't care.

He changed out of his soaked suit in the locker room. The tie was ruined, but the suit could be dry-cleaned. The one-piece shop floor coverall felt better anyway. He was just zipping it up when the locker-room door slammed open.

"Hey, it's the college basketball star! Oh, wait. He knocked up a cheerleader. That's one way to be a star."

Prime glanced once at Carson and his pack of high school buddies, but he didn't say anything. His heart was thudding in his chest, and sweat ran down his side from his pits.

"How are those pom-poms, Rayburn? They still jiggly?"

Prime didn't reply. There were six of them, and it was just him, late for third shift by five minutes and the last one in the locker room.

"Nothing to say? I didn't think so."

Carson turned away, and that drew a spike of white hate from Prime's heart.

"Carson!" Prime said. He turned. "I found something of yours last night at my apartment."

An odd look passed across Carson's face.

"A cat," Prime said. "Thought it was yours, since that's the only kind of pussy you can get."

His friends laughed weakly, glancing at Carson, who glared.

"Keep laughing, Rayburn."

Prime felt a moment of coldness as Carson walked off. He'd faced the bully down, but there was no joy in it. Things he'd have found satisfaction with were dull.

He pulled on his safety shoes and walked out to the shop floor.

Casey was sitting at the table, Abby bouncing on her knee, still awake, when he got home at midnight.

Her hair was disheveled, she wore a sloppy T-shirt that read: "Cheerleader," and there were dark circles under her eyes. Still his breath caught as he saw her. Passion combined with respect, and longing, and feelings he wasn't sure of filled him.

"What?" she said. "What's wrong?"

"I— I love you," he said simply. He'd never been sure what that meant.

Casey smiled and it was a sight that stopped him in the doorway.

"Yeah, well, I love you too," she said. "Even if you feel trapped."

"I was wrong about that, Casey," Prime said. "I was so wrong."

"You got that right," she said.

He leaned in and kissed her. Abby grabbed at his collar with chubby hands.

"How did the meeting in Toledo go?"

"Worst possible outcome," he said.

"I'm sorry, John. Maybe if I'd given you more free time yesterday . . ."

"Wouldn't have mattered. They'd already made up their minds," Prime said. "We don't need them."

"I'm—"

There was a scratching at the door, perhaps a pen digging into the wood.

"Damn it, Carson," Prime said.

"Carson—?" Casey started.

Prime threw open the door, and there was Ted Carson, something metallic in his hand.

"Listen, John—"

Prime reached for whatever was in Carson's fist—a knife, a gun, a weapon. Carson jerked back, but Prime had his wrist. Only the meaty hand was sweaty and Carson pulled free. Teetering on the step to their landing, he grasped out for some hold. Prime's hand refused to move, refused to grab Carson's collar or his other hand. He was within reach, but Prime let Carson flail. In slow motion, Carson wheeled his arms and crashed down the stairs.

"What'd you do?"

He could have—

"Did you push him?" Casey asked.

Carson lay unmoving at the bottom of the steps. Casey took them two at a time and knelt next to him. She reached tentatively toward his neck. Prime watched as she felt for a pulse.

"Don't touch him!" he cried.

She turned on him.

"What have you done? What have you done?"

"What do you mean? He was here to hurt us? It was self-defense. He fell!"

"He's not armed!" Casey whispered shrilly. "And now he's dead."

"Dead?" Prime shuddered. Dead?

"You killed a man. You killed Ted Carson, and now the police are going to take you away."

"No." Prime scrambled backward until he was up against the table and chairs.

"What am I going to do when you're gone?"

"He had a knife, didn't he?" Though as Prime said it, he wasn't sure. Carson had used it to dig at the door. He'd had it in his hand.

Prime scrambled up. Where was the knife?

There was nothing on their landing. There was nothing next to

Carson's body. Prime descended, and stepped over the body. Was it on the stairs? Was it under the body?

He saw it, then, a glitter of metal under Carson's leg.

Prime rolled the body over. It was Carson's car keys.

Prime's heart thudded. He stood there, desperate, angry, helpless. It was over. He'd ruined it all.

He stared wild-eyed at Casey.

He took a step for the stairs.

"Stop."

He looked at Casey. She was staring at him with hard eyes.

"Turn around. Grab him under the pits and drag him inside the apartment."

"What?"

"Do it!"

Prime turned and maneuvered the hulking corpse up the stairs and through their doorway. A trail of slimy blood, mixed with urine, slid over the doorjamb.

"Onto the tile. Don't leave him on the wood."

Prime dragged Carson into the kitchen. The blood glimmered red on the gray tile.

Casey returned from the bathroom with a roll of paper towels and a spray bottle of cleaner. She bent down and started scrubbing the floor.

"Take a shower," she said over her shoulder.

"I can't—"

"Do it!"

"What are you doing?"

"I'm betting Carson didn't tell anyone he was coming here," she said simply. "I'm betting no one heard the racket. And I'm betting on your doing everything I say."

Prime found himself stripping down to nothing, climbing into the shower, and turning on the hot scalding water. He scrubbed himself clean, rubbing at the dashes and dots of blood that covered his arms and hands.

When he pulled back the shower curtain, his clothes were gone, replaced with a simple white T-shirt and jeans. The apartment was empty except for Carson's corpse. A note on the fridge said Casey'd be right back.

The apartment smelled of bleach and blood. Prime leaned against the door and stared at the body.

He jumped at the sound of keys in the lock.

Casey stood there.

"Where's Abby?" Prime asked.

"With my mom," Casey said.

"Isn't she suspicious of why she needs to watch Abby at midnight?"

Casey shrugged. "That's what moms do; they do what needs to be done, and needle their daughters about it for the next month."

She tossed a bag from Hoffman's on the kitchen table. Inside was a solid blue shower curtain and more cleaning supplies. The superstore had gone in near the interstate six months earlier, causing consternation among local shopkeepers, but none of them were open twenty-four hours.

Casey handed Prime Carson's car keys.

"Find his car. Pull it around to our driveway, with the trunk even with the walk."

Prime nodded.

The car keys were heavy in his hand. Two Hewitt keys adorned the ring, as well as a generic house key. A piece of polished metal proclaimed "Stud" in black metal. There was no remote car lock. Of course Carson would have the most common brand of car in this universe.

Prime ran down the stairs and looked up and down the street. There were dozens of cars lining both sides. A lot of them were Hewitts: Trojans, Tempos, and Zeros, the cheapest cars on the road.

He tried the first one in front of him. The door didn't open. He tried the next. His fingers caught on the door handle, and he cursed.

A car crossed the street two blocks down, and Prime realized it was a police car. Had the officer looked his way? Would he back around for a look? Prime realized he couldn't just walk down the street and try every car.

Which car was Carson's? Prime stepped up onto the sidewalk. He walked slowly down the length of the block. Then back again. His eyes fell on a car with a factory parking-lot sticker, just like his sticker. The key fit; the door opened.

There were open beer bottles on the passenger's seat. The car smelled of mold. The dashboard was peeling. Prime hoped the car would start. He sat down and tried it.

The car turned over without starting. He pulled back the key, taking his foot off the gas. He didn't want to flood it. He tried again. Nothing. Once more.

The car started, rumbling to life. Great, he needed a new muffler.

Prime put it into gear. He realized he could run then, leave it all behind. He didn't have the device, but he knew how to make a new identity. He could be rid of Casey, Abby, and Carson's body. Run for it.

The car purred as Prime goosed the accelerator. He pulled the car into the driveway of the apartment building, edging the trunk alongside the front path.

He sprinted up the steps. Casey was at the door with the corpse wrapped in the shower curtain.

"Take his feet," she said. She left him there, walking past the door of their neighbor, listening for any noise. She shook her head. "All clear."

They dragged him downstairs, certain that at any moment someone would open the door and ask what they were doing. But no, the apartment was silent for once at one o'clock in the morning.

Prime popped the trunk and they stuffed the corpse in among the nudie magazines, spare tire, and bow-hunting equipment.

Casey slammed the trunk, and they stood there, watching the

dark windows of their street. Prime saw nothing, heard no one. A long way off, a siren howled.

"Get in; drive," Casey said.

Prime threw the car in reverse.

"Slow down!" Casey shouted.

"Oh, right."

"Don't act stupid now."

Prime nodded.

"Where to?"

"Your parents."

"My parents?"

"Just do it."

Prime nodded, steering the car toward the south end of town. The streets were empty. No one was out on a Thursday night. Findlay was shut down, and not even the police were patrolling.

Prime hoped Carson didn't have any outstanding tickets on his car. Now was not the time to be pulled over.

Prime rolled down his window as they hit the county roads. Bugs spattered against the windshield. The cold October air cleared the stench from the car. He glanced over at Casey. She was staring straight ahead.

They came to the turnoff toward his parents' farmhouse.

"Stop here. Don't pull in."

Prime pulled off into the gravel. Casey took the keys, opened the trunk, and together they levered the corpse into the grass. They were on the edge of his father's land, in the patch of trees where Prime had met Johnny Farm Boy the year before.

Casey tossed the keys back at Prime.

"Dump the car in the quarry. Roll down the windows. Pop the trunk. Push it over the edge. Roll it fast enough that it doesn't snag on the way down."

Prime looked at her. "Have you been planning this?"

"Of course not!" she said. "But I do read mysteries. Go."

Prime pulled away and in his rearview mirror he saw Casey dragging Ted Carson's corpse into the trees. The quarry was right across the road, but the entrance was off Brubaker. Prime had spent a lot of time exploring the quarry; he knew it well.

The gate was chained shut, but when he got out he saw that it wasn't locked. The chain was just draped over the two ends of the gates. He pushed it open and drove the car through. He hoped no kids were hanging out drinking beers. He drove past the two prime spots for drinking. No sign of anyone. Then he drove the car to the overlook. The topsoil was gone, and the granite was white in the moonlight. Prime killed the headlights, dropped the car into neutral, and rolled down all the windows. He popped the trunk, then tossed the keys back onto the front seat.

Then he got behind the car and pushed.

At first, the car wouldn't budge, and he had a moment of panic. What if the car was stuck? Then it shifted and began to gain momentum. The car rolled, faster, faster.

He gave it one last push and it sailed into the abyss.

He ran to the edge.

The car splashed into the water. Bubbles erupted around it. Slowly it sunk. Prime watched the taillights disappear, and then waited until the roiling was smooth, until the car was totally submerged and on its way to the bottom.

The quarry was one hundred meters deep. No one would find that car.

Prime exhaled. They were halfway done. He turned and ran across the white stone. It gave way to green-black lichen, and then he was in the weeds, which smacked him in the thighs.

The road was deserted. He paused, listening. Nothing.

He ran across, pausing at the ditch.

"Casey?" he called.

Had a police officer come by, asked her what she was doing hauling a corpse? Had Ted Carson come back to life and throttled her?

Prime stuffed down a nervous laugh.

He heard the scrape of a shovel on dirt.

He pushed through the row of wild blackberries. There was Casey, digging into the earth of a clearing among a half-dozen trees. The corpse lay beside her, motionless, still dead.

There was another shovel on the ground. Prime picked it up, and he realized that Casey had raided his parents' barn to get tools. There were two shovels and a pickax.

"Is the car gone?" she asked.

"Gone."

"Good."

"Casey," Prime started.

"What?"

"You're doing a lot for me."

She stopped digging and stared at him. "For us."

"I'm sorry, Casey, that I've disappointed you. I'm sorry we had a child without—"

"Shut up, John," she said.

"Casey," Prime cried. "I'm not who you think I am."

"I think we've learned things about each other tonight that have pushed the limits," she said.

"No, I'm not John Rayburn," he said. "I'm not from . . . this world."

She stepped out of the shallow hole she had started. Prime stepped in and picked up where she'd left off.

"What do you mean? You're some kinda alien? What?" Her voice was shrill.

"No! I'm human. I'm from another Earth, like this but different."

"What do you mean?"

So Prime told her as he dug Ted Carson's grave. Prime started from the beginning, when he first met his own John Prime and was tricked into giving up his life. He told her about Oscar and Thomas. He told her about all the times he'd almost died. He told her about his schemes and ideas. He told her how he'd stolen this life from Johnny Farm Boy.

When Prime was done, he was a foot and a half deep. She still stood outside the hole, staring at him, shovel in hand.

"When?" she asked after a moment.

"What?"

"When?" she repeated. "When did you exchange places with my John?"

"A year ago."

She raised the shovel. "Was it before we . . . ."

"Yes! Goddamn, yes. It was before he even talked to you. It was at the church dinner!"

She exhaled, dropped the shovel. "Then you're my John. He was never my John."

"He was here first. . . ."

"He never even talked to me! He never knew me."

"But—"

"All your ideas— You stole them." She laughed.

Prime frowned, then laughed too. "Yeah, I'm just a thief."

She hopped into the hole on the far side of the grave and sunk her spade into the dirt.

"I'm glad you're you," she said.

"Casey—"

"Dig."

They managed to dig a grave one meter deep and one and a half meters long. Casey stripped Carson of his clothes, tossing his wallet on the ground. Prime rolled the body into the grave, feeling a moment's nausea at the cold skin. Then Casey poured a bucket of lye over the body. Prime's father had some in the barn, which he used to correct soil pH.

"Fill it in," she said.

Prime pushed dirt over the top of the corpse with the shovel head. The sound of clods on flesh was nauseating, but he didn't stop. When they were done, the grave was a ridge of dirt in the clearing.

"We'll throw some grass seed on it this weekend," Prime said.

"Your father never comes over here, does he?" Casey asked.

"I don't think so."

They stood for a moment; then Prime dragged the tools back to the barn. It was nearly 5:00 A.M. They were dirty, sweaty, and shivering now that the physical effort was over. Prime felt giddy.

"I did it. I got away with it." He barked a laugh, realized it made him sound maniacal, and stuffed it back down his throat.

Casey took his hand. "Let's go."

They started walking into town, keeping to the edge of the road.

"We did it," she said softly. "We killed a man."

"We got away with—"

"Shut up, John!" Casey cried. Prime realized she was crying.

"Casey—"

"Shut up! We killed a man. Whether right or wrong. We—both of us—killed a man tonight. We're murderers, and God will judge us in heaven."

"There's a million of him that are still alive," Prime said.

"What?"

"Across all the universes, Ted Carsons are still alive out there."

"But this one, right here," she said, "is dead. You and I took a life."

"It was just me," Prime said. "I'd say that in court."

"It was *us*! We're in this together."

Prime bristled. "Did you help me so that you could tie me down?"

Casey snarled at him, "Go, if you want! No one is holding you down. Go use your stolen ideas to make a fortune, and keep it all for yourself. I really don't care."

They walked in silence.

"I didn't mean that," he said after a while.

"It's been a stressful night," she said.

"The police will come looking," he said. "He might have let people know where he was going."

"It was just talk," Casey said. "He never showed up at our apartment."

"What about our dirty clothes and the mud on our shoes?" Prime asked.

"Your father owns a farm, doesn't he?"

John nodded.

"You scare me," he said.

"Me too," she said. "Let's go home. You have work in a few hours."

CHAPTER 21

John picked Casey up at eight on Saturday night. In fact, he was there at seven thirty, but he stopped at the Burger Chef not far from her house and sat in his car in the parking lot. He considered being fashionably late, but the stress on his nerves with just showing up on time was bad enough. At five till, he drove over.

Her little brother, Ryan, opened the door.

"Yeah?"

"I'm here to pick up Casey," John said. Saying it to a little boy was a lot easier than saying it to her parents.

"You're not Jack."

"I'm John."

The boy eyed him, then swung the door open. "I guess you can come in." He yelled up the stairs, "Casey, your stem is here!"

From upstairs came an answering shout: "Shut up, you little puke." Then, "Hi, Johnny." She poked her head around the bannister on the steps leading upstairs.

"Hi, Casey," he managed to say.

"Be right down."

Ryan disappeared into the kitchen and John heard: "Casey's date is here. Are you going to grill him?"

"Hush, dear," Mrs. Nicholson said.

Mr. Nicholson appeared from the kitchen and

approached John with his arm extended. "Hello, John. I'm Casey's father."

"Uh, good evening, Mr. Nicholson." It wasn't easy remembering that this wasn't the Mr. Nicholson that John had met once or twice at church and nodded to in passing. He had never met this man.

"Casey has been a bit reticent about you, so you'll have to give me your detailed curriculum vitae and the last six years of tax returns." He paused, then laughed. "Just kidding. But do tell me about yourself."

"I go to the University of Toledo. I'm a freshman, from Findlay. My major is physics."

He guided John to the living room, nodded. "Uh-huh. Physics. Very respectable. I'm an insurance salesman myself. Tried suffering through calculus and couldn't."

John nodded.

"John, hello. I'm Casey's mother. Can I get you a pop?" Mrs. Nicholson was chubbier than he remembered. She offered him dry hands to shake.

"No thanks, ma'am."

"Do you have proper insurance on your car, John?" Mr. Nicholson asked.

"I think so."

"Alex!" Mrs. Nicholson said.

"Just checking to make sure he's covered," he said quickly.

"Dad, enough of the grilling," Casey said from the entryway. She was dressed in a short black dress. A jeans jacket hugged her shoulders. "Let's go, John."

"Honey, have a good time."

Casey grabbed his hand and dragged John out the door.

"My parents are so embarrassing."

"They're not so bad."

Casey gave him a look.

"Your brother told me I wasn't Jack."

"Well, you're not." As John opened the door, she slid into the car. "Let's go eat."

Hilliard Avenue, the main drag, was teeming with life. Teenagers were dressed in all sorts of clothes to attract the opposite sex. Cars cruised the street. He felt a homesickness so sharp he almost felt ill.

A body bounded from the curb sidewalk, and John slammed on the brakes, though he was only going fifteen kilometers per hour on the packed street. His heart thudded in his chest. The seat belt slowly unloosened.

A sweatshirt-hooded teen slammed his palm on John's car, then flashed him the bird with both hands.

"Hey, Casey!" the teen yelled. He grabbed his crotch.

John realized with a shock that it was Ted Carson.

John gripped the steering wheel with viselike hands. Ted Carson.

"Hey, Casey! Come on out and play!"

"He's drunk," Casey said.

Rage seethed inside John. He leaned on his horn, blasting the street with the Trans Am's alarm.

Carson lifted his foot and slammed the fender of the car. John took his foot off the brake and the car jumped forward a few centimeters.

Carson jumped back but not out of the way. John steered around him and past.

"What an asshole," Casey said.

"Carson is that."

"You know him?"

"I've run into him a couple times," John said, remembering the fight the two of them had had, how his mother had manipulated John's mother into taking Carson's side, and how he'd been cornered into writing an apology letter for beating the crap out of Ted.

But that wasn't this Ted Carson.

"He was a year behind me," Casey said. "He's dropped out, I

think, still in town. I think he works with his father at the appliance plant."

John watched in the rearview mirror as Carson shot him a double bird again. His friends were laughing from the sidewalk.

"Some things never change," John said.

"You said it."

During dinner, at a small restaurant called the Riverview, Casey said, "That Ted Carson really burns me up."

John shrugged. "He's a loser, always will be."

"He tried to hit on me once," she said.

John felt a moment's jealousy. "Yeah?"

"At a party in town," she said. "He grabbed me. I kicked him in the crotch."

"Good response."

"It works for most grabby boys," she said.

"I'll keep that in mind."

"You probably won't have to worry about it," she said. John wasn't sure if that meant she trusted him not to touch her or she was going to let him if he tried.

Remembering what John Prime had told him, he said, "I heard Carson tortured animals."

"That's not a nice thing to say!" Casey said.

"During dinner or at all?"

"At all."

"What if it's true?" John asked. What was true in one world was probably true in another.

"Have you seen the evidence? With your own eyes?"

"Where there's smoke, there's fire."

"Have you heard 'innocent until proven guilty'?"

"How many squirrels need to be dissected while still alive for us to know someone's a bad egg?"

"How many innocents should suffer to capture one bad egg?"

John grinned; then Casey grinned back. She said, "I don't

agree with you, but you're a lot more interesting to talk to than Jack."

"Jack?"

"Jack would have jumped right out of the car and laid into Carson."

"Who the hell is Jack?" John asked. "And why do people keep bringing him up?"

"My ex-boyfriend."

"Uh-oh. I thought he was just some frat boy from college."

"He'll probably be at the dance we're going to."

"Dance?"

"Who needs a movie when we can dance?" She smiled. "Oh, wait. I just remembered you like that country and western crap. Too bad."

John said, "I hear that *The Revolutionary War Witch* is a great movie."

"Uh-huh. We'll catch it next week at the U."

"So we're going out again," John said as casually as he could.

"Despite your views on Ted Carson."

The dance was at a warehouse next to the railroad tracks over on the east side of town. The warehouse was empty, hidden behind two other buildings, isolated, and perfect for a party.

The music was the rock-and-roll stuff that he usually heard on the radio, bouncy fifties music, and not the hard reverb that would have been impossible to dance to. The teens in his universe would be listening to heavy metal. Here they listened to songs the Big Bopper might have written and sung.

"I suppose you're gonna tell me you don't know how to dance," she said as they walked in past a hulking doorman who waved them right in when he saw Casey. Apparently she was well known at these things.

"I know how to dance," John said. He didn't know the bouncing dances that the kids on the floor were doing, but he had been in a play during his sophomore year when he took drama. The play had been called *Sock Hop,* big on Broadway during the seventies. It featured a number of fifties-style dances, and he'd had to learn the jitterbug. "The question is if you do."

She looked at him with mock outrage. "Johnny, you amaze me." She grabbed his arm. "Let's go."

He showed her the slow-slow-quick-quick step twice, and she mimicked it gracefully enough; then he grabbed her in promenade and launched into it.

She stumbled once and then she had the hang of it. She'd been a cheerleader and studied dance when she was younger, and the basic steps of the jitterbug were easy. When he spun her out, she squealed, but when she came back in again, her face was lit with a smile.

They danced three dances straight, John adding moves as they went. He was rusty at first too; it had been three years since he'd done it. When he'd learned it for the play, his mother had danced with him in the kitchen, his father looking on and laughing. At least until John's mother had taken his father's hand and shown that he too knew the double lindy.

John noticed that people were watching them. They were frenetic and different enough in their moves that it drew interested attention. A small circle formed around them. Apparently the jitterbug had been forgotten here or it had lapsed into the junkyard of fads.

"Enough," Casey said, pushing him away. She was breathless, her chest heaving, and John wanted very much to clutch her to him again. He settled for slipping his arm around her waist and leading her to the makeshift bar. She didn't shrug his arm off but instead leaned closer to him. If they hadn't been dancing for twenty minutes, John would have retracted in fright, stiff at her encroachment. But there was an intimacy that had formed between them suddenly. Dance had its social function, and John was suddenly glad he'd worked so hard to learn those dance steps.

"Two ice waters," he said to the bartender.

Casey took hers, dipped her finger in, and wetted her right cheek. Impulsively, John wetted her other cheek from his own glass.

"Told you I could dance," he said.

"I've never done that before. Where'd you learn that?"

"For a school play," he said truthfully.

"That was damn fun." She flickered the water from her finger at him.

"Hey, Casey," someone said behind him, and he turned to see a tall, dark-haired young man standing there.

"Jack," Casey said.

"You wanna dance, Casey?" he said, edging past and in front of John.

"Too tired, Jack. Besides, John has all my dances tonight."

Jack turned and looked at John. He was three centimeters taller than John, perhaps six foot two. His shoulders were broad, and John felt his guts twist. How many fights had Jack been in during the last year? John hoped that Jack was a sensible person but smelled alcohol on his breath.

"Yeah? I saw that crazy dance he was doing. Must have learned it from his grandmother."

John sighed but remained quiet. Jack probably had a half-dozen friends to back him up. John had no one.

"Beat it, Jack. You're boring me," Casey said. She drained her water.

"I didn't used to bore you," he said. "I used to make you real happy."

"So does a good dump. And you're about as smelly."

John choked on his drink of water and sputtered a half laugh, half cough.

Jack turned red and then instead of throwing a punch or insult as John expected, he turned and walked off.

"Did you have to taunt him?"

"Oh, yeah. I did," she said with a smile. She looked over John's shoulder. "Uh-oh."

John turned and saw the red-blue flashing of lights coming through the warehouse windows.

"Cops."

"Better go," Casey said.

She grabbed his hand and headed behind the bar. There was a sheet metal door there with an unlit exit sign. They pushed through it into the cold night. John's ears seemed cushioned by the sudden silence.

"Car's on the other side of the building," John said.

They edged along the building. The music suddenly died and he heard screams from inside. The raid had commenced.

There were three police cars out front and a dozen patrolmen coming in. Two started their way to cover the side exits.

John and Casey ducked behind a Dumpster and watched the two officers jog by.

"Let's go," John said, and they dashed to the first row of cars.

Two more patrol cars pulled into the lot, and one stopped next to his Trans Am.

"Shit," he said.

"They're probably not gonna bust us," Casey said. "Just give us a warning."

"Yeah, I can't take the chance," John said. He didn't know how well his ID cards would hold out against a thorough search.

"You can't?" Casey asked.

"No, I can't. I can't get caught."

"Really, John. Three surprises in one night. I haven't been surprised three times on a date since I was a virgin."

John couldn't help laughing, and he stifled it by clamping a hand over his mouth.

"Stop it. We have to get out of here."

"We can't leave the car, so let's wait here a few minutes."

Officers started leading kids out of the warehouse, some of them cuffed. The patrolman in the car next to John's car finally got out and walked toward the front of the building.

As he passed them, John and Casey went around the car they were hiding behind and dashed across the open space to the last line of cars. They slid into their seats and doused the dome light quickly.

They watched, holding hands, until the police all had gone inside the building or left with their collars.

"Coast is clear, Johnny."

"Coast is clear," he agreed, and started the car.

As he drove her home, he considered and discarded a dozen strategies that would allow a good-night kiss. He need not have bothered. She grabbed him around the neck as they reached her porch and kissed him with a warm, half-open mouth. It lasted ten seconds, and John felt her slide against him and fit like she belonged there.

"Good night, John," Casey said, looking solemnly into his eyes. "See you tomorrow."

CHAPTER 22

John Prime was exhausted the next day, yet hyper-aware of every sound, every person at his shoulder. He kept hearing people saying "Carson" over and over again, but when he focused on the conversation they were saying "cars" or "cartoon" or "Khartoum." He almost ran from the building twice.

Sweating, almost gagging, he took his break in a stall in the locker room.

"Keep it together. No one knows," he whispered to himself. "No one even knows he's missing yet."

At the end of the day, Prime saw Carson's father talking to one of the foremen in the parking lot. Prime averted his gaze and got into his car.

Abby cooed at him when he got home, as if nothing had happened, but Casey looked at him with hollow eyes. There was no smile, no hug, no twinkle in her eye. When he neared her, his guilt merged with hers into a black swirling mass. What had they done?

They spoke not at all over dinner, and when they climbed into bed they lay as far apart as possible.

He was just nearly asleep when she spoke.

"So, we've only killed one of an infinite number of Ted Carsons," she said.

"Just the one," Prime said. "And he deserved it—"

"Don't do that," she said. "Don't justify it."

"Isn't that what you're doing?"

In the darkness, he felt her lift her arm to her face and rub at it. She was crying.

"It had to be done," she said. "Didn't it. If we hadn't, Abby would have had no father."

"He wasn't coming to talk," Prime said. "He was coming to attack. We just did what had to be done. It had to be done."

Casey sighed. She rolled over, hooking her legs around his.

"Why did you pick me, of all the Caseys?" she whispered.

"I always pick you," Prime said.

"Why me? Why this me?"

Prime shrugged. "You're . . . you. I mean, you're beautiful, and interesting, and really hot."

"Just because you think I'm sexy?"

"No! We were meant to be!"

"Why me and not some other me? Maybe you were meant to be with her."

"This is where I ended up. It must have been fated."

"What about that other John? What if he and I were fated to be together and you ruined it?" Casey asked.

"He never even talked with you!"

"No, he never did. Not more than a dozen words," she said. "Even though I gave him a lot of chances."

"I talked to you the first day," Prime said.

"At the church dinner," Casey said. "You were suddenly different."

"I was."

"It was the first thing you did?"

"Pretty much."

"And then you got expelled."

"Yes."

"And you started your big Cube idea."

"Yes."

"But I was first," she said.

"Yes."

"What if you went to some other universe, and some other Casey was there, would you want her?"

"Casey, don't—"

She rolled over on top of him, and he felt how hot her sex was near his.

"I deserve some answers! Would you date any Casey you came across?"

"No, some are . . . better than others."

"Better?"

"Sometimes you're not . . . you. You've dropped out of school, or gotten pregnant—"

"Like here?"

"—or you've run away from home. There you're not as beautiful, or as . . . interesting."

"How many Caseys have there been for you?"

Prime didn't answer.

"Tell me," she said, thrusting her hips against him. He groaned.

"Ten," he said.

"Ten? You fucked ten of me?" She nipped at his neck. "What do they have that I haven't?"

"Nothing," Prime said, responding, "You're the best."

She bit him. "Now I know you're lying."

He yelped, and their lovemaking turned silent, angry, and desperate.

The next Monday, a group of workers combed the plant and assembly area. Prime couldn't help but hear the rumors: Missing boy. Hadn't been seen in thirty-six hours. Car missing.

Prime focused on his work, assembling his parts without regard for the person in front of him.

"Slow down, Rayburn!" Sid whispered. "You're making me look bad."

Prime glanced at the six partially assembled washing machines hanging on straps between him and Sid. There should have been one.

"Sorry."

"Hey! You hear about this Ted Carson kid?"

Prime shook his head, though he had.

"Missing for a week now." Prime bit on his tongue at the incorrect information. "They think he was crushed under a crane. Didn't have any of his safety quals, but his dad is some union muckety-muck and got him a floor job. Big mess."

A shop warden came by and asked if anyone wanted to help search the warehouse after shift. Prime grunted noncommittally.

"What, Rayburn? You too good to help look?"

"I've got plans after work."

"More of that Cube business?" the shop warden said with a laugh.

Prime should never have bragged about it. He shook his head.

"We searching on the clock?" Sid asked.

The warden laughed. Sid didn't volunteer either.

That evening, Casey and Prime almost acted like normal. He caught her glancing at him more than once, but he ignored it. It was easy to lose themselves in caring for Abby, in the mundanity of married life. Without the time he'd spent on the Cube, his evenings were more free than ever, and he had no interest in the novel anymore.

It was as if he had lost everything that he had held sacred up to a week ago, but when it was possible he might lose Casey and Abby what he really valued became clear.

The next day at work, a police officer was questioning the people who had worked with Ted Carson. They led each of Carson's posse of friends into a small office, one at a time. After fifteen or twenty minutes the next one was led in. Prime had a good view of the office from his position on the line, but they never called him.

He caught one of Ted's comrades staring at him twice during the day, but he looked away when Prime focused on him.

Was it his imagination?

In the locker room, he found himself standing next to Ted Carson's father. The room was suddenly empty.

Prime turned and faced him squarely.

"Yeah?"

"I hear there was something between you and my son."

"So what?"

"In case you haven't heard, he's gone missing. If you know something, you need to tell the police."

Prime barked down a laugh. "I have nothing to say."

"If you know something—"

"Nothing!"

Carson's face turned a blotchy purple. Prime wouldn't have survived a punch if he'd thrown one. The man was squat and muscular, twice the width of Prime.

"I'll remember that when you need someone to help you," Carson said. He turned and stalked off.

There was a police car out front of their apartment when Prime got home. For a second, he considered driving on, but he pulled the Trans Am into a street spot.

A uniformed officer and a plain-clothed detective stood in the kitchen. Casey, Abby in her arms, glanced up as Prime entered.

"John, these officers are here to ask about the guy that disappeared."

"Detective," the plain-clothed detective said. "Not officer. Detective Duderstadt." He didn't offer his hand.

"I'm sorry," Casey said.

"Ted Carson," Prime said. "You're here about Ted Carson."

"Yes, you know him?"

"Vaguely."

"Enough to have at least one fight with him," the detective said. The officer stood with arms on his hips, glaring at Prime. The detective was shorter, with a pencil-thin mustache.

"That was a long time ago," Prime said, and another John entirely.

"You were expelled because of it."

"I was expelled for not writing a letter to his mother. It was a matter of principle."

"Motive could be a matter of principle."

"Motive for what?" Prime asked. "Didn't he run off?"

"Could have," the detective said. "You two had words at the plant too, I hear."

"He said rude things about Casey," Prime said. "I didn't let him get away with it."

"I see."

"Carson is a punk. He's a bully. I learned last year he's not worth messing with," Prime said.

"Did he stop by on Thursday night?" the detective asked.

"No," Prime said. He paused. "Why would he?"

"Seems he was bragging to some comrades how he was going to teach you a lesson. He'd have to stop by to do that."

"Or he was just flapping his gums," Prime said.

"Or he was writing a check he couldn't cash," the detective said.

"He did—does—that a lot."

Prime changed his reply in mid-sentence. He had used the past tense. The cop was using the present tense. Had he given himself away?

"He seems that sorta fellow." The detective glanced around the apartment. "So, you haven't seen Carson since . . . ?"

"I dunno," Prime said. "Work on Thursday, I guess."

"Where you had words in the locker room."

It wasn't a question.

"I guess."

"And you haven't seen him either?" the detective asked Casey.

"Why would I?"

"If he came around, you'd've seen him, right? You here alone taking care of the baby. You'd have seen him if he came by."

"I would have," Casey said. "But I didn't."

Prime looked for some sign, some tic on her face to give away a shred of guilt. She looked like a bored housewife, uninterested and cool. Prime felt himself relax in reaction.

"Anything else you want?" Prime asked, motioning toward the door.

The detective gave him a pointed stare. "No, I guess that's it." He glanced at the other officer. "We'll be going then. If you happen to suddenly remember seeing Ted Carson on Thursday, you let me know."

Prime showed them to the door and watched them clomp down the stairs. A sudden squawk from Abby made him jump. He shut the door too quickly and it slammed.

Casey looked at him, her face pale. "We're going to have to move the body," she said. "They're on to us."

Prime shook his head. "No way. Someone will notice if we have to dig up that ground again."

"I need to sow some wildflowers then," she said. "Something to cover up the dirt."

"It's too late in the season for flowers."

"Something!"

"Calm down!" Prime said. "They were here to see what we did under pressure. If we run now, it'll be apparent!"

"But—"

"They haven't found the car, and they haven't found the body," Prime said. "He's just a runaway kid."

She nodded. Prime took Abby and bounced her on his hip. She gurgled and cooed. She had no idea her parents were murderers.

He found himself reassigned to overflow the next day, which meant he sat in the overflow room with six other workers waiting for the assembly line to back up. It meant idle time, nearly all day long. The workers in the overflow room were union advocates, since it was considered a cushy job. The six just stared at him, and he guessed that Ted Carson's father had something to do with his reassignment.

It drove Prime crazy to sit idle. He was getting paid for doing nothing, but under the scrutiny of grizzled old workers.

He didn't even try opening a conversation with any of them. He ate his bagged lunch in silence, watching the six play euchre with rules that were a little different than he remembered.

At the end of his shift, he couldn't wait to get out of there.

When he got home, Casey was in the shower while Abby slept.

Dirty clothes hung over the chair backs: overalls, plaid shirt. Dirty sneakers sat by the door, covered in mud.

"Where have you been?" Prime demanded as Casey stepped from the shower. "Where have you been?"

Casey gave him a cold look. "You wake the baby, you put her back to sleep."

"'Where have you been?' I said!"

"Yeah, I heard you the first time."

"Well?"

"With your mother, planting bulbs and shrubs."

"You didn't—" Prime had been sure she had moved the body.

"No, of course not. But our friend has a spruce sticking out of his chest, as well as a new blanket of mulch."

"You . . . mulched him?"

"I bought a few extra trees, and when we ran out of room around the house, I suggested one by the road. You can't even tell the dirt was dug up now."

"Will it take? I mean a dead tree is like a spotlight."

Casey shrugged. "The guy at the tree nursery said it would."

Prime sighed.

"Can I dry my hair now?"

"Yeah, sorry."

Prime sat on the couch and stared at the wall. It scared him that he needed Casey so much. It terrified him that he was relying on her competence. He hadn't relied on anyone but himself since . . . since he couldn't remember.

He found himself shaking. All the fear and frustration seethed within him. He forced himself to breathe.

"Let it go," he whispered. "Let it go."

He exhaled again, slowly, staring at the wall.

"What's wrong?"

Casey stood wrapped in a towel, rubbing her hair dry.

"What?"

"You're crying."

"I'm crying?" He felt his face. It was wet with tears. "I didn't re-alize—"

Casey slid into his lap.

"What is it?"

Prime looked at her incredulously. "We've killed a man, is what. *I've* killed a man. And I was wrong."

She squeezed him. "Yes. That's all true."

"I'm so sorry, Casey. I'm sorry for what I've done to you. And what I've done to others," Prime said. He felt a sharp pain for what he had done to the Johnny Farm Boy from this universe, sending him alone into the unknown, never to return.

Prime looked into Casey's face. She was staring at him.

"What now?" he cried.

"I don't think I've ever heard you say that."

"What?"

"That you're sorry."

Prime was silent. "I am sorry."

"Because you're suffering?"

"No!"

"Then why?"

"I've— I've done bad things to people. Murder aside. I've hurt a lot of people."

Casey nodded. "That's true. A lot of different Caseys."

"Yes."

.   .   .

The next day at work, there was a rush job and everyone in over-flow was called to the floor, except for him. He'd brought a book, however, so opened it to read. If they were going to pay him to sit, he'd at least entertain himself.

But an hour later, Ted Carson's father came by, glared at him, and said, "We're not paying you to read, Rayburn!"

"You're paying me to do nothing!" Prime replied.

"And you'll do just that!"

"Why can't I be on the shop floor?"

Carson stared at him. "I don't think I like your attitude, Rayburn!"

"Good!"

"You mouthing me, boy?" Carson said. "Because if you are, we can go out back and finish this off."

Prime's chest thudded. How had he gotten so far over his head again? If he could have returned Carson's son, he would have.

"Forget it!" he said. Prime grabbed his book, his lunch pail, and his jacket.

"You walk out this door, Rayburn, and you're done here!"

"Good."

Prime pushed past him onto the floor. It seemed the entire factory was watching him as he walked down the aisle. His heart thudded. What was he doing? But he couldn't stay. He'd find another job. Casey could find a job, and he'd watch Abby.

He didn't bother to change, just clocked out and went to his car. The parking lot was alien, with all the cars motionless and empty. Usually the lanes were packed with cars heading for the bars and home. At mid-morning, the place reflected the fall sun off a thousand windshields.

The apartment was empty when he got there. He sat in the chair in the dining room, feeling at ease yet hyper-aware, wondering how Casey would take it all. She'd understand, he knew. He was suddenly proud of how strong she would be. The phone rang. He ignored it, letting it go to the machine.

He listened to Casey's voice on the tape, asking the caller to leave a message.

"Hello, Mr. Rayburn. This is Yolanda Kemp. We met at your lawyer's offices last week. I realize it wasn't the best of circumstances. Something's come up, and frankly, we'd like you to help us. The sum of it is, the firm we've hired to build the Cube doesn't *understand* it. We've had some issues over your actions, but we've never doubted your enthusiasm. We need you as a part of the organization. An integral part. Call me when you get this message. You have my card. Thanks."

CHAPTER 23

"Is this what you were talking about?"

John looked at the hulking black box, sitting in the corner of the Student Union basement, next to the eight-lane bowling alley. He peered into the hooded display. A square ball moved slowly across the screen. Grace spun a dial to move her line to hit it, bouncing it against a stack of blocks that disappeared when hit.

"It's Breakout," John said.

"No, it's Electrux," Grace said. "It's got a ball, like you said, and a flipper, paddle thing like you said. So I figured this is what you were talking about."

In his universe, this type of video game would have been laughed out of any arcade. It seemed to have come from the seventies. An arcade and any decent bar would have a bunch of complex video games and pinball machines.

"Nope, this is definitely not pinball. Pinball is mechanical, not electronic."

Henry grunted. He reached out as the ball went past Grace's flipper. She jumped out of the way.

"You play it then!" she cried.

Henry did, racking up a high score. John wasn't too impressed.

"So," Grace said. "It's mechanical. Henry can't find it in the literature."

"Yeah," Henry said.

"It's not like we don't believe you," Grace began.

"I don't care if you believe me," John said, suddenly hot.

"Right," Grace said. "But we want to see one. How it works."

"So, it was some one-of-a-kind thing," John said.

"I think we should do it," Henry said.

"Do what?" John cried.

Grace rolled her eyes at him. "Build a pinball machine, of course."

"What? No!"

"It's not like you can stop us," Grace said. "You already explained it to us. We'll just do it without you if you don't want to do it."

"But—"

They were almost to Benchley Hall. Grace stopped suddenly. "You're going the wrong way," she said. "You live over on the other side of campus."

"I'm meeting . . . someone," John said. It was his and Casey's first date in a week, since the dance. She'd been busy with a project, and every time he'd called he'd gotten her roommate, and finally he'd just stopped calling, until Casey called him. He felt so . . . stupid with the emotions running through him.

"Who?" Grace said.

"My . . . friend," John said. He wasn't even sure how to refer to her. What were they? Friends? A couple, after just three dates?

"Your friend who?" Grace said.

"Casey," John said.

"Oh, Casey," Grace said.

"What does that mean?" John asked.

"Nothing."

John glanced at Henry, who was staring off into the trees.

"John!"

He turned to see Casey walking down the sidewalk behind him.

She lunged at him, wrapping her arms around him and kissing his cheek. He felt suddenly embarrassed.

"Hey, Casey," Grace said. "So . . ."

"Let's go," John said.

"So, what?"

"So, you two dating, I guess? Going steady?"

Casey said nothing, and John felt himself color.

Casey finally said, "Oh, I don't know. He's just a rebound boy, so I doubt there's any hope."

"I'm standing right here!" John cried.

"Well, you should know these things," Casey said with a smile. She kissed him again. "What are you guys doing?"

"Nothing," John said.

"Discussing our pinball project," Grace said.

"Oh, yeah, pinball," Casey said. "That sounds interesting." She looked at John. "Let's go get something to eat. I'm so done with dorm food."

"Right," John said, happy to lead her away from Grace and Henry.

A few dozen meters away, Casey asked, "Explain this pinball thing again?"

John groaned.

They sat across from each other in Giovanni's, sipping milk shakes.

"You perplex me, John Rayburn," Casey said after a few moments of silence.

"Me?"

"Yes. You can dance, which I like. You're smart, which I also like. You have a cool car, which is a small plus. Yet . . ."

"Yet?"

"Your reaction to the police."

"It's no big deal—"

"Hold on. The police show up, and the worst that would happen is a ticket, and you run us out the door, where we hide in the shadows, then drive off out of there. What gives?"

John shrugged, searching for something to say. "I just don't like that kind of attention."

"What kind? Police kind?"

"Yeah, I don't want to be hassled by the police."

"Why?"

"I just don't. I had some run-ins with the law, and it's better if I don't have any more," John said, the lie coming off his lips too easily.

"'Run-ins with the law,'" Casey repeated.

"Yeah."

"That's so *Glitzdale*," Casey said with a laugh.

"Glitzdale?"

"Didn't you ever watch that? It was on in the nineties. 'What evil lies in the heart of suburbia?' Olena and Magdelene? You never watched that?"

"I must have missed it," John said. The TV show didn't ring any bells with him at all.

"Did you live in a cave?" Casey asked.

"While I was running from the law," John replied, trying to take a light tone.

Casey laughed.

"No, really?" she said.

John realized she wasn't going to let it go.

"I was a bad boy, you know," John said. "I brewed my own black powder. I wired my own detonators."

"You didn't!"

"I did," John said. He had. Everything up to that point was true, and what he was about to say was almost true. "But I made too much."

"How much?"

"Enough to blow up my dad's barn."

"You didn't!"

"I blew it up. Completely."

"Were there animals inside?"

"No, it was empty, and mostly ruined. I got arrested. And my dad was so mad, he wouldn't bail me out. The local FBI agents investigated, and I got booked for terrorism."

"Terrorism?"

"Yeah, it was a mess. I'm on probation," John said. "For another couple years. So I can't get in trouble, at all."

"Oh," Casey said. "Well, that makes sense."

"Yeah."

"I shouldn't have taken you to the dance," Casey said. "But you didn't tell me!"

"It's embarrassing," John said. "And we were only on our first date."

Casey nodded, grinning. "It's dangerous for you to be out anywhere," she said. "We need to get you to a safe place."

"Like what? Canada?"

"No, I bet Grace would hide you in her closet."

"Stop it!"

"Oh, you've been dealing with this all your life, I bet. Handsome farm boy, a bit of a rebel, explosives expert, smart. You must have to beat the girls away with a stick."

John blushed. "Not really. Not like you."

"A few girls, but mostly boys," Casey said with a grin.

John blushed deeper. "I meant—"

"I know," Casey said. "Now that she knows about us, maybe she can focus on Henry."

"Henry?"

"You're a little oblivious, aren't you?"

"I guess so. Henry and Grace?"

"He's crushing, big-time."

"I guess," John said. It was his turn to be sly. "What does Grace know about 'us'?"

"We're dating, didn't I tell you?"

"I couldn't even get ahold of you all week."

"I do go to school," she said. "But the weekends are all yours. Until you screw it up."

"Won't be long."

Casey grinned, and their conversation turned to other things. At the end of the evening, he found her in his arms on his grungy couch, her lips on his.

The lab was huge: a football field–sized enclosure off the engineering building, with additional bays. The main area housed a dozen experiments: the subcritical nuclear pile that was roped off, a miniature tokamak, a medium energy collider, a supercool lab, a metallurgy lab, and a machine shop. One of the bays was the freshman lab, broken into six benches, all of them labeled and cluttered with junk. One said: "Pinball."

"You already got us a lab area?" John said.

"If I didn't, someone else would have taken it," Grace said. The table was empty, except for a pile of empty boxes some other team had thrown on it. "There have already been inquiries on our space. Use it or lose it, you know."

John shook his head. "Do you just not have any other ideas for projects?" he asked.

Grace grinned. "We have lots of ideas. They all stink," she said. "So, what do you think?"

John looked around the labs. There was a Geiger counter on one table. An X-ray machine was roped off across the bay. Light microscopes sat atop workbenches. A scanning electron microscope was hidden somewhere. He realized that his poking at the device with a jeweler's tool kit was a waste of time. Here were tools that he could use to probe the inside of the device, without opening it up.

And he could have access to it all.

"Fine," John said. "We'll do it."

He sat at the table in his apartment and stared at the blank page of the notebook. The device was on the table. It grinned at him, its teeth an LED green. The jeweler's kit lay open but unused. It was his habit to sit every night and think about the device, what it did,

and what he had done with it. All of that was written in the notebook. But tonight his mind was elsewhere.

He found himself drawing freehand, not the device but rather a
pinball machine. He'd played it so much in high school. There'd
been one at the Lawson's where he bought comic books. He'd ride
into town on his bike, spend his meager allowance on books and
pinball, milking high-score extra games from a single quarter. He'd
played a lot of games, and he remembered once when the machine
was broken the repairman had had the front open like the hood of
a car. Inside had been a hundred lights, a mile of wire, and a lot of
dust. Mesmerizing, but that didn't mean he knew how a pinball
machine actually worked. But when it came right down to it, it was
freshman physics.

It was a ball on a slanted plain. Gravity was the enemy. When
he thought of it that way, it became an experiment in classical
physics. He had been reminded of pinball during physics lab, because the ball followed Newtonian laws of motion. The ball was
easy: It was ball-bearing. The plane was easy: It was a slab of wood
with obstacles. Add lights, flippers, bumpers, and scoring and you're
there.

John started making a parts list under the drawing.

He jumped when the doorbell rang.

"John, it's me!"

"Shit!" It was Casey. He stared at the device sitting on the table.
She couldn't see it. He couldn't explain it if she did. He grabbed it
and ran to the bedroom. He shoved it into the lockbox and turned
the key.

"John!"

"Coming!" He threw the lockbox onto the floor of the closet.

As he ran past the kitchen table, he realized the tools were still
out. He folded them up in their leather satchel.

"John, I see you through the peephole! Open up!"

"I'm . . . I'm cleaning up."

"Don't bother. We're going out."

John tossed the tool kit on top of the refrigerator, then unlocked the door.

Casey was dressed in a miniskirt and leather jacket with dangling leather bangles. John couldn't say he liked the local styles, but Casey looked good enough in anything.

"You're not dressed," she said flatly.

"I— Uh, I was . . . working?"

"Yeah, I figured." She waved her hands. "Go, go on; get dressed. We have to be there in an hour."

"Right."

John jumped in the shower, sprinkling more than showering. When he came out of the bathroom, Casey was paging through his notebook. He'd left it on the table.

"What's this?" she said.

"Just a notebook." He reached out to take it from her.

"These are pretty elaborate drawings," she said. "Very crisp, very clear."

"It's nothing!" John cried. He snatched the notebook from her hands, slapping it shut. He threw it through the door of his bedroom, where it sailed with a ripple of pages.

Casey looked at him calmly. "Fine, it's nothing. You ready?" There was a tone to her words that chilled him, that ebbed his anger and made him feel cautious.

All night Casey was aloof, hardly dancing at all. Instead of going back to his apartment, she asked to be dropped off at the dorm. John watched her enter Benchley Hall and realized he'd made a superb mistake in letting her see the notebook. No one could know about the device.

"Here's the parts list I came up with," John said. It'd been relatively easy to come up with. Flippers were a chunk of wood attached to a solenoid. Bumpers were plastic wrapped in rubber with a solenoid inside. The coin box could be bought from whoever made them for vending machines. The balls were steel ball bearings. The launcher was a spring and rod. He'd need a sheet of glass, power, a stand, wood. The first design would be simple.

Grace looked at the list, then reached for his drawing.

"Your perspective's off," she said.

"I barely got a B on my first drafting assignment," John said.

"I'll get someone to redraw these," she said. Henry took the diagram from Grace and grunted.

"Machine shop," he said.

"Yeah," Grace said. "We'll need some time on the lathe and we'll need the soldering tools."

They were standing at their table in the lab. All around them was the sound of voices and tools clinking. The thrum of some equipment somewhere vibrated the floor. Casey had wanted to join them but had begged off at the last minute. "You guys can handle the tech. I'll handle the other stuff." What other stuff was there? John wondered. And how had she gotten on the team?

"Why is it called pinball again?" Grace asked. "There's no pins on this list. I see a ball, but no pins."

"Steelball," Henry chimed in. John realized he was suggesting a new name.

"I don't know why they call it pinball," John said. "They just do."

"I'm sure it'll become apparent as we move forward," Grace said. "Where's Casey? Everything all right between you two?"

"What?" John said. "She had something to do, okay? Why do you think there's something wrong?"

Grace looked at him strangely, and John realized he'd yelled at her.

"Sorry. Didn't mean to raise my voice."

"Yeah, no problem."

"Hold on," Henry said. He disappeared into a storeroom. John heard things banging around. Henry emerged with a huge piece of fiberboard. He hauled it over to their lab table and John helped him heft it onto the table.

"Can we use this?" John asked. It was about the right size for the play board.

"Everything in there is fair game," Grace said.

John took out a measuring tape. He marked off a rectangle a meter wide and two meters long. He held his hands along the width and flipped imaginary flippers. Maybe a little skinnier, he thought.

"We'll need a lacquer to smooth the surface, and paint," he said.

Henry had found a block of wood in the skunk works room. He propped the first plank up, giving it a five-degree angle. Then he grinned at Grace and John. He pulled a steel ball bearing, about two centimeters across, from his pocket and held it at the top of the plank.

"Ready?" he asked, then let the ball go.

It rolled down the plank, gained speed, and flew off the end. John caught it in his palm.

"Cool," Henry said.

"I love potential energy," Grace said.

John found himself grinning too. It had been no sort of test at all, no prototype of any value, but the physics was true. It could work.

They missed dinner, and by the time they looked up from their drawings and list of parts, the lab was empty. They agreed to meet daily after class, then parted company.

John went back to his apartment, retrieved the device, and returned to the lab. Since Casey was busy that night, he figured he'd do something he'd been meaning to do for a long time.

The lab was still empty when he unlocked the door. Now that he had a key, he could stop by any time he wanted. He walked the entire length of the room to be certain, but it was truly empty.

John sat at the row of light microscopes and turned the first one on.

He removed the device from his bag and placed it under the microscope.

The light microscope only gave an increase in resolution of a few times, but it was better than the magnifying glass he had at the apartment.

He peered at the gray surface of the device, looking for anything that was out of the ordinary, looking for any clue.

Centimeter by centimeter, he examined the surface.

One hand on the scope, one hand holding a pencil, he drew close-ups of the controls. But even with the microscope, he saw nothing that he hadn't seen before.

Then he turned it on its side. The line was a hair-width wide, and ran the circumference of the device's disk. Was this how the device came together? he wondered.

He spun the device slowly under the scope, following the line. It remained the same hair-width wide, but then he saw the scratches.

They were tiny, but a dozen of them radiated from the crack, as if a tiny tool had been used to dig there. Why?

The door opened and John jumped.

"Hello there, working late, I see."

John reached for the device to hide it but then felt that would look too suspicious. He turned, smiling. Professor Wilson stood by the door.

"Uh, yeah," John said. He'd had almost no contact with his advisor and didn't want any now.

"You're the other Wilson, aren't you?"

"Yeah, I am," John said, regretting for the umpteenth time that Wilson was the name he'd latched onto when he'd met his faux father in this universe.

"What's that you're looking at?" Professor Wilson asked.

"Nothing, nothing important."

Wilson peered around John at the device sitting on the microscope's stage. He stared at it, then nodded slowly. John refused to explain or say more or remove it from sight.

"How are classes? Too hard? You were admitted with just a GED, correct? You and I had some question on how you'd handle the core physics classes."

John gritted his teeth. He'd had no question of how he'd do, but Wilson had.

"No problems," John said. "I've aced all the quizzes in physics and physics lab."

"Good, good." Wilson paused, still staring at the device. "Carry on."

After Wilson had disappeared, John packed up the device and exited as quickly as he could.

They built the prototype out of the wood plank. Henry found a dozen more ball bearings at a local industrial supply store. John carved flippers out of wood and placed them so that a player could flip them from underneath. It was more work than an electric flipper, but it got the idea across. As he used the rasp and the file to carve the flipper, John realized that the shape and length of the flipper could be varied. The prototype was done by the end of the week.

It was clunky and hard work to play, but it was fun. John's wrists ached after whacking at the flippers all afternoon. The crew—Henry, Grace, and John—spent the evening talking about how each component would work. Casey was busy with a project, but John kept glancing at the door, expecting her to show. After the first night, John added a spring launch mechanism, so they didn't have to drop the ball in at the top.

"This is a lot more fun than those video games," Grace said, referring to the ghastly Pong-like Electrux game in the Student Union.

"The prototype just proves that the ideas work," John said. "Now, we have to ramp it up, so to speak."

"That was bad," Grace said.

"Grace," John said. "I want you to build a flipper prototype. When the player presses a button, the flipper will move, about thirty degrees from here to here." He showed her the angles with his hands. "Use a solenoid. It needs to be strong enough to launch a steel ball bearing two meters up an incline plane of ten degrees.

"Henry, I want you to build a prototype bumper. When a ball

hits a bumper, it triggers a solenoid that bounces the ball back in the opposite direction." He drew a diagram on the chalkboard, a triangle. "The first one should be about this size, but we'll want to be able to make any shape of bumper. I'm going to work on sound, operation, and scoring. We'll worry about flags and other crap later."

"Flags?" Grace asked.

"More ways to score points."

"How can you know so much about these things when I've never even heard of them?" Grace said.

"I spent a lot of time playing pinball . . . in Vegas," John said.

Grace had a flipper done first, and John suspected that she had worked on it when she should have been working on her lab reports. They were all three working in the lab after dinner two days later when Grace called John over. She showed him a small red button mechanism that she held in her hand. Wires passed from it to a block of wood, where one of John's carved wooden flippers was mounted.

"Watch this," she said, and pressed the button. The flipper spasmed, the block of wood jumping.

"Wow. Kinda powerful."

"Yeah," she said, smiling at the thing. She made it hop a half-dozen times.

"Let me try," John said. He took the button from her and pressed it, holding it down. The flipper jumped and came back to the starting position. "Is there any way to keep the flipper up while the button is depressed?"

Grace frowned. "That wasn't in your list of requirements, John."

"I'm sorry. I forgot that one. But I like this. It's exactly what I had in mind otherwise."

When John looked over Henry's shoulder to check his work, he pointedly stopped what he was doing.

"You may want to tighten that. . . ."

"It's not ready yet."

John shrugged and let him have his peace. Managing a team was tough work, he decided, so he returned to tracking down a quarter box and designing an underlaying physical and electrical framework. He could have used Casey's help, but she had begged off again.

Henry was a mechanical engineer. He'd worked in his father's auto garage as a kid, and knew how to weld. He built a table in no time, one that opened up as John suggested so that they could easily work with the electronics underneath the table.

"Every solenoid that clicks may need to trigger a sound and a score," John explained.

They built a row of bells and buzzers into the base of the thing, and a backboard that housed a small analog scoreboard. Within a week their prototype could rack up a score and emit sound when they touched various triggers on the play field.

Two weeks later, Henry put two of Grace's flippers into the play field and they played for an hour before the right flipper's solenoid burned out.

"Crappy equipment," Grace said, pulling the mechanism out and poking at it with a soldering iron. "It worked for a while. Not bad, I say."

"Neat," Henry said. "I'll have a bumper for tomorrow. We can put it here." He pointed to a spot next to the flipper. A wooden bumper sat there now.

"This is coming along very nicely," John said. "We need a ball return mechanism." When the ball fell out the bottom of the play field, it landed in a cup. Players manually picked it up and put in the launch lane.

Henry nodded. "I've got some ideas on that."

Grace said, "Why don't we have two boards back-to-back for double play?"

"What?"

"Pinball is fun, for one person. Why not put two boards together, with a player at each end, with the goal of trying to get the ball in the other person's drop area?"

"Mechanical soccer," Henry said. "Neat."

"That's not traditional pinball," John said.

"So?" Grace said. "We don't have to build a traditional pinball machine, do we?"

John nodded. "I guess we don't. We're doing this for fun."

"All right."

The next night, they tore off the backboard and built another play field. They decreased the slope a bit.

"You know," Grace said, "it would be better if there were several sets of flippers; then you could pass the ball back and forth."

John shook his head. "Let me tell you about foosball," he said with a laugh.

"Yeah?"

"Never mind."

The next time he came to the lab, John did so after midnight. He wanted no one to interrupt him, especially Wilson. The lab was dark and empty. John opened his lab book on his desk and scattered some experimental data around to act as cover if anyone came in. Then he turned on the spectrometer. He'd seen it on one of his casual tours of the lab: a brand-new gamma ray spectrometer from Aggison-Hewlett.

He'd borrowed the spectrometer notes from a guy who'd taken the nuclear physics lab class the semester before. It had a simple procedure for calibrating the spectrometer, then taking and printing a spectrum.

John calibrated it with the cesium sample, then set the device under the detector. He started it and waited.

It took a while, but a peak began to grow. He let it sit for an hour, nervous that someone would disturb him. To occupy his mind, he started filing at a new flipper; he'd made a dozen styles for the pinball machine, and to swap them the player could simply lift off the old flipper and replace it with a new one with the same mounting.

The spectrometer beeped. John examined the screen; there was a single sharp peak. He printed the spectrum, and used a ruler to figure the center of the peak. He guessed it was about 510 keV. Just one peak meant just one isotope inside, usually.

He opened the nuclear physics book and started working through the list of elements and their gamma ray energies.

He worked his way through the list eliminating anything with a half-life less than a year and anything with a gamma ray not within 50 keV of 510. He ended up with Kr-85, which had a half-life of 10.3 years and a gamma ray of 540 keV.

He wondered if he had calibrated the device wrong.

John started over, and calibrated this time with a Cobalt 60 isotope, which had two distinct peaks at 1330 and 1170 keV. Again he put the device under the detector. Again he saw the same peak, and he calculated it to be at 510 keV.

Frustrated, he put the two spectra in his backpack and walked home. Could it be that the device contained an isotope that no one here had discovered?

The next day he wandered over to the spectrometer when someone was using it.

"Excuse me, can you help me with something?"

"Sure," the guy said in a Slavic accent.

John showed the spectrum to him, and asked, "What isotope makes a peak at 510 keV?"

The student looked at the spectrum and said, "None. You have annihilation peak here."

"Annihilation peak?"

"Sure. Gammas interact by three mechanisms. . . ."

"Photoelectric effect, Compton scattering, and pair production. Of course!" John laughed as he realized what he was seeing.

"I'm Alex Cheminov, by the way," the student said. "You know your stuff. We could make a decent nuclear physicist out of you easily enough."

"John Wilson," John said, shaking hands. "I may have a few more questions. Do you mind?"

"Not at all."

John realized that the peak at $510\,keV$, really $511\,keV$, was from the gammas produced when a positron hit an electron and disappeared in a burst of radiation: two equal energy gammas at $511\,keV$. He was seeing the tail end of the pair production interaction of gamma rays in matter.

It only happened when the gammas were highly energetic, the spontaneous breakdown of a gamma ray into an electron and positron, antimatter, as it neared a nucleus. The positron would then bounce around, slowing down until it found another electron to interact with and generate the annihilation gammas. And that was what he was seeing.

John stopped. But the annihilation radiation was the tail end of a reaction. It was seen in addition to other methods of interaction. He should have been seeing at least one higher energy peak. But he wasn't.

Unless the positron wasn't being created by pair production. Unless there was another source of the positrons. Unless there was antimatter inside the device, powering it.

He laughed. It made sense. To move between universes required a lot of energy. And what better form was there of compact energy than antimatter? The device was powered by antimatter. It was a sound hypothesis.

One more mystery of the device fell before the sword of science.

"Science!" he cried, and as he was in the lab, not a single person looked up in surprise.

John watched Casey smile, and his heart jolted. They were standing on the edge of a chasm in Old Shady Park. Water had etched a

fifteen-meter jag into the bedrock, already scraped clean of topsoil
by glaciers. Autumn leaves tumbled around them. Browns, reds,
oranges, and yellows covered the ground.

Casey wore no makeup. Her hair was pulled back into a pony-
tail. She was the most beautiful woman he had ever seen, and he
hated himself for coming to desire her so. He was leaving this universe one day and would never come back.

"Let's go down," she said. She caught his look. "What's wrong?
You look . . . pensive."

"I'm okay."

There was a stair that led them to the bottom of the gorge. The
iron rail was wet, and the damp pulled the heat from John's hand.
The steps were carved into the rock but patched with cement in
places. Still they were mossy, and the footing was slick.

Casey slipped, exhaled sharply, and grabbed John's arm. She
tensed, then relaxed into him.

"Thanks," she said.

"Sure."

The park was empty this early in the morning on a weekday. She
had skipped her abnormal psychology lecture, and he had no classes
on Wednesday morning. She had told him they needed to spend
some quality time together.

Something rustled in the leaves on the other side of the rail. A
chipmunk raised its head to look at them, then scampered away.

"Look!" Casey cried, before it disappeared into a hole somewhere.

From below, the U-shaped falls seemed to close in on them.
The sprinkle of water splashed in a small basin of rust-colored
rock. John looked up into the falling water, past the trees, and into
the cloudy sky. The moisture tickled his nose.

"I feel claustrophobic," Casey said.

Her voice echoed around the carved-out cavern behind the falls.
John leaped across the weakly flowing stream. Graffiti was scrawled
across the rocks behind the falls. A pile of beer cans were tossed in
the dry grotto. It was clearly a hangout for local kids.

Casey hopped across the stream and joined him, hanging on to his arm.

She looked at the garbage and said, "People are so stupid. Look at this."

"Yeah."

John walked around the cavern. The floor had been rubbed clean and smooth over the years. During heavy rains, the place would fill up.

"Listen, John."

He turned. Casey was standing back a couple meters, hands in her pockets. He nodded.

"I'm really sorry for, you know, reading your diary," she said. "I shouldn't have done that. It was really rude."

John shrugged. He didn't want to talk about it and had hoped that she had forgotten all about it.

"I mean it," she pushed. "I am sorry."

John nodded.

"Don't you accept my apology?" she said.

"Yeah, yeah, I do."

John was worried she'd keep at him, but she seemed satisfied with his reply.

"So, are you ready to meet my parents again?"

"Huh?"

"For Thanksgiving. You're coming for dinner."

The holiday was only a few weeks away.

"Casey, I don't think—"

"John, you have to. They want to meet you again, especially since they never liked Jack so much."

John sighed.

"No, I won't be able to go," John said firmly.

"Where else will you be going? You don't have family."

"The Rayburns will have me."

"You're not even related!"

John's face flushed, but instead of yelling back, he said quietly,

"I don't want to go to your parents' house. I don't want to spend Thanksgiving with you and them."

Casey's retort died in her mouth. "You don't—?"

"No. I'm busy with pinball stuff."

"Pinball stuff?"

"Yeah."

"You have got to be kidding! You'd rather spend time with your friends on that stupid game than with me?"

"I thought you were a part of it?"

She rolled her eyes.

"If I wasn't I'd never see you. It's either the pinball machine or whatever you have locked in that box."

"Hey!" John cried. He hadn't realized she knew about the box.

"It's like I'm not even a part of the important stuff in your life," she said. "It's like you keep everyone at arm's length."

"That's not true!"

"Then what's in the box?"

John didn't answer.

"What?"

"It's not important," he said. "Casey, I'm new at this. I've never had . . . I've never been this close before."

"You're not that close now!" she cried. Tears were falling down her face.

"I've never done this before!" John replied. "I don't want to hurt you or make you angry or hide important things from you. But—"

"But you do."

"Casey, don't be unfair to me!"

"Me unfair to you?" She forced a sharp laugh. "I'm your girlfriend, remember? We're supposed to share things. Be together. For holidays and things."

"Fine, I'll go to your parents' for Thanksgiving."

"Too late. The offer is null and void!"

"Don't be petty!"

"Don't cave just because I cried. You should have wanted to come." Her cheeks were bright red.

"Stop playing games!" John cried. "Stop pressuring me! I have a say in what we do, don't I? If I don't want to go to Thanksgiving dinner, I shouldn't have to!" A point that had been inconsequential was now a bone of contention.

"You think—" She stopped herself. "John. It doesn't matter. You don't have to come to Thanksgiving."

She turned away, stepping over the stream into the open.

"Casey."

She walked down the path parallel to the stream.

"Casey." John ran after her. He grabbed her arm. "This is silly," he said. "I want to come to your parents' house. I do. I don't know why I said I didn't. It's just stupid of me."

She wiped snot from her nose on her sleeve. "Yeah, that's true."

"You didn't have to agree so fast," John said with a smile.

"I think I did."

John slipped his hand in hers and they walked the length of the trail in silence.

The prototype was ready three weeks later, a complete head-to-head pinball game, with a digital scoring system, various bumpers, and six sets of flippers per player.

John won the first ten matches, mostly because he knew how to work the flippers while the others couldn't get the hang of catching and holding the ball. But Henry learned fast, and he was the first to beat John.

"And there was much rejoicing," Grace said when Henry scored the game point.

"Whose side are you on?"

"Not yours."

The flurry of bells and screaming could be heard throughout the lab, and before long a grad student wandered by and asked to join in. He dropped in a quarter, and when John heard the clink of the coin in the money bucket he caught Grace's eye and smiled.

Henry kicked his ass in two minutes.

The next night they had ten people there. The third night it was standing room only in the lab. That weekend they had the first tournament. Henry won against John in the finals, ten to nine.

It was a smash success. So much so that John decided they would try the next step. He should have known better; he should have remembered his ultimate goal was to understand the device. Instead he was caught up in the idea of the pinball machine and didn't realize what he was about to do.

Seeing the bars in the light of the day was like seeing a news anchor without his or her makeup and cue cards. The places smelled of stale beer and echoed their footsteps as they entered. John and Casey stopped in a small bar called Woodman's not far from campus, which had a video game and a couple of pool tables. John and Casey had been there once. John was always surprised not to be carded going into bars, but the drinking age in this universe was eighteen.

"We're looking for the manager."

A guy was hauling a keg of beer up a conveyor belt from the basement through a hatch in the floor. He said, "In the office. Past the bathrooms."

Casey followed John down the hall to a door marked: "Authorized Persons." John knocked and a rough voice answered, "What do ya want?"

John pushed the door open onto a cramped office. A balding man sat behind a desk, smoking a cigarette.

He looked up at them and said, "I ain't sponsoring any homecoming float."

"That's not why we're here," John said.

"Good thing. What then?"

"We have a game. We'd like to put it in your bar."

The guy looked at them, then said, "I don't want any trouble, so I don't run any slots here."

"It's not gambling," John said. "It's like a video game, but mechanical, sort of like pool."

"A game." He pulled a long puff on his cigarette. "You got a license from the city?"

"No."

"You work with the gaming union?"

"No."

"Then I don't think so."

"But . . ."

"I'm sure it's great, kids, but, one, I don't have the room, and, two, I don't have the time for the trouble it'll cause me." He lifted his hand, pointing to the door. "Thanks for asking."

John turned to go, but Casey said, "We made fifty bucks in one night, and that was when it was in a lab on campus."

"Fifty bucks?"

"In quarters," she said.

"My jukebox makes seven dollars a night. How could you make fifty? You're shitting me."

"You want to see it?" Casey asked.

"You got it open to the public tonight?" he asked.

"A small crowd," John said. "We can't keep it where it is."

The man nodded. "I'll stop by."

Outside on the sidewalk, John said, "You did good, Casey."

She smiled and said, "I know."

The lab bay was packed and John was worried that it would attract campus security, but it didn't. And the bar owner finally showed up, wading through the throng.

"Ray Paquelli," he said, offering his hand to John.

"John Wilson."

Ray looked around, counting the people. He didn't look too closely at the game, and John suspected he didn't care.

"How long is a game?"

"Three minutes, seven max."

"How much per game?"

"Fifty cents. They play to ten."

"What kind of deal you want?"

"We split the money fifty-fifty."

Ray nodded. "You'll need a license from the city."

"I've already got the paperwork."

"Deal."

They shook.

CHAPTER 24

John found himself thinking more and more about the antimatter source in the device. Somewhere within the device was a pinpoint of gamma radiation, perhaps used to power it. He didn't have the equipment to take an X-ray of it, and at first he had worried that an X-ray might harm the device. But he knew that a tomogram of the interior of an object could be taken by using a point source passed through the device at various angles. The images of the sections were put back together to make the tomogram. Why couldn't he use the source within the device as the source for the tomogram? Because he had not the first clue how to do it. He did know one grad student who might know.

When John asked Alex Cheminov about his idea to use tomography for a special project, Alex listened emotionlessly, his hands in the pockets of his tattered jeans, then said, "You'll need collimated beam."

"Why?"

"You've got a point source, right?" He held up a pencil. "Eraser is source. Radiation comes out of source in all directions isotropicly, decreases with one over r-squared. Further you get from source, more scatter your detector picks up from gammas that don't come directly from

194

PAUL MELKO

source. Collimator blocks those scattered gammas, reduces noise. You'll get a better image. Clearer. I worked on same in Russia."

"How long will my collimator need to be?"

"Fifteen centimeters, maybe twenty."

"What should I make it out of?"

He pointed to the storeroom. "Some in there. Take one. Fits right over the detector."

"Thanks, Alex."

He shrugged, his face slack. "No problem."

John borrowed the whole setup, collimator and detector. From what he'd read, he'd need to take long measurements because his source was so small. And he'd have to take many measurements. He decided that he'd need a measurement every fifteen degrees around the diameter of the device. That was twenty-four measurements. He decided to do one per night.

Where he would do it was a problem. He couldn't do it at his apartment. Casey was staying over every few nights. And after he'd reacted the first time she'd seen his notebook, he couldn't afford to let her see any more. The lab bench that the team was using for the pinball machine, however, had a deep drawer. He could set the device in there for twelve hours each night and get a decent reading, he hoped.

Then he would reconstruct the inside of the device. Anything that looked interesting he could reconstruct with finer detail or at oblique angles. It would take a while, but he would have an image of the inside of the device, without ever opening it up.

The calculations were not particularly hard, but there were a lot of them. And there was more than one type of tomography reconstruction algorithm. He found himself begging off two dates in a row with Casey to struggle through a textbook on the subject, but by the third day he seemed to have worked out the equations he'd need to build the reconstruction.

He started taking measurements, showing up late to set up the counter. He had to make clear notes on what angles he took the measurements on and be precise on what the counts were at the exact twelve hours in length.

After he had six measurements, John sat down with a calculator and started figuring. He wished he had a computer, but the computers in this universe were like those from the sixties in his universe, big hulking things used for inscrutable government activities. He had to do the calculations by hand.

The result of three hours of number crunching was a grid of blobs. He realized quickly that having too few measurements produced false images. He saw six regularly spaced blobs inside the device, and he couldn't determine which were false and which were true. He filed his drawing away.

Two weeks later, he tried it again, only this time it took him two days of work to back out the results. But it was much more successful. The inside structure was clearer. There were two main round areas of attenuation inside the device, one near the center, under the middle button, and one halfway between the center and the lever. There were also a number of smaller lumps.

Studying the drawing, he noted that the device was mostly empty space, or very weakly attenuating material.

He decided to do the same set of measurements at a slightly higher plane. John had a cross section of the things at the midplane, but he didn't know if the shapes were cylindrical or spherical.

He returned to the device one morning to find his drawer empty.

A wave of panic passed through him.

The device was gone!

Fuck! I should have locked it!

John spun around. The lab was empty, except for someone making a racket with the lathe in the bay one over.

John ran over there. A grad student was at work on a piece of wood, carving into it a series of grooves. She looked up when he waved his arms.

"I'm sorry for disturbing you," John said. "Did you see anyone in that lab bay over there?"

"No, sorry," she said, bending back over her work. Then she stood back up. "Well, Professor Wilson was there, which was odd since it's so early in the morning."

"Wilson!"

John turned and ran out of the lab. He ran down the connecting hall to McCormick Hall, then up the stairs two at a time. Wilson's light was on, his door closed.

John paused to knock, then instead pushed the door open.

Professor Wilson looked up. On his desk was the device. He had a screwdriver out and was attempting to lever the device open.

"What are you doing?" John cried.

"Is there a radioactive source in here?"

"'What are you doing?' I said," John repeated. He stepped forward and reached for the device.

Wilson pulled it back. John had a moment's flashback to the arguments he'd had with other versions of Wilson. John didn't want to play games.

"You can't have a radioactive device in the lab without permission," Wilson said. "And don't try to attack me. It'll be the end of your academic career."

"Watches use radium. Bananas have potassium," John said. "Those are no more radioactive than this. You're just trying to hide the fact that you stole my equipment. Hand it over."

"It's my lab; it's my equipment," Wilson said.

"You know that's a lie," John said.

"Don't speak to me that way!"

John stared at Wilson and reached across the desk. Wilson jumped back, but John grabbed the phone. He spun it around.

"I'm calling the police," John said.

"Do it. Campus security will see things my way."

"The real police," John said. He hit 9 to get an outside line. The phone emitted a steady tone.

Wilson just stared at him.

John dialed 911.

"This is the operator. What is the nature of your emergency?"

John paused.

Wilson stared at him.

"Mr. Wilson? Is there an emergency?"

Again neither moved.

"I'll send a patrol car to investigate."

John opened his mouth to urge them to hurry, but Wilson spoke up. "I'm sorry. This is Professor Wilson. I seem to have hit the wrong button by accident."

"Thank you, sir. Have a good day."

The line went dead.

John held out his hand.

Wilson smiled meekly, then placed the device onto John's palm. He shoved the device into his backpack and turned to go.

"What is it, John?" Wilson asked. "Tell me."

"I told you once, and you didn't believe me."

He'd left the collimator and the detector in Wilson's office. He didn't bother to get a new one. He had enough measurements to do the to-mography calculations. He set to work on them with his calculator.

The result showed that the blobs were ovoid. Not cylinders, not spherical. Were the lines wires? No, they seemed to clump to-gether at the ends like spiderwebs. Were they even real or artifacts of his calculation? He wished he had an industrial tomograph. Then he could produce a high-resolution tomogram. He didn't have the time or the facilities for that. But he wasn't unhappy with the results. He had vision into the inside of the device. Even his run-in with Wilson couldn't dim that elation.

He made a final drawing, one with perspective, and filed it in his lockbox.

John had his first inkling of the inside of the device, and now he would continue to dig at it until all the mysteries were solved. The answers were still far, far away, but he had some hope that he would one day discover them.

CHAPTER 25

Henry wrote out a note and taped it on the lab bay door: "Pinball Machine Moved to Woodman's." Then they managed to drag-carry the thing to the loading dock, where they maneuvered it into Henry's truck.

"Note this down," John said. "'Add wheels.'"

"And let's make the next one out of plastic," Grace said. It barely fit.

"It's going to fall out the back," Grace said, and she proceeded to wrap a hundred yards of red rope around the machine and the truck.

"Relax, Grace," Henry said as he started the truck.

"I'm riding in back with it," she squeaked, climbing in.

"Fine."

John followed in the Trans Am.

They unloaded the machine onto the street, and Grace stayed with it while Henry and John parked. Then they wrestled it into the back room, complicated by the three steps that connected the room to the bar area. Luckily, the bartender was there, a hefty fellow named Lou, and he helped get it up the steps.

"Can I try it out?" Lou asked.

"Sure. We just have to get it set up," John said, getting his level out. "We need to prop that side up."

Henry slid a shim under the leg nearest him. "How's

that?" He wrote something in his notebook. "We should build screw levels right into the legs. There's no telling what kind of floor these things are going to be on."

"That's level." John took the gaming sticker out of his pocket and stuck it to the glass. "I think it's ready. Plug it in. Grace, do the honors."

Grace found an outlet in the floor and the game started up with a bit of Mozart's *Eine kleine Nachtmusik.*

"I like that," John said.

Henry smiled. "Grace wouldn't let me do 'Caveman Rock.'"

"And right she was."

Lou played a quick game against John. John easily passed the ball from flipper to flipper and slammed it down the center of Lou's play field.

"Fuck!" he yelled as the tenth straight ball went down his outlet. "Damn. That was fun. Let's go again."

Lou played John again and managed three scores. He stood up, and said, "You guys should start making a few more of these right now." Then in a whisper, he said, "Ray splits thirty-seventy with the jukebox people. He's ripping you guys off."

John nodded, then shrugged to his three companions as Lou walked back to the bar. "Oh, well."

"Back here at what? Seven?"

"Yeah. It's a Wednesday night. Who goes to bars on a Wednesday night?"

"People with quarters, I hope," John said.

The game was sitting unplayed when they got there that evening. Henry checked with the bartender.

"No one played it," he said.

The bar was relatively empty. A couple locals were playing pool and a few people were watching a baseball game on the TV above the bar.

"That's 'cause they don't know how," Grace said. "Come on, John. Let's make some noise."

They played three games, and by the end of the third everyone in the bar was standing around them.

"I've got winner," someone said.

Woodman's was the place to be, and Ray had to open his doors at noon for the college students who wanted to play pinball. They cleared close to one hundred dollars one day.

"We need to redesign the flipper," Grace muttered. "It keeps burning out." They were sitting at the Burger Chef, eating a quick lunch.

"You showed Lou how to fix it," John said.

"Yeah, but if it was properly designed, he wouldn't have to fix it every other night."

John finished with his calculator. "One hundred and twenty-two dollars and fifty cents apiece."

"What?" Henry said.

"That's a chunk of change," Grace said.

"Not bad for two weeks," John said. "But I didn't take out anything for parts. I assume we donated that stuff for the good of the project."

"Is it a project still?" Henry asked.

"What do you mean?"

"Maybe it needs to be, I dunno, a company?"

"Why?" John asked.

"One machine brings in three thousand bucks a year. Ten machines bring in thirty thousand. One hundred machines bring in over a quarter-million dollars per person sitting at this table!"

John nodded. "Do we want to do that?"

"Maybe we have to," Grace said. "To protect ourselves."

"How much time are we going to have to do this during finals? And next quarter is even tougher than this quarter," Henry said. "I know I won't have time to run a company."

"You may be right," John said. "Let's give it another week and see if this fad sustains itself."

"We've got the tournament this weekend," Grace said. "I'm putting up flyers." She showed them the electric orange flyer she had designed. It showed a huge ball speeding past a flipper. It read: "Pinball: The Best Game in Town. Tournament, this Saturday, Woodman's. Bring your quarters." She grinned.

"Looks good, doesn't it?" she said.

"And bright," John said, shielding his eyes. John blinked. He wasn't sure what he was seeing. Through the glass he saw Casey getting out of a car. She was smiling, leaning down with one hand on the top of the car to speak with whoever was driving.

Casey had said she was studying, John remembered.

And then the driver stood up, and John recognized Jack. His stomach clenched, and he felt the food he'd just eaten begin to rise.

Grace glanced over her shoulder, looking for what John was staring at.

"Oh, man," she said. "I was hoping you wouldn't find out."

John felt a surge of anger. He slammed his cup down and rose.

Henry put a hand on John's shoulder, but he was already up and headed toward the door.

His eyes were riveted on Casey and Jack. She had taken his arm and was leaning heavily on him. John swung the door open in Casey's face.

She flinched, then saw who it was.

"John!"

"Casey," he said coldly. "Jack."

"Hey, dancer," Jack said. "Excuse us."

"Jack, let's go someplace else," Casey said.

"I thought you were studying," John said.

"No, I want a Big Shef," Jack said.

"Listen, John," Casey said. "I didn't want you to find out, but . . ."

John looked at Jack's smirk and Casey's pale face. She wasn't upset, just embarrassed. He realized they'd been cruising toward this inevitably. In fact, he felt a moment's relief. He didn't ever have to explain to her about the device. He didn't ever have to hide it from her again. It was really for the best.

"Sure, yeah, I've been seeing other people too," John said. "It's for the best. See ya."

He pushed past the two and got in his Trans Am. His heart was thudding. There were a million other girls in the world anyway. There were a million other Caseys for that matter. This one didn't even matter. This one could date Jack for all he cared. He'd have his choice of Caseys one day.

A local high school student won the tournament, beating Henry in the finals ten to eight. Henry sulked for an hour, then challenged the kid, pockets lined with the one-hundred-dollar prize, to a rematch.

"We should do this every weekend," Grace said, her voice slurred from alcohol. She leaned heavily against John. "I love organizing these things."

"You did a good job." The music blared from the jukebox, and he felt her hopping to the beat. It reminded him of the dance he'd gone to with Casey. It seemed a long time ago. He hadn't seen her since the Burger Chef, and that was fine with him.

Grace must have been thinking about Casey too, because she said, "John, I didn't bring it up 'cause of Casey and that."

John looked at her. "Bring what up?"

She looked away. "I wanted to let you get over it."

"Grace, what do you mean? It was last week."

"I love you, John." She finally looked him in the eye.

He recoiled from her, and her face fell.

"I'm sorry," she cried, and fled, running back toward the bar.

John stood stunned for a moment, then followed her, jumping down the three steps to the sidewalk, but she had disappeared into the street.

"Damn it all." He sat at the bar, which was relatively quiet compared to the back room.

"Hey, John," Lou said.

"Hey, Lou. Give me a Coke."

"Sure." He poured it and then leaned close. "I want to let you know something."

"Twice in ten minutes," John sighed.

"Ray had a few people in to look at the pinball machine. Arcade people. I didn't eavesdrop or anything, but he was talking about selling it out from under you."

"What?" John stood up.

"Calm down," Lou said. "Sit. You didn't hear it from me, but you need to protect your interests." He slid John's money back at him. "This one's on the house."

John drank the Coke, struggling to sort his thoughts. Grace . . . loved him. Ray was trying to steal the pinball machine. John's mind couldn't get around either problem.

Henry came out of the back, his arm around the guy who had beaten him in the tournament.

"Hey, John!" Henry called. "Did you meet Steve? This guy is good."

"Yeah, I met him." Both of them were drunk, and John realized that Steve was underage, even for this universe. "Steve, you better crash at my place tonight. That okay with your parents?"

He nodded, looking a bit nauseated.

"Henry, we need to meet tomorrow. Tell Grace."

Henry mock-saluted him. Drunk, Henry wasn't so dour.

"Come on, Steve. You should have celebrated in moderation."

"I know," he gasped, his face white.

Grace wasn't at the meeting, but Steve had tagged along. They met in the empty lab bay.

"Where's Grace?" Henry asked.

John shrugged, but he assumed she was avoiding him. He hadn't given the question of her feelings much thought. He liked Grace, but he couldn't say he felt any sexual attraction for her. She was a friend, with many bizarre qualities. And frankly, he now had no interest in another relationship with any woman in this universe. Not after Casey.

"So, here's what I know. Ray is trying to sell the machine to an arcade company."

"Son of a bitch!" Henry said. "Let's go get it right now."

"Hold on," John said. "He doesn't know we know."

"You can't let him steal it," Steve said. "That game is the greatest thing since . . . since . . . I don't know what. It may be the greatest thing ever."

"Here's the thing," John said. "The machine is just so much equipment. Losing it would be bad. But what we really need to protect is the technology."

"We need to patent it," Henry said.

"Right."

"How much does that cost?" Henry asked.

"Does it matter?" John asked.

"I guess not."

"And I think we need to form a corporation," John said. "For our own protection. Like you said."

"Can I work for you guys?" Steve said. "I have some ideas. I can help too. I'm good with a soldering gun."

"The corporation is not yet ready to hire employees, Steve," John said. "But we'll keep your résumé on file."

"Thanks!"

"Should we pull the pinball machine out?" Henry asked. "It would hurt us to lose it. The stuff we did could be reverse engineered. Any electrical engineer could figure it out."

"But it doesn't matter if we have a patent, I think," John said. "If we pull it, we lose the revenue. We may need to pay an attorney."

"We could put it somewhere else," Henry said. "At seventy-thirty like we should have in the first place."

"Ray will not be a happy man," John said.

"He can't stop us," Henry said. "We didn't sign a contract. We own the machine. By word of mouth we can fill up any place we put the device around campus."

"You guys should open your own arcade," Steve said. "Right next to the high school."

John said, "Here's the plan. Tomorrow, I'll find a lawyer who can help us. Henry, you scout out some of the other bars around campus and see if we can get another place to put the machine. Steve, can you watch the bar to see if anyone tries to mess with the machine?"

"Sure. I've got a fake ID."

"Steve, you're five foot one," John said.

"Lou'll let me in. And I won't drink." He looked suddenly queasy. "Never again."

John called Grace's dorm room, but no one picked up. He would have gone over to see her, but Casey's room was on the same floor and he didn't want to chance running into her. Grace wasn't in the lab, since he had just come from there. He tried the library, and found her reading a paperback at a study desk.

"Hey," he said softly.

"Hey." She didn't look up from the book. John pulled a chair over and sat beside her.

"Grace, you've turned into my best friend," he said.

"Don't say it," she said. "I don't want to hear it."

"Grace, you're my best friend," he said again, taking her hand. "There was a reason I should never have gotten involved with Casey, and that same reason applies to you."

"Oh, please."

"I'll tell you why someday, but till then we've got to stay just friends."

Grace wiped a tear from behind her glasses. "I was just drunk, John. It didn't mean anything."

John let the lie slide.

"We've got a crisis, by the way."

She sat up, her eyes bright and wet. "Oh, I love a good crisis. Do tell."

Henry found a bar on Secor Avenue called Adam's All-Star Cavalcade that would take the pinball machine for seventy-thirty. The manager had heard about it and one of his bartenders had played in the last tournament, losing to Steve in the first round.

They met on the next Monday in the lab bay to plan the extraction.

"Ray leaves by ten each night. Lou or someone else closes up. We can be there late, then take it out the door," Grace said.

"Will Lou help us?" Grace asked.

"What do we do with the machine then?" Henry asked.

"Bring it back here," John said.

"Take it to Adam's right away," Grace said.

"All the bars close at the same time," John pointed out.

"So we leave it in a pickup truck until the next day."

"In the open?" Grace said. "No way."

"Here," Henry said. "No one will bother it."

"Sounds good," John said. "So here's the revised plan: Tonight we close Woodman's and we take the machine with us. We drive it to the lab. Then tomorrow we drop it off at Adam's All-Star Cavalcade."

"It's a plan," said Grace.

They were yawning by twelve but managed to stay awake until closing time, drinking Cokes and eating tortilla chips. Lou wasn't working that night; another bartender, Chip, was closing the place. But Ray left by ten as usual.

"Cha-ching!" he cried as he passed them on the way out.

"Yeah," Henry said. "You said it."

At ten to one, the bartender yelled, "Last call." But the place was empty except for a couple career drunks. No one was playing pinball.

"Let's go," John said.

They went in back, unplugged the machine, and lifted it.

"God, it's heavy."

They maneuvered it down the steps and past the bar.

"What the fuck you doing?" Chip yelled. "Put that back."

"We need to make some repairs," John gasped. "We'll have it back tomorrow."

"No way!" Chip stepped around the bar to block their way. Grace, on a front corner, set her side down and kicked him in the shin. As he bounced away holding his leg, they pushed the machine through the door.

It took them five minutes to load it, but it took Ray four to run down the block from his house, dressed in a robe that flapped behind him.

"What the hell do you think you're doing?" he yelled.

"Taking our machine," Henry said.

"Put it back, now."

"No," John said.

"I've called the police."

"Why? It's our machine."

"Listen, we had a deal, you stupid fucks," he said, trying to climb up onto the truck bed.

John grabbed his shoulder and set him back down on the sidewalk gently. "We know you tried to sell us out, Ray."

His mouth slapped shut. "I was trying to make you guys a deal. Do you know how much money this thing is worth?"

"Make us a deal?" Henry cried. "That's a load of bull."

"Sorry, Ray. Our deal is finished," John said.

Grace climbed into the front, while John steadied himself and the machine in back. Henry started the truck and drove away.

CHAPTER 26

John Prime watched the late November snow fall from his corner office in the McClintock Building in downtown Toledo. The production reports were on his desk, above the sales projections, and he needed to review them before he went home to Casey. To their new house in Sandburr. In his new Unic XK.

Prime grinned at the partial reflection in the mirror. Everything he'd ever wanted he had now. Not exactly according to plan, but here he was, president of a corporation, marketing one of his "inventions." In just two months, he'd gone from murder suspect to corporate wheeler-dealer.

He should have been going over the reports, but he was still flying from the marketing meeting. They'd managed to get the kid on *Late Night with Garofalo*. That's all they'd need. Just sixty seconds of the kid solving the Cube, a "wow" from Garofalo and her sidekick, Nealon, and every kid in the world would want a Cube. It was selling, sure, but it wasn't the sure-fire hit he'd hoped. There were a dozen other toys kids in America were asking for instead of the Cube. But with a month until Christmas, they could still have the stores stocked nationwide. He hoped.

He turned back to the production reports.

Prime opened the first folder and his phone buzzed.

"Mr. Rayburn, a Mr. Ismail Corrundrum on line one," Julie said.

"Who?"

"Mr. Corrundrum, sir. Says he knew you when you were a kid. Says it's important."

Prime rolled the name around on his tongue. It didn't ring any bells, but who knew who Johnny Farm Boy had in his past? Prime glanced from the reports to the blinking light. He didn't really want to go over the reports.

"Hello?" he said. "This is John Rayburn."

"It's not 1980," a voice said.

"What?"

"It's not 1980. The Cube is usually out by 1980. You are late by twenty-five years."

"Who is this?"

"A fellow traveler," the voice said. "Apparently."

"What are you talking about?" Prime said, pretending to be as confused as possible. But inside he was cold. The man on the line was implying he knew the Cube was the result of cross-universe movement. He knew about traveling across universes.

"You're going to attract a lot of attention," the voice said. "Good thing I found you first."

"I'm hanging up, you crackpot," Prime said. He slammed down the phone. "Julie!" His assistant stuck her head in. "No more calls from Corrundrum!"

"Sure thing, boss."

He glanced at the reports again. Now he was definitely in no mood for them. He pulled on his coat and gloves. It was late enough that the roads would be clear. The snow wasn't sticking; it was still too warm, but Prime guessed that the thought of snow alone was enough to snarl all of rush hour.

He took the elevator down to the parking garage. The Unic beeped to life, its engine starting from afar as he stepped off the elevator.

A man leaned against the car. He hadn't even bothered to move when Prime had unlocked it with the remote. For a moment Prime thought it was Corrundrum, but then he realized who it was: Vic Carson.

"I have a restraining order against you," Prime said. He reached for his cell phone. "I'm calling security."

"Sure, if you can get a signal down here."

Carson pushed off heavily from the car with his buttocks. Prime saw he carried a crowbar in his left hand. It swung loosely from his ham fist.

"But I doubt you'll get a signal, and if you do, I bet the call won't go through."

He whipped the crowbar through the air.

Behind Prime five meters, the elevator door slammed shut. Prime turned and lunged at the call button, but the elevator was already gone.

Carson slammed the crowbar against a concrete beam. It rang out.

"If the police aren't going to do something, I will," Carson said. He staggered, then took a step toward Prime. Carson was drunk, but even so, Prime was half his weight and unarmed. If the crowbar touched him, it would break a bone.

"Your son just ran off," Prime cried. It was the story he'd been telling himself for so long, he almost believed it.

"He wouldn't a done that."

Carson lunged, and Prime jumped back.

"You're a fool. If the police had evidence, they'd arrest me."

"Police are the fools. They been bought off, with your fancy money."

"That's just your sorrow talking," Prime said. "I know you feel like you lost a son. But don't take your anger out on me."

Carson stumbled to a stop, his shoulders stooped. He seemed to consider this. Then he grunted. "Ain't coming back. Neither are you."

Prime leaped back from the horizontal swing. He dropped his

briefcase and the papers spilled out. Carson swung again, and the blow glanced off Prime's forearm. He grunted and stumbled back. Carson was on him, trying to beat him down with the crowbar.

Prime kept going backward, away from the elevator and away from his car.

Prime ran up against something, a car. He tried to dodge to the left, toward his own car, but Carson blocked the way. Prime was forced right, deeper into the maze of cars and empty spots, away from the elevator.

Prime turned and ran, circling a car, putting it between him and Carson.

Carson leaped over the hood of the car, and Prime was again face-to-face with the man.

The blow caught Prime in his temple, and he staggered back, almost falling. The next swing caught his thigh. He cried out. His stomach erupted bile and acid. His thigh was jelly. Dizzily his body shuddered toward the wall. There was nowhere to go.

The elevator dinged.

Carson stared, expecting someone to come off the car, but it was empty.

Prime realized it was the car he'd called.

He took a step toward the elevator and Carson ran to intercept.

But Prime was feinting. He ran toward his car instead, to the opposite side.

Carson swung, but too late.

Prime's dress shoes skidded on the concrete as he reached the Unic. Falling, he slammed his head against the car door. The concrete was icy cold; he clawed at the door handle, but his angle was off.

Prime pulled himself up, his shoulder blades itching. He yanked the door open and slid into the seat, slamming the door shut behind him.

The crowbar smashed into the car window. It starred, obscuring the image of Carson.

Prime dropped the car into gear and pulled through his spot, leaving Carson to swing wildly at his taillights. He ran over his own briefcase as he accelerated toward the gate. Curse words formed on Carson's lips, but Prime couldn't hear anything.

Shaking, exhilarated, he drove up the ramp, through the gate, and onto the downtown streets of Toledo.

He didn't even remember his drive home, whether the streets were full of early evening commuters or clear. He didn't remember if the snow was falling or not. He hadn't bothered calling the police, so he was confused when he saw the cop prowler in his driveway.

Someone must have found my briefcase, Prime thought. The police were there to check up on him.

He pulled into the garage, sliding past the patrol car. As he stood up from his car, a hand grabbed his arm.

"Mr. Rayburn, step out of the car."

"It was just Vic Carson, violating the restraining—"

"Put your hands on the top of the car, please."

Prime twisted around to look at the officer. His partner stood behind him with a hand on his gun.

"What's going on?"

The officer used his hip to push Prime against the car. Prime splayed his hands on the roof. Snow slid between his fingers. The cop cuffed his right hand, brought it behind him, and cuffed the left.

"John Rayburn, you are under arrest for the murder of Theodore Carson. You have the right—" Prime tuned out as he was Mirandized, thinking to himself, They've found the body. I'm doomed. I can't let them drag Casey into this.

An officer on each arm, they guided him to the car. Casey shot out of the door and grabbed Prime's head.

"Mrs. Rayburn, please."

She whispered into Prime's ear, "Don't say a damn word. Do you hear me?"

One officer pulled her away, while the other pushed Prime into the car.

"Do you hear me, John?" Casey yelled.

He looked at her, nodded slowly.

In his mind, he gave himself over to her completely and utterly.

CHAPTER 27

The second time John noticed the tall blond man, he was talking with Grace at the all-university tournament. John couldn't remember the first time exactly, but the man definitely stood out. He was tall, over two meters tall, with nearly albino features. His close-cropped hair was almost white. His eyes were sled dog blue. He was so distinctive, John knew he had seen him elsewhere but wasn't sure exactly where.

Grace turned toward John and gestured as she explained something. She couldn't stop talking with her arms and hands. The tall man stared at John, and a feeling of being examined under a magnifying glass passed through him.

The ball slammed against the glass, and John turned his eyes back to the game. Henry was beating the crap out of a freshman English major who'd bet him twenty dollars. The back room of Adam's All-Star Cavalcade had four pinball machines arranged back-to-back, and it was nearly impossible to move in the room with all the people. A lot of students were going to fail their finals, John thought.

John glanced up from the game. The man was on his way over. It bugged John that he couldn't remember where else he'd seen the man. He worked his way through the crowd, pushing between people who gave him dark looks that he didn't seem to care about.

He reached John's side and said into his ear, "This pinball was your idea?"

"What?"

"This pinball," the man repeated, waving his hand at the machine. "It is your idea."

John shrugged. The name was the same, but no one from his Earth would confuse it for the pinball that he knew. It had ended up more like foosball, with its head-to-head action. "It was a team effort."

"The name is your idea?"

John didn't like the man's demeanor.

"I don't remember," John said.

"What was the source of the name?"

"I told you, I don't remember. It was a brainstorming session," John said.

"It is quite important for me to know." The man had an odd accent, almost Germanic but not quite.

"Listen, people are waiting to play," John said. "If you're not here to play, move on."

The man gave him a dark look, then reached into his front pocket and handed John a card. It read: "Ermanaric Visgrath, Investments." There was a Columbus address and phone number. "Perhaps another time then, and we can discuss your invention in detail. My firm is always interested in financing exciting and innovative ideas."

He turned then and disappeared out the door. John filed the card away in his pocket and thought no more of it.

They filed the patent application on the day after they freed the machine from Ray's bar with the help of a young law student, studying patent law. Kyle Thompson had come out to Adam's All-Star Cavalcade, played and lost three games to John, and then agreed to work on their patent with them.

"I can't charge for my work, which may delight you or worry you," he said.

"Delight," Grace chimed in.

"Worry," added Henry.

"But all my work will be looked at by one of my professors. And I will do good work."

John liked his serious, polished manner. He'd played his games without so much as a smile but with intensity. His finger had been white on the flipper buttons.

"How long before we have the patent?" John asked.

"It varies, six to ten weeks."

"How much will it cost in fees?" Henry asked.

"To file the application with the Patent and Trademark Office, it costs two hundred and forty dollars. If they accept the patent, it costs an additional four hundred and twenty-five."

"That'll about wipe out our profit so far," Henry grumbled.

"I'll need access to the machine. It helps that you built a working prototype. I'll also need your time to fill in the details. It won't take long. Part of the problem in patent applications is visualizing the item." He pointed to the pinball machine. "We'll have no problem visualizing."

They heard no more from Ray but saw Lou once at Adam's All-Star Cavalcade. He said that Ray was mad and wouldn't talk about it. Lou grinned. "Serves him right."

After cleaning out the lab bay, they decided to keep using it to work in. John wanted to do the stand-alone model that he'd talked about at the start. He also wanted to build a phase two prototype. There were a lot of improvements that six weeks of play had caused them to consider.

Steve, the high school student who'd won the first tournament, came and worked in the lab after school every day, testing and making suggestions for playability. He also had a knack for soldering, as he'd said. He became Grace's arms and legs. They had the two new machines built in three weeks. Grace almost failed her finals, but then they had all of Christmas break. The lab was deserted.

They had no problem finding a home for as many machines as they could build. When the students had discovered it at Adam's All-Star Cavalcade, they'd managed to keep the place packed day and night.

"Maybe we should offer one of the new ones to Ray," Henry said.

"No way," Grace said. "I say we put one on campus, next to the bowling alley."

"In front of the Electrux game," Henry added.

"That's a great idea," John said.

They stood in the student lab, a week before Christmas. They had taken over three more lab tables during break. Their parts inventory was strewn across the floor. John's apartment was filled with boxes and electronics. Grace had had to move everything out of her dorm when her roommate complained to the RA.

"We need a better place to build," John said. "We need a factory or a warehouse."

"How do we pay for that?" Henry said.

John shrugged.

"We form a corporation, we make a business plan, and we get a loan," Grace said.

"What?" John said. "Where did you get that?"

"I was in Teen Professional," Grace said. "In high school. I designed and built a kickstand for your bike that was also a bike lock."

"A kickstand lock?"

"Yeah. I lost two hundred dollars, and I still have a hundred SecureStands in the attic at home."

"How reassuring," John said.

"This is a way better idea," Grace said. "Probably."

"I have no idea how to do a business plan," John said.

"I'll do it," Grace said. "It's all pretty pictures."

"Are you taking this seriously?" John asked.

"No, are you?" Grace replied quickly.

John couldn't help himself, and he began laughing. "Good point."

"What do we call ourselves?" Henry asked.

"I dunno," Grace said.

John couldn't help himself. "Pinball Wizards," he said. There was no Pete Townshend in this universe, no super rock group called the Who. He'd checked. There was no Beatles either, which made John feel a little silly whenever he hummed "Hey Jude."

"Pinball Wizards," Henry said, rolling it around in his mouth.

"I like it," Grace said. "Anything with wizards in it is cool."

Every place John looked at was too expensive for their shoestring budget. They finally found an abandoned factory on the far side of the river. The neighborhood was decrepit, but the place had strong locks on all the doors. John signed a six-month lease, with a down payment of most of his savings. If they didn't start bringing in more money, he'd be flat broke.

If it came to that, he'd have to drop classes and get a job. He'd be detoured from his goal of understanding the device. What a mess, he thought as he surveyed the freezing-cold factory floor. He was setting himself up for failure in his primary goal. He should just cut Henry and Grace loose, let them ruin their lives here. Yet the pinball machine was some last vestige of John's own universe. Pinball didn't exist here. He had brought it into being, an idea passed tenuously between worlds. A simple, silly game.

An hour later, Henry and Grace appeared with Henry's truck filled with parts and pieces of pinball machines.

"We need heat," Grace said, rubbing her hands on her shoulders.

"You want to pay that bill?" John asked.

"No. Maybe we need a trash can fire," she said. "Or space heaters."

"We do need electricity," Henry said.

John moaned. He hadn't thought of utilities when he'd signed the lease. "Let me call Toledo Edison right now," he said. "Do you think they'll turn it on without a deposit?"

"They might," Grace said. "We are a business after all."

They hauled two more piles of parts from the lab that afternoon. As they did so, John calculated they had enough pieces to build maybe three more machines.

On their last trip, they stopped by the three bars where their machines sat and the Student Union and drained the coin bins of quarters.

"Sixty-seven dollars and fifty cents," Henry said. "Plus fifty cents Canadian. I gotta work on the foreign coin rejection system." He looked up. "But it's got to wait."

"Why?" John asked.

Grace chimed in. "The parents want him home for the holidays. Mine too."

"When do you guys go?" John asked.

"Day after tomorrow," Grace said. "I have a train ticket to Athens."

Henry nodded. His family was in Columbus.

"I guess it's just me for the next three weeks," John said.

"I bet Steve would help you."

John laughed. "That's all right. I have work to do on a couple new features." His eyes rested on the huge crane hanging from the ceiling. He remembered the scratch on the edge of the device, and wondered how much pressure would be needed to pull the two hemispheres of the device apart. With Grace and Henry gone . . .

They ordered pizza delivery, but the driver wouldn't bring it to their neighborhood. Instead Henry went out for it and brought back a steaming pie that they ate in their coats in the dusty office.

Grace raised her can of cola. "To Pinball Wizards, Incorporated. May our balls always roll!"

"Hear, hear!" Henry said.

John laughed but felt a moment's regret that Casey wasn't there to share the toast.

With electricity—kindly turned on by two coveralled workers the day after they ordered, no deposit needed—they worked through the night and finished two more machines. Henry drove Grace back to the dorm to pack in the morning but came right back with her, waving a letter.

"We're official!" Grace cried.

"What?"

"Our articles of incorporation, notarized and accepted by the great State of Ohio," Grace said. "We're a company!"

John opened the letter. Inside were their boilerplate articles and a form signed by the deputy secretary of state. It listed Grace as CEO, only because neither Henry nor John wanted the job. Casey would have been a great CEO, John thought.

"Aren't you two going to be late for the train?" John asked.

"Yes!" Grace cried. "Let's go!"

"Merry Christmas!" John shouted as they ran from the building toward Henry's truck.

John turned back toward the machine he had been hips deep in, one of his single-player models. Their first machines were head-to-head, but he'd wanted from the start to build a traditional one, just like he remembered from his universe. He reached in and triggered a credit. He popped the ball into play and bounced it around for a few minutes. John had to admit that the old type of machine that he was used to was not as fun as the competitive version.

They'd gone through six flipper designs until Grace was happy. They had a hundred different bumper configurations that could be built from the simple plastic parts that Henry had ordered. If they could build ten machines a month, if the money came in for each of them the same as the first machines, they could keep the factory and they might even have a little extra for salaries.

John let the ball fall into the slot at the bottom of the machine. He was tired of solenoids, flippers, and ball bearings. He turned to his briefcase, sitting innocently on the table near the crane controls. Inside was the device.

The real estate agent said the crane worked, and to John's surprise it lowered when he pressed the switch, shuddering as it unrolled the steel cable. The iron hook slammed into the floor, sending a shard of cement skittering to the far side of the factory.

He'd need vise grips to hold the device in place. He'd have to be careful; he couldn't afford to destroy it. Did he even dare try this? he wondered. What if the device ripped apart? What if it ceased working?

He'd still have the parts. He'd still have his slowly garnered knowledge. The alternative—his own slow experimentation with the physics of multiworlds after ten years of physics study and no guarantee that he would be able to make the breakthroughs necessary—was too daunting. He had a working device right here. The marks on the edge seemed to indicate it had once been opened. He could do it again and have access to the internals.

John took the device from his briefcase. He placed it on the floor near the crane hook. His stomach twittered. If he destroyed it, he might be stuck here forever in a universe where he'd ruined his chances with Casey.

He was suddenly angry at what he had wasted and scared of what he might be giving up if he broke the device. He placed it back in his briefcase and locked it. No, he thought. I'll not do that yet.

John found two letters in his mailbox when he got home that evening, the first, a letter from the city of Toledo, from the Department of Treasury. He recognized the address, the same one they'd used to apply for gaming licenses for all their machines.

He opened it and read the notice. "It has come to our attention that the game licenses (see attached sheet for a complete listing) issued to Pinball Wizards, Inc., are for gambling devices. Gambling devices are not allowed within the city limits, and as such must be removed within twenty-four hours from their locations. Failure to do so will result in a one-hundred-dollar per day penalty for each offending device."

They weren't gambling devices! John thought. But how do we prove that?

He opened the second, thicker envelope. It had a return address of a law firm in Toledo. The document inside was dozens of pages thick and, at first, John couldn't parse the legalese. Then he realized that the Ray Paquelli in the document was Ray from Woodman's and that he was suing them for breach of contract and theft.

John sat heavily on a kitchen chair. How would they deal with this? They had forty-eight hours from the postmark on the letter (yesterday!) to remove the machines, and they had no more than a handful of quarters in the bank. And Henry and Grace were at home on winter break.

He called Grace and Henry the next morning on a conference line from his apartment.

"Call our student lawyer," Grace said.

"No, we need a real lawyer this time," Henry said.

"How will we pay for that?"

"Call Kyle Thompson!" Grace said. "He filed the patent for us; maybe he'll do this too."

"He's probably on winter break," John said.

"At least try!" Grace said.

"Maybe Casey can help," Henry said.

"No," John replied quickly. That was the last person he wanted to see for help.

"I mean, she's in Findlay—"

Grace cut him off. "If John doesn't want Casey, Henry, don't push it."

"Okay. I'm just saying . . ."

John said, "I'll contact Kyle. Maybe he's still in town."

"Do you need us to come back?" Grace asked. "I mean, I can turn around. My parents would understand. . . ."

"Don't even think about it," John said. "It's just a game."

"Sure," Henry said. "Call anytime. Even on Christmas. Good luck."

Kyle didn't answer his phone, but the message didn't say anything about being out of town for the holidays. It didn't note a second number either. John drove over to the law school. The door was locked, but a pair of students pushed out through the double doors and John slipped in after them. Kyle had an office in the basement, called the Bench, an open space of dozens of desks and chairs jammed together in what may have been optimized use of space or just plain chaos. Surprisingly, the place was nearly half-full with law students. One of them was Kyle Thompson.

"Ah, the intrepid Pinball Wizard," he said as he saw John approach. "Nothing back from the Patent Office yet, so no news to give you."

"It's not that," John said. "It's these." John handed the letters to Kyle.

Kyle leaned back in his chair, instantly absorbed in the documents. He seemed to forget that John was there, and John began pacing in front of Kyle's desk. When Kyle turned the last page of Ray's suit, John said, "Well?"

"It's not my speciality," Kyle said. John sighed. "I don't do municipal law. And I can't advise you on this lawsuit."

"That's okay," John said. He reached for the documents. "Thanks for—"

"But—" Kyle placed his hand on the documents. "I think we can still help."

"We?"

"Hey, Angela!" Kyle called. A brunette looked up from her desk. "You interned in the mayor's office, didn't you?"

THE WALLS OF THE UNIVERSE   225

"Yeah."

"Can you take a look at this?"

Angela was a foot shorter than Kyle, dressed in a wool sweater and gray skirt. She skimmed the letter from the city, then threw it down on Kyle's desk.

"They can't do this," she said.

"They can't?"

"No, Department of Treasury has no jurisdiction over gambling. That's the Department of Gambling Control. That's Able Swenson. Treasury can garnish wages for back taxes, but it can't order a cease and desist."

"What can I do about this?"

"Do? You fight these bastards for trying to muscle you!"

"Sure," John said. "But how?"

Angela wrote down a number. "This is Able's number. Call him. He'll know what to do."

Kyle took the number from Angela. "I'll do it," Kyle said. He picked up his phone, and Angela took the suit document. She started quizzing John.

"Did you have a contract?"

"We shook on it."

"Anything written?"

"No."

"Did Paquelli contribute to the business?"

John shrugged. "He provided a place for the machine."

"In exchange for a cut?"

"Yeah."

"What about working on the game? Did he help? Did he give you ideas?"

"I don't think he ever even played it," John said. He tried to remember a time when Ray was in the same room as the pinball machine, and couldn't except for the time he showed up at the lab to watch the first time.

"Where did you get the idea, anyway?" Angela asked.

John felt himself flush. "Well . . ."

"Don't answer that!" Angela said. "It doesn't matter. He doesn't have a leg to stand on. But that's the good news."

"There's bad?"

"Do you have any money? Do you have the cash on hand to fund a long legal battle?"

"Of course not!"

"Ray probably is guessing that, and thinks you'll be an easy mark."

"Couldn't Kyle . . . ?"

Angela shook her head. "We're just students. We can't argue in court. Well, we could, but it's six kinds of felonies." She turned toward Kyle. "Have you heard of Paquelli's lawyer?"

"What's the name? Panderstack?"

"Per Panderzelder."

"Nope. Could be from Columbus."

"We just rented a warehouse," John said. "All our cash is tied up in parts."

"Do you have orders?" Angela asked.

"We do. A couple more bars want machines. And we had an inquiry from a firm in Las Vegas."

"No booked orders?"

"No, I guess not." John realized they'd been doing everything haphazardly.

Kyle slammed the phone down. "Good news!" he said.

"But there's bad news too," John said. "I'm beginning to get the pattern."

"Yeah, but good news first," Kyle said. "We got a hearing with the Department of Gambling Control. Swenson said that Treasury has no authority to order them off, but he does."

"When's the hearing?"

"January fifth."

"So we can keep them in the bars until then?"

"Well, bad-news time. Swenson wasn't convinced they were

nongambling devices. He needs to see them. If he thinks they are, he'll ask you to pull the plug until the hearing."

"When is he coming to look?"

"He wouldn't say, but within the next three days."

"That would mean the end of our cash flow, if the games were shut down," John said.

"They need a real lawyer, Kyle," Angela said.

"I know!" Kyle seemed exasperated. "I feel responsible for you guys. Freshmen, building a business in one quarter."

"With quarters," John said.

"For quarters," Angela added.

"I'll call around for you," Kyle said. "We'll need a lawyer who'll take the case pro bono. But I know some people."

"Me too," Angela said. "You guys have appeal. College students, entrepreneurs, inventors. There might be public interest." She snapped her fingers. "We could paint Ray as the bad guy here. Too bad the school paper won't publish another issue until next year, but this won't show up on a docket for a month or more."

"That's a good idea," Kyle said. "You guys need some marketing help. You need some exposure."

"I don't know about that."

"Of course not, you're an engineer," Angela said. "Yours is a great story."

"Thanks for your help, guys," John said. "This is all too much."

"You said it," Kyle said. "We'll get you through this."

On the way back to his apartment, John's mind roiled. For a moment he was ready to chuck it all. What did this have to do with understanding the device? Nothing at all. Yet he couldn't abandon his friends. Nor could he bring them closer to himself. All this running around, all this legal maneuvering, seemed like so much bullshit. It meant nothing in his universe.

The next day—a week before Christmas—John spent in the factory. He'd left the device at the apartment, unwilling to have the temptation nearby. Their cash box was empty, save a couple rolls of quarters he had to deposit. He'd swing by the machines later, but with school out he doubted there'd be more than a few dollars' worth of coins. Having all their machines near campus seemed like having all their eggs in one basket. Sure, it was easy to service the machines and collect coins. But they had saturated the market. And they were at the whim of the local climate: When school was out, they wouldn't get any traffic at all. Furthermore, they were under the thumb of the Toledo municipality, as seen by the hearing they had with the Department of Gambling Control.

The nibbles from the casino in Las Vegas hadn't come to anything yet. A company called Typhoon Gold wanted to take a closer look, however; they supplied casinos with games. If Pinball Wizard could get a larger order there, there'd be no complications with local laws. They could ship the machines anywhere.

Working on a machine in gloves and winter coat proved too cumbersome. He moved all the equipment into one of the smaller offices, which had a woodstove in it. The chimney pipe fed through the window. Using cardboard as tender and broken pallets as fuel, both of which the factory had in oversupply, he stoked the woodstove enough so that he could work without a shirt.

The door banged open after noon, and John jumped up from his wiring, startled. He peered around the doorway to see Steve—the high school champion of the first tournament—standing there stamping off a dusting of snow from his feet.

"Hello?"

"Steve, what are you doing here?"

"Grace said I should come over and help."

"Don't you have school?"

"No, water main break," he said with a smile. "I'm here to help. I can solder, I can game test, I can—"

"Can you sweep?"

"What?"

"We have customers coming in three days after Christmas, and this room is a mess."

Steve's shoulders sagged. "Yeah, I guess."

John smiled at him. "Then you can help me with the soldering."

"All right!"

By evening, they managed to get the room cleaned out, swept, and half-painted with a utilitarian light gray. John realized that Steve had ridden his bike through the slush to get to the factory, so he threw the bike in the trunk of the Trans Am.

"What are those two guys doing?" Steve said.

John saw the black car then, parked in the alley that led to the factory. Two blond men wearing dark glasses sat in the car. John wouldn't have noticed them if Steve hadn't said anything, but now that he saw the car, it seemed out of place for the location.

"Watching," John said.

"Why?"

John had no idea. Maybe they were private detectives hired by Ray Paquelli. Maybe they were innocent bystanders, just waiting. Maybe they were employees of the Department of Gambling Control. No, not in that car.

Suddenly bold, John pulled right next to the car. He stared at the two, but they kept their heads facing straight ahead, as if they didn't see John and Steve staring.

"Maybe they're like one of those fake security systems," Steve said. "You don't spend the money on the system; you just buy the sign. They couldn't buy real security teams, so they bought some manikins."

"But they aren't manikins," John said.

Finally he pulled away.

Kyle called the next morning.

"Good news," he said. "Able Swenson saw no need to close the machines down."

"So we're good until the fifth of January?"

"I think so," Kyle said. "But he did say something interesting."

"What?"

"He said you had some odd enemies," Kyle said.

"What does that mean?"

"I dunno, but I assumed he meant he butted some heads with the Department of Treasury. But he wouldn't say for sure."

"Maybe Paquelli pulled some strings," John said.

"Maybe," Kyle said.

Immediately after, John dialed up Henry and Grace, giving them the summary.

"So both legal items are deferred until next year," Grace said. She sounded relieved. "Now we can focus on Typhoon Gold." They'd hinted at an order of one hundred machines.

"Steve and I painted the 'showroom,'" John said with a chuckle. "We're building three demo models, including another stand-alone one."

"You and that stand-alone model," Henry said.

"I'm a purist!"

"Yeah, but everyone likes the head-to-head ones," Grace said.

"Just because we built that one first," John grumbled.

"Three demo units," Henry said. "That should be fine."

"I'll be back the week after Christmas," Grace said. "In time for the Typhoon meeting. I told my parents I wanted to start studying early."

"Did you even sign up yet for classes next quarter?" John asked.

"I think so. Did you?"

"Uh-huh." Though John wondered how they would juggle time between Wizards and class.

John drove to the factory afterwards. Unlocking the door, he immediately noticed the drift of snow under the far window. Someone had broken the window. There were tracks in the dirt. Someone had broken into the factory.

John rushed to the showroom. He couldn't tell if anyone had

been there. Steve's sweeping had left the floor dirtless. The machines were all as John had left them, as far as he could tell.

He returned to the main door and looked up and down the alley. The car with the two men wasn't there. Could it have been them? He shook his head. It was just kids. Especially in this neighborhood. He found an old piece of plywood and nailed it to the open window frame.

He kept expecting Steve to walk into the factory, but he was alone with the machines and the tools all day. He found himself drifting off into a daydream of Casey, and he shook his head. What was she up to? John wondered. Not that it mattered. She and he were finished.

He sighed and put the wrench down.

He put everything down, locked the factory, and drove to the nearest gas station. From their pay phone he called Casey's parents' house in Findlay. Surprisingly, she answered.

"Hello?"

"Uh. Casey."

"John," she said. She didn't sound angry or even interested. Perhaps resigned.

"You free tonight? You wanna see our factory?"

There was a pause. "Yeah, I'm free."

CHAPTER 28

John Prime had been in police stations before. There'd been the time he'd been arrested for vagrancy. Just the once, but that was amazing given the number of times he'd slept in the open, unable to obtain local currency and too scared to move to the next universe without trying to make a go of it. Then there'd been the time he'd been pulled over in the rental because he'd thought the speed limit signs were in miles per hour instead of kilometers an hour. There'd been a lot of almosts too: the time he'd skipped out just as the treasury agents bashed down the door of his hotel room and the times Casey's father had called the cops.

This time was different. There was no easy way out. Worse, he'd done it, with no mitigating circumstances. He'd killed a man, and they had him. His only hope was to trust Casey.

"Look at me, Rayburn," Detective Duderstadt yelled.

Prime continued to stare at the floor.

"You think this is all going away if you ignore it? Is that it?" Duderstadt turned to the one other cop in the room, a uniformed officer, standing by the door with his arms crossed. "He thinks I'm not here. Thinks I don't exist."

The other cop said, "Don't I wish. You haven't showered in seventy-two."

Duderstadt shrugged his shoulders at the cop, said to Prime, "He's a comedian, Eckart is. He finds this funny. Me, I take murder very seriously. The people of Findlay take it very seriously. How do you take murder, Rayburn?"

"Ask my lawyer," Prime said. His throat, dry after the booking, the mug shot, and the hour in the hot room alone, broke his voice.

Duderstadt laughed. "Apparently you do find this humorous too. Your lawyer isn't here, at least not for the next twenty-three hours."

"Twenty-two hours and thirty minutes, hoss," Eckart said.

"Right. Law says we can hold you incommunicado for twenty-four hours until we let you see your lawyer."

Prime shrugged. The laws of arrest, interrogation, and trial varied slightly and constantly from universe to universe.

"I have nothing to say," Prime said.

"I'd expect so, if you were guilty," Duderstadt said. "I'd say very little if I were guilty, eh, Eckart? I'd not want to incriminate myself."

"If they don't speak, it means they're guilty," Eckart said. "First rule they teach in detective school."

"Ah, yes," Duderstadt said. "Silence equals guilt. We're just going to assume you're guilty when you don't talk."

"I want my lawyer," Prime said.

"He'll be here, he'll be here in what?"

"Twenty-two hours and twenty-eight minutes," Eckart finished.

"So, my throat is going to get a little dry if I do all the talking during that time. But I'm willing to start us off. I'm willing to explain why you're here. You just jump in when I get it wrong."

"Lawyer."

"Here's how we see it. Ever since this expulsion thing in high school. What? A year ago?"

"About that," Eckart said.

"And how about that? High school student to president of some crazy toy company. And here you're throwing it all away over some punk. I can't fathom it. I can't fathom why you'd do it."

"Because I wouldn't," Prime said, instantly regretting.

"Ah, yes, but this all started before you were rich and famous. This all started when you were just a punk yourself. Two punks, with a grudge. The end is always bad for two punks and a grudge."

"Black eye, broken leg, punctured lung," Eckart said, ticking off his fingers. "Gunshot to the leg."

Duderstadt turned back to Prime. "And that was all this week!" He took his coffee off the table, sipped it slowly. There'd been no offer of coffee to Prime. "Two punks and a grudge. Never works out. So, Carson comes to work during the summer with his dad. He sees his old nemesis. Tempers flare. Words are exchanged. He insults your wife. You accuse him of torturing animals." Duderstadt paused. "How did you know that, by the way? How did you know that bit of information? Ted Carson, animal torturer. That's perplexing, unless you were in league with him."

Prime's face jerked up, but he held his tongue.

"Ah, perhaps not. Perhaps you knew, and you feared for your wife's life, because you knew what he could do. You knew you had to act to save your family, so when he came to your apartment, threatening you, you did what you had to do. You did the only thing possible. You killed him before he could kill you."

Prime met Duderstadt's eyes but remained mute. The detective was too close to the truth, but Prime wouldn't let him know how close.

"It was probably justifiable. It'll make it easier on you if it was. The boy had it coming. No doubt about. I'll stand up in court and let the judge know about his . . . activities. You might get no jail time at all. You might be back to that beautiful family of yours before Christmas." Duderstadt looked him square in the face, the perfect confidant, the perfect friend to help a wayward soul through turmoil.

"I think you want to tell me what happened, Rayburn. I think you do."

Prime opened his mouth, closed it again.

"Come on; you'll feel better when you do."

Prime nodded. "Go fuck your fag buddy, and get me my god-damn lawyer."

Eckart actually laughed. Duderstadt's face turned purple, and he slammed the back of his fist against Prime's cheek.

Prime grinned and let the blood flood over his lips and onto his shirt.

"You'll have to explain that to my lawyer too," Prime said. He grinned with what he hoped were ghoulishly bloody teeth.

"You were already worked over when you got here," Duderstadt said.

"By your patrolmen," Prime said. "What a lawsuit I have."

Duderstadt grunted and stood. "You'll wish you confessed. You'll wish you confessed before this is all over. Keeping all that inside you, Rayburn, it hurts. I've seen what a good confession will do for a man. I feel just like a priest sometimes."

Prime bit down on his first response. He wanted to tell Duderstadt to piss off and let him sleep. But the bastard was right; how much better he would feel if he just confessed.

To get it all off his chest—

"No confession today, Father Duderstadt. Why don't you go and let me sleep."

The detective stared at him, then nodded to Eckart. They left, slamming the door behind them.

Prime awoke with a start. Duderstadt had slammed the door. Prime glanced at the clock. He'd slept in the uncomfortable chair for three hours, an amazing feat considered how worked up he'd been after the questioning. But the fight with Carson, the trip in the back of the patrol car to Findlay, the hours of tension had drained him of energy.

Prime relaxed his face, forced himself to yawn.

Duderstadt slapped a pile of papers down onto the table.

"What is this shit?" Duderstadt said.

"What?" Prime asked.

"Even your wife didn't have the combination," Duderstadt said. "We had to get a cracker in from Detroit to open it."

Prime stared at the pile of paper. He saw the newspaper clippings; one from the *Findlay Bee* was on top. In this universe the Findlay newspaper was called the *Gazette*.

"Articles on the mayor, on the council members, plans for crap, bric-a-brac, toys." Duderstadt spread the material across the table. "And here's the file I care about, one on Ted Carson. Clippings of him being arrested for killing a cat. Only this never happened." Duderstadt shook the paper in Prime's face. "What is this shit?"

Prime couldn't help it. He started laughing. "You broke into my safe for some old fake newspaper clippings? What a bunch of idiots."

"Fake? These look real."

"Real? Whoever heard of the *Findlay Sentinel*?"

"What are these for?" Duderstadt cried. He was a deep shade of purple.

Prime grinned. "A book," he said. "I'm also a writer. A science fiction murder mystery."

"A book."

"There'll be a police detective character, but I think he'll die early in the narrative."

Duderstadt glared at Prime. Then he swept up the materials into his arms and pulled open the door. Eckart stood there.

"Send him to the pit," Duderstadt said. "Let him rot there until his lawyer comes and gets him tomorrow."

"You got it, hoss," Eckart said.

Prime relaxed. Now he could get some more sleep.

"Hey, Duderstadt," Prime said.

The detective turned.

"Just throw all that junk away," Prime said. "I don't need it anymore."

CHAPTER 29

Kyle set up interviews with three lawyers before Christmas, but though all were sympathetic and believed the cases were winnable, none had time to work on them. Though John was depressed, Kyle assured him that someone would take the case.

"There's a requirement for pro bono work," Kyle said. "We just have to find the right lawyer who has the right time to work on this."

"Sure," John said.

"And even if we don't find someone before the January fifth meeting, I'll be there," Kyle said. "Though I can't say anything. Or be your lawyer. I can at least be there to make suggestions."

"I appreciate that."

On Christmas, John drove down to Bill and Janet's farm. He had small gifts for them, and though they welcomed him warmly and it looked like home, it wasn't. John left early and drove over to Casey's street. She had told him to pick her up at three thirty, but it was only one. He parked next to the curb in the slush one block up and sat in his car. He was afraid he was in love with Casey.

She'd been impressed with the factory, looking it over, commenting on the paint job. She'd played the stand-alone version and said it was fun. But when he'd gone to kiss her, she'd deflected his face with a hand and asked him to take her to the dorms.

"I have to pick something up," she said.

He'd driven her back to Findlay after that.

"Can I see you again? I'll be down on Christmas Day to see Bill and Janet," he'd said.

She'd looked at him with an odd look that John hoped wasn't pity. He felt so desperate asking, but looking at her, he couldn't help himself.

"Sure, my parents are having an open house. Come by after three thirty," she'd said. Then she'd pecked him on the cheek and disappeared into the house.

Colored lights adorned the eaves of the house. The huge pine out front was covered in flashing bulbs, at least as high as Mr. Nicholson's ladder could reach. Electric candles flickered in each window. There was even a small menorah in an upper-story window. Cars were packed in the driveway, and someone had built a snowman. The rising temperature had exposed swatches of brown grass and forced the snowman to a thirty-degree angle.

"What am I doing here?" John muttered. He should have been back at the factory. He should have been working on what he would say at the hearing with the Department of Gambling Control. Instead he was here waiting outside Casey's house.

He almost drove away. He almost got out and knocked early. Just as he pulled the handle on his door, the front door swung open. There was Casey, in a white fur-trimmed red dress that came halfway up her thighs. Then someone followed her out the door, his arm around her waist.

John's heart jerked.

Jack leaned forward and kissed her. She reached around his neck and held him tightly as she kissed him back. His hand reached around her and under the dress.

John looked away.

Then he looked back, gripping the steering wheel with both hands, leaning forward to see through the fogging windshield. He felt sick.

Jack finally let Casey go and sauntered down the path. He waved once from the end of the walk, then climbed into his car and drove away. Casey watched him the whole way. Finally, she turned and went back inside.

John, his hands shaking, started his own car and began the solitary, vivid drive back to Toledo.

The day before the Las Vegas team was to arrive, Grace and Henry returned. The weather had turned suddenly dark and windy. Drifts of snow covered the alley and the Trans Am got stuck. Henry and John spent three hours shoveling the brickwork, only to have it fill in again later that day. Grace spent the same time sweeping the empty factory, throwing cardboard boxes and pallets into the incinerator, and scrubbing the new rust from the old rust. The gas company had agreed to service on credit, and they had the furnace in the basement cranked up to at least ten degrees Celsius.

"I hope they don't have to use the bathroom," she said. "It's still frozen."

"The showroom looks good," Henry said. And it did. A second coat of paint and two floor lamps had made it seem almost cozy. The bare bulbs were gone, as well as all the cobwebs, and the stove kept that room, if not the whole factory, at a toasty temperature.

"I hope they can make it in tomorrow," John said. Sleet pounded against the window. He rubbed the frost off the pane and looked out at the six more centimeters that had covered his car. The alley was empty; John hadn't mentioned the break-in or the stalking duo to Henry or Grace. It didn't seem to matter.

"It'll clear up—"

"It'll clear up—"

Grace and Henry spoke on top of each other. They glanced at each other and giggled.

"It'll clear up by tonight," Grace said. "They come in this afternoon."

Henry put a quarter in the stand-alone and started playing a game lackadaisically.

"This is growing on me," he said.

"See?" John said.

"With all that capital," Grace said, "we can afford to heat this place."

"We can afford to pay some workers," Henry said.

"We could hire a lawyer," John said.

"We could buy a decent soldering gun," Henry said. "And get a decent supply of Plexiglas."

"We could hire a salesman," Grace said. "And a receptionist. And we could have a lunch for everyone's birthday."

"We could countersue Ray," John said. "We could pay Kyle." I could buy something for Casey, he added silently. Something more than Jack could ever afford.

"So the plan is to hang at my apartment," John said. "They'll call when they land and rent their car. And then we can go to the factory and meet them there."

The snow tapered off by sundown. John drove Steve home and Henry and Grace to the dorms. There was a message from Casey on his machine when he got home.

"John, sorry you couldn't make it on Christmas," she said. "Something come up? Call me."

John deleted it and went to bed.

The phone rang.

John jumped. Grace dropped her book and grinned sheepishly. Henry nodded his head.

"It's them," he said.

It was ten minutes before the Typhoon Gold people's plane was supposed to land.

"They're early," John said. He picked up the phone. "Hello?"

"Hello, is this John Wilson?"

"Yes, this is he."

"This is Brad Urbeniski, Typhoon Gold."

"You've landed then?" He grinned at Grace and Henry.

"No, not exactly."

"Huh?" They couldn't be calling from the plane. Weather? The airport was open. Maybe they'd been snowed in somewhere else.

"We figured we'd give you a call," Urbeniski said. "We're not going to make it."

"What did they say?" Grace whispered.

"What? Why not?"

"We've heard that the game has been encumbered."

"What does that mean?"

"Someone else has a claim on the technology," Urbeniski said. "There's a suit in court. It makes your game less interesting to us."

"But that's all a mistake," John said. "No one else has a claim on this!"

"Sure, but until the mistake is fixed, we can't make an order. You understand."

"But—"

"When the problem is fixed," Urbeniski said, "we'll consider another arrangement." The line went dead.

"What?!?" Grace cried.

John placed the phone in its cradle, then sat down on the couch. "They heard about Paquelli's suit. They won't make a deal with that hanging over us."

"But it's crap!" Henry cried.

"Yeah, I know."

"They can't do that!" Grace cried. "That was a huge order! That would have made it all right!" She looked close to crying.

John just shook his head.

"We're doomed," Henry said.

"We'll win our case," John said. "We'll deal with the city of Toledo. We'll get another big order."

Grace said, "I don't think so. This was a stupid idea!" She stormed off to the bathroom.

Henry looked on in surprise. John couldn't blame her. This was all his fault for getting them into this. He remembered then the card he'd gotten from that guy at Woodman's. What was his name? Visgrath? Ermanaric Visgrath? He'd been weird looking and he'd acted funny. But he'd wanted to invest. He'd probably be as leery as Typhoon Gold was. Where was that card?

There was a bowl of crap on his kitchen counter, next to his keys and his wallet. He dug through it, tossing aside receipts and pieces of paper.

"Here it is," he said. The business card was crumbled and folded, but the name and number were still visible.

"What?" Henry said.

"What if we got an investor?" John said. "What if someone would fund us?"

"You want to bring someone else in?"

"They have money, and we don't."

"Yeah, but . . ." Henry seemed to consider it.

"We're not only going to lose it all," John said. "We're going to lose it to Ray Paquelli."

Henry gritted his teeth, as if he found the idea abhorrent. "I dunno." He glanced at the bathroom door.

John picked up his phone, then put it back down.

"Should I call?" he said. "Should I find out if they're still interested?"

Henry shrugged.

John felt a moment's anger at Henry's ambivalence. He picked up the phone and dialed the number.

"Mr. Visgrath's office," a male voice answered after the first ring.

"This is John Wilson. Mr. Visgrath gave me his number. . . ."

"Ah, yes, the Pinball Wizards," the voice said. "Just a moment."

"They remember us," John answered.

"Why would they remember us?" Henry asked.

A deeper voice spoke into the phone. "Mr. Wilson, so good of you to call. What can I do for you?"

"You— You said you'd be interested in financing our pinball machines."

The door to the bathroom opened and Grace came out looking perplexed.

"Who's he talking to?" she whispered.

"Investors."

"Yes, we're interested, though your circumstances have changed, have they not?"

"How so?" John asked.

"The lawsuit, of course, by Raymond Paquelli," Visgrath said. "And the problems with the city of Toledo."

How could everyone know their business so easily? John wondered. How had Typhoon Gold and Ermanaric Visgrath both learned of it?

"Those things will go away in no time."

"So you say."

"They will," John said. "Paquelli is grasping at straws and the city thing will be cleared up next week."

"But orders are down," Visgrath said. "And time is short for you."

"Are you interested or not?" John asked.

"We are."

"On what terms?"

"For fifty-five percent of the stock of the company, we will give you capital of two million dollars," Visgrath said.

Two million!

"Hold on," John said. He set the phone down on the back of the couch and motioned Grace and Henry over. "He's offering two million for fifty-five percent of the company."

"That's a majority," Henry said loudly.

John shushed him. "But two million is huge!"

"We could do everything we wanted," Grace said.

"But we're giving up ownership."

John realized Henry was right. He picked up the phone.

"We don't want to give up ownership," John said.

"That's not negotiable," Visgrath said.

"Why not?"

"Look at it from our perspective," he said. "We are investing a huge amount of cash in a company run by three teens without college degrees. We must maintain control of the company in case the situation deteriorates."

It made sense, but John was reluctant.

"I don't know."

"We have no interest in running the day-to-day aspects of the corporation," Visgrath said. "You have shown remarkable capability so far, but we must have assurances, and a minority share for us is not any assurance."

"We'll want more cash," John said.

"We're willing to raise our offer to four million, but no more."

John raised his eyebrows. "We'll have to think about it."

"Of course. I'd expect no less." Visgrath cleared his throat. He seemed suddenly distracted. "You have my number. Of course, the sooner the better, for you as well as me. Money makes a lot of problems disappear. Good-bye."

John hung up the phone.

"Who was that?" Grace demanded.

"You spoke with him," John said. "Visgrath. Ermanaric Visgrath. He was at one of the tournaments. You sent him my way, and he gave me his card."

"Yeah, just to get rid of him," Grace said.

"What kind of name is that?" Henry muttered. "Visgrath."

"We're not taking any offer!" John shouted. "We're just looking at options. We can walk away, we can fight city hall on a shoestring budget, or we can take their four million and hire the big guns."

"Four million!"

"It was just two million," Grace said.

"The fifty-five percent is nonnegotiable," John said. "But the cash part wasn't."

Grace sat down on the couch heavily. Her shoulders sagged. "This is all too much in one day. Too much." Her eyes were still bloodshot. John almost went over to her, but he recalled suddenly the drunken revelation of her feelings. And before he did, Henry took a step, stopped, then stepped toward her to place a hand on her shoulder. Grace suddenly sobbed and grabbed his hand.

"What should we do?" she said, her voice breaking.

John shrugged heavy shoulders. "I dunno."

Henry just shook his head.

"I don't—," John started to say. He stopped, swallowing. "I don't want to lose it all. And if that means asking for help from, from . . . professionals, so be it. We're just kids. We don't know how to run a company. Ermanaric Visgrath does. So they want something in return. So be it. But we've gone from nothing to four million dollars in four months."

"So you want to do it," Grace said.

"I don't want to lose it."

"I don't either!" Grace cried. "But . . . but . . ."

They were silent for a while. Finally, Henry said, "Let's do it."

"What?" Grace said.

"How often does a chance like this come along?" he said. Grace shook off his hand. A stricken look passed across Henry's face, but he continued, "Four million dollars to build a company. We can do . . . everything we want to do."

Grace grabbed her coat.

"Fine," she said.

"I'll drive you home," Henry said.

"No, I want to walk," she said. The door slammed behind her.

John shrugged his shoulders. "I'll call him tomorrow and arrange it."

. . .

"It's like this," Kyle said. "You have three people on the board, and they have four. They can fire Grace as CEO any time they want and elect one of themselves to the position. But the day-to-day stuff they aren't involved in."

John and Henry were in the basement of the law building again, where Kyle was examining the investment agreement Ermanaric Visgrath had sent over. Again the Bench was filled with law students. John wasn't sure if they ever took a break.

"So they ultimately control it all," Henry said.

"No, they control fifty-five percent," Kyle said. "All that means is that *if they wanted to* they could force a new chairman of the board and a new CEO. You see, investment companies like this don't want to run your company if it's doing well. They want to make money. But they want the reassurance that if you screw it up, they can step in and take over."

"That's why they won't budge on fifty-five percent," John said.

"Exactly."

"So," John said. He glanced at Henry, who shrugged. "So, what do we do?" John finally said.

"John, you know I can't offer legal advice," Kyle said.

"Yeah, but what do we do?" Henry said. He sounded as desperate as John felt.

Kyle sighed. "There's nothing in here that looks outrageous," he said. "And . . ."

"And?"

"And it's four million dollars. Jeez!"

"We know," Henry said.

"We're conflicted," John added.

"You should be." Kyle wrote down a number and a name. "Professor Andropov, in the business department. He taught our business contracts class. Ask him to look at it."

"A Russian?" Henry said.

"If you want a balanced opinion on Capitalism," Kyle said, "ask an Americanized Russian."

. . .

Andropov was a bespectacled man in a tweed coat. His office was lined with tomes, in Cyrillic and English.

"Here," he said. He handed the contract to John. It was marked heavily with red ink.

Henry looked over John's shoulder. "Are there any words left from the original?"

Two hours before, Professor Andropov had listened to their story with a blank face. John was certain he didn't care at all.

"In four months, you have gone from prototype to moneymaking venture?" he asked.

"Some money," John said.

"In quarters," Henry added.

"And now you have an offer for four million for majority ownership."

"Yes," John said.

"And we don't know what to do," Henry said.

"Why should you? You are engineers," Andropov said. "But engineers can do well in business." He took the contract. "I'll read it. Come back in two hours."

"Did it suck?" John asked, flipping through the pages.

"No, pretty good," Andropov said. He pulled a sandwich from his desk drawer. It was dark outside; John and Henry had spent all day in the law school and the business school. "Some weak language. One bad encumbrance. Otherwise, it's okay." He took a bite of his sandwich. "Oh, someone other than an American wrote this."

"What?"

"The syntax is off in places," Professor Andropov said. "Grammar is correct, but phrasing is odd." He shrugged. "No big deal."

"They asked for fifty-five percent," John said. "Is that too much?"

"For four million, they should have asked for ninety percent," Andropov said with a laugh, the first John had seen from him. "It's a good deal."

"So we should take it?" Henry asked.

"That I can't answer," Andropov said. "But think of this. You made one company in three months. If this doesn't work out, you can just make another one."

On New Year's Eve, John, Grace, and Henry sat at John's table. The revised contract lay before them. Ermanaric Visgrath's legal team had accepted nearly all of Andropov's changes. A ballpoint pen sat atop the fresh contract.

"So," John said.

"So," Grace replied. She grinned nervously but otherwise had nothing more to say. Unusual for Grace.

John slid the contract in front of Henry.

He opened the contract to the last page. "Signing it all away for fifteen percent," he said. He signed his name with a flourish.

Grace took the pen from his hand and signed her own name.

"Our new president," Henry said.

John took the contract then. He smoothed the page. It wasn't permanent. It wasn't forever. And it was only binding in this one universe anyway.

He signed his name.

"Pinball Wizards, Incorporated," he said, "is flush with cash."

CHAPTER 30

The barred door clanged shut behind him. In the two days he'd been in the Hancock County Jail, John Prime hadn't learned to ignore the finality of the sound. But it would be over soon. Casey had found a bail bondsman to handle the bail. It was just a matter of time and he'd be out of there.

He stood for a moment looking for Casey in the visiting booths cutting the center of the room. None of the visitors on the far side of the Plexiglas was her. When he'd heard he had a visitor, he'd assumed there was some last-minute question on the bail agreement, or some consultation with his lawyer.

"Number three," the guard said.

Prime took a step toward the third chair involuntarily.

A man sat behind the glass, a plain man wearing a wool coat, a hat, and glasses. A beard covered most of his face. Prime was sure the man was wearing a disguise. He looked too . . . different.

"Go on," the guard said.

Prime paused again, then took three steps, pushing himself down into the plastic chair. He studied the man, but disguise or no, Prime was sure now that he'd never met him before.

"What?"

The man grinned suddenly. He leaned forward and spoke through the perforated opening in the Plexiglas.

"Too bad you can't just leave all your worries behind," he said. "Isn't it?"

"I don't know you," Prime said. "What do you want?"

"We've spoken before."

"When?"

"Not long ago."

"Do you get your jollies off visiting prisoners in jail?" Prime said. "Because I really don't care for it."

"No, not any prisoner," the man said. "But you, yes. This seemed like a very controlled way to visit. What with your volatile temper. I'm sure jail hasn't relaxed you any."

"Who are you then?"

"We spoke two days ago." He paused, expecting Prime to guess. Two days ago he'd been arrested.

"So?"

"I called."

A light dawned on Prime.

"Ismail Corrundrum," he said.

"Yes!"

"You crank-called me. So?"

"I'm just surprised you've gotten away with this for so long."

Prime thought for a moment he meant Ted Carson's murder, then remembered what Ismail Corrundrum had said on the phone. He'd mentioned that the Cube usually came out in 1980.

"I don't follow."

"They watch for these things, you know," Corrundrum said. "Any sort of technology like that. I can't believe no one noticed. But maybe because it's a game, and maybe because you screwed it up, they didn't notice."

"I really don't know what you're talking about."

"Is this an exile?" Corrundrum asked. "Is that what you're doing here? Me too, in a sense."

Prime shook his head. "You've made a mistake," he said. He stood.

"Wait!" Corrundrum called. "Maybe it's not an exile. Maybe you've got a . . . way back."

Prime turned, staring hard at the man.

"That hardly seems possible," Corrundrum continued. "How could you have a device? Well, if you did, you don't have it now, do you?"

"I'm leaving."

"Maybe it's at home with that lovely wife of yours," Corrundrum said. "Does she have it?"

"You go near my family and I will simplify all your questions," Prime said. He turned and walked to the barred gate, waving the guard to open the door.

Prime paced the corner of the TV room, his mind racing. He knew people were exiled in universes without devices. He'd run across them before; he'd killed two, Oscar and Thomas, when they'd tried to steal his device. What if there were exiles everywhere, in every universe? Who was exiling them? And why?

He kicked the bolted chair.

"Hey!" one of the guards yelled at him from the overhang.

"Sorry," he muttered. He sat down.

Corrundrum was one of those exiles. Or he seemed to be. He seemed to know a lot. He'd indicated that Prime had made a mistake in marketing the Cube. That it would draw attention. Whose attention? Corrundrum was watching; he'd detected it. But Corrundrum had said they watched for any technology.

Damn it! He was just trying to get along! Why wouldn't everyone leave him alone?

He felt the urge to hide, to run. But he wasn't going to give it all up, not after he'd finally made it with the Cube. He and Casey had expenses now: the house, the cars, the nanny. He had a career. No way was he running out.

The fear of prosecution for Ted Carson's death had faded away. Ted Carson was alive somewhere in the multiverse; if one of him was dead, so what?

What else did Corrundrum know? Could Prime use it? What if there were observers? What if there were other devices? Could he get his hands on one?

Corrundrum had come to see him in disguise. He'd been careful, because he feared detection. Perhaps he feared Prime. He didn't know if Prime was an exile or an innocent or a traveler. Corrundrum had felt safe when Prime was in jail or when he called Prime at the office. But Corrundrum was playing it safe. What did he fear?

How would Prime lure him out? How would he get the information he needed?

If he had a device again, he wouldn't have to worry about Ted Carson.

What would Corrundrum find irresistible? A device, of course. If someone was trapped in a universe, he or she'd do whatever it took to escape. Hadn't Prime done the same?

Now how to get hold of Corrundrum?

Casey was silent on the ride back to Toledo. Prime didn't feel like talking either. He needed a shower; he needed some new clothes. In the backseat of the SUV, Abby slept.

Finally, halfway home, Casey spoke.

"You didn't tell them anything, right?" she said.

For a second, Prime thought she was talking about Corrundrum.

"How do—" Then he realized she meant the police. "No, nothing."

"They haven't figured something out, have they? They don't have some new evidence? Something we missed?"

"No," Prime said. "They expected me to admit it. They were fishing."

Casey exhaled. "They searched the house."

"I know."

"They took your . . . papers."

"I know."

"There wasn't anything in there. . . ."

"Casey, they've got nothing. They took a gamble, that they could scare me, and when they couldn't they threw me in jail. They don't have a case."

"That's what the lawyer said," Casey said.

"Then why did you ask?"

"I needed to hear it from you." They turned off at their exit. "The office called."

"What did you tell them?"

"Family emergency," she said. "But it's been in the papers."

Prime shrugged. "It's only been two days. It'll be all right. Money makes everything all right."

"Does it?"

"Absolutely," Prime said. "It bought us this house, didn't it? And this car."

Christmas lights hung from their eaves.

"What do you think?" Casey said. "I wanted something special for when you got . . . home."

"It looks nice," Prime said. "You didn't . . ."

"Dad came over and helped."

"What did you . . . tell him?"

"The truth. That it's all a horrible misunderstanding. He gave us half the bail money."

"It is a horrible misunderstanding," Prime said. He pulled into the driveway, looking up and down the street. There were a couple of dark cars, but Prime couldn't tell if they were occupied. Could Corrundrum be watching? Prime caught a flash of movement in one of the cars. They pulled around the back of the house into the garage.

"Has Carson's father been around? Or . . . anyone else?"

Casey shrugged. "Not that I've seen. I haven't been here, really."

"Yeah."

She grabbed Abby and climbed the three stairs into the back foyer. Prime sat in the car for a moment.

"Coming?"

"In a moment," he said. "I want to walk around front. Look at the lights. Can you unlock the front door?"

"Sure."

Prime walked out the garage door and waited until Casey had shut the inner door. Then he slipped through the hedge into his neighbor's yard. He sprinted across the back lawn, dodging the piles of snow. Between the neighbor's house and the next, Prime saw the car. From his vantage, he saw someone within, someone who could watch their house from where the car sat.

Prime hid behind a tree trunk. Then he dashed across the driveway, coming to rest behind a shrub not far from the car. A man sat within, his eyes on their house. Was it Corrundrum? He couldn't tell for sure. The man had been wearing a disguise at the jail visiting room. It could be the police.

Prime stood and walked over to the car. He leaned in and stared at the gaping, surprised face. It was Corrundrum.

Prime rapped on the window and waited until Corrundrum rolled it down.

"So?" Corrundrum asked.

"You have information I need," Prime said. "What do I have that you want?"

CHAPTER 31

EmVis allocated office space for them at the headquarters in Columbus. They had desks, phones, and doors in a corporate office building on a wooded plot on the north side of the city. The main office was a three-story glass building that seemed half-empty, except for the guards who manned the front desk and cruised the halls regularly. John saw more of the guards than he did of any of the EmVis personnel. Behind the main office was a fenced area within which was a second and third building. The only way through the barbed-wire enclosure was via a double-gated tunnel.

"What do they do in there?" Henry asked, looking out John's office window.

"Clearly we're not the only business EmVis funds," Grace said. "Maybe weapons research."

"Development of a better mousetrap?" John suggested.

"Reusable toilet paper!" Henry cried.

"You don't reuse yours?" John asked.

"Ew!" Grace replied.

They'd spent the last couple days at the office, working on project plans, and sales projections, and business plans. Not a minute had been spent on anything related to the pinball machines. It chafed Henry the most.

"School starts next Monday," Henry said. "We won't have to come down here as much. We can spend our time at the new office."

They'd moved out of the dilapidated factory as soon as they could, into a new building in Winterfield, one with an office and reception in one corner and the rest of the ten thousand square meters shop floor and production facilities. John had moved the lease of the old factory into his own name.

John's intercom chimed.

"Mr. Wilson?" It was Stella, his no-nonsense secretary. John had tried to kid with the beehive-haired woman on the first day, but she'd stared at him blankly. She seemed always poised to respond to anyone's next need, as if that was what she was programmed to do.

"Yes?"

"Mr. Charboric is ready for you."

"Charboric," Henry said softly. Henry did not like the second of the four board members from EmVis. Visgrath was palatable, in his sincerely intense way. Charboric, similar in Nordic features to Visgrath, was brooding, angry, and mean—at least in appearance. He'd had contrary suggestions already on design and implementation that Henry took personally. The two other EmVis board members were Mr. Alabathus and Mr. Zorizic, neither of whom they had met yet.

"What does he want?" Henry asked. "More ideas for flipper design? The perfect coin box?"

"Henry," Grace said. "Be nice."

"Patent stuff," John said.

"Great."

John grabbed a notepad from his desk. "Be back in a bit; then we can head back to Toledo."

"Sure."

Stella was standing outside the door to his office. He wondered if she listened in on them so that she could time her appearance perfectly. Perhaps she had just been standing there waiting. Her subservience disturbed him.

"This way, sir."

"I think I can find it."

"No, I insist, sir." She took his arm and led him down the hall to an elevator bank. She kept a strong grasp on his bicep while they waited for the elevator. An EmVis employee passed them, and neither acknowledged the other, though John gave the man an unreturned nod and half smile. The conference room was down one floor. Charboric was already there, sitting at the head of a table. A video camera was pointed at the chair to his left.

"Sit," Charboric said, pointing to that chair.

John took the chair to Charboric's right.

Charboric looked at him for a moment blankly, then stood and adjusted the camera. John resisted the urge to move.

"I will record this meeting," Charboric said.

John shrugged.

"We are here to discuss the patents for pinball," Charboric said, his Germanic or Slavic accent even heavier than Visgrath's. "We need to determine any instances of prior art."

"What do you mean?"

"Before we file patents, we must know if there is prior existence of similar devices."

"Shouldn't the lawyers be doing this?" John asked.

"They will," Charboric said shortly. "This is for their benefit. Now, are there prior art examples for pinball?"

"You know there are."

"What?"

"I saw pinball machines in Las Vegas when I was a kid."

"Where?"

"Las Vegas," John said. He felt Charboric's anger growing.

"Where in Las Vegas?"

"A casino."

"Which one?"

"I don't remember."

"Was it called pinball?"

"Yes."

"Which casino?"

"I don't remember."

"Think."

"I told you I don't remember."

"We need to know!"

"I'm telling you, I was five years old. I barely remember."

"They would not allow a five-year-old into the casino."

"It was outside the gambling area."

"Was this with your parents?"

"Yes."

"Who have died."

"Yes."

"Their last known address?"

"None of your business."

Charboric stared at him. He seemed like a man used to getting his way.

"Your reticence has been noted."

"Good," John said. "Your assholedness has been noted."

Charboric colored.

"You know nothing of business!" he hissed. "You think you're a smart know-it-all because you made something pretty. You think we're here trying to steal it. Our goal is to run this like a business. And we need this information to protect ourselves. To protect you."

John slowly shook his head. "You think you understand me, but you don't." John stood up.

"I'm not done here!" Charboric cried.

"I am," John replied. "If you need anything else, send me a

memo." He slammed out of the conference room, startling Stella, who had been sitting in a stiff-backed chair by the door.

"Done already, sir?" she asked.

Charboric grabbed the door before it slammed shut.

"Get back in here and answer my questions!"

John laughed. "Not in this lifetime."

"We own a majority of you! You have to."

"You own a majority of Pinball Wizards," John said. "You don't own me at all."

John headed for the elevator. Stella ran after him. Her face was pale. She seemed to be muttering under her breath.

"What's that, Stella?" John asked.

"Mr. Charboric is upset, sir."

"You think so?"

"Yes, I can tell."

John thought she was being sarcastic; then he realized she was sincere. She had seemed a highly competent, highly focused administrative assistant. Now John wondered if she was mentally defective.

Grace and Henry looked up when John entered his office.

"That was quick," Grace said.

"Charboric and I had an . . . a heated discussion," John said. "We're done. Let's head back to Toledo before it gets dark."

As they were walking toward John's car, Grace said, "Do you think we made a mistake?"

Henry paused but said nothing.

John shrugged. "I don't know," he said. "But we're better off than we were two weeks ago. We've got cash flow. We've got a business plan."

"We've got partners," Henry said sullenly.

"But we can sell and leave anytime," John said. "We can just go back to being students, and no one can stop us. But . . ."

"It's a chance we take. I know," Henry said. He crawled into the backseat of the car, hitching his feet onto the seat. His legs were too long for the car otherwise.

"Let's enjoy it while we can," John said. He hoped his words seemed jovial and positive. But as for himself, he was worried. Charboric was scrutinizing John's past. And that was something he couldn't let happen. He had no past in this world.

CHAPTER 32

Corrundrum sat nervously across from John Prime, spinning his coffee mug in his hands. It was two hours later, and three miles east, in a small coffee shop in a strip mall. Corrundrum had yet to say anything. Prime said nothing either; he was the one bluffing here. He expected that he had nothing Corrundrum wanted, while Corrundrum had information Prime needed.

"Corrundrum. That's a funny name," Prime said.

Corrundrum shrugged. "It's not from around here," he said.

"Around here?"

"You know what I mean."

Prime grunted. He didn't know what Corrundrum meant. He had always assumed that the universes where humans lived would be similar enough that everyone spoke a common set of Indo-European languages.

"Is it a contrived name?" Prime asked. "Did you make it up?"

Corrundrum looked up from his coffee, staring at Prime.

"No, of course not. What did you think?"

Prime didn't want to appear like he knew nothing, so he remained silent.

"I'm a singleton, of course," Corrundrum said.

"Sure," Prime said, unsure what he meant. "Tell me how you got . . . where you are." He tried to make the request innocuous yet filled with context, if Corrundrum chose to interpret it a certain way.

"How does anyone ever end up in a backwater like this?" he mused. "Everyone has a story, they're all different, and they're all the same."

"Sure."

"Anthropology expedition," Corrundrum said. "I thought the guy was funded and legit, but he was just a Prime seeker. He had some wild idea that there were artifacts in some universe, but he told us he was doing culture relativism studies. He had us up and down the moraines, coring samples, testing for traces. I had no idea what he was really looking for."

"What?"

"Prime artifacts, I said."

"Only we must have done something stupid, because a group of paths found us," Corrundrum said. "We were camped at the edge of the North American Craton in the Appalachians when the whole place was rousted by a pack of paths. They drove us out of the tents, shot some of us. Kryerol was gone, not in his tent, and his transfer was gone too. I thought he flashed out, but he had actually been at a farmhouse down the road, entertaining one of the local wives. He liked that sort of play."

"Kryerol?"

"Yeah, he was the 'expedition lead.' The paths stripped us and shackled us in a mass mover. It was old tech, and probably the only transfer they had. The thing was humming and we watched this shaved-head tech with welts on his back getting it back online and synced to wherever they wanted to go."

"Where was that?"

"Hell if I know! Whichever universe they used as home base, I guess."

"Don't get upset," Prime said. They weren't the only patrons in the coffee shop.

"Right. I get a little crazy when I think about how close we were to being dead. When you're a singleton, it means a little more, ya know." Corrundrum sipped his coffee. "Kryerol came back and they almost got him, but he slipped out. They were angry. They blew the brains out of the girl next to me. I thought I was next. Then Kryerol was there, materializing out of nowhere in the middle of the mover. He was firing his weapon, but the paths were armored. It was enough to drive them out of the bay.

"He knelt down in the middle of us and began fiddling with his transfer.

"'Didn't think I'd leave you, eh? You're my buds.'

"He must have used all that thing's juice. He whipped us all out of there."

"To where?"

"To here, of course. This universe. I turned around to thank him. Only he was choking on his own blood. One of the paths must have got him just as he transferred. Only he got the device too. The projectile had passed through the control deck into Kryerol's chest."

"So you were stranded here," Prime said. "All of you. Where are the rest?"

"You really don't know?"

"I only see you. Did you kill them?" Prime asked with a false joviality. What Corrundrum was telling him was nearly impossible to assimilate quickly. But he needed to keep Corrundrum talking.

"We headed for the beacon near the Serpent Mound," Corrundrum said. "This world isn't dead, at least. We didn't have to walk. But we didn't realize it was infested. The Primes had abandoned it long ago, and a band of paths had the beacon area under surveillance. They captured the rest of us. But you know that, don't you."

"What?"

"You'd have to know that," Corrundrum said. He leaned back, pulling his winter coat back to reveal the black handle of a gun.

"This is a public place," Prime said. "What do you think you're doing?"

"I have no illusions they're still alive. It's been ten years. But I want in on it," Corrundrum said. "I want a piece of this."

"What are you talking about?"

"You can't be so stupid to try and do this and not be a part of them," Corrundrum said. "But you're in trouble now, so I have leverage. This murder thing. You can't get out from under it. Why not? These paths are making billions here. You could buy your way out of anything. So you must be an offshoot. You must be making some play that you don't want them to know about. So I have something over you."

"I got another idea," Prime said. "You're psychotic. You're spinning science fiction tales in a coffee shop with someone you've been stalking. Maybe you're the person in trouble now, mentally."

"No, I've been watching you," Corrundrum said. "You believe my story. You're second generation at least, but you've heard the stories. You understand what I'm saying. You people owe me." Corrundrum stood up. "If you don't give me what I want, I'll tell them. I know where they are. Or at least where they're looking. They'll be interested in knowing what you're doing with the Cube, I bet."

"Sit down," Prime hissed. When he didn't, Prime grabbed Corrundrum's wrist and slammed him into his seat. Corrundrum could have reached for his gun, but he seemed shocked that Prime had resorted to violence.

"You've got it wrong, you fuck," Prime whispered. "I'm trapped here just like you."

Corrundrum shook his head.

"I had a device," Prime said. "It was broken. It got me here . . . there, I mean. I . . . gave it away. It's gone."

"You had a transfer? And you stopped in this shithole universe?"

"This is what I was used to."

Corrundrum leaned back, confused. Then he laughed. "You're not even a singleton, are you?"

"What?"

"You're some backwater kid who got a transfer and you don't even understand what you had." Corrundrum stood up, his face dazed. He began to laugh. "You have no idea, do you?"

"I didn't before," Prime said. "But I think I'm getting it."

Corrundrum said, "You're worthless to me. You're not even an original." He didn't wait for an answer. "So long, kid. Sorry for bothering you. Good luck. When they find you, don't tell 'em you know me."

"Hold on!" Prime cried, but Corrundrum was already out the door. Prime watched as he started his car. Corrundrum gave him a shrug and a roguish smile.

Prime wrote down the license plate number as the car disappeared into the cold night.

CHAPTER 33

Regardless of Charboric's dire demand for the source of the pinball idea, the lawyers decided that the head-to-head versions of the pinball machines were so different from anything that John had seen that the patent work could go forward. They filed several more patents on different pinball technologies in January.

Visgrath sent them dozens of tall Aryan men who spoke little English but came with glowing references from him or Charboric. They didn't bother hiring any of them, and instead brought on a squat, reserved shop foreman named Viv, who seemed to inspire a fear of death in her workers. She had her own recommendations for workers that resulted in a fifty-person staff on the floor by February, working at 100 percent capacity to fill the orders they had coming in. The Vegas deal had come through after all, as had a dozen smaller orders.

As classes picked up, John's time became sparse. At first he didn't notice, but when Grace missed class for the third straight day, he realized something was up.

"What gives?" he said. "You missed thermodynamics again."

Grace shrugged. They were in an office on the fore-man's deck, overlooking the factory floor below. Because of their school schedule, they ran the floor from the afternoon to midnight.

"Yeah, it's boring," she said.

"We have a test on Friday."

"Henry told me."

"You need to come to class."

"I don't!"

"Okay, okay," John said. "Sorry. I'll get you my notes if you want."

"Don't bother."

"Why?"

"I dropped the class," Grace said, looking away. "I dropped all my classes."

"You what? All?"

"Yeah, college dropout, that's me."

"You should have told me you were going to do that, so I could have—"

"—talked me out of it?"

"Yeah."

"Well, I didn't."

"Why?" John said.

She spread her arms. "This, of course."

"This? Pinball Wizards?"

"Yeah," she said. "It's working. It's really working. Our accounts receivable are huge. I mean millions of dollars. I could double the shop floor size based on the projections. It's that big."

"You didn't have to drop out."

"You can't run a million-dollar business part-time," Grace said.

"We could have hired someone."

"We already have Visgrath to deal with," Grace said. "No way am I dealing with a CEO who isn't one of us."

"Then Henry or I could—"

Grace shrugged. "It's better if I do it."

John marveled at how different Grace was. Her clothes were different. Her manners were different. He remembered suddenly her drunken admission three months ago.

"You've changed; you've become a businesswoman," John said.

"Yeah, I'm different. I feel all grown-up."

John was aware of her shapely body. Her skin was clean, and she had used perfume. That wasn't the Grace he had met in September.

"Grace—," John said.

Suddenly she turned away, and John felt awkward. She handed him a package. "I almost forgot. Kyle dropped this off. Just for closure, he said."

"Yeah." The lawsuit and push back from the city of Toledo had all just faded away as if they had never happened. John remembered how tense December had been, how desperate they were for a solution, and how Visgrath had been their savior with the infusion of cash. In hindsight, their desperation seemed so trivial.

John slit the envelope open with his thumb. Inside were a dozen legal-sized documents. When he looked up, Grace was at the door of the office.

"I have to— I have to go check in with Viv," she said. "See ya in a bit."

John nodded, then sighed. He pulled out the documents and, plopping down in an old leather chair, started paging through them.

The lawsuit from Paquelli was last. John almost tossed it aside; then he saw the name of the codefendant in the suit. He sat up, his mind cold. If it had been Smith or Jones, his eyes would have skimmed right over it. But how many Charborics were there in the world?

They'd been played.

At first John was stunned; then he felt just plain stupid. It was probably his own embarrassment at arguing so vehemently for the deal with EmVis that decided him against telling Henry and

Grace. He rationalized it. Grace would have confronted Visgrath. Henry would have turned inward into a dark mope. Better for all if he hid it away.

John stuffed the papers in a rusty filing cabinet in the old factory, and tried to forget about them.

But every time he saw Visgrath, every time Charboric sent an infuriating memo, every time there was a conference call on the latest sales projections, John felt the grip of their manipulation on his neck.

He stopped coming to meetings. He skipped one board meeting, then another, and when Grace pressed he told her to vote his shares as needed. John's roost became the old factory, where he tinkered with pinball machines of the traditional kind. When Visgrath asked, John complained of a large workload at school, finals.

The phone call from Janet Rayburn was a surprise. He'd sent them a couple letters, a Christmas card, and a huge basket of apples when his first check came in from the company. But otherwise, he'd stayed away. The year with them had been too gut-wrenching. They weren't his parents, and though they would have let him be a surrogate son, he wouldn't allow it. His parents were elsewhere.

"How's the farm? How's Bill?" John asked.

"Fine, fine, he's fine. Spends time in the barn, mending and fixing. Spring is around the corner, so everything needs to be right," Janet replied.

They chitchatted for a few more minutes, and then Janet said, "Someone was around to ask after you."

"Who?"

"Foreigner of some sort," Janet said.

John didn't ask what kind of foreigner, but he guessed the man had a Slavic or Germanic accent.

"Asked if we knew where you came from."

"What . . . what did you say?"

"Didn't say nothing," Janet said with a laugh. "Some people

should mind their own business. We never asked where you came from or what you were running from. We know good people when we see them. And this guy was no-good."

"Thanks for that," John said.

"Sure, but maybe you'd like to come down for Easter, bring that girl, Casey Nicholson. She's nice."

"We're not . . ."

"Oh, right. You kids and your quick relationships. Bill was the only man I dated. Did I tell you that?"

"No, I didn't know that."

"That Casey is a nice girl. You should call her up, see what she's doing tonight."

"I'm sure she's with her other boyfriend, Jack," John said, harsher than he'd wanted to.

"Oh, she's one of those girls," Janet said. "Better done with her then."

"Exactly."

"Well, come over for Easter dinner by yourself then," Janet said. "We'd love to have you."

"I'll think about it," John said. He hung up the phone. He had no doubt who had been snooping around, looking for dirt on him: Charboric or Visgrath. What did they hope to find? John had a moment's nausea, a pounding of agoraphobia that forced him to steady himself on the kitchen table with his hand.

If it got bad enough, if the tension from EmVis and Pinball Wizards, Inc., and Casey and Grace and Henry got to be too much, he could just leave. He didn't have to be there. He didn't have to be in Toledo or part of the board at PW. He could just leave. If he wanted to, he could leave the universe.

He paused. Yes, it was true. He could just go. This was the hundredth-some universe he'd passed through, some much more quickly than this one, but this one was ultimately transient just like the rest.

Could he leave Henry, Grace, and Casey? Why not? There were

millions of each through the universes. What made these instances any more important than any other? If he wanted to he could befriend a dozen Graces, he could seduce a dozen Caseys.

With that thought he felt relief from his panic. He could just ditch it all whenever he wanted.

Charboric was just trying to keep his investment safe. He was just being diligent. No more. John chalked it up to the man's paranoia, and his own.

Then came the lawsuit, the patent claim against their pinball machines from some company in Pennsylvania.

"This is bullshit!" Henry cried. They sat around the table of the conference room in Columbus. John and Henry had blown off classes to be there on a Wednesday. Henry had worked himself into a lather over the lawsuit on the drive down. Grace had fretted with a loose thread on her shirt, and now the string was ten centimeters long. She looked flushed and tired.

Charboric and Visgrath watched Henry's outburst with calm.

"This is exactly what I said would happen," Charboric said. "We weren't careful enough with the patents." He stared at John.

"Our machines are nothing like the machines John saw as a child!" Henry cried. "They're head-to-head, for Christ sake! That's nothing like the pinball machines he saw."

"The name is the same," Visgrath said.

"Is it a trademark? Has it been defended?" Henry said. "We couldn't find a sign of them anywhere. They didn't keep their trademark current, and they lost it."

Visgrath shrugged. "We must now exert energy to defend ourselves legally."

John had said little, and as Visgrath said the last word, the lawsuit leveled by Paquelli came to mind: the one secretly funded by EmVis. Was this not just more of the same?

"Who owns this company?" John asked.

"It's not important!" Charboric said.

"Sure it is. We can buy them out. We have the cash. You have the cash."

"They are too big," Charboric said.

"How big? What's their name?"

"It's . . ." Charboric glanced at Visgrath, who remained passive. "It's called Grauptham House."

"They can't be that big," Henry said, "if I haven't heard of them."

"They are too big," Charboric said. "They think they have us."

John finally spoke up. "If they are businesspeople, they'll take a deal, won't they? If they've sat on pinball for years and done very little with it, why would they pass up an opportunity to make some money? Aren't businesses supposed to maximize profits?"

"They won't deal," Charboric said.

"How do you know?"

"I know."

"Who's their lawyer? Who's their CEO? What other products do they market? How many employees do they have? It seems," John said, "that we are getting worked up for nothing."

"It is a disaster!" Charboric cried.

"Only if we stay in the business and lose," John said.

"What are you saying?" Charboric said.

"We can always walk away, can't we? We have free exit, do we not?" John said.

Visgrath smiled. "You would walk away from your creation?"

"There's always more creations," John said.

"Such as?"

John smiled. "That'll cost you," he said. "You know, the last time we had legal troubles, they seemed to just fade away."

"This is not the same," Charboric said.

"Why not?"

"That was a small-time bar owner," Visgrath said. "This is a real company."

"I'd like to know exactly what this company does," John said. "Do you have its prospectus, its filings? Anything?"

"It is privately owned," Visgrath said.

"They must have filed some paperwork with the state," Henry said. "We had to."

"I don't—," Charboric began.

Visgrath cut him off. "John and Henry make a good point," he said. "I will ask our legal team to provide a report. It is good to go down all avenues."

Henry sat back, smiling. "Yeah, exactly."

John nodded too, but he had no interest in letting EmVis do the digging on Grauptham House. Not after last time.

"I need help."

"What? To spend your money?" Kyle said with a smile.

"No, that I can do fine," John said. In fact, he had made a large purchase for his warehouse that day, a precision micrometer, light microscope, and X-ray machine. "This company. How do I learn about it?" He handed Kyle a sheet of paper with the name "Grauptham House" on it and the address from the affidavit they had filed.

"Pennsylvania, hmmm," Kyle said. "We'll have to send a letter to the state requesting information on its business license."

"Can't we just do a computer search?" John asked, before remembering that the Internet didn't exist in this universe, that the smallest computers were used by the CIA and NSA here and still fit only in barns.

Kyle laughed. "Not with any computer I have access to. Do you have some resources I don't know about?"

John almost said, Yes, but instead shook his head. Why had he stopped in this universe instead of one where they had decent computers?

"You'll need to write a letter," Kyle said. "Get the address of the secretary of state's office. Just send them the name. Do you know their ID?"

"No, this is all I know."

"It should be enough."

"Thanks, Kyle," John said.

"No problem. I love the game. I've been playing. Won the law school tournament."

"Really? That's great."

"The machines on campus are packed. You guys really did something special."

John wrote the letter as soon as he got home.

Six weeks later, he received a reply, an envelope from the secretary of state of Pennsylvania in Wilkes-Barre. He opened it, reading the list of vital statistics on the company of Grauptham House in Pittsburgh. The CEO didn't happen to be Visgrath and Charboric wasn't on the board of directors, but as John read the names, he began to suspect: Fritigern Wallia, Athaulf Chindasuith, Reccared Gesalex. No one he knew had names like that . . . except for the employees of EmVis. There wasn't a single normal name or a female name on the list of owners and principals, unless Chintila Ardo was a woman, but he found it unlikely.

He dialed the number on the sheet.

"Grauptham House, Incorporated. How may I direct your call?" answered a female voice.

"Can you send me information on the company, please?"

"I'm sorry. Grauptham House is a privately held company not interested in seeking investors at this time."

"I'd just like to know what you guys make."

"I'm sorry, but that information is confidential."

"Fine, thanks." He hung up the phone.

A company couldn't just be a black hole. How far was Pittsburgh from Toledo? Maybe five hours. It was time for a road trip.

For a moment he considered calling Henry and Grace, but then he would have to explain his suspicions. He'd have to excuse his push to take the capital from EmVis. He didn't want to do that yet. If he could find evidence that Grauptham House was a front for

EmVis, or vice versa, then he'd let his friends know and they could work against Visgrath's plan, whatever that was.

That Friday, John drove across Ohio to Pittsburgh, windows down, radio blaring. He pulled into the tree-lined drive mid-afternoon, coming to a stop at a gate.

"Can I help you?" asked a stone-faced, blond-haired, hulking man.

"Is this Grauptham House?" John asked.

"Yes, what is your business?"

"I'm doing a report for school. Can I get some literature on what you guys do?"

"I'm sorry, no. Perhaps you should do your report on the ketchup company."

"Please? It's due on Monday and I can't change the subject," John said.

The guard stared at him, then turned around in his guard shack, rummaged around for a moment, and handed John a dog-eared pamphlet.

"That's all I can do for you," he said. "Turn your car around."

John sighed, backed out of the gateway, and swung the car around. The entrance to the drive was across from a wooded, hilly area. There was a hunters' road there, and he pulled into it, giving himself a clear view of the entrance road.

The pamphlet was unhelpful. "Grauptham House: Company of the Future" was involved in high tech. Defense, electronics, mining, and deep-sea salvage were listed as the main areas of activity. Otherwise, the pamphlet was all marketing mumbo jumbo.

He waited three hours, and not a single car came in or out.

"Is there a back entrance?" he asked aloud.

The building was hidden behind a hill and trees. He'd caught a glimpse of it from the guard shack.

John started his car and tried to circumnavigate the parcel of land the building sat on. The terrain of Pittsburgh was against

him, however, and he found himself lost after the left turns that
should have brought him back to the entrance. Grauptham House
seemed hidden in a valley with just the single entrance, though he
couldn't be sure.

John stopped at a local bar at an intersection of two winding
roads. A trailer park crawled up the nearest hill, and an old strip
mall sat across the way. A half-dozen locals were drinking their afternoon away inside.

He ordered a beer, and when the bartender brought it he said,
"You know anyone who works at Grauptham House?"

"Grauptham House?" The man rubbed his chin. "Is that a furni-
ture store?"

"No, it's a company up on Glencoe."

"Glencoe? There's not much up that way," the bartender said.

"Glencoe?" someone else at the bar said. "There's that one place.
Charlie got run off when he went hunting up there." He turned and
looked for Charlie. "Said the place was surrounded by twelve-foot
barbed-wire fences and motion detectors."

"What good's a motion detector when there's deer running
around?" someone else asked.

"Motion detectors between the fences," the first one explained.

"Do you know anyone who works there?" John asked.

The bartender scratched his chin. "No, can't say that I do."

"It's the fifth-largest company in Pittsburgh," cried one of the
regulars at the bar. "You must know someone!"

"Do you?" the bartender shot back.

The regular shrugged. "They have a plant in McKeesport. My
brother has a friend who knew someone who worked in their plant.
Sure did."

"Right."

John listened as the stories rustled around the bar. It was soon
clear that nobody knew anyone personally who worked there but
that there were plants and factories scattered around Pittsburgh,
though no one could say what the factories made.

John got directions to McKeesport, paid for his beer, and drove the ten miles through the hills of Pittsburgh. He found the Grauptham House factory, this one fenced in and guarded too, but here cars filled a parking lot and people entered and exited the buildings. It was nearly five, so he drove to the nearest bar and again asked about people who worked for Grauptham House.

He was more successful. It seemed everyone in the bar worked in the Grauptham House factory. When he asked what they did, however, they turned their eyes toward their beers.

"Sorry, I didn't mean to intrude," John said.

The man next to him grunted.

The bartender spoke up. "I've never seen a group more close lipped about what they do," he said. "You'd think they're building bombs over there."

"Shut up, Howie," the man said.

Howie nodded at John. "They make underwater breathing things," he said. "It's no secret."

"Howie! You know we all signed contracts not to talk about it!"

"I didn't sign no contract, Tom," the bartender said.

"Well, who else would you get the information from?"

"Underwater breathing devices?" John said. "You mean scuba gear?"

"How'd you know that name?"

"Everyone has heard of scuba," John said.

"How could you?" Tom cried. "We only started producing them a couple years ago. Our only client is the military." He slapped his hand over his mouth. "Oh, shit!"

"I've heard of scuba before," John said. "It's no big deal."

"You're probably working for security," Tom said. He stood and moved off, giving John a dark look.

"You've heard of scuba, haven't you?" John asked the bartender.

"Just from these folks."

"Don't people go diving around here?"

"Snorkeling, you mean? Not in Pennsylvania!" he said with a laugh.

"No, I guess not," he said. "Do you know of any other Grauptham House factories?"

"Sure, there's one in Trafford and one in Plum."

"What do they make there?"

"Hell if I know."

John paid and left.

By midnight he had visited bars near four more Grauptham House factories. The one in McKeesport manufactured scuba gear. The one in Trafford made defibrillators. The one in Plum made Velcro. The one in Latrobe published music. It had a storefront and was the only Grauptham House location open to the public. John parked outside the store; a dozen people entered and exited the shop in the half hour he watched the Latrobe Music Shoppe.

He entered the store. A blond man stood at the register. Racks of tapes and LPs lined the walls, all of it classical music. A woman fingered through the selection of records. Beethoven's 9th played on the tiny speakers overhead. She hummed along.

"I love this part," she said. "This new symphony is just splendid."

"New?" John said. "You mean, new recording?"

"Oh, no," she said brightly. "This is Witt Chindasuinth's brand-new symphony."

"This is Beethoven's Ninth," John said.

The woman looked at him for a moment blankly; then she laughed. "Beethoven's Ninth! How funny. He only wrote six! What happened to the other two if this is the ninth?" She turned away to make her purchase, but the cashier was looking at him.

"What did you say?" the cashier asked in an accented voice.

"What?"

"You've heard this before?"

John shrugged his shoulders at the ceiling. "Uh, I thought I had."

"Maybe you did hear it," the cashier said. He stepped around the register toward John. "Somewhere else."

John shook his head. "No, my mistake." As he ran out the door, the bell chimed frantically. From his car, he watched the cashier pick up a phone and call someone.

John sat in the parking lot of an Eat 'n Park. It was nearly midnight. He was exhausted and frightened. It was clear that Grauptham House was doing the same thing John Prime had wanted to do, the same thing he had done inadvertently with the pinball machine. They had set up shop in a new universe and were using gadgets from other universes to make money.

They probably had hundreds of patents and inventions, and pinball happened to be one of them. But if they knew about pinball, then they knew that John, Grace, and Henry hadn't invented it here; they must suspect that John pilfered it from somewhere else. What was their game?

He broke out into a sweat. He'd brought himself to the attention of others: people who knew about other universes. But was that bad? Maybe he could ask for help in getting home. Only why did they lock everything away? Why were they so security conscious? Because they didn't want anyone to know, like the U.S. government.

But now Pinball Wizards was elbowing in on their racket. They were fighting back. Or were they nervous that someone else was mining this universe? Would they ask him to leave? Would they force him to leave? Would they just kill him?

John had a device. Why didn't he just move on?

"Damn it!" he said.

He'd done what he'd told himself not to do, get involved with the locals. He couldn't leave Grace and Henry to fend for themselves. He couldn't leave Casey, though he hadn't talked to her in months.

He couldn't leave. As tempting as it was, he couldn't leave his friends in a lurch. Not when there were nefarious forces against them. And what of his goal to understand the device? He'd have to start from scratch if he moved universes. He'd have to reestablish his identity. He'd have to start back in school. The money from the pinball company was nice; he'd never have been able to buy the scientific equipment he had without the cash flow from Pinball Wizards, Inc.

No, he had to figure out what was going on. He had to keep his friends safe. And if that meant giving up Pinball Wizards, so be it.

But how could he find out what Grauptham House was up to? How could he find out if they were travelers like him, without tipping his hand?

CHAPTER 34

"John, can I speak with you, please?"

John, solder gun in hand, was wiring a new flipper into a prototype game. He looked up, startled not just by the interruption but by Visgrath being at the factory on a Sunday. Visgrath and Charboric had visited once; the other board members, not at all.

"Sure, hold on," John said. He'd been spending most weekends in the lab, as they called it. It was the smaller bay behind the factory floor, where they put together the prototypes and demo units that might become new models. He'd slept in on Saturday after his long hours on the road Friday afternoon and Saturday morning to and from Pittsburgh. Now he was there late on Sunday finishing his work, trying to figure out what he was going to do. This surprise visit from Visgrath was unsettling. John stood, leaving the flipper hanging by its wires.

"What do you want to talk about?" John asked.

Visgrath smiled. John didn't remember ever seeing the man smile.

"So easy to pretend with an outsider, I forget how to speak frankly," he said.

"What do you mean?"

"We traced your license plate number," Visgrath said, meeting John's stare directly.

John felt perspiration break across his back. They had him.

"What do you mean?"

"Please. Give us some credit. Your trip to Pittsburgh," Visgrath said. "You know what we're doing. You know why we're interested in you."

John realized he was face-to-face with Visgrath's mass of assumptions; neither of them was what the other thought he was. And John was certain his life hung on how he answered. Denial wouldn't work.

"Beethoven's Ninth," John said with a smile. "Nice touch."

Visgrath laughed, and John was frightened again at the sight of his bleached white teeth. "Some things make easy money. Beethoven is one of them. It does require a bit of infrastructure to pull off. We need an orchestra. We need certain technologies. Pinball," he said. "We never would have done that. But it's ingenious."

John realized then that Grauptham House and EmVis were in league, if not the same company. "You, I mean Grauptham House, holds a pinball patent."

"Not really," Visgrath said.

"Oh, I see. More pressure, just like the city of Toledo thing and the Ray Paquelli suit," John said. "You use the same tactics over and over again."

Visgrath nodded. "Apparently we are a race of repetitive minds," he said with a laugh. "You caught us. I will have Charboric killed if you like, for his lack of original thinking."

John shook his head. "That won't be necessary."

"Of course."

Visgrath looked at him, and John returned the stare. After a moment Visgrath spoke again. "I assume some commonalities between us, yes?"

"The exploitation of stolen technology?" John asked.

"Yes, that, of course. But hardly exploitation," Visgrath said. "It's more regarding how . . . we came to be here."

John nodded. "Yes, how we came to be here." John's mind

churned. They were exploiting technology. They were hiding. But they were on the lookout for similarly exploited technology. They'd discovered his pinball machines. How was their situation like his own? Then he realized.

"You're stranded," John said.

Visgrath laughed. "Would we stay in this hellhole otherwise?"

John realized his play. "You said it. We gotta make the best of what we've got."

"Exactly. You understand us then."

"How long have you been here?" John asked.

"Decades. I was stranded with an initial group of twelve. Myself, Charboric, and ten you have not met. It was rough, of course. These barbaric universes are so far behind the main line. And the philosophies here aren't like we expect. You understand, to each his own, which is why we didn't object to Grace being named president." Visgrath paused. "I'm surprised you allowed it, however."

"Why do the work when someone else can?" John said.

"True, but jump-starting in a new universe can be hazardous. You are brave to allow her to lead the endeavor. We thought she was the stranded, not you at first. It is just you, is it not?"

"They don't know anything," John said quickly. "Why would I tell them?"

"Yes, why would you?"

"So, scuba, defibrillators, music. Grauptham House is a busy little company," John said. "You all must be rolling in the dough."

"We have enough to make ourselves comfortable but not quite enough to act with impunity," Visgrath said.

"Is that your goal? To have enough to do whatever you want?"

"Our goal is to get back to our home universe," Visgrath said, "and to punish those who put us here."

"Who put you here?"

Visgrath grinned. "Bad luck, fate, enemies within and without." He waved his hand. "Does it matter?"

"No."

"Who put you here?"

"Someone I trusted," John said.

"Indeed." Visgrath nodded. "It is always the case. So then, we understand each other. We have common cause, more common than before, and more secret. You understand our secrecy."

"Of course."

"Our goal is money and comfort, while we perhaps wait to be rescued. If such happens, we would take you with us. And if those who stranded you or those who await your return were to come here for you . . ."

"Yes, of course. That seems fair."

"Excellent." Visgrath paused. "We have used all the ideas we could think of. We have run short on them after fifty years. Your pinball was something we knew of, but not enough to exploit. You are from another world and more current on certain things. If you have ideas that we could exploit, EmVis would be able to do so effectively, and for a more even distribution of wealth." Fifty years? John thought. How old was Visgrath? He didn't look older than thirty-five or forty.

"I wasn't prepared for being marooned," John said. "I really don't have a list of ideas." He thought for a moment of John Prime's Cube.

"Yes, of course," Visgrath said, standing. "Perhaps we can discuss it again. There may be ideas that you aren't remembering clearly."

"Perhaps."

Visgrath extended his hand. They shook. "I'm glad we have shared our positions. Charboric said we should have eliminated you, but I felt that we can gain from partnership."

"Remind me not to send Charboric a Christmas card."

Visgrath laughed. "Why would you?" he said. "I knew that you'd be more valuable to us alive. This pinball is just one example. There's probably more you don't even realize you know that can be exploited."

"I don't know about that. . . ."

"It really is for the best," Visgrath said. "And I won't take no for an answer."

"Maybe we should keep this relationship more formal," John said.

Visgrath paused. "I don't want it anything but," he said. "But we are two dogs in the same kennel, and it is best if we work together. If not, you can deal with Charboric."

John felt himself recoil. "Is that a . . . is that a threat?"

"Of course it is, John!" Visgrath said. "It is us travelers against them, the mundanes. You are a traveler; therefore you are with us. Do you understand?"

"I do now," John said. "I do now."

"Good. I will make an appointment for you to visit the inner compound," Visgrath said. "You will be interested. Startled perhaps, even envious of what we have wrought from nothing."

"I will, I'm sure."

Visgrath left then, and John watched the door for long minutes until he heard the outer door swing shut. His heart was racing. His face felt flushed. What had he gotten himself into? He had just wanted to study physics. He had just wanted to go home! Now, Grace and Henry were caught up in this fiasco.

He wanted to drive home, grab the device, and leave. Leave this fucking universe and find a new one. Damn it! He should have been careful! He'd broken his own rule, getting involved.

He could just leave. No way could Visgrath follow him. They were trapped. They had no transfer device.

But then Grace and Henry would be at Visgrath's mercy. Even Casey and Bill and Janet were at risk if John fled. He wouldn't put it past Visgrath and Charboric to take their anger out on his closest.

"Damn it!" he cried. He picked up the phone. He put it down. He picked up again and dialed Grace.

"Grace," he said when she picked up. "I need you here right now. The factory. It's important." He hung up and called Henry.

The truth didn't faze either of them. They took the facts of John's testimony in stride. That was the best part of his admission.

"You *betrayed* us!" Grace cried.

"I didn't—"

"You fucking lied to us!"

"Not on—"

"You aren't even who you say you are!"

"I'm still me—"

"Just shut up and stop defending yourself!"

"Grace!"

"What?"

"I didn't mean for this to happen!"

"Of course you couldn't. You're too self-involved to see anything around you!" Grace cried.

Henry thankfully said nothing.

Grace started sobbing. "Why did you even get us into this mess?"

"I'm sorry, Grace." John held open his arms, but she glared at him and sagged instead onto Henry's shoulder. He looked uncomfortable with it.

"Grace. I need—"

"You're fired."

"You can't fire me!"

"I can; I'm the president."

"But I own fifteen percent of the company."

"That doesn't mean you get a job here!" Grace cried. "Get out!"

John stood up. "I understand if you hate me. And I understand if you want me out of here. But we have a real, serious problem."

He walked out the door of the office. Behind him, he heard Grace sobbing. He heard Henry say something, but it was too soft to hear. John walked across the silent factory floor. How had he ended up here? He'd tried to make the best decision in every case. But here he was, losing his friends, losing his company. He had already lost Casey. And even his life was in jeopardy. All because . . .

All because he had hidden the truth and lied to the ones he loved.

He cursed, slamming open the door. The parking lot was empty except for their three cars. He sat heavily in his front seat. What now? He'd lost the friendship of everyone who could help him. He'd placed all his friends in jeopardy.

He leaned his head against the steering wheel. His mouth was dry, his face hot.

"Damn it."

Someone tapped on his passenger side window.

He looked up to see Grace. She pulled open the door and sat beside him.

"So," she said, then didn't say anything more.

"So," John said.

"Were you going to leave us?" she said.

"I could have. I thought about it," John said. "But I couldn't."

"I read a lot of science fiction," she said matter-of-factly, "so this is not as much of a shock as it should be."

"The tough part is how I used you guys," John said. "I never meant that to happen. It just snowballed."

"Sure, I understand. If I didn't know you were the biggest Boy Scout ever, I wouldn't be out here now," she said. "So, thousands of universes, you end up here. The bad guys end up here. They find you. They don't know you have a device. We're in the thick of it. Is that the skinny?"

"That about sums it up."

"And now you need some help," she said. "From your friends."

"My only friends."

"That's true enough," Grace said. "John, I'm not giving up the company. I'm not giving up Henry. I'm not letting Visgrath or Charboric take it all away. And that means . . ."

"Yeah?"

"We're going to help you."

John let out a breath.

"What do we do? Do you have an idea? I've been struggling for so long with this alone. . . ."

"Show us the device. I want to see it."

"Sure," John said. "Does that mean I get my job back?"

"Don't push it."

"That's it?" Henry asked.

"Yeah."

Henry stared at the device, ran a finger over the metal edge. "It looks like a piece of equipment from *Space Lords*."

"It's a Virbidian Shift Modulator," Grace said, with a squeal.

"It's not," John said. "It's a powerful device that rips holes in the walls of the universe."

"It looks like a toy," Henry said.

Grace took it in her hand. "Feels like aluminum. Is it?"

"I don't know."

"You haven't run a spectrograph on it?"

"No. I did a tomogram," John said.

"What's that look like?" Henry asked.

John showed him the diagrams. "Cool. What are these things in here?"

"I haven't a clue," John said, laughing. He felt joyful to be sharing it with his friends after hiding it for so long.

"Is this a seam in the cylinder?" Grace asked. She ran her finger along the edge of the device.

"You have sharp eyes," John said. "It is." He handed her a magnifying glass.

"I felt it."

She peered at the edge. "There's marks here."

"I know."

"Someone's opened this," she said.

"Probably, to build it, of course," John said.

"Not necessarily. You say the device doesn't work," Grace said. "We can't test that?"

"You'll have to trust me," John replied.

"But a device like this would have fail-safes," she said. "It shouldn't break. Unless . . ."

"What?"

"Isn't it obvious?"

"Uh."

"Sabotage."

"What?"

"Sure! Suppose you're some guy in a high-tech, world-hopping society. You have a rival for your affections. What do you do? Murder? No way. Not in a high-tech, panopticon world. No, you sabotage the unalterable. You rig the unriggable. You make his trip across the universes one-way."

"You think," John said, "that this device was deliberately broken, for some reason."

Grace shrugged. "We know the devices are rare. We know people are punished by banishment to backwater worlds. We know the technology is controlled. We know the technology is advanced. There have to be fail-safes. There have to be redundant systems. No advanced society would risk all they have. Isolation would be worse than death. Someone deliberately broke this thing."

"I think you're extrapolating too far," John said.

"Why else is it broken?"

"Parts wear out."

Grace harrumphed. "You're going to trust your life to a device that wears out?"

"Cars wear out."

"Make a car with an order of magnitude more technology. Two orders of magnitude," she said. "Whoever made this is not burning fossil fuels to get around!"

"But we can't say this was sabotaged!" John said.

"Then let's do what we have to do," Grace said.

"What's that?"

"Let's open it up."

John's stomach dropped. He said, "No!" before he could think of anything else.

Grace stared at him, and he looked away.

"I thought you were staying," she said softly.

"I am, but . . ."

"But what?"

If they took it apart and it broke, he'd be stranded forever.

"I know what you're thinking," Grace said. "But how bad could that be, living here with us for the rest of your life?"

"What about Visgrath and company?" John said.

"Those ass clowns?" Grace laughed. "We'll fix them!"

"But . . . ," John said. He sighed. It wasn't like some other Casey would love him when this one didn't. It was clear they weren't meant to be. "Okay. Let's open it up. But carefully."

Grace smirked at him. "Just like physics lab. Careful as can be."

"And we can't let Visgrath know."

"A tangled web we weave," Henry said.

"You're the one, John," Grace said, "who has to be careful. He thinks you're something that you are not, and will act according to his assumptions."

"He thinks I'm stranded just like they are," John said.

"He's made assumptions you can't betray," Grace said, "or we're doomed."

"I don't know how long I can keep it up," John said.

"Avoid him," Henry said. "At all costs."

After buying supplies and equipment, they met the next Saturday. That should have been a factory day, but the three put Viv the foreman in charge and met at John's old warehouse.

"So, tell us what you know," Grace said, "from the beginning."

John brought out the spectrum that he'd collected earlier in the year. He showed them the spectrum of the radiation being emitted by the device, and explained its significance.

"Cool! Antimatter," Grace said.

He showed them his drawings of the outside of the device. They each looked at the seam with the light microscope. Henry examined the device millimeter by millimeter.

John explained the tomograph and how it depicted two ovoid shapes within the device.

Henry shook his head. "That's ingenious, John. I'd never have thought to use tomography."

"I wouldn't have either if I hadn't talked with the radiation engineers in the lab."

"How do you think the thing comes apart?" Grace asked. "Do you think it pulls apart at the seam?"

John shrugged. "I assume the two halves come apart there."

"That's a tight fit," Henry said, squinting at the line.

"Yeah. Whoever built this thing were machining gurus," Grace said.

John could tell both of them were excited about opening the device. But he felt a twinge of trepidation. He spoke on what he had been thinking about for the last week: "It's possible that we may destroy the device in the course of opening it up. I can deal with that, though this is not my home universe. I will regret not ever seeing my parents again. I will regret not getting back to John Prime. But I accept the consequences of what we are about to do."

Grace smiled. "Don't worry, John. We build and take apart delicate machinery for a living."

"This is not a pinball machine!" John said.

"Sure it is," Grace said. "You're the ball and the multiverse is the play field."

"You're a bumper," Henry said to Grace. He bounced his hip off hers and said, "Boing!"

"Funny."

One of John's purchases was a set of vises. They took the device and placed it in a vise that gripped the base of the device. The vise had rubber grips that squeezed the thing evenly. John then lowered a similar vise from above. This vise was attached to a lever and pressure gauge so that they could measure the exact force they were applying to the device.

"We'll start with twenty newtons of force," John said.

"This *is* just like physics lab," Grace giggled.

"Applying twenty newtons of force."

Henry watched the seam on the device. They had precision calipers on both sides to measure its width.

"Nothing."

"Applying forty newtons."

"Nothing."

John worked slowly to 200 newtons, with no change in the width of the seam.

"Maybe we need to relieve the pressure inside before it comes open," Grace said.

"But how?"

"Cracking it open is probably not an option," Henry said.

"Not yet," John said.

"Lubricant?" Henry suggested.

They sprayed a liquid lubricant along the edge. "Not too much."

Then John tried 200 newtons of force again. Then 240. "I can't do any more than that evenly," he said.

"Then let's use pulleys," Henry said. "You have a four-pulley assembly." With four pulleys they could quadruple John's force.

They hung the pulley assembly from the crane.

"Three hundred newtons. Three fifty. Four hundred."

"Stop!" Henry cried. He slid the caliper against the line. "I've got half a millimeter movement here."

"Me too," Grace said from the other side.

"Now that it's started, you may not need as much force," Grace said.

John tried 80 newtons, then 120. With a soft pop the front of the device came off.

"Hold it." The two halves hung separated by a small crack.

"Flashlight, please," John said.

He shined the light at the crack but could see nothing.

Henry said, "There's hinges on this side."

There were, small hinges where the two halves came together.

They disconnected the upper vise and moved the pulleys out of the way. Gingerly John lifted the upper half away, and it opened like a compact mirror, revealing the inside of the device.

Inside were what looked like two marshmallows covered in mold.

"It was meant to open like that," Henry said. "If it has a hinge."

John looked into the inside of the device and examined the marshmallow things closely. "Take a picture from every angle, of everything. Use two rolls. I want redundancy." If he screwed it up, he wanted to know how.

The fungus attached to the two shapes was actually tiny threads. As he looked closer, he saw that the marshmallows themselves were made of tightly bound layers of the stuff.

"That doesn't look like anything made by a human," Grace said. "It looks alien."

John had seen the diversity of the human universes and he was willing to bet that humans, however bizarre they might be, had built this. It just didn't look like anything Grace knew of in her universe.

Henry loaded a new roll of film and repeated all the same shots.

Dozens of threads ran between the two marshmallows, connecting them. Threads also ran from the marshmallows to the hinges and then to the back sides of the controls on the device's lid. Threads ran to all of the buttons, dials, and switches. In fact, below each of the buttons were smaller fuzzy marshmallows.

"The threads comprise the control system," Grace said. "They must be the electronics of the thing."

Of the two fuzzy marshmallows, one was near the center of the device and the other was to the upper right. That one was the source of the gamma radiation. John noted that there was a white spine, perhaps a half centimeter in diameter, jutting into it. The center mallow had no such spine.

"That's the power source, I assume," John said. "Maybe that spine houses the antimatter."

"How can you house antimatter?" Henry asked.

"Magnetic field, I assume."

Grace pointed the flashlight at the edge of the bottom half. "Look there." John peered closely and saw a small strand of the fiber lying unconnected. "Do you think it fell off? Do you think that's why the device is broken? Or perhaps you've come around to my hypothesis of sabotage!"

"I don't know. Do you have . . . something?" He made gripping signs with his hands.

Grace handed him long, thin tweezers. Carefully, John slid the thing through the web of threads and caught the stray thread. He pulled it out and put it in a plastic bag.

"Let's see what this is made of," he said.

He placed it under the light microscope, and they took turns looking at it.

"Fiber?" Henry asked.

"I have a laser," Grace cried. "For presentations." She held it carefully to the end of the small thread. John couldn't see coherent light coming from the other end.

"No, I don't think so."

"Maybe it will run current," Henry said.

They attached a voltmeter to the ends of the thread. It showed a few ohms of resistance. "Maybe they're like wires," Grace said. "That whole mass is a large electrical circuit."

"That doesn't get us anywhere," John said, sighing. He wasn't sure what he'd expected inside the device, but the mass of threads wasn't it.

"Why not?" Grace cried. "We just have to figure out what these balls do."

"And fix where it's broken," Henry said.

"How?"

"I dunno," Grace said. She peered closely at the masses. "If we could map it out . . ."

Henry clicked a few more pictures. "There's no way to figure out what's connected to what."

Grace shook her head. "There's always a way." She pointed to the single thread that they had retrieved from the device. "We'll start with this."

There wasn't anything else for them to do with the device, so John closed it back up.

"I'll send the thread to a lab and get an analysis done," Grace said.

Charboric called three times that week asking for a meeting. John dodged the call all three times, having the secretary say he was in class, though he wasn't. Grace called him on Saturday just as he was getting ready to head into work.

"Charboric is here," she said. "Head to the old factory instead. I have news."

John sped to the old factory. He couldn't continue avoiding Charboric. The man would grow suspicious, if he wasn't already. The man was paranoia incarnate.

Grace was already at the old factory. She handed John a stack of paper. "Lab report," she said. "This stuff is cool."

"Did the lab technicians have any questions?" John asked. "Were they suspicious?"

Grace shrugged. "Who cares? This stuff, its walls are a dielectric material. Its inside is glass."

"What does that mean?" John asked. In his universe, he knew fiber-optic wiring was common. Here most electronics used copper.

"Who knows?" Grace cried. "But that's not the cool part. I mean, it's cool, but it's not the coolest part. Hit the lights." John turned off the overhead fluorescent bulbs while Grace pulled the shades down to the room. She clipped a wire to the end of the thread. The other end of her wire was attached to a nine-volt battery.

The thread glowed a ghostly blue.

"Cool, but so what?"

Henry slammed through the door. "What'd I miss?" he said, puffing.

"Lab report, glowing thread," Grace said. "But not the climax."

"Go!" Henry said.

"We can map out the marshmallows with this," Grace said.

"Oh," John said. "I get it. We can apply a voltage thread by thread to the device and figure out the diagram of its workings."

"Yes!" Grace cried. "Then we just have to engineer material to match the thread's characteristics and—voila!—we've reverse engineered the device."

"Easier said than done," John said.

"Most things are," Grace said. "Let's get started."

It was a slow, painstaking process. They marked up an enlarged photo of the masses, and worked through each mass, tracing each thread's faint glow, applying a voltage and measuring the resistance. They found that threads could be arranged in parallel or series, much like typical electronic circuits that Grace understood. They could also be arranged in elaborate sequences that reminded John of human nerve cells connected together in three-dimensional lattices.

They cataloged a thousand threads that weekend, and John estimated that the device held a hundred thousand such threads. But they got faster as they went along. John was worried that they wouldn't be able to reach the center threads, but Henry and Grace showed him that she could move the threads out of the way with tweezers. The masses were not glued or otherwise bonded together.

"This is going to take a long time," Grace said, wiping her forehead.

"I know, but it seems the best way," John said.

"Agreed."

"We can't make this go any faster," Henry said. "Only one pair of hands can reach into the device at a time." He'd been drawing the diagram of the thing as they went, labeling it, snapping photographs.

John said, "But sooner or later, we have to turn that diagram into physical components."

"I don't know where to begin," Henry said. "It's one thing to draw it."

"We can make some assumptions, maybe," John said. "We can assume that the threads are homogenous. We can assume that they use current and that they have a capacitance and a resistance."

"Unless they also have semi-conductor characteristics," Henry said.

"Let's find out!" Grace cried. She spent an hour on the phone with a company out of Canada that was open on Sundays, ordering oscilloscopes, transistors, diodes, semi-conductor materials with various dopings. John looked up when she said, "Just charge it to my corporate card."

"How much is that costing?"

"Does it matter? Wealth has no value now that we know a million universes exist," she said.

Henry grunted. "How many *Mona Lisa*s exist?" he said. "How many diamond mines in South Africa that are known elsewhere and not here? How many worlds in which pinball doesn't exist?"

"There's no value in material goods," Grace said, "if material is infinite. The only good is personal happiness."

"That's a rather odd philosophy for a CEO of a corporation to take," John said.

"You've changed everything, John," she said. "Again."

They finished up for the weekend, without John getting anywhere near the pinball factory. Suddenly it seemed irrelevant. The longer he could avoid Charboric and Visgrath, the better.

Unfortunately, when John got home there was a dark SUV in the street in front of his apartment and Charboric was leaning on the rail of his apartment steps smoking a cheroot.

"Good evening, John. Let's talk."

CHAPTER 35

"Charboric."

"If I didn't know how stupid it was, I'd think you were dodging me," he said. He stamped the cheroot out on the cast cement stairs. There were at least half a dozen of the stubs littering the ground.

"It would be stupid, wouldn't it," John said. "But as you know, I have engineering school and a job and a life as well." He opened the door to his apartment, considered for a moment not inviting the man in, then thought better of it. John was keenly aware of the device in his backpack. He let Charboric in in front of him.

"Why do you even bother with the backward physics of this world?" Charboric asked. "It's not even worth knowing."

John shrugged off his backpack. He walked it into the bedroom and laid it carefully on the far side of the bed.

"How long have you been here, Charboric? Fifty years?" Charboric nodded. "How long do you plan to live?" John asked. "I don't rate my chances high of ever leaving."

Charboric eyed John, then nodded again. "You understand something that Visgrath sometimes forgets." Charboric's expression softened, and for a moment John almost felt sorry for him.

"Engineering is a philosophy of science," John said. "Even if the science changes, the process remains the same."

"Indeed," Charboric said. "But we sometimes lack the patience for study."

"Knowledge is power," John said.

"Power is power," Charboric replied.

John shrugged.

After a minute, Charboric added, "Visgrath has explained our situation, has he not?"

"He has."

"We've been trapped here for a long time awaiting rescue—we are not going to debate the benefit of that strategy. In that meantime we have made ourselves as comfortable as possible by exploiting what we know from other . . . locations."

"Scuba," John said.

"Local law limits the length of time we can exploit our ideas."

"Patents."

"The time frame for patents in this universe is twelve and a half years."

"But you can still market a product after the patent time," John said.

"The most profit occurs in the time of monopoly," Charboric said. "Afterwards we sell the patent and adjunct company. We have little patience for competitive markets."

"So after decades you're running out of ideas," John said.

"We've accreted a rather extensive entourage beyond the original dozen," Charboric said.

"Thus your interest in pinball."

"We knew it was an extra-universal technology. We of course know how to exploit technology here. The decision to invest was obvious."

"But you don't do competitive markets," John said.

"It was a strategic decision," Charboric said with a smile and nod toward John. "You've been mainline much more recently than we have. An alliance would allow us to exploit everything else that you might know."

"But I'm not that old," John said. "I don't know that much."

"You'd be surprised. You've been immersed in a highly techno-logical world for your lifetime. There are hundreds of objects—inane in that universe—that are valuable here."

John struggled to come up with some argument. "Yes, but every-thing was so different there."

Charboric shrugged. He reached into his jacket pocket and pulled out a small spiral-bound pad of paper and a pencil. "Carry this with you. Write down anything you think of. Ideas will come to you when you're driving or in the shower or taking a shit. Keep this with you. Write down what you remember."

"Uh, okay," John said. He took the pencil and pad. The pencil had teeth marks near the eraser.

Charboric stood up. "We'll talk again in a week. Don't dodge my calls. This is important. I'll expect you to have ten ideas on that list. Ten good ideas."

"Sure."

Charboric paused at the door. "I don't need to remind you how important secrecy is. Your business partners should know nothing of this."

"Of course."

John listened as the car door slammed shut on Charboric's SUV. He looked down at the pad of paper in his hand.

"What the hell am I going to do now?"

He opened the pad and wrote: "Rubert's Cube" at the top of the first page.

"What a dumb idea."

He scratched it out.

Henry and John took turns going to class the next week. The one not in class spent hours hunched over the opened device in the old factory, tracing threads with the voltmeter. Slowly the neural mapping within the marshmallows took form. Grace drew the connections as they went along and John or Henry verified them so that there were no mistakes. If they made one, there was no way to correct it unless they started from scratch.

"I don't understand these at all," John said, staring at the diagram.

"We need an electrical engineer," Grace said.

"Electrical engineering is not till junior year," John said. "We can't wait that long."

"I'll buy the textbooks," she said with a laugh. "They'll be here next week."

They finished another thread. While Grace drew it on their huge sheet of drafting paper, she said, "Casey keeps asking about you."

"What?"

"Casey, remember her? Tall, blond, broke your heart."

"I remember."

"She says you two broke up over a big secret," Grace said. "You wouldn't share."

"Yeah."

"Is it this same secret?"

John sighed. "I guess so."

"Well, the cat's out of the bag on that one," Grace said.

"What do you mean?"

"You can tell her the truth, can't you?"

"Too many people know already!" John said. "It could put you in danger."

"What will happen to her if we build a device and leave?"

"Nothing." John found the next thread within the device. Beside him the Geiger counter clicked a single beat. They kept it nearby in case, but there'd been nothing but background radiation. "Besides, she's probably with Jack." He remembered the sight of her and Jack on Thanksgiving Day, kissing and groping in front of her house.

"She hasn't seen Jack in months! Not since . . . Thanksgiving. She dumped him on the day before Thanksgiving."

"She did?"

"Yep. Jack was a total asshole."

"I agree with that."

"So go see her," Grace said.

"She's probably dating someone else," John said.

"She's not."

"How do you know? You moved out of the dorm." Grace had moved into an apartment near the factory when she stopped going to class.

"I still keep in touch," Grace said defensively. "I still go back for lunch at the cafeteria. It's really good mac and cheese."

John laughed.

"Call her; see her," Grace said. "Talk to her. What can it hurt?"

"Everything."

John said no more, but his mind churned over their last argument, his last view of Casey. Not now, he told himself. It was too complicated, too wrong.

But when he left Henry and Grace to go to Dynamics, he drove past Casey's dorm and parked in the nearest commuter lot. Instead of stopping and calling her from the lobby, he walked on to class.

On the way back, after a lecture on rigid body torque, John paused again in front of her dorm. It was nearly five in the afternoon. She was likely to be studying or getting dinner. If he had really wanted to talk with her, he should have stopped by before class. Now it was too late.

"I'm an idiot," he whispered to himself, and headed toward his car.

"John?"

He turned. Casey was standing three meters behind him on the sidewalk with two other female students John didn't know. They peered at him curiously.

"Hi, Casey."

"What are . . . ? How are you doing?"

He shrugged. "Busy."

"I hear. Grace keeps me up-to-date, and I read all the newspaper articles."

He was full of words and not sure where to start. The two friends, eyeing him as if he were a toad, didn't help.

"Listen. . . ."

"Yeah."

"You want to go to dinner?"

"Casey," one of the women said. "Don't you have—"

"It's okay, Sheryl," she said. To John, she said, "Let's go."

It was easier than he expected to tell her the truth. And far easier to wake up next to her the next morning in his apartment.

"I'm not saying I believe it," she said, propped up on one elbow.

"Then why are you here?" John said.

"Because you clearly believe it and you think keeping it from me is what drove me away."

"Didn't it?"

"Yes, but I need to decide if the secret of cross-universe travel is any different from the secret of harboring a paranoid delusion of cross-universe travel," she said.

John smirked. "Henry and Grace believe me."

"Yes, smart people can behave irrationally. Insane people can be incredibly smart."

"We have a device. We've taken it apart."

"Does it work?" she asked.

"Yes!"

"Have Grace and Henry seen it work?"

"Uh, no. I've seen it work."

"So your experience is your only evidence."

"Charboric and Visgrath know."

"Who witnessed your conversations with those two?"

"Uh, no one."

"So you see my dilemma?"

"Not really."

"Can I still love you if you're a psychopath?"

"Is paranoia really a psychosis? It's more of a neurosis. And everyone has neuroses."

"No, I think dedicating your life to your delusion is a psychosis."

"It's brought prosperity."

"So pinball is part of the psychosis. I assumed it was just a good idea you had that you had to justify due to an inferiority complex."

"I do not have an inferiority complex. I'm very good at most things I do."

Casey laughed. "You're a very attractive psychopath."

"See? I have no reason to feel inferior. I'm not short like Napoléon. I'm going to college. I own an explosively growing company. I have an above-average . . . you know."

"How do you know?" Casey said. "About that last one."

"I've read scientific articles. In scientific magazines."

"Did they come with color pictures and pullout centerfolds?"

"No. Black-and-white bar charts. Many, many bar charts."

Casey laughed again and straddled him.

"I appreciate your scientific process," she said. She slid him inside her. "I've decided to give you the benefit of the doubt."

"You believe I'm not—huh!—lying?"

"No, I don't believe it matters as long as you're honest with me."

"I won't ever lie to you again."

"That's what I wanted to hear."

They stopped talking after that.

Huge crates of materials—everything that Grace had ordered—arrived at the old warehouse the next morning.

"What are we going to do with this stuff?" John asked.

"Henry is going to model our diagram."

"I am?" Henry asked.

"Sure."

"I don't know anything about electronics," he said.

"You didn't know anything about pinball before either," Grace replied.

"I can't argue with that."

They were at the point where they could do a couple hundred threads in an hour. The slowly evolving circuit almost made sense, but then John'd turn his head and it would all dissolve away. It was alien and yet familiar. Like thermodynamics.

John looked up suddenly, his bladder near to bursting. The sun had set.

"Where's Henry?"

"He went to class," Grace said.

"It was my turn."

"You were in the zone, John."

John stretched, then ran to the bathroom.

"I think we're halfway," Grace called.

"Mapping it," John called back. "We still have to build it."

"Look at what Henry did."

John came out of the restroom and stared at the wired-up machine on the workbench. An oscilloscope blipped. Wires extended from component to component. A lab book lay open on the table. John flipped through it; the first fifty pages were covered in tables and equations.

"He did this today?"

"We were *all* in the zone."

"You didn't go into the office today. We barely made it into school. Are we wasting our time here?"

"Listen," Grace said. "We—not just you—have gotten ourselves into trouble. The source of that trouble is this device. We need to understand it. We need to reverse engineer it. Then we have all the possibilities in the universe. And then some."

"I hope you're right."

"I'm always right," she said. "I'll go into the factory tonight. In fact, I've got to run."

Grace gave him a quick hug. She said slyly, "So, you saw Casey yesterday . . . and this morning."

"How do you know these things?"

"If you don't come home to the dorm, the *girls* know!"

"But you don't even live there anymore!"

"Everyone knows where everyone sleeps every night," Grace said. "It's a rule of the women's dorm. Or else there'd be nothing to talk about at breakfast. See you tomorrow."

John pulled a sandwich and a soda from the fridge, then sat down with Henry's notebook. He had to keep referring to the textbooks. Luckily, physics lab had exposed him to Henry's cryptic handwriting. Henry had started with the thread, the lab report on it, and the test bench. With as much data on the thread's characteristics as possible he had tried to reproduce its physical parameters. The mess on the lab bench was his first attempt.

They'd estimated there were one hundred thousand strands in the device. Henry's prototype would require about ten million dollars in parts.

"It would bankrupt us," John whispered. Unless there was a simpler way to model the threads with this universe's components. Could they design a circuit that modeled the thread and then custom-order one hundred thousand of them?

He started rearranging Henry's circuits.

John looked up when the door to the warehouse opened. He expected to see Grace or Henry. Instead it was Casey.

"Oh, crap!" he said. "Did we have a date?"

"Not for another forty-five minutes, but you didn't answer your phone, and Grace said you'd be here," she said.

"So I didn't miss it."

"No, but I'm not saying you wouldn't have," Casey said. "I just didn't want to give you the chance to blow our relationship again so soon after we've decided to give it another shot."

"So you're here as a precaution for our relationship," John said.

"Yep, and I brought Chinese."

John looked at the cold sandwich he had half-eaten and swiped it into the trash can. "Excellent."

"So this is the device, huh?" Casey peered into the innards, squinting. "Looks like a toy."

"It's an intensely powerful device, capable of ripping holes in the universe," John said.

"Or you just think it is."

"Entirely possible, from your point of view, but wrong."

"You would say that."

John sighed. "If you are going to assume that there's no difference between me believing what it can do and it actually being able to do it, can we drop the argument until definitive proof is available?"

"Sure," Casey said. "You got any plates around here? Napkins are probably out of the question." She glanced around. "Good thing they included plastic sporks."

"It's an old warehouse. There's paper towels in the bathroom. I'll clear off a spot on the table."

Casey came back with a handful of towels. "So this is where you guys moved to after you relocated from campus."

"Just for a few weeks. Then we got better facilities."

"Grace is giving me a tour tomorrow." Casey looked into one of the pinball frames that stood in the corner.

"We have sporks there," John said. "Don't worry."

"And napkins?"

"We have waiters ready to wipe your lips as needed."

"Oh, posh."

"Mmm, good food," John said around a mouthful of noodles. "Where're we going tonight?"

"Your place."

"All right."

John pushed his worries away. He had a meeting with Charboric in a couple days. He had the device open on a workbench, possibly ruined. Visgrath had threatened him with harm if he didn't comply. But Casey was back in his life, and that was all that mattered.

CHAPTER 36

"I think so, if the current doesn't exceed half an amp," Henry said.

"We can't guarantee that," John said.

"Not until we test," Henry said.

John paged through the circuit board catalog. "These IMCAL 212 boards seem to be what we need—"

The phone rang, and they looked up from the workbench filled with circuitry. They had spent the morning trying to simplify Henry's model of the thread. Grace was at the factory, giving Casey a tour.

"Hello?"

"John, this is Grace. Visgrath is here. He's angry."

"What? Why?"

"The circuits and equipment showed up on my corporate bill. He's suspicious."

"Stall him. We're coming."

"What is it?" Henry said.

"Visgrath. He's suspicious because Grace bought all this on her corporate card."

"Oh, shit."

"Yeah."

Henry ran for the door. John looked at the device, sitting there in the open.

"I need to lock this in the safe," John called.

"I'll meet you there," Henry said.

John placed the device gently in the huge safe in the warehouse office. No one was getting in there.

When he reached his car, Henry was long gone. John sped toward the new factory, zipping past the noonday traffic on the highway. The factory was only ten minutes away.

The undercarriage of the Trans Am smashed against the speed bump as John came into the office complex. He slammed on his brakes as he came around the corner. An ambulance was in front of the building. Henry's car was parked in the fire lane, with its door open. There was Grace's car.

Paramedics were working on a body in the middle of the road.

John threw open the door of the car.

He ran.

As he neared the fallen body, he made out a woman's shoe. He came to a halt, his heart thumping.

Lying on the street, blood flowing from a wound in her abdomen, was Casey.

"Casey!" John cried. He tried to get closer, but a paramedic blocked him.

"Let us work, buddy," she growled.

John stumbled back, tripping over the curb. What had happened? Where was Grace? Where was Henry?

He saw Viv, the shop foreman, coming out of the door of the Pinball Wizards factory.

"Viv!" he shouted. "Where's Henry and Grace?"

She looked confused, shrugging her shoulders. "Not here."

"Where?" John cried.

"They left just a few minutes ago," Viv said, confused. "They left with Casey and the gruesome twosome."

"Who?"

"You know, Visgrath and Charboric. They were all locked up in the office for a while, then Henry came, and then they all left." She peered around John's shoulder. "What's happening?"

"Casey," John said numbly. "She's been . . ."

"Is that blood? Jesus, that's Casey," Viv said.

John felt his knees buckle. Viv, with legs thick enough to be mistaken for tree trunks, lifted him to his feet. "Hold on there, John. Let's get you inside."

John shook her off. His vision seemed to crystallize. They'd shot Casey. Visgrath and Charboric were on to him. They had to be. Something had forced their hand. Realization struck. They wanted the device. If they didn't know about it, they soon would. And John didn't have it. It was at the old factory.

He brushed past Viv, ignoring her squawk of outrage. His car was still idling, with its door open. He drove between the ambulance and the row of parked cars. His heart twisted as he saw Casey lying there. He hated himself for leaving. What else could he do?

There was a dark SUV outside the warehouse when he got there. He pulled the Trans Am around the corner of another alley and sat there shaking. He should have taken the device with him. Then he could have . . . What? Run? Not this time.

He popped his trunk, rooted around inside, and pulled out the tire iron. It felt cold in his palm. Useless and limp.

He snuck down the alley, taking the back way to the warehouse. He peered down the cross street and saw no one in the front seat of the SUV. He felt foolish. Lots of people parked in the alley. He'd probably seen that same SUV a dozen times.

He came to the padlocked rear door of the warehouse. He of course didn't have the key; it was in his dresser at home. He could see nothing inside. The window was crusted over with dirt and grime. John would have to go in the front door.

A Dumpster, half-rusted and smelling of foul water, blocked most of the alley. Beyond it were piles of pallets. Technically he owned all of this, but he hadn't bothered to clean it up.

He made his way along the wall of the warehouse. The sun blazed down on him—it was hot for an early May day—and he cast no suspicious shadows over the windows.

At the corner, he glanced around quickly. The SUV was still empty, and the door to the warehouse was open. Someone was in his warehouse.

The device was in there.

Peering around the corner of the warehouse, he tried to get a good look inside. He heard voices.

"Get the torch."

He dodged back.

A man exited the building, tall and blond, one of Visgrath's men undoubtedly. He opened the back of the SUV and pulled out a blowtorch and canister. Grunting as he lugged it over the door sill, he called, "Help me with this."

John heard the canister being dragged across the cement floor. They were definitely heading for the office where the safe was.

"I don't know why we can't wait for a combination," the man who had fetched the torch said.

"You know why."

"We'll find him sooner or later."

The second man said something in a language John didn't recognize.

The tire iron suddenly slipped in John's sweaty palm. He snatched at it and barely caught it before it clanged on the ground. His heart thudded. What was he doing?

He had to stop these men. Call the police? How long would that take? Grace and Henry were in danger. Casey had been shot. John didn't have time to wait around. Everything they were working on was in that warehouse. And these two goons were breaking open the safe that held the device.

John waited five seconds, then ducked down and crawled toward the door. If the two men were in the office with the safe, they had no direct line of sight of the door. He slipped inside.

The office was ten meters from the warehouse door, past the workbench where the electronics sat.

He carefully and swiftly ran to the wall next to the office door,

plastering himself there. The two men were muttering to themselves. John heard the clicking of the ignitor but no burst of flame
from the torch. Good.

Then there was a whoosh as the torch caught. The two men
laughed.

John counted to five again, determined to rush in on five. When
he got to ten, he almost laughed aloud.

"Come on, John. Now."

He dodged into the room.

The two men, goggled, were bent over the safe.

John slammed the tire iron into the shoulder of the closer man,
the man who wasn't wielding the torch.

He grunted, collapsing to one knee.

John raised the iron over the second man.

He cursed in that odd language and tossed the torch aside.

John brought the iron down, but the man blocked it with a forearm. The arm bent at an odd angle. The man grunted, pulling it to
his chest. John had broken it.

The other man wasn't down. He swung at John, his fist connecting with John's jaw.

Staggering, John saw blotches of light. The tire iron fell from his
hands, and he reached to pick it up. The first man landed a punch
to the side of John's head, a glancing blow.

John kicked with his foot, catching the first man in the knee. He
went down hard. John found the handle of the tire iron and swung
it madly at the first man. It connected with his skull. A dull, sickening thud knocked the rising man flat. He didn't move.

John swung the iron backhanded at the second man, the one
with the broken arm. He jumped back, but that brought him to the
wall. John swung again and caught the man's shoulder. He grunted,
twisting, trying to get past John. John slammed the iron into his
thigh. He fell like clothes off a hanger.

John paused, his chest heaving. His enemies were both down,
one unconscious, one clutching his thigh. John raised his iron to

knock the second one out, but the man cringed before him, and he found he couldn't swing his iron on a defenseless, prone man.

The smell of smoke rose in the room. The torch had landed on a pallet, among some old newspapers. The tip, still hot, had caught the papers aflame. Already the papers were engulfed, and the pallet was next.

John thought for a moment whether there was a fire extinguisher, but he couldn't remember where. He turned to the safe.

Placing the tire iron on the top of it, he touched the lock with a finger.

Suddenly his brain wouldn't work! He couldn't remember the combination.

"Damn it!"

He glanced at the rising fire. He ducked his head below the smoke that was collecting at the ceiling. His lungs kicked and he coughed.

John placed his hand on the dial. He closed his eyes and relaxed. Turn, spin the dial to . . .

He remembered, or rather his fingers remembered for him. He dialed the combination.

The safe popped open, and he grabbed the device.

The conscious man cried out.

John turned, expecting him to be lunging at him. The man was still on the floor, having crawled his way to the door. He was staring with amazement at the device in John's hands.

"You have a ——." He used a word John didn't know. "You have a goddamn ——."

The man started crawling toward John. He grabbed the tire iron and swung it, but the man wouldn't be deterred. John couldn't swing on a prone man, and now he was blocking the door with his body. Smoke continued to fill the room.

John leaped over the man, running for the door. He stopped at the lab table. He scooped all the electronics, all the notes, into a box, laying the device on top of it.

He turned slowly and surveyed the warehouse. There was nothing left here. Casting one last look over his shoulder, he saw the two men, one dragging the other, struggling out of the burning room. John turned and ran.

John's mind raced. He slowed the car down to the speed limit. Getting pulled over now would be bad. What could he do? What had happened so suddenly? He drove past the exit he'd usually take to his apartment. They'd be there for him now. He drove past the school. They'd look for him at class.

Casey was shot. Casey may have been killed. Visgrath had Grace and Henry. They'd kidnapped Grace and Henry! John's breath came in short breaths. He pulled off the highway, found the first parking lot.

Dare he go to the police? What would he say? Grauptham House was a billion-dollar company. They had a security force. They had weapons. They used their money to buy secrecy. What could he do against them? He had no allies.

What could he do?

His eyes found the familiar logo of his bank across the street. That was one thing he did have. Money. His bank account had swollen with cash in the past few months and was still high even after the purchase of all the equipment for the lab.

It was time to make a withdrawal. He drove across the street and entered the bank.

The cashier looked at John oddly.

"Gold? You want gold?" she said.

"Can I withdraw everything as gold?" John said again.

"We don't have . . . At least I don't think we have . . . ," she said. "Let me check."

The cashier—Molly according to her nameplate—entered another office. Through the window, John saw her point him out to another woman, presumably Molly's manager.

"Sir," the manager said when she emerged from the office, "you want to withdraw your five hundred and fifteen thousand dollars and receive it in gold?"

"Yes, please." John was feeling a little nervous suddenly. "Yes, and quickly."

The manager took a calculator and tapped it for a moment. "Sir, we don't have forty kilograms of gold here."

"How much do you have then?"

"Just a few coins."

"I'll take what you have, then," John said. "And the rest in cash."

"Sir?"

"Cash."

"Yes . . . , sir. Wouldn't you rather have a cashier's check?"

"No, cash. And can I see your phone book?"

John paged through the book, looking for metal dealers. If he was going to carry forty kilos of gold, he'd prefer not to do it in coins. They'd jingle a lot. Ideally, he'd prefer gold wire or foil, which he could wear easily on his body. He found a coin shop nearby.

The bankers managed to find sixty thousand dollars in American Eagle coins of assorted weights between one-tenth and one troy ounce. The seven kilograms couldn't go in his pockets. He'd need a backpack. He jotted down a sporting supply store's address near the coin dealer.

John left the bank with a satchel of cash and coins. He felt conspicuous, and he guessed he was, carrying a heavy bag from a bank. All the customers behind him in line watched him leave.

The coin dealer had no wire, only more coins, but the man knew where John could get some bullion bricks. He did have a few thousand more coins to sell John, as well as rolls sized for the gold coins.

"Most people don't roll these," the deater said. "They keep them for display."

"I'm keeping them for an investment."

The man shrugged. "You'll get better return from a good bond fund."

"Not where I'm going."

At the sporting goods store, he bought a huge camping back-pack, a hunting knife, a switchblade, and a first-aid kit. He looked at the display cases of guns but chose against it. John remembered the sickening thunk of the crowbar on a skull. He would have to use his wits to beat Visgrath.

His next stop was an electronics store.

"IMCAL 212 boards?" the shop man said. He opened a catalog. "We've got one. In our store at the Chaney Mall."

"One?" John asked. "I need . . . more." Several thousand more.

"That's all we have," the clerk said. "Cutting-edge stuff."

"Where do you order them from?"

He turned over the catalog. It was from an electronics supply firm in Detroit.

"Can I have that number?"

"Sure."

"Can I see your phone book?"

"I wrote the number down."

"This is for something else."

The clerk handed the book over. John paged through to the list-ing of hospitals. His stomach had been churning as he'd made preparations. He needed to know how Casey was.

The closest hospital to the factory was Ardenwald. He wrote the number down next to the number for the supply firm. There was a pay phone on the sidewalk outside the shop. He dialed the hospital.

"I'm calling about a Casey Nicholson. Was she admitted?"

There was a pause while the woman looked. "I don't see that name here."

"She just came in, a gunshot wound."

"Oh, her. That paperwork hasn't come through yet."

"I'm her boyfriend. Can you tell me how she is? It's important."

"Hold on."

John waited, his heart thudding. He should have stayed with her. But Visgrath and company would have come back. If John had waited they might have opened the safe and gotten the device. It was his only edge. He wasn't even sure what he could do with it. Trade it, he hoped for Grace's and Henry's lives. He needed a safe base of operation. He needed—

"Sir?"

"Yes, is she all right?"

"She is. The doctor says the bullet is in her shoulder. It missed the arteries and bone. She's in stable condition."

"What's her room number?"

"She doesn't have one assigned."

"Thanks."

He suddenly felt better. Casey was all right. She wasn't dead. She wasn't in danger. For the moment she was safe, and that was enough. He dialed the next number.

"Foley's Electronic Supply."

"I need as many IMCAL 212 boards as you've got."

"Well, how many do you need?"

"How many do you got?"

"We have thousands, buddy."

"Are they right there in your store?"

"Yeah, in the warehouse."

"How late are you open?"

He could just make it. Then he'd find someplace safe to hide, and he had an idea of where.

The boxes were piled so high in the Trans Am that he couldn't see out the passenger's window and he had to use his side mirror instead of the rearview mirror. It was dark when he pulled into Bill and Janet's, but the lights were still on. If he'd arrived an hour later, they'd have been in bed.

"Hello, John!" Janet cried, hugging him.

She's not my mother, John repeated to himself. "Hello, Janet. How are you? How's Bill?"

"Good, good! We're watching *Matlock* reruns," she said. "You caught us just before bed. Bill! John's here."

He sat with them for a few minutes. They didn't seem to have heard the news about Casey and he didn't want to get into it right then.

"I need a favor."

"Of course. What is it?" Bill said.

"I need to use the second barn."

"The second barn? Whatever for?"

When Bill and Janet had bought a few acres across the road from the Walders', it had included a dilapidated house and a barn. The house had been razed, but Bill had decided to keep the second barn, in case he ever tried cattle again. He never did, and the barn was empty. It had electricity, however, which was one of the reasons John wanted to use it.

"I need to do some work."

"Pine ball work?" Bill asked.

"Pinball. Sort of."

"Well, all right," Bill said. "I think I left the key in the box." He groaned as he rose and hobbled on shaky knees. John wanted to know how his parents were, whether arthritis was slowly creeping in on them as it was for this Bill and Janet, whether they watched *Matlock* reruns in the evening before going to bed at eight thirty. Nostalgia overwhelmed John, and he swallowed it down as he took the padlock key from Bill.

"Thanks. If someone comes looking—"

"—you aren't here," Bill said. He shook his head. "The youth of today with all their secrets. Probably building another pine ball empire in there. I saw a boy put six dollars in quarters into one of those machines the other day. Amazing. You get a cut of that?"

"We do."

"Good for you."

"Can I use your phone?"

He dialed the hospital and asked for Casey's status: stable and now she had a room number. He considered calling Visgrath, then refrained. Not yet, not until the device was safe. Not until he had thought his move through.

He bid the Rayburns good-bye and drove the Trans Am across the road and onto the dirt path that led to the second barn. It loomed black on black, obscuring a patch of stars from the sky as he neared it. Leaving the car running, he got out and unlocked the door. He drove the car into the barn and began unloading the boxes. An old workbench became his lab bench.

Cobwebs clung to the beams. The dim bulb cast weak shadows into the stalls and loft. He ticked off a list of things he'd need: extension cords, lamps, soldering gun, breadboards, wires, a box of resistors and capacitors.

He debated for a moment what to do with the device. Then he placed it in the backpack, along with one hundred thousand dollars in gold coins, and hid the backpack in the loft.

Locking the barn behind him, he drove as fast as he could toward the hospital in Toledo.

It was just fifteen minutes before the end of visitors' hours, but he convinced the attendant to let him go up the elevator to Casey's room.

The ward was dark and quiet except for an occasional lit room, a faint TV, and the *beep-beep* of hospital equipment. He found Casey's room at the end of a cul-de-sac of rooms. The room was dark, and she was asleep inside.

A nurse suddenly appeared.

"You are?"

"Her boyfriend."

"Oh, visiting hours are almost up."

"I know; I had to see her."

"I understand," the nurse said. She paused. "She's stable. The bullet has been removed, and we've given her something to sleep. Do you know her family?"

"Yes, I do."

"We've contacted the university to get hold of them. But no one has come yet, except her uncle."

"Her uncle?" Casey's mother and father were only children.

"Yes, he just left. Sat with her for an hour, waiting. Said he'd call the parents, but he never picked up the phone."

"Tall man, blond?"

"Yes."

"Don't let him back in."

"What?"

"It wasn't her uncle," John said. "Have the police been here?"

"Police? Briefly. They said to call when she awoke." The nurse suddenly looked worried. "Is she in danger? I can— I can call security."

"Do that."

John felt a moment's panic. He should have been thinking of Casey. They might come back for her. John sat in the chair next to the bed. Looking at Casey's pale face, John felt sick. She had been shot. Because of him. He felt no anger at Visgrath. They did what they did, but because John had meddled. He had to set things right.

John reached forward and grasped Casey's hand.

"I'm sorry, Casey," he whispered. Perhaps she moved; perhaps she squeezed back. John wasn't sure.

"Touching."

John bolted upright. Visgrath stood in the doorway of the room. He was dressed in a suit. A blond bodyguard stood behind him.

"Get out," John said.

"Or what?" Visgrath laughed. "John, our fates are bound now. You can't shake me." He took two steps into the room and sat in the other chair. The guard blocked the doorway.

"You were not entirely forthcoming to me when last we talked," Visgrath said. "It didn't come up in our conversation that you had in your possession a transfer device."

"You didn't ask."

Visgrath laughed. "You played me, for what reason I don't know. But now we're here together, and we both have things to trade."

"Henry and Grace."

"They're not even singletons!" Visgrath said intensely. "I don't know why you care. But clearly you do, and I will use it to my advantage."

"Singletons?"

Visgrath paused.

"Yes, singletons. Surely you've heard the term."

"No."

Visgrath laughed. "Again I have made assumptions about you that are wrong. A singleton, like me, is a person who has no doubles in the universes. We are the special ones, the unique ones. Don't you understand that?"

"No."

"Look at her! There's a thousand of her next door! What does she matter? You feel some . . . lust for her, so sate yourself, use her, and move on. Any one of them is worthless."

"What are you talking about? She's a human, just like you."

"Value comes from rarity!"

John shook his head. Visgrath's manner, the reason for his disdain for anyone not in his inner group, was suddenly clear. "I'm not a singleton either. I'm just some kid from Universe 7533."

Visgrath looked at John blankly, then began to laugh. He glanced around the room for some weapon. John had not brought a gun or the tire iron or anything else into the hospital.

"A kid! From 7533!"

"And singletons or not, you've kidnapped my friends, and I want them back."

Visgrath's face went stone flat.

"Yes, the crux of the matter," he said. "You will give me the transfer device and your friends will live."

"I'll go to the police!"

"And your friends will die. You know what we are. You know how much money we have. We own this world."

"And if I give it to you, what assurances do I have?"

Visgrath's face twitched. "I said I would do it."

"But we're not even singletons like you," John said. "We have no value."

"My honor is of value to me! Give me the device and your friends live. If you are obstinate, then you will get one of them back and the other will die."

John realized he was dealing with a monster. He could not trust Visgrath or deal with him in any way.

"No," John said.

Visgrath rose, his face a mask of fury. "I can just take it! And if you don't have it, you'll tell me soon enough." He motioned to his bodyguard. John stood to confront him.

"That's enough."

A young uniformed man stood behind the bodyguard, his hand on a holster. His voice quivered as he spoke, but he stood solidly.

"This woman needs her rest, and visiting hours are over," he said.

The bodyguard glanced over his shoulder, then at John, and finally at Visgrath.

Visgrath nodded slightly and the bodyguard seemed to deflate. John took a breath.

"Indeed, she needs to recover for her next . . . tribulation," Visgrath said darkly.

"You harm any of my friends and you'll never get the device," John said softly.

"You don't give me the transfer device and you'll never see your friends alive," Visgrath replied civilly. At the door, he added, "You know how to reach me."

John watched as Visgrath and his bodyguard left. He listened to their clicking steps down the hallway. The young guard watched too, his face slick with sweat. The elevator dinged, and finally John relaxed.

"You better go too," the nurse said, suddenly appearing. "It is past visitors' hours."

"Yeah, sure."

"We'll make sure she's safe."

"I appreciate that."

John cast one look at Casey's slack face. He was vulnerable be-cause she was. Visgrath already had Henry and Grace. John couldn't let him get his hands on Casey. He had to do something.

First, he needed allies.

The spring night left the barn cool. The space heater hummed when John turned it on, emitting the sharp stink of burning dust. He set it under the bench, where it toasted his feet. The halogen lamp he'd bought cast sharp shadows, but still the barn was dark in the corners. There was nothing to be done for it.

He unrolled the diagram and laid it on the bench. His heart beat too fast, and he felt a moment's panic as he stared at the diagram.

"Damn it!"

It was like a physics problem he didn't have the tools to solve. Too big and too hard. He had no idea where to start.

He had to start somewhere. This was his only weapon, and Vis-grath didn't know it was broken.

Or did he? Would Henry or Grace tell? Would Visgrath force them to speak?

John shuddered. He was playing a violent, crazy game and he had only half the rules.

He stood over the diagram, and his eye caught the set of circuits that tied to the display. They had to be simple. It was just an LED. He decided to try to model that first.

An hour later, he grunted in frustration. He had no idea what went with what. John popped another can of cola. It was his sixth, and he was beginning to feel jittery. At the same time, he felt in-flated with knowledge and drive. He turned his attention to the next nexus of circuits. Something had to give.

John's first breakthrough came when he found that the dial on the side of the device was tied to the power system. The dial had always been placed on the most counterclockwise position when he used the device. John Prime had said that he had no idea what the dial did. But John suspected that it regulated the strength of the device's field. Wouldn't power correlate positively to strength? It made sense.

He remembered how the cat-dog had been cut in half. The dial might well extend the range of the field, so that larger volumes of material could be transported. He wondered how large of a volume it could move between worlds. An entire building?

Then he began wondering why the field was not a sphere, with the device at the center. If it had been a sphere, he would have always scooped up an arc of dirt every time he transferred. But no, he only transferred to his feet. The field seemed to stop at the edge of his body, with his clothes included, but not beyond. The cat-dog had been gripping his leg when he'd transported through from that universe. He had been lying on the grass; the cat-dog had been attached to his calf. Yet none of the prairie he had been lying on had come though with him. Just himself, his clothes, and half the cat-dog.

Clearly the field followed some topology rules when it determined what passed through to the next universe. Perhaps whatever was in contact with the device up to a certain radius was included in the transfer, but earth material and air were not. Perhaps it was based on density. Only objects with a density near one were transported.

John wondered if that was a property of the field or it was determined in some fashion by the device. Perhaps there were circuits built into the fuzzy marshmallows to calculate the passenger's topology. The thought that complex intelligence was built into the device daunted him. How would he reproduce that with simple diodes, resistors, and transistors? Then he wondered if he even needed to. Perhaps he could simplify it to the bare essentials needed to move between worlds.

The buttons on the front that incremented and decremented the universe counter also were easy to understand. He realized that one nexus of circuits kept the counter; they tied into the display and the toggle switch. These circuits modified the state of a complex three-dimensional circuit that John figured must determine which universe was the destination. John noted that the decrement and increment buttons did change the state, as did the third button. The first and second buttons changed it to a new one each time, while the third button changed the state to a fixed one every time.

John assumed that the third button represented some kind of reference universe. Perhaps it set the device to transfer to universe zero. If so, John wondered why it didn't reset the display.

John paused, realizing it was nearly dawn and that he had actually simulated several functions of the device. Sure, they were smaller functions, but he had done it! Groups of circuits began to make sense in his head. He started to see the logic of it grow. A glance at a ganglion told him what it might do. It was slowly starting to make sense!

He'd covered the whole workbench by then, and had to place some of his circuits on the ground or the hood of his car. He'd need some card tables. He rubbed at his eyes. He needed sleep. He needed food, but he wasn't leaving until he'd made more progress.

The basic controls, such as the field radius control, were easy to duplicate. The eigen matrix, as he came to call it, was the most complex. The hardest part of the neural mass was that connected to the trigger mechanism. It seemed to wrap around on itself like an Ouroborus eating its tail.

As he was turning to pick up a new circuit board, his foot caught the leg of the bench and he nearly sent all his work flying. He steadied himself, his chest heaving, his heart racing. He needed rest. He'd done enough.

John checked his watch: nine. He'd visit Casey again.

"John."

"Casey! You're awake."

"Yeah, I'm awake and sore, but I think I'm okay."

"I'm so sorry you got messed up in this," John said.

Casey looked confused. "What are you talking about? Wasn't it some crazed worker? Where are Henry and Grace?"

John lowered his voice. A nurse was standing outside the door to Casey's room, and the same security guard was sitting on a bench watching.

"It was Visgrath," John said. "He's kidnapped Henry and Grace. He was here last night. He threatened your life."

"What? That's nuts."

"What happened yesterday? When Henry showed up? What did you see?"

Casey shrugged, then closed her eyes. "Grace and I were in the office talking when that weird guy showed up."

"Visgrath."

"Yeah, that's his name. She was apologetic to me, but Visgrath had to see her right then. He looked angry. They disappeared into her office, and I didn't eavesdrop, but there was no missing that they were yelling."

"About what?"

Casey shrugged again. "Dunno. I heard 'circuit boards' and 'transfer device.' I figured it was a pinball issue and none of my business."

"If only."

"And then Henry shows up, and he goes right in. They're in there for a while, so I wander around. For five minutes or so, and then I see them leaving, only Visgrath is dragging Grace and another guy is dragging Henry. They don't look happy. I run across the factory floor, but by the time I get there, they're in a black mini-van. I yell, 'Hey! Wait! I'm calling the cops!' or something like that. It was clear Grace and Henry didn't want to go. Then I get hit, and, man, did that hurt. I woke up in the hospital."

"Who shot you?"

"I don't know. Nobody in the first minivan. The doors and windows were closed."

"The first?"

"There were two, but I didn't look at the second."

John shook his head. Visgrath had found out about the circuit boards that Grace had charged on her corporate card; that was apparent. He'd confronted her and she'd let out or he'd deduced that they were building a transfer device. He'd taken Grace and Henry, thinking perhaps they were travelers too, thinking they had knowledge of building a device.

"Do you believe me now?" John asked.

"About what?"

"My paranoid delusions!"

"I guess even paranoids can be right about someone out to get them," Casey said, with a slight grin.

"Thanks for your support." John paused, then said, "Casey, I may be gone for a while, or something might happen to me."

"John! What are you going to do? Just go to the police!"

"We can't. They'll kill Grace and Henry. I've got to do this in a different way."

"What way?"

"I can't say, in case they get to you."

"John!"

"I'll do everything I can to win this, Casey. I promise."

"Oh, John. You're a big paranoid idiot."

"I can't argue with that." He bent over and kissed her dry lips. "See ya."

John slept through the morning in the barn, his dreams filled with circuits like mazes that he ran down. The capacitors were huge balloons that slowly grew until they exploded. The resistors were thin sewer lines that he had to crawl through. He reached the end of the maze, only to discover that the last door opened onto a huge white fiber labyrinth even larger than the one before. He awoke covered in sweat.

His back stiff, John stood again before the array of circuits and wires. He didn't know where to begin. A wave of panic crept through him. Things that seemed clear the night before were vague in his mind in the light of day. It was a Rube Goldberg contraption; he was a fool to think he could understand the device's logic.

He wrung his hands, and then turned his attention to a single circuit. Break the problem down, he thought. Start with a simple thing. Then go to the next thing. Don't hold the whole problem in your head at once. Just the part you need to look at first. Then it would be easier to add to the whole later.

As he was staring at the diagram, a piece of it suddenly clicked. He started placing pieces together, soldering, wiring. He didn't have to understand it to duplicate it. Understanding would come later. Maybe ten years later, when his friends' lives weren't in jeopardy.

John looked up from the circuit board. His stomach rumbled. His breath tasted stale in his mouth.

"How long . . . ?" he muttered.

The circuitry before him was a mess. He couldn't remember anything he had done an hour ago; he was blindly connecting things, leaving taped notes to himself to help him remember what would connect where. He had no faith in it, however. What chance was there that he had pieced it all together correctly on the first try?

None at all, he thought to himself. It was useless. It would never work.

His mind turned toward Casey, then toward Henry and Grace. He felt sick to his stomach. Maybe he should just hand the device over to Visgrath. Maybe he should just do whatever it took to get his friends back instead of trying to be tricky.

John, anxious and frustrated, picked up the old rotary phone Bill had installed in the barn and dialed Visgrath's office number in Columbus. Visgrath picked up on one ring.

"I need to know they're okay," John said as soon as Visgrath answered.

"You think you're in control here?" Visgrath asked sharply. "You think you can call the shots? Think again. We have no compunctions. You clearly do."

"You want the device, I need to know they're fine."

"Come here now, or we kill one of them," Visgrath said.

John swallowed against a dry throat. "So? They're not even singletons," he said.

Visgrath laughed. "If you truly believed that, you wouldn't care about them."

"I've growth accustomed to them," John said, trying to sound haughty.

"Do not pretend to be what you are not. It won't work a second time," Visgrath said.

"I talk with them before we make any deal," John said.

Visgrath was quiet for a moment. Then he said, "Call this number in ten minutes." John wrote it down, then hung up.

John paced the barn floor as he waited. If Visgrath answered the phone, John knew where Henry and Grace were. They'd have to be in the fenced compound behind the Columbus site. They weren't in Pittsburgh; John had dialed Visgrath's office directly. The only secure place for him within ten minutes was the fenced area.

John dialed the number Visgrath had given him.

"Hello?" The voice was heavily accented and not Visgrath's.

"Give me Visgrath," John said, his voice breaking.

"He's not here."

"I need to talk with him." If Visgrath wasn't there, John had no idea where he was holding Grace and Henry.

"Who is this?"

"He told me to call here."

"This is . . ." There was a pause, the sound of something away from the phone. "He's here."

John sighed. They were in Columbus.

The phone switched hands, and there was a long pause. Finally a faint voice came on the line.

"John?"

"Grace! Are you all right?"

"John?"

"There. You have spoken with her," Visgrath said. "Now bring the device."

"What about Henry?"

"He is fine as well."

"I want to speak to him!"

"No!"

"Then no deals!" If Henry couldn't talk, John had to assume the worst.

"If you don't bring the transfer device to us now, I will kill them both," Visgrath said.

"Forget it," John said.

"Don't test me!"

"Don't fuck with me!" John's voice was shrill. Looking at the old analog phone line strung along the wooden beam above him, John suddenly wondered if Visgrath had the power to trace his call. John felt dizzy with panic.

"I'll deliver the device, but on my own terms," John said. "If either Grace or Henry is harmed, I'll leave and never come back."

Visgrath said nothing for a moment. "When?"

"I'll call you in two days."

"Too long!"

"You've waited decades! You can wait forty-eight hours!" John slammed down the phone.

As if an automaton, John finished the wiring of the transfer circuit, which was the last critical control system that actually caused the transfer to occur. Many of the subsystems he'd ignored, hoping they weren't absolutely necessary for the device to work. He made guesses, on intuition and feel, hoping he was cutting the right stuff. He didn't study what he was doing, just strung the boards, capacitors, and resistors together in what he hoped was the right sequence based on Henry's modeling of the thread properties. It was as if he were in a daze of wires and circuits. For a moment it all made sense, and then it collapsed into dream logic.

John knew it was a long shot. But he couldn't expect to deal with Visgrath as a human being. The man would kill him and his friends to get the device. Visgrath was depravity incarnate.

At dawn John placed the final pieces and examined the completed machine.

It filled three tables in the barn, a hundred times larger than the device he wore. It wasn't portable. It was stuck where it sat. Two-by-fours, wired with equipment, jutted out into the middle of the barn. The transfer field would be generated below the cantilevers, he hoped. John expected—guessed, prayed?—the device to generate a sphere-shaped field with a radius of two meters, but it was just as likely to explode. The physicist inside him chided him for encumbering his experiment with too many variables. Too many things were unknowns. But he didn't have time for testing one thing at a time.

"Now we skip unit testing and rush headlong into production," he muttered. John stopped as he spoke. How long had he been up?

John felt the same hyper-alertness he'd felt when he'd tried to kill his one-armed self. The nausea threatened to buckle his stomach again. No, Visgrath and company weren't even human, though John knew as he thought it that it wasn't true. They were monsters, killers. They had kidnapped his friends. They deserved to die, to be punished. John realized he was psyching himself up. Just as when he'd confronted Ted Carson.

John pushed it all aside and powered the machine, instantly smoking a dozen resistors.

He replaced them, and traced their destruction to a loose wire he had knocked from one end of a capacitor. He powered the thing again, and felt the contraption hum. He set the eigen matrix to Universe 7649, one universe back.

The lights flickered.

Did he have enough power?

John grabbed an old wheelbarrow with a broken handle and rolled it into the center of the field area.

Then, with a shrug, he activated his device.

With a pop, the wheelbarrow disappeared. In place of the wheelbarrow was a hemisphere of dirt, like a large model of the lower hemisphere of the Earth. As he watched, it slumped into a mound.

"Ha! Ha! It worked!" He realized as he capered around the lab that he looked like a mad scientist. Perhaps he was.

John ran outside and looked at the topography around the barn. In the faint light of the morning, he noticed where the land had been flattened and cleared. Maybe Walder had dug out the side of the hill to make the barn rest on flat ground. In the universe where the chair went, there was no barn. There was a field with a two-foot-radius hole in it, and in that hole was an old wheelbarrow.

John chortled and went back inside. He used a shovel to clear the transfer zone of dirt, dirt from another universe.

When he was done cleaning the transfer zone, John took the rolled-up plans for the device, his gold, and his backpack.

He stopped, his hands shaking. He hadn't slept in days. His friends' lives were in his hands. He'd built a crazy transdimensional device while in a delirium. What did he think he was doing? Did he think he was going to do this by himself? He couldn't.

He needed help. Perhaps Grace and Henry from some other universe? No, they'd have no idea who he was. Who could even begin to understand his plight?

He could think of just one person.

He set the universe to 7533.

If there was one person who could understand, it was the John who got him into this mess.

"Here goes nothing," he muttered. He powered the machine; then with a ten-foot pole he pressed the trigger.

CHAPTER 37

The same dawn sun filled the same barn through the same barn windows. Only it wasn't the same. He was back home: Universe 7533. He'd done it!

Something rustled in the dark stalls.

He spun, but it was only a horse. This was Walder's barn. John remembered that they used it in this universe. His father had never bought it from Walder here.

John crept to the back door and pushed it open slowly. There was no sign of Ernst Walder in his fields. All was quiet. John ran toward the road, pausing at the berm. There was his house. The lights were on. Steam rose from the kitchen vent. Mom was up, cooking breakfast for Dad.

John ached to go inside.

Dare he?

He needed transportation. He needed to know where John Prime was. Perhaps he was in that house right now. Prime had stolen John's life after all.

John walked across the road and up the drive toward the house. His nose caught the familiar smells: fresh hotcakes, sizzling bacon, coffee. Even the chicken coop smelled good to him: It was home.

He walked around to the back of the house.

The screen door swung open suddenly. His mom had

a dustpan of dirt and was about to toss it into the trash can just outside the back door.

"Johnny! You scared the heck out of me."

"Hi . . . Mom."

"What are you doing down here? Where's Casey? Where's Abby?"

"Uh." Casey? Had Prime gotten together with his Casey? Who was Abby? "At . . . home."

"You should have brought them," his mom said. She leaned the broom against the door frame and with her other hand still holding the dustpan hugged him awkwardly. "We hardly get to see you these days. With that Carson business and all."

"Uh, right." John felt he had to write everything down to make sense of it. He was disquieted to realize this wasn't his life after all. Eighteen months had passed.

"Why are you dressed like that? What is that under your shirt? Have you been camping?"

John just shrugged and followed her inside the kitchen. He sat heavily in his seat. Home.

"Bill!" his mom called. "John's here." She turned to him. "You just caught him. He's on his way to the fields to plow." She poured John a coffee. "You take it black now, don't you."

"No, cream is fine," he said automatically.

"I thought you liked it black." She set the cup and saucer in front of him and he smelled the aroma. It should have been like any other cup of coffee, but it wasn't.

"John, where's your car parked?" his father said. "It's not in the driveway."

"Um, well," John said. "I need to borrow your car."

"Did that damn Japanese thing break down?" his father said. "A good solid pickup truck is a status symbol too."

"Yeah, it broke down. Tow truck dropped me off."

"You should have called," his mom said. "We would have picked you up."

"No, I didn't want to wake you."

"You know we'd be up," his father said. He took the car keys off the hook and tossed them at John. "Your mom and I can come up to Toledo tomorrow to get it." Toledo! That's where Prime lived.

"Thanks."

"How are Casey and our cutest granddaughter?" he said. Granddaughter! So that was Abby. Casey and Prime were married here and had a daughter.

"Fine."

"We hardly ever see them these days."

"That's what Mom said," John replied.

"This Carson business." His father shook his head. "The way people talk about it. You'd think the trial was over already."

John kept his face straight. Carson? Trial? What the hell had happened while he was gone?

"The papers say the trial has been postponed again," his father said. "Probably because they don't have evidence."

He nodded, but he felt his face flush. He had to find Prime.

John finished his coffee in one gulp that burned his throat. Holding the key tightly, he said, "Thanks. When you come get the car, stay for dinner."

"Oh, that'd be nice," his mom said.

John hugged his mother and shook his father's hand. Then he stiffly walked to the old Ford pickup and started north toward Toledo.

The neighborhood was nice. Prime had done well for himself. At the same time, he'd jeopardized it all, somehow. What trial had John's parents been talking about?

John had stopped at a gas station on I-75, dialed information for Toledo, and found the home address. He passed the house once, caught the digits on the mailbox, and turned around in the next driveway. Someone opened a curtain in the neighbor's house, a balding man. He waved at John, as if he saw him every day. The man probably did. John waved back.

He parked in the driveway. There was no sense of familiarity. No sense of home. But the house was exactly what he would have chosen. How odd.

He rang the doorbell, and he felt silly for doing so. If anyone in the neighborhood saw him doing it, he'd look like an idiot. Forgot his keys, he'd say.

The door opened, and he caught his breath.

"Why did you ring the doorbell?" she said. A dozing baby slept on her shoulder. She wore a gray sweatshirt with the sleeves cut off.

John stepped in.

"I—"

Casey handed him the baby.

"Hold her," Casey said, turning away.

The baby's eyes fluttered as he held her in front of him. What was he supposed to do with her? She was beginning to wake, so he put her up on his shoulder.

Casey was halfway down the front hall when she stopped. She turned, her eyes sharp.

She ran toward him and took Abby off his shoulder. John backed away, feeling her tension.

"Which one are you?" she said. "Which one?"

"You know?"

"He told me everything," she said, her voice angry. The baby began to squirm.

John held his hands up. "I'm the one that was here," John said. "I'm the . . . original from this universe."

Casey's face contorted, and then she burst out crying. She jumped forward and cast her arms around John's neck, squeezing the baby between them. Now, Abby did wake, crying out at the sudden motion.

"You're different," Casey said, her voice muffled in his shoulder. "You smell different. A little, but enough."

"I'm sorry for . . ." He didn't know what he was sorry for.

"It's okay," she said. She kissed him a peck on the lips and John was startled at the sudden arousal he felt. This wasn't his Casey.

"Why are you here?" she said. "John said the device doesn't work."

John grinned, stepping back to put distance between them, a little bit at least. "The original is still broken. But I took it apart and built a new one."

"You built a new one."

"With the money we made from pinball."

"Pinball."

"We invented pinball in the next universe," John said with a shrug. It sounded rather silly saying it. "Not really invented, I guess. Made something called pinball and based on pinball but really different."

"Like John's Cube."

"John's Cube," he said. "Oh, yeah. Rubert's Cube. Is that what got you all this?"

"Yeah, all this," she said. John felt a lack of emotion in Casey, or rather a shutting down of emotion.

"You've done well with this John," he said. "Better than I could have done for you."

Casey frowned, then smiled slightly. "I know when it happened. The day before the church potluck. Before that you never talked to me."

"I was very . . . nervous around you."

"But you finally got up the nerve with the Casey next door?"

"She—," John said, remembering. "She asked me out, to a dance. Remember *Sock Hop,* the play we did two years ago?"

"I remember."

"That's how they dance in my— The universe I ended up in," John said.

"Women love a man who can dance," Casey said.

"I love Casey," John said. "It's why I'm here. I need help."

"You're not here to—"

The sound of the garage door opening stopped her.

John felt his pulse race. He was finally about to come face-to-face with Prime. His fists balled involuntarily.

"What are you going to do?" Casey said hastily, stepping back from him to stand in front of the garage door. "You're not going to—"

"No, I told you I need him." He stepped toward her.

The door opened, and Prime said, "What's Dad's truck—"

He stopped dead in the doorway, his eyes on John.

John found he couldn't speak. All the emotion he'd built up around him was gone. Instead he just felt a moment's kindred spirit. There was a heaviness in Prime's face, a wariness and a resignation. Perhaps even desperation.

"This has been one crazy year," Prime said with John's voice. "I didn't think it could be any crazier."

"Guess what?"

John found himself laughing, and with him Prime joined in.

Casey shook her head. "You both are nuts," she said.

"You fixed it?" Prime asked after he had caught his breath. "You figured out how to work it?"

"Nope, still broken, you fucker."

"Okay, I deserved that."

"I built a new one. I reverse engineered it."

Prime walked past John into the living room, where he sat heavily in a chair. "I knew we could figure it out."

"We?"

"Yes, we," he said. "You gotta remember I was a year younger than you. I hadn't had physics yet. I couldn't have done it. But you did. I had faith."

John held his tongue.

"Now, why are you here, if not to punch my lights out?" Prime asked.

"I'm here for that too." John sat across from him on the couch. Casey disappeared into the kitchen. John smelled coffee brewing after a moment. "But I'm really here because I've run afoul of some renegades. They know I have a device, and they want it."

Prime nodded. "I know the type," he said. "The devices are rare or controlled. Some worlds, maybe all worlds, are used to dump exiles. Here too."

"Did you—"

"No, I don't think they've even noticed me. Yet."

"You're in danger, then."

"Less in danger than in a legal mess," Prime said.

"Carson."

Prime looked at him sharply. "How'd you know? What do you know?"

"Dad let it slip. Not what, just that something had happened," John said. "What's the story?"

"Carson's missing," Prime said. "They think I had something to do with it. They've charged me with murder."

"Did you?"

"What do you think?"

John studied Prime's face and saw nothing there that he didn't see in the mirror every day. Murder? "You had the chance to murder me and keep the device. You chose . . . the lesser evil. But you still chose evil."

"Carson deserved whatever he got," Casey said from the doorway. She handed John a cup of coffee. "Wherever he is."

"I'm sure," John said. "I knew him too, remember? Know him, I guess. He's in the universe I'm in too. I saw him once."

Prime and Casey shared a look that John couldn't decipher. This John and Casey had been together longer than he'd been with his Casey.

"Why are you here, John?" Casey asked. "What do you need?"

"I need help. I have to save my friends," he said simply.

Prime and Casey shared another look. Finally, Casey nodded.

"Anything," Prime said. "It's the least I can do."

"Wait here," Prime said. He'd parked the truck in John's parents' driveway while John parked Prime's car behind his. They were dropping the car off, ostensibly. John was nervous, but the windows of the Unic XK were tinted; he doubted his parents would look out the windows, and if they did, they couldn't see him in the driver's seat. Still he didn't want to have to explain to them what was happening.

"What are you going to tell them?" John asked again.

"Camping trip, I said."

"Right. Is that going to work?"

"I've borrowed his rifle before. Why won't he give me the handgun too?"

John nodded and Prime headed for the house. He waited, turning the dial on the radio. None of the songs were familiar, but the call signs and radio voices were what he remembered. This universe had rock and roll. He found that he missed the twanging songs of 7650, and he flipped the radio off in disgust.

They had hammered out a plan in Prime's living room. Casey had figured out John's idea the quickest.

"Surprise attack," she said. "They don't exist in every universe. Anything that comes from another universe or is built by someone from another universe is probably unique."

"That's what I think," John said. "I don't think their facility will be there in this universe. I checked the phone directory. There's no mention of EmVis or Grauptham House here."

"Oh, I get it," Prime said. "We have the device." He chuckled. "I don't know how I feel about using it."

"We'll do it carefully," John said.

"You sure it won't . . . cut my head off?"

"I understand it better than you do," John replied. "At least I know what some of the knobs do."

"We come in the back door," Prime said. "And the back door in this case is this universe."

"Yeah."

"We'll need firepower," Prime said.

"Why? We can just sneak in," John replied. He had no interest in killing anyone, not even Charboric.

"Sure, sneak in, and what happens when the plan goes off the rails? You wanna call a time-out, while we regroup?"

"No."

"Luck favors the prepared, brother," he said. "Let's be prepared."

"Fine."

"And speaking of prepared," Prime said. "I need to call my insurance agent."

"Now?" Casey said.

"Yeah." He picked up the phone and dialed a number.

"Nancy? John Rayburn here. We have a policy with you on our cars." He paused. "Yeah, that's our number. Bit of an embarrassment really. My car got dinged in the parking lot. I saw it happen. But the guy drove off." He paused again. "I have the license plate. . . . Yeah, CDDA-92. . . . Yeah, Ohio plate. . . . Great. . . . No, just the rear panel is dented. All cosmetic. . . . Great. . . . Yeah, that's it." John seemed poised to set down the phone. "Oh, one more thing. The police want the guy's name for their report. Can you run that plate through the DMV for me? Great, thanks."

"What are you doing?" John asked.

"Social engineering," Casey said.

"Kent Corriander? And the address? In Columbus? That's awesome. Thanks, Nancy."

"Why would the police need the insurance company to run a plate?" John asked. "She's going to be suspicious."

"She's going to remember that she was incredibly helpful," Prime said. "She won't remember anything else. People just want to be helpful."

Prime came out of his parents' house carrying a rifle in its padded wrap. He headed toward the barn then and came out a few minutes later, rifle slung over his shoulder, carrying a bundle in both hands.

"Pop the trunk."

He piled the gun and the bundle into the trunk. John saw him remove a pistol from his pocket, as well as two boxes of ammo. He felt misgivings about using weapons. It could only end badly for someone.

"What was in the bundle?" John asked as Prime slid into the passenger seat.

"Let's just say that you'll want to avoid any rear-end collisions," Prime said.

"Dynamite?" John cried. His father always kept a few sticks for tree stumps.

"Yep."

"I don't—"

"We're going into battle, John," Prime said, his smile gone. "Don't forget it. You asked for my help, and this is how it works."

John nodded, but he wasn't convinced. "Now what? Columbus?"

"One stop."

They drove the eighty miles to Columbus, but instead of the office park where EmVis existed in 7650, they drove to the south side of town, to a run-down apartment complex downwind from the trash-burning power plant.

"Pull in here," Prime said.

It was a first-floor apartment.

"Here's what you do," Prime said. "Give me two minutes, then knock on the door."

"That's it?"

"Yeah, that's it."

"What do I say?"

" 'Hello,' 'How are you?' 'Remember me?' "

"Fine."

Prime slipped out of the car and around the side of the building. John counted to 120 and then trotted up to the door. He pounded on it, ignoring the doorbell.

He heard sounds within and ducked his head away from the peephole.

"What is it?" came a voice through the door.

John pounded again.

The door came open fast. "Goddamn it! What—"

The man was shorter than John by a foot. He looked up into John's face, went white, then turned and ran, slamming the door.

John caught it with his foot, pushed it inward, and watched as the man scrambled over his couch to get into the kitchen and through the sliding door there. It must have led to a back patio, but the man stopped short there.

As the sliding door opened and the aluminum blinds clanked against the glass, he came face-to-face with Prime.

"Corrundrum," Prime said. "We have some questions."

"Christ, you two are so screwed! Doppelgangers? The vig are going to fall on you like bricks."

Prime motioned John in, grabbed Corrundrum, and steered him toward the couch.

"We need some information," Prime said. "You were wrong about me. I don't know what's going on."

"Then how'd he get here?" Corrundrum cried, pointing at John.

"We have a device," Prime said. "We have more than one. We built more."

Corrundrum choked on a laugh. "Build them? You're punching unauthorized holes?"

"Holes?" John said.

"You built a device?" Corrundrum said, staring at him. "Your own device?"

"Yeah. I modeled it on the broken one."

"They don't break! You two are talking crap!"

John shrugged. "Your understanding is wrong." He turned to Prime. "This guy doesn't know anything. Let's get out of here."

"Wait," Prime said. He turned to Corrundrum. "We can get you home, if you help us. That is what you want, isn't it?"

Corrundrum's forehead broke with sweat. He stared at Prime. Finally he said, "I hate this fucking universe! The food is crap! The entertainment is only TV! They have diseases! It's—"

"So you'll help us?"

"What do you want?"

"Just information."

Corrundrum chuckled. "There are rules, you know."

"You talked enough before."

"I didn't know you were a fucking native!"

"So?"

"The vig kill people who talk."

"Why?"

Corrundrum looked at him with wild eyes. "You won't get it. You won't ever get it. You're just a fixture." He waved his hand. "You're a set piece. A goddamn coffee table."

"You're talking like this is entertainment," John said.

Corrundrum laughed. "It's worse than that, for those of us who know."

"Visgrath? Charboric?" John said. "Ever hear of them?"

"Sound like Vandals."

"Spray paint?" John asked, confused.

"Capital V."

"Huh?"

"Goths. In the Yankee Doodle universes, the Goths sacked Rome and then a few years later Clovis sacked the Goths. Yay, Europe. Yay, America. You think it's great, but only because it's all you know. When the Goths win, even less great. Goth universes are some totalitarian places. In 2119, they got hold of some transfer technology. Tried to spread their way of life across a couple dozen universes. They were crushed. Some got away. This was a few decades ago. Sounds like you ran into some of the meaner ones."

"Visigoths," John said, shaking his head. "They're Visigoths."

"The descendents of Germanic tribes that defeated Rome," Corrundrum said. "But if anyone asks, I didn't tell you that. Oh, screw it. Did you run up against some Goths?"

"I guess so."

"Do they know you have a transfer device?"

"Yes."

"Well, how'd they let you get away?"

"I ran."

"To him for help?" Corrundrum nodded at Prime.

"Who can you trust, if not yourself?"

Corrundrum snorted.

"What do they want?" John asked. "What can I give them if I negotiate?"

"Restore the Alarian Empire. Do you have twelve universes to spare?"

"We have the device, don't we?"

"That's what you think."

"What can I do?"

"Run away. Leave them alone. You have a device. Go somewhere else they aren't. Far away. Take me with you."

"I can't."

"Why not?"

"They have my friends."

Corrundrum looked at John solemnly. "Hopefully they weren't singletons."

"You're an ass," John said. "Let's go." He stood.

Corrundrum stood up too. "Hold on; hold on. We can reach an arrangement where I get out of here, right?"

"How can you help us?" Prime asked.

"I'm no fighter," Corrundrum said. "But I know more of what you're fighting against than anyone. I'm a strategic asset. You've gotta take me with you."

"I don't think the device can take that many."

"Of course it can. It's a Mark Three? A Four?"

"How would I know?"

"Show him," Prime said.

John wasn't sure if they should.

"Go ahead. What do secrets matter now?" Prime added.

"I had the same thought recently," John said. He lifted up his shirt, showing Corrundrum the device strapped to his chest.

Corrundrum stared at it. "What the hell? That's not a—" He cast a hard glare at Prime. "Are you guys screwing with me? That's not a transfer device."

"What do you think a transfer device is?" John asked suddenly.

"It's a machine to move material and people between universes, what else?"

"That's what this does."

"It's not like any transfer device I've ever seen," Corrundrum said. "Where'd you get it?"

John shrugged toward Prime.

"Where'd *you* get it?"

"Another John Rayburn gave it to me," Prime said.

"Gave it or tricked you into using it?" John said.

"Does it matter?" Prime said.

"Yes, it does."

"Just like you," Prime said.

John sympathized with Prime. He couldn't deny that he might have acted in the same way Prime had if he'd been in the same situation. In fact, he almost had. If the one-armed John hadn't been there . . .

Corrundrum rubbed his head. "You know, there are universes that are off-limits to us."

"Who's 'us'?" John asked.

"None of your business."

"You want help or not?" Prime said.

"It doesn't matter!" Corrundrum said. "Your Goths are going to kill you. Take me back to my universe first, and then I'll help you."

"No way!"

Corrundrum shook his head. "You don't get it. Alarians have one hobby: killing non-Alarians. They get together and ask each other who they killed recently. How bad do you think your Goths are to get exiled by other Alarians?"

"We don't know they were exiled by their own kind."

"All the Alarians were wiped out when they were defeated. If there's any around still, it's because they were lost before the final battle. They don't negotiate. They don't deal. They take what they want and destroy what they don't need. You two against a strong-hold of Alarians who've had five decades to entrench? You two are walking dead men."

"So you're not going to help us?"

"I just did! Walk away!"

"We can't," John said.

"Then if you come back, remember me," Corrundrum said. "I don't belong here."

"Come with us and make sure we succeed," Prime said.

"Didn't you hear me? You're gonna die there."

"Better to try and die than live in vain," Prime said.

"You natives! You think life is to be sacrificed," Corrundrum said. "Sacrifice is for Christers. Life is to be cherished and not wasted."

"Isn't your life wasted here? How long before you die, alone, in an alien universe?"

"I have years ahead of me, more than your science can provide."

"What about Kryerol? He risked his life for you, and died!"

"Don't bring him up! He knew what he was doing. And he shouldn't have brought us there for some Prime treasure hunt. He deserved to die!"

"He saved you, didn't he? Sacrifice is what he did, for you and the rest of your team."

"Lotta good it did them," Corrundrum said.

Prime exhaled heavily. "Fine. I thought we could help you, and I thought you could help us. I guess not." To John, he said, "Let's go before it gets dark."

They were halfway to the front door when Corrundrum cried out, "All right! All right. I'll come with you. It's nuts, but what the heck. It's not like there's a rescue party coming from home uni-verse." He hauled himself up from the couch. "Let me get some stuff first."

Corrundrum disappeared into a back room. John felt Prime tense up. His hand was in his pocket where he had put the pistol.

"Don't you trust him?" John whispered.

"He's not like us," Prime said. "He may be half-mad from exile here."

"I believe it."

Corrundrum came out with a black duffel bag. He tossed it on the coffee table and rooted through it, pulling out a black handgun and a box of bullets. He loaded the gun and put it back into the bag.

"More guns," John said.

"They'll kill us if they can," Corrundrum said. "Most people in this multiverse will for what you have on your chest. These people more than most."

"We should go," John said. It was already three thirty. If they didn't get to the site soon, there'd be no light to search by.

"George Washington? Executed as a traitor usually," Corrundrum said. "Napoléon? Unified Europe five times out of twelve. Christ, a minor prophet for Mithras one in twenty times." He had been reciting useless universe facts for ten minutes.

"Shut up," Prime said.

"Yeah, the truth sucks," Corrundrum replied.

"Who cares what the truth is?" Prime cried. "It all depends on which universe you're in."

"True," Corrundrum said. "Unless it's home universe." He paused. "South wins the Civil War one percent of the time. The South will not rise again; they can't even rise the first time."

"Shut up!" Prime shouted.

"Fine, all right."

John pulled into the parking lot, driving upstream through the five o'clock commuters. The office complex looked just like the one that EmVis rented in Universe 7650.

"This is it."

John pulled to the edge of the parking lot. He sat staring at the wooded lot beyond, where the fenced compound should have been. A biking path threaded its way through the trees.

"Is this it?" Prime asked.

John paused. "Maybe."

"Maybe?" Corrundrum cried from the backseat.

"Maybe, I said." John looked to the right, at a duck pond that hadn't been there in 7650. He got out of the car, walked a short distance to the left.

"I can't tell," he said. He turned and looked over at the office building. If this had been Grace's universe, his office would have been the one there on the corner. The view of the compound had been clear from there.

"We need to get inside the office building," John said. "We need to look out of that window."

The door was open—no key pass or other lock barred them—but there was a guard at the front desk. John just shrugged and walked past. The guard glanced at the three, perhaps because John and Prime looked like identical twins and how often did one see adult identical twins out and about?

John hit the elevator button for the third floor. The elevator door didn't close.

"What the—?" Corrundrum said.

John pointed to the sensor below the elevator buttons. "We need a key card to activate the elevator."

"Damn!" Corrundrum said.

Just then a woman sprinted on, waving her key across the sensor and pressing 5.

"Could you get us to three, please?" Prime said. "We've forgotten our keys."

"Sure," she said, swiping again and hitting 3.

The elevator opened on their floor. Stepping into the lobby, John was momentarily disoriented. He had expected to see an austere receptionist's desk. Instead there was a huge wall-mounted fish tank and an arrangement of orange chairs and geometric shapes.

"This way," he said, turning around. "My office was over here."

The door to that wing of the building was locked.

"Damn it," John said. There was nobody around to let them in.

Prime picked up a phone mounted to the wall. A list of numbers was taped next to it. He dialed an extension.

"No answer," he said, dialing another.

He was through six numbers when a door on the other side of the elevators opened.

"May I help you?" a young bespectacled man said. He was carrying a briefcase.

"Uh," John said. "We—"

"Yeah," Prime said, cutting him off. "Josh in Facilities said to meet him here at five. We're supposed to tour the floor. Can you let us in? We have only a bit of time before we have to see the next place."

"Oh, yeah? Touring?"

"Yeah, they're building a third building, you know, and it's going to have this pattern."

The man nodded and keyed open the door for them.

"It's a great space. We've been here for a couple years now."

"Awesome," Prime said.

The door shut behind them, and Prime exhaled. "Too easy."

Corrundrum said, "A social engineer."

"Make it a big lie," Prime replied.

"I agree."

John sped down the hallway. The layout was the same, and his office a hundred universes away was in the spot he expected. Luckily, it was empty.

The view was nothing like he remembered, however. Of course there was no fence, no building. But even so, the landscape wasn't right.

"Does it ring a bell?" Prime asked.

"No."

"No? What the hell? If we come in anywhere but—," Corrundrum cried.

"Quiet!" Prime snapped.

John leaned on the window glass with his forehead and jammed his eyes closed. He visualized the view from his office, the slope of the land, the trees. He tried to remember it without the fenced compound.

He opened his eyes. Yes, he had it. This universe's parking lot extended too far. It had thrown him off.

"See that big oak tree?" he said.

"Yeah."

"About six meters to the east and three meters to the north."

"Got it," Prime said. "Inside the fence, outside the buildings?"

"Yeah."

John marked it in his mind.

Back in the parking lot, Prime and Corrundrum climbed into the car while John took a hazard sign from the car's trunk. He found the oak tree and walked off six steps east and three north. Using a rock to keep it in place, he placed the orange flag on the ground in the spot, his best guess across universes. Then he went back to the car and dozed in the front seat. They had a couple hours at least.

Someone nudged him awake.

"What?"

"Shh!"

Corrundrum was in his face. "Out of the car," he whispered.

"What?"

Corrundrum pulled the gun from his pocket. "Don't make a sound."

John got out of the car. He considered nudging Prime, but he was snoring in the backseat, beyond reach.

"Over there."

The air was damp and dewy on his cheeks. His breath came in a white cloud.

"What are you doing?"

"Keep going," Corrundrum said. The man glanced over his shoulder at the car.

"Corrundrum! We had a deal."

Corrundrum chuckled darkly. "You're not even singletons. You don't deserve a transfer."

"You can't do this!"

Corrundrum nudged him with the pistol barrel. "Remove the transfer. Give it to me."

"No!"

"It doesn't matter to me, except it will take longer to remove from your dead body," Corrundrum said. "Give me the transfer. Now."

"I can't," John said. "My friends will die."

"Fine." Corrundrum raised the pistol.

There was a pop.

John tensed, but there was no pain. That wasn't so bad, he thought. Then Corrundrum pitched forward.

Prime knelt ten meters away, gun held in a two-handed grip.

Corrundrum rolled over on his back, gasping for breath. Blood welled up black behind him.

"Jesus!" John said. "You shot him."

For a moment, the handgun was still pointed at John's chest. He stared down the barrel into Prime's eyes. Then Prime slid the gun into his pocket.

"I don't think I can ever trust anyone," he said. "Except for you, except for Casey."

"You shot him."

John rushed forward and lifted Corrundrum's neck. Blood and snot gurgled in his nose.

"Fuck'n— Fuck'n—," he gasped. "Fuck'n dups."

Corrundrum exhaled once more; then he died.

"He's dead," John said.

Prime shrugged, but his fingers were fists. He was shaking.

"Him or you, brother."

"Don't call me that!"

"We're closer than brothers, but there's no words for it," Prime said. "Grab the body. We need to move. It's past midnight."

John stood up and walked past Prime. "You grab the body, bro," John said.

He went and stood next to the transfer point marker. Had it been a mistake to ask Prime for help? Corrundrum was dead. Prime was armed. John felt naked, even with the device tucked under his shirt.

He turned as he heard the sound of Prime dragging Corrundrum's body down the hill toward him. Prime grunted, then sprawled onto the ground. John felt a moment's pity for him, then decided lugging Corrundrum's corpse was penance for killing him.

Prime finally managed to get Corrundrum near the marker.

"Thanks for the help," Prime gasped.

John said nothing.

"We'll need to take him with us, to hide the body."

John grunted. He dialed the machine to 7650, while Prime dragged Corrundrum's body close to them. John shivered at the nearness of the corpse.

John found the dial that increased the radius of the field. He set it to the maximum radius.

"What are you doing there? What does that do?"

"You don't know?" John asked.

"No!"

"Increases the radius of the field."

"How do you know?"

"I took this one apart, remember? I built one from scratch."

"Right."

"Ready?"

"No."

John looked again at Prime. He had one hand on Corrundrum's shoulder. The other was rubbing Prime's scalp. Even in the cold night air, he was sweating. He was genuinely scared.

"You don't want to do this, that's fine," John said.

"No way. I'm coming. I owe . . . people."

"Fine. Let's go." John stepped next to Prime, face-to-face with his twin. "Seven-six-five-oh, here we come."

CHAPTER 38

John's ears popped, and the moonlit gray was replaced with pitch-black.

He fell, maybe a half meter, landing awkwardly on his left ankle. Nearby he heard John Prime land against something that rattled metal on metal.

"Flashlights," Prime hissed. "We should have brought flashlights."

"Let's go back and get some," John replied.

"God, I hate this," Prime said. John listened in the darkness to Prime's fast breathing, the stress in his voice.

"You're okay, man," John said. "We're okay. You can calm down now."

Prime laughed, almost hysterically. Then he paused and said, "Yeah, thanks."

John spun slowly around. The air was moist. They were underground, not in the open at all as they had expected. Perhaps this was just as well.

"We missed the parking lot," Prime said.

John reached out, felt cold cement blocks.

"We're lucky we missed that wall," he said.

"Shit."

John reached along the wall. His elbow knocked into something that clattered, and then his fingers found a light switch. The room lit up.

It was a basement room, twenty meters long, filled with odds and ends, buckets, mops, old equipment, scuba gear. Rows of shelves were stacked with boxes. It was empty of any people, Goths or otherwise, save dead Corrundrum.

"Oops," Prime said.

"What?" John asked.

"That's how big it is." The device's field hadn't quite reached Corrundrum's feet. The corpse had been amputated at the shins. "Someone is going to get a surprise tomorrow morning."

Blood flowed across the floor in a wave, reeking of iron. John's stomach flipped and he looked away.

"I had been twenty-five percent sure he'd turn on us," Prime said. "Guess I was right."

"There were other ways to deal with him," John said.

Prime stared at him for a moment. "This cleans up a lot of loose ends for me."

"Let's get out of here."

There was a single metal fire door. John twisted the knob and pulled it open. It squeaked like old bedsprings. John paused, peering beyond the door into darkness. He could just make out stairs leading up. He jerked the door open, turning the long, slow squeak into a quick squawk.

"Upstairs," Prime whispered. "It's where we gotta be."

The steps felt slick under his boots. The stairway smelled of mold.

At the top was another metal fire door. John placed his ear against the door but heard nothing. Prime knelt at the base of the door and pressed his eye against the crack.

"I don't see anything," Prime said.

"Nothing to hear," John replied. He nodded and opened the door.

They were in a dim hallway, lit by sconces every few meters. There was a half-glass door across the hall, leading into a dark office. Prime slipped across the hall and tried the door. It opened. They stepped inside.

Prime turned the small desk lamp on. John hoped no one would notice the light; the window shades were drawn.

"'Arturto Ildibad,'" Prime said, reading the name off the placard on the desk.

A manila folder lay open on the desk. A credit card receipt lay atop the papers, and the name on it was Grace's.

"Look at this!" John cried.

"What?" Prime said.

John handed him the credit card statement.

"So?"

"That's the part list for a transfer device. That's how they found us out," John said. "Grace put it all on her corporate card. They noticed."

"Maybe, or they went looking after they found you guys out," Prime said. "Don't knock yourself out. These guys are professional assholes. Look at all this junk."

Ildibad's desk was cluttered with newspaper clippings and journal papers. Most of the clippings were from the U.S. *Examiner,* one of those disreputable tabloids. John noted the large number of UFO stories. There was also one about a modern dinosaur roaming Columbia, South Carolina. The accompanying picture showed a Tyrannosaurus Rex grabbing a Volkswagen Beetle in its teeth.

Also on the desk were pictures of the Rayburn farmhouse, close-ups of the barn, the fields, and John's parents.

"These guys are rather thorough," Prime said.

"Wouldn't you be if you were obsessed with getting home?" John said pointedly.

"Uh, yeah." Prime actually looked guilty for a moment.

Prime pulled open Ildibad's desk drawers, looking for something of use. He found a brochure for the company and inside was a map of the campus, including the fenced-in areas.

"Why do they have a brochure?" Prime asked.

"I dunno," John replied. "Do they actually hire anyone from the outside?" John guessed no person from this universe had ever set foot inside the fenced area. Except for Henry. Except for Grace.

John looked over Prime's shoulder. Building One was labeled "Administration." The buildings beyond it were labeled "Laboratory One" and "Laboratory Two." Walkways attached the three buildings.

John looked up and saw an emergency drawing. It showed the office, the corridor, the nearest fire exits, and a silhouette of the rest of Building One. A "You Are Here" sign indicated that they were on the eastern side of Building One.

"We're in Building One. I think we need to get to the laboratories," he said.

"If I were part of an evil group of renegades, that's where I would store my hostages," Prime said. He knelt down in front of the bookcase and pulled a thick volume out. He checked the table of contents, then put the book in his bag.

"What are you doing? What was that?" John said.

"Concise encyclopedia," he said. "You never know what might be useful back home."

"Right." John hitched the duffel on his shoulder. Prime would never change. Yet he was here now, helping. "Let's find my friends."

The hallway was still empty. Prime led them in the direction toward the laboratories. As they neared a set of double doors, one of them swung in and a security guard stepped through, oblivious to them.

He stopped dead in his tracks, staring at the handgun in Prime's hands. Prime motioned him forward silently.

"Come on," Prime whispered. "In case there's someone behind you." The guard came forward, but no one followed him. He was alone. Prime slid the man's pistol out of his holster, handing it to John. It was cold and heavy in his hands. He held it awkwardly for a moment until he slid it into his pocket, safety on.

"This way," Prime said, and they led the man back to Ildibad's office and pushed him inside.

"Where are my friends?" John asked the man.

He sneered, then said, "Zulo! Marikoi!"

Prime said, "I guess that means he doesn't want to tell us."

"What language was that?" John asked.

"The Language, you ass," the man said. His English was accented just like Visgrath's.

"Well, he speaks English, as well," Prime said. "That means he'll understand when I say he better start talking if he doesn't want to die with a bullet in the head." Prime raised the pistol, aiming at the guard's forehead. John almost reached out to push the gun away. But they needed to know, and John assumed—prayed!—that Prime was bluffing.

"Pikutara joan!"

"Listen, you dumb son of a bitch. To me, you're just an animal that needs to be put down. Speak or face oblivion."

"Your friends are dead. Just like you'll be."

"Not the right answer!" Angry, Prime slammed the side of the pistol against the guard's face.

"What are you doing?" John cried out.

"Quiet!"

"Me be quiet?" John stuck his head out the doorway, looking both ways. Empty. "You can't torture this guy."

"Watch me," Prime said. "Isn't this why you brought me along? For the dirty work?"

Blood welled up at the guard's mouth. He spat at Prime, who dodged it with a smirk.

"Where are they?"

"Kabroi! You can't stop our glorious return to Alara. We will take your transporter and leave your bodies for the dogs." He spat again.

Prime smashed his face again with the gun, and this time the guard collapsed unconscious. John looked down at the bleeding man, his head spinning.

"That was going nowhere," Prime said.

"You could have killed him," John said. He crouched down and felt for a pulse.

"Leave him," Prime said. "He's garbage."

"Listen to yourself! It's not about being fierce, or killing, or attacking. Calm down."

Prime looked at John. There was coldness in Prime's eyes that frightened John. "I've seen this type before. They'll do anything to get what they want. We have to attack them or die!"

John put a hand on Prime's shoulder.

"I know how you feel, John," he said. "I want to kill them all too. They've shot my Casey. Consider that. But we need stealth and speed. Violence and anger will get us killed."

Something changed in Prime's face, and he nodded.

"Yeah, you're right. Sorry," Prime said. "We aren't really the same anymore, are we?"

"Not that far apart," John said. "But it's been two years."

Prime cuffed the guard with his own handcuffs, then dragged him behind the desk. He turned and headed back toward the double doors. Prime waited with his palm against the cold metal until John caught up. Prime listened at the door for a moment, then pulled it open. Beyond was a set of glass doors leading outside.

"The lab buildings," John said.

"Halt!"

Prime turned at the sound. Someone was running down the hallway toward them.

John pulled Prime inside the atrium and slammed the door shut. Prime paused for a second, then kicked it open again, and fired into the hallway three times.

"Stealth wasn't working," Prime said, with a grim grin.

John rolled away with his arms around his ears. Prime was going to get them killed!

Prime kicked the door again. John glanced up when no bullets came flying and saw the body of the guard, dead, lying in the hallway. Prime ran forward and rifled through his pockets, finding a set of keys.

"Come on. They know we're here now."

Prime led the way outside, following a sidewalk that joined the buildings. A metal door leading into the Laboratory One building opened, and Visgrath stepped out.

"Hold it," Prime said, his gun trained on the man. He stopped and raised his arms. Instead of fear, the man's face showed a smirk.

"Visgrath," John said. "Where are my friends?"

"The brave John Wilson. Two of you. How interesting."

"Where are they?" John repeated. His anger was boiling up inside him. He reached into his pocket for the pistol.

"Not here."

Prime pointed his handgun at Visgrath's elbow. "This is going to hurt, and I have no qualms doing it."

Visgrath blanched. "How can there be two of you? Your device is broken. Unless you've been successful in—"

Prime touched the gun to Visgrath's elbow. "Where are his friends?"

Visgrath stared at Prime closely, perhaps deciding if he had the guts. He clearly valued his life more than the guard did, because he finally said, "They're in Lab One. Right here."

"Let's go get them," John said. "Keep your hands behind your head."

John took a quick look around him. He hated being in the open. The shots Prime had fired should have drawn a lot of attention.

"Hurry."

"How can I open the door if my hands are behind my back?"

"Open the damn door."

"You'll never get out of here. There's fifty armed guards. Certainly more guards than you have bullets."

They stood in an atrium similar to the one in Building One. "Which way?" There were two pairs of doors.

"Through there." Visgrath nodded his head.

"Go."

Visgrath hesitated.

"Go."

John Prime saw Visgrath hestitate and knew he was planning something. Prime opened his mouth to order Visgrath away from the doors.

Visgrath glanced back once at Prime, then yelled and dove out of Prime's arc of fire.

Prime pulled the trigger and splattered the door with three shots. His face stung and his ears rang. He pushed at the door, and got a glimpse of the lab within.

Three technicians in white coats turned at the sound. And there was a woman, naked and strapped to a table. Blood dripped from the red lines drawn across her arms and torso.

Farm Boy cried out in rage, and Prime was shocked to see him aim his gun and fire on the technicians. The closest man crumpled with a spray of red. Prime fired three more shots, then paused to reload.

He had no idea where Visgrath was, but he wasn't focused on that. The two remaining technicians turned to run. Prime ran into the room, leaping over a tray of scalpels and surgical instruments. He caught the second man in the back with a shot. The third slipped behind a row of cabinets, and Prime's shot missed his head by centimeters, thunking into the concrete wall with a spray of powder.

Prime scanned the room, caught the closing door as Visgrath skittered through. He was the leader of this group of renegades, and he might bring reinforcements. Prime dashed across the room and opened the door slowly.

Beyond the door was an empty hallway. Visgrath had disappeared. He walked slowly past doors, checking the knobs. They were locked, and the labs beyond were dark. What were these bastards doing? Probably just what he'd done. They were trying to make their marooned lives better while trying to get their lives back. But these people were nothing like him. They tortured and killed. . . .

He killed too. He had killed Oscar and maybe Thomas. They had been the first, a hundred universes away. He had killed Corrundrum and Ted Carson. And he had done despicable acts to get his life back. What anyone would have done. Even Farm Boy had tried it, though he'd failed at the last minute.

Prime paused in the hallway to pull the rifle from his shoulder. Ahead of him, the hallway bent to the right, and he heard running feet approaching. He pushed himself into a doorway on the right side.

Two men, carrying nasty machine guns, rounded the corner.

Without hesitation, he fired his rifle into their chests, once each. They crumpled, each face marked by an O of surprise.

You never expected to die coming around a corner, Prime thought. He took one of the machine guns and stowed it across his shoulder. He was trading his ordnance up, he thought with a smile.

Did these two guards have wives? Prime wondered. Had these two gone native to find women, or did they have a partner among the renegades? Perhaps they were themselves lovers. Prime chuckled grimly. Add two more to his total. Two more fucking bodies.

He edged around the corner, but the hallway jagged again to the left and was empty. He took the next corner slowly too but found that the hallway ended in a set of windowless double doors.

He turned the knob slowly and pushed the door open, then stepped back. Nothing. The door hushed shut.

He pushed it open again and stepped through.

Prime was in a warehouse connected to a loading dock; it was piled high with boxes on pallets. There are a lot of places to hide in here, Prime thought.

Counting the stacks of boxes, Prime realized that these renegades were busy. They were acting. They were watching. It was as if they expected to find someone like Farm Boy, expected to exploit

something, expected to find someone with a means to get to—
what had Corrundrum said?—the Alarian Empire.

Prime was struck by the invisible threads of action just below
the horizon of the universes. Who put these renegades here? Who
were they waiting for? Where was Corrundrum from? Universe
zero? What was at the beginning of all this?

Movement in the warehouse caught Prime's eye. He ducked behind a pallet, and watched as two men moved from stack to stack
surreptitiously.

Prime edged along the outer wall of the warehouse, trying to
flank the two men. He heard voices as he neared, heard whispered
orders. He hoped one of the men was Visgrath. He wouldn't let him
get away again.

Prime glanced around a box and saw two men crouched and talking. One of them was Visgrath. Prime stepped forward and a weight
landed on his shoulders. The rifle in his hand discharged and then
spun away from him.

He tried to roll, but the weight pressed against the back of his
neck. Someone had ambushed him by jumping from the stacked
boxes. They'd baited him.

"Crap," he huffed, barely able to breathe.

From his prone position, he watched the smiling Visgrath approach until all he could see was Visgrath's shoes.

"Finally, the elusive John Wilson."

"Rayburn."

"I know you have built a new transfer device. I know you have
another one in your possession. You are not of the Aratoan, yet you
vex us." Visgrath squatted and looked Prime in the eye. "Well, we
will have much time to discuss these matters."

Prime knew the veiled statement meant torture.

"Listen, Visgrath, I'm not the John you want. But I can get him
for you. There's no need for torture."

Visgrath laughed. "You kill several of my men, you try to kill me,
and now you want to strike a bargain."

"I had to. John has the device. He shanghaied me to get me to help him. He's worse than you. I think I can help you guys."

"I know you can help us. And you will." He barked orders to the man holding Prime down in that same language the guard had used. "The sincerity of your offer will be tested soon."

The man on top of him cuffed Prime's hands behind his back and dragged him to his feet. They searched him quickly, lifting his shirt, looking for the device.

"Now we will find your twin."

CHAPTER 39

John spun around, surveying the room for Visgrath and any other targets. He saw none. The gun handle was slick with sweat. His heart was pounding, and the smell of gunpowder was overpowering.

John Prime was missing. Had he gone after Visgrath?

The lab was crowded with equipment, so others might have been hiding, but there were three other doors leading out of the room. John heard a door swing shut and assumed it was the third lab technician. Where was Visgrath?

John put the pistol next to Grace on the table, within reach, and began to work on the leather buckles binding her arms and legs. His rage boiled when he saw what they had done to her.

"Grace! Grace!"

Her eyes were closed, but she breathed. Her bloody chest rose and fell. John could not bear to look at the savage cuts on her body. This was all his fault!

He undid her arms and then her legs.

"Grace, are you okay? Can you hear me?"

Her eyes fluttered, then opened. She didn't focus at first, and then she smiled with a smile missing one front tooth. "Johnny," she croaked.

"Everything's okay, Grace. Are you okay?" He realized he was babbling.

Grace grinned. "I'm not dead yet," she whispered. "It's just a flesh wound."

John's eyes burned as the tears came, and his sob turned into a foul-sounding guffaw.

"Goddamn it, Grace. Don't make me laugh."

"Got to," she said, sitting up on the table.

John pulled the lab coat off one of the technicians and draped it around Grace's shoulders. She looked shaken and pale, but her eyes were focused now.

"Grace, we need to find Henry," he said.

She looked around the lab, then grabbed John's shoulder to steady herself. "I feel woozy." She pointed to one of the doors. "They brought me through there. I never saw Henry, but I guess he was in a cell near mine."

She glanced down at the gun next to her. Then she took it in her hands.

"Can I have this?" she said.

"I have another one," John said. Corrundrum's gun was in his other pocket. "Do you know how to shoot?"

"I'm a city girl," she said. "All I can do is dial nine-one-one. But I'm willing to try it today."

"Be careful, but if it isn't one of us, then shoot," John said. "And John Prime is in the building too." He made sure Corrundrum's gun was loaded.

"John Prime? You went back to get John Prime?"

"Yes. I needed help." Grace's face was pale. "Are you okay?"

"Don't worry." She knelt down to turn over the corpse of the second technician. She spat on his face.

John saw her ferocity. He knew that she was a competitor, that she could be angry and fierce. But not till then did he recognize the stamina that bolstered her, and it made him fear for any Visigoths they came across.

"Grace, I'm sorry for getting you into this."

She stood and said, "Not as sorry as these fuckers are going to be."

He helped her across the room, and while Grace rested against the wall John listened at the door that she had indicated. He heard nothing. There was no window to look through.

"Out of the way of the doorway," he said, motioning to the left side. He turned the knob and flung it open. Nothing.

John slipped into the corridor. It went about ten meters before a right turn. Three doors lined the right wall.

"That one's mine," she said. Grace pointed to the middle cell. John tried the door on the left, but it was locked. He pounded on the door.

"Henry?"

Nothing.

He tried the one on the right, but there was no response there either.

"They've taken him away," John said. "Let's go."

John led Grace down the hall. The right turn was into a short hallway ending in double doors. John listened, then kicked the doors open. Beyond was another lab.

Visgrath stood in the middle of it with Henry in front of him, a gun pointed at his temple. Henry's lip was crusted with dry blood. His eye was black-and-blue. He looked tired, as if Visgrath was holding him upright. Prime, his hands cuffed behind him, lay at Visgrath's feet.

"Nobody move," Visgrath yelled. "I want the transfer machine," he said simply. "If I don't get it, this man dies. And then this other one dies. It's your choice."

The man was five meters away and the path between them was clear. He was dressed in a lab coat and dark trousers.

John said, "Calm down. I have the device here and I'm willing to trade." John pointed the handgun away from him.

"I am exceedingly calm. Now put your gun down."

John slowly lowered the gun to the ground. He saw the man visibly relax. The gun lowered a centimeter from Henry's temple.

"You have chosen wisely. Now hand me the device."

Grace took three strides and was face-to-face with him, her own gun muzzle touching his nose. John realized that the man had paid no attention to Grace, had not even regarded her being armed as a concern.

"Put the gun down," the man said. "Or I shoot your lover."

Grace smiled. "The choice is no longer mine. If you shoot Henry, I will shoot you. If you let him go, I will not shoot you. The choice is now yours."

John picked his gun back up, unsure of what would happen. Grace had raised the stakes with her brave move.

"Grace?" Henry said weakly, but she ignored him.

"You'd risk your lover's life?" the man said, but his face had paled.

"No, I'm not risking anyone's life. You're risking your own." She pushed the muzzle against the man's nose. "If you don't lower the gun, you will die. It's that simple."

"And him with me."

"No. I think that as this bullet passes through your brain, you'll have no inclination to pull the trigger on your own gun. In fact, as this bullet cracks your nasal facial bone and shatters your ethmoid bone into a hundred razor-sharp shards that explode through your brain, into your frontal lobe, which controls your abstract thinking, aggression, and sexual behavior, into your medulla, which controls your heart, into your hypothalamus, which controls your breathing, in that fraction of a second while your brain is disintegrating I am betting that you will not contract your finger. I'm betting you will simply wet your crotch and shit your drawers, because your body will be dealing with more important matters. Your last thought as your personality implodes, as your occipital lobe erupts out the back of your head, will be 'I'm a little teapot' and 'I want my mommy' and nothing—not one blessed thought—will be about shooting your gun." Her finger whitened on the trigger. "So, what do *you* choose to do?"

The man's eyes were locked on hers, and John could see the sweat shining on his forehead.

Slowly he brought the gun away from Henry's head.

"We have a draw."

As Henry turned and backed away, Grace smiled coldly and said, "You have chosen poorly," and fired into the man's forehead.

"Grace!" John yelled, but it was too late. Visgrath's face was pulped, a mess of red, as he tumbled, stumbled into a lab table and over it.

John's heart hammered.

"Grace," John said. She seemed focused on the corpse.

Henry gently spun her around and placed his handcuffed arms around her neck. John helped Prime to his feet.

"How are you guys doing?" John asked.

"I've been better," Henry said. "I think that corpse has the keys."

John rifled through Visgrath's lab coat pockets and found a set of keys. He unlocked Henry's cuffs, and then helped Prime.

John said, "We have to get out of here now."

Prime handed Henry Visgrath's handgun. Henry looked at it oddly, then put it in his pocket with a shrug.

"Are you all right?" John asked Henry. "Did they . . . ?"

Henry looked away. "I'll be fine. What's the plan? I mean, there's more to this plan than just rescue Henry and Grace, right?"

The ironic smile caused John to choke back a laugh. "We need to leave here," he said simply.

"Obviously," Grace said. "We can't stay in the bad guy's lair."

"If we have to, we can leave this universe," John said.

Grace looked at Prime, her eyes going wide. "John, you built a device! You had to or else you couldn't have gone back for him."

"I did."

She hugged him. "I knew you could do it."

"Come on, guys," Prime said. "Let's put some distance between us and this place."

John picked a door out of the lab at random, and he kicked it open into an empty hallway. Slowly, they worked their way down it, checking the doors they passed, most of which were locked or led into small laboratories: dead ends. One opened into a greenhouse that had a door to the outside.

"Here."

They ran through the rows of plants. John stopped and looked suddenly at the fruit-covered vines. "What fruit is this?"

He grabbed one off the vine. It was red at the top and blue at the bottom, fading between the two colors in the middle. It was about the diameter of an apple but had indentations around the outside, giving it a six-pointed star–like shape. John pocketed it and ran on.

The door from the greenhouse opened onto a larger garden. John said, "This way," leading them to the northeast. He figured they'd circle around to the parking lot and try to steal a car.

"Ow!" Grace said, and he realized she had no shoes. Henry helped her, taking an arm to lead her over the ground.

To the west, about fifty meters away, was a loading dock where a tractor trailer sat. To the east, the building curved into the darkness.

"This way," Prime said, pointing to the east.

Hugging the cement wall, they ran to the corner of the building. John peeked around, blinking in the bright spotlights of the parking lot. Three security vehicles were sitting at the entrance to Lab One. Men with nasty-looking weapons were entering the front.

He saw a group of three spread out and head toward them.

"Here they come. Everybody down," John whispered.

They crouched in the darkness near the building. John was ready to shoot, ready to kill if necessary, but through luck the two guards passed within three meters of them and didn't look in their direction once.

They waited until the two guards disappeared into the greenhouse.

"Let's try for one of those Jeeps," John said.

They ran through the grass, and as they approached, a gun barked, sending a bullet zinging off the hood of one of the Jeeps.

The team that had entered the lab was coming back out, joining the search outside the building.

Henry fired his gun wildly at them, his face a mix of horror and glee, and they dropped for cover. Henry helped Grace and John into the back of the Jeep. Henry took the wheel and Prime took the front passenger seat.

Henry dropped it into reverse and backed away from the lab. Prime fired his gun again, then reloaded. John laid down a spray with his pistol.

"I'm out," he said. Henry tossed him his gun as he bucked the Jeep over a rise and toward the front gate.

"Gate's closed," he said.

"Ram it," Prime yelled.

Henry pressed the accelerator as John saw the spike stripes. The Jeep hit them and seemed to collapse. Smoke rose up from the shredded tires, and the Jeep lost momentum, bouncing weakly against the fence.

"Crap."

Gunfire from the guard shack shattered the windshield, and Henry cursed, grabbing his hand.

Prime pulled him out of the Jeep on his side, away from the guard shack. Grace slipped to the pavement as well. John fired three rounds into the hut, shattering its windows and sending the guard for cover. Behind them John heard the approach of more Jeeps.

"Pinned down," Henry said. There was no way through the fence while the guard was there. And the rest of the security force was approaching in Jeeps. John looked around for some avenue of escape.

John said, "I'd hoped we could get out the old-fashioned way. But, Henry, we're not pinned down."

Grace understood instantly and said, "John has the device."

"Well, you can get out of here at least," Henry said. "What about the rest of us?"

"We're all going." John pulled up his shirt, wincing, as he struggled to do it with one arm. He realized his shoulder had been grazed at some point in the escape. John turned the dial that specified the field radius as high as he could. Then he set the device to 7651.

"We need to gather close," he said.

"Don't!" Prime yelled. "There's no way for me to get back to my universe if we do this!"

Lights from the approaching Jeeps lit his face for a second.

"What choice do we have?" John asked.

Prime cursed.

Huddled behind the Jeep, the four hugged one another.

"Here we go," John said.

CHAPTER 40

John approached the old barn with trepidation. Bill and Janet had said there'd been a break-in. John knew what that meant, but he had to make sure.

They'd been gone six weeks, enough time to convert his gold to local currency in Universe 7651 and build a bridge device from scratch. Luckily, 7651 had been advanced enough in electronics for it to be a relatively easy job. No detailed breadboard soldering. They'd just designed the circuits they wanted and ordered them in bulk.

They'd sent John Prime home first, John and he traveling together to 7533, along with Prime's huge trunk.

"What have you got in here? A body?" John had asked.

"You promised not to ask," Prime said.

"Yeah, but . . ."

"You know me. Books and toys and gimmicks," Prime had said with a shrug. "I used up all my ideas from my last trip between universes."

"It doesn't seem fair," John said.

"You did it with pinball."

It was true. John had stolen an idea from one universe and made a lot of cash off it in another. How could he fault Prime? They'd done the same things.

"Fine."

They'd built the gateway device on the site of the

abandoned quarry pit in 7651. The result was that they were only a few hundred yards from the farm when they transferred through.

"You gonna be all right?" John asked. Prime was hyperventilating.

"I hate it," he said. "Every time."

"Do you want me to help get this over to the farm?" John said, nodding to the trunk.

"Naw." Prime pulled out his cell phone. "I got it taken care of. I missed a court date, but I think it's all going to work out."

"I can drop you anywhere," John said. "Any universe. Maybe even back where you came from. . . ."

Prime seemed to think it over. Then he shook his head. "No, thanks. This is where I live now. Unless you want it back."

"No, not anymore," John said. "Up till a few weeks ago, I'd have taken it all back, but . . ."

"It's a big universe out there."

"Yeah."

Prime stepped away, dragging his trunk across the bare stone.

"Get back to your own Casey. I bet she's worried," Prime said.

"Yeah, I bet she is."

"Just do me a favor," Prime said. "Check in on me in a few months. I might need a ride out of this dump."

"You think?"

Prime shrugged. He reached out his hand, and John took it. They shook once solemnly.

"Good luck."

John had then used the portable device to transfer back to 7651, where Henry and Grace waited with the newly built transfer gate.

"Not too bad," Henry had said. They'd smoked the nearest transformer the first time they'd powered up the transfer gate in 7651. They'd lost a week while the electric company fixed it. "It was the range module, like we thought."

John glanced at Grace, sitting in the corner of the quarry office. They slept on cots in the same room with the transfer gate, so John knew she'd had nightmares since the death of Visgrath, since her torture. John had broached the subject just once.

"There's probably, uh, psychiatrists in this universe—"

Grace had shot him a hard look.

"—or, you know, drugs to help you sleep, at least," John said.

He thought she was going to bark at him or, worse, turn away in silence. Instead, she shook her head and said, "John, I just need time and distance."

He'd not asked again.

The only times she left Henry's side were to take a pistol into the shallow quarry and fire at a row of cans she lined up meticulously. John hoped getting her back to 7650 would solve her problems, but there was no telling what Charboric had done while they were gone.

"Ready?" John said.

Grace nodded, standing up. She was dressed in army fatigues they had bought, along with all the electronics, machine guns, dynamite, and bulletproof vests. She hefted a duffel bag full of munitions near the transfer gate.

Just like the gate that John had first built, the transfer gate in 7651 was a fixed structure that transferred anything within a few-meter radius between 7651 and any other universe. A cantilever hung above the transfer area, and duct-taped to it were the electronics that projected the spherical field below. The field was not as subtle as the one from the portable device; it seemed to wrap around whatever it was attached to. But the subtlety of those circuits had been sacrificed in the drive to finish the device in time. The spherical field required them to be careful that nothing was outside the radius of the field when it was activated.

John and Grace slid a wood platform into the field area. The platform—half in and half out of the field—would keep their feet firmly in the field radius. Anything outside the radius—arms, feet, legs—wouldn't be going along for the ride when they transferred to 7650.

"Let's go," Grace said.

"Do you really think we'll need all the ammo?" Henry asked again. "We'll just be able to call the police, right?"

"Do you want to take that chance?" Grace asked flatly.

John nodded, though he worried at Grace's willingness to kill. "Until we know for sure what has happened there . . ."

Henry started the timer—big LED numbers counted down from 30. They hunkered down on the platform with their gear. At 0, John heard a rising buzz that suddenly cut off. Bright daylight, and they dropped a foot as the platform—once a rectangle, now a circle—collapsed. John, ready for the drop, steadied Henry and Grace with a hand.

They stood on the stone cliff above the quarry in 7650. A warm wind blew through the grass that sprouted in clumps. There was no one there.

And when they trotted across the road to Bill and Janet's farmyard, Janet burst into tears of joy at their appearance.

"Where have you been?" she cried.

"Hiding," John said. "Have you heard from Casey Nicholson? Do you know if she's all right?"

"She was here," Bill said. "They let her out of the hospital a week after you disappeared."

"Can I use your phone?" John said.

John dialed her dorm room, but there was no answer. He glanced at the wall calendar. It was summer break, of course! He hung up and dialed her home number.

"Hello?"

"Casey!"

"John! Where are you?"

"Are you all right?"

"The police have been looking for you. It's a kidnapping, they say. And that company that funded you, EmVis, it's been in the news all month."

"Are you all right?" John repeated again slowly.

"I'm fine, damn it! But what about you?"

"We're all fine."

"Who? Grace and Henry?"

"Yeah, we're all fine. We had to run, and things got complicated, if you know what I mean."

"I knew it wasn't a kidnapping," Casey said. "I'm just glad that you made it back. Where are you?"

"At Bill and Janet's. I'll come see you in a while."

"Sure you will. Because if you don't get here by sundown, I will track you down and kill you," Casey said cheerfully.

"I know you will."

He hung up, everything suddenly okay in the world.

Henry called from the TV room: "John, you have got to read this."

"What?"

Henry was reading a copy of the *Saturday Evening Post*. Grace had a copy of *CapNews*.

"EmVis has imploded," Henry said. "All the management and owners have disappeared."

"They mention us in here," Grace said. "One line. We disappeared too."

"Disappeared?" John said. He glanced out the front window but couldn't see the old barn from there. "What's happened in the last six weeks around here?"

Janet shook her head and sighed. "What a mess it's been. With you missing, and someone breaking into the old barn . . ."

"Someone broke into the old barn?"

"We thought it was kids, but all your things that you'd spent so much time on look busted up," Bill said.

John, Henry, and Grace shared a look.

"I better go see."

John pushed open the door of the barn and hit the light switch. Nothing happened. He pulled the door all the way open, fishing for the flashlight in his duffel. He flicked it on.

His first transfer gate had been taken apart and removed. John knew by whom: Charboric and his cohorts.

They'd found out from Grace that John was building a device, and when Visgrath had died and John, Henry, Grace, and Prime had escaped to the next universe Charboric had been free to search until he'd found the device. John appearing with Prime had been proof that John had succeeded in building a gateway.

Once Charboric had found the gate, he'd moved it to one of EmVis' labs and used it to transfer his entire team back to where they needed to go.

They were gone.

John sighed. It was for the best for Grace and Henry. They were safe here now if Charboric and all of the EmVis bastards were gone. Casey was safe now. John was safe to stay too.

But no, that wasn't a choice anymore.

The Visigoths had a gateway now. If they'd reversed engineered his device, they knew how to build more. John had released a menace on the universe, and he wasn't going to let that cancer linger.

He owned the technology now. It was time to make things right.

Ted Carson was certain he was going insane.

His father was dead. He remembered the funeral. Yet here was Dad, big as life and not dead from a heart attack at forty-nine. Ted felt his stomach knot with fright whenever he stared him in the face.

"You all right, Ted? Have a beer."

"No, I'm not all right," he said.

He and the man who looked like his dad sat side by side in the living room Ted didn't remember, watching a TV he didn't recall, in a chair he'd never sat in before. His "dad" placed a meaty hand on Ted's thigh. He forced himself not to flinch.

"It's an effect of the amnesia, the doctors said. A fugue, they called it."

"Yeah, whatever, but you were dead," Ted said. "And I live somewhere else." That wasn't amnesia. He had memories that didn't actually seem to have happened. Amnesia was when you *didn't* have memories.

He didn't want the beer, but his mom, ten kilograms lighter than he remembered, brought one in an iced mug anyway.

He sat back in the recliner and held the mug against his head.

None of this was right.

He'd been getting high in his basement apartment on Winslow. There'd been a knock on the door and some guy was there with a taser. After that Ted didn't remember much, just the claustrophobia from being hog-tied in a coffin. He'd been certain it was those punk dealers who wanted their cash. If only they had given him a chance to pay, to explain! The next thing he remembered was being pulled out of the trunk by Casey Nicholson and led into the police station. Ted's pants had been wet. He'd vomited on the cops' floor. They'd taken him to the hospital, and the newspaperman showed up.

And then Ted's parents, and he'd screamed in terror. The nurses had had to drag his dad out of the room before Ted calmed down.

There'd been tests and questions, and Ted had answered what he could. He remembered the last two months clearly. He had a job at Lawson's. He worked nights. He had a car. He knew his address. The doctors had written down notes and nodded.

Then they'd taken him to the corner of Hodge and Staley where the Lawson's should have been. It had been a used-car place. Then they'd taken him to his apartment, but some Mexican family lived there and it looked like they always had. No car, no apartment, no job. But his dad was back. After ten years.

Ted wasn't sure if it was a fair trade, because he seemed to have traded in his sanity with all the rest of that stuff.

"The doctor's been through all that, Ted," his dad said. "It may not come back to you for a while, or it never will. But you're safe and home now."

"Yeah."

"And all this nonsense is behind us."

"All this nonsense" included Ted appearing in front of a judge and stating his full name for the record. He'd had no driver's license, no Social Security card, so he'd had to affirm he was Ted Carson, and his dad and mom had affirmed too, and when that was all done there was Casey Nicholson hugging that guy who had tasered him. Only now he was standing with three lawyers and was dressed in a suit.

He'd met Ted's eye and smiled, as if he'd just gotten away with something.

But for the life of him, Ted couldn't figure out how his life had been stolen.

"Fuck it," he whispered, and downed his beer in one gulp.